What will they gain—or lose—with

THE SCOFIELD DIAGNOSIS

DR. JEAN SCOFIELD

Unswerving in her dedication, rebellious despite all opposition, she can live with the hidden truth while Bobby Tatum dies from it, or she can reveal it—and give up the dream of her very promising career.

HORACE CAMERON

Powerful in the electronics industry and Chairman of the Board of Trustees of University Hospital, he rules both worlds. In one world, he controls Bobby's father. In another, he controls Jean Scofield—until she decides to fight him with his own fire.

DR. LARRY BRAHAM

Bobby's pediatrician and Jean's lover, Larry would do almost anything to keep his romance with Jean alive. Yet it's precisely what he <u>won't</u> do that could destroy the woman he loves!

Books by Henry Denker

The Experiment
The Kingmaker
The Physicians
The Scofield Diagnosis
The Starmaker

Published by POCKET BOOKS

THE Scofield Diagnosis

HENRY Denker

PUBLISHED BY POCKET BOOKS NEW YORK

**POCKET BOOKS, a Simon & Schuster division of
GULF & WESTERN CORPORATION**
1230 Avenue of the Americas, New York, N.Y. 10020

Copyright © 1977 by Henry Denker

Published by arrangement with Simon and Schuster
Library of Congress Catalog Card Number: 77-22599

ISBN: 0-671-81645-4

First Pocket Books printing November, 1978

Trademarks registered in the United States and other countries.

Printed in the U.S.A.

ACKNOWLEDGMENTS

For the scientific and medical research that serves as a basis for this novel, the author wishes to express his deep appreciation to Dr. Sumner R. Ziegra, Professor and Chairman, Department of Pediatrics, and Dr. Michael G. Blackburn, Associate Professor of Pediatrics, Director of Neo-Natology, Medical College of Pennsylvania, Philadelphia; Dr. Peter Carmel, Department of Neurosurgery, Columbia Presbyterian Medical Center, New York City; the late Dr. Peter Lake, Director of Education and Research, The Eisenhower Medical Center, Palm Desert, California.

To DR. PETER LAKE,
whose life was devoted to
literature and medicine, the science
which failed him in the thirty-sixth
year of his life.

one

Dr. Jean Scofield, Associate Professor of Medicine in Neurology, raced down the long corridor of University Hospital in answer to an urgent call from Emergency Admitting. In her late thirties, and of average height, she seemed both younger and smaller in her long, white, starched lab coat.

"Disarmingly small" was the way old Hans Benziger, Chief of Neurology, liked to describe his protege after watching her in determined confrontation with some of her male colleagues. But, even in those moments, her warm green eyes and her auburn hair endowed her with a softness decidedly feminine and unusually attractive. So attractive, that many who worked under her, especially young physicians and student nurses who knew nothing of her past, always wondered why such an obviously handsome woman was not married. Most assumed it was due to her total dedication to her profession.

Actually Jean Scofield had been married once. But the marriage had ended abruptly and tragically. Whatever it had done to her personal life, it had not diminished her unique effectiveness as a neurologist.

She had almost reached the Emergency Room when the beeper in the breast pocket of her lab coat buzzed insistently. She picked up the phone at the nurses' floor station and announced herself to the operator.

"Dr. Scofield speaking."

"Doctor, Administrator Carey has been trying to

reach you. He's in conference in his office with Dr. Benziger and he would like you to join them."

"Sorry. I'm on my way to Emergency. I'll see Mr. Carey as soon as I'm free."

She hung up and continued toward the Emergency Room. Even before she reached it, she heard the sound of a young child crying in great pain.

The admitting resident was Dr. Preston Guylay, a young black man who had been a student in her neurology class at University Medical School. He was examining a black child who, to judge from appearances, was some fourteen or fifteen months of age. Jean noted that in the far corner of the room, on a white metal stool, sat a young black woman of no more than twenty. She was staring, seemingly impassive, except that she nervously twisted a tattered handkerchief. When Guylay spied Jean Scofield he left his anguished little patient to speak to her privately.

"Sorry to bother you, Professor. I know you've got a hell of a schedule. But I need help. Not only medically, but legally. This can become messy and I don't want to make any mistakes."

"What is it?" Jean asked, staring past Guylay at the whimpering child on the examining table.

"Glove burn. But there may be more. I need your opinion on any neurologic deficit."

Jean moved to the tiny patient, at the same time casting a glance at the young black woman in the corner, whose eyes followed her with an expressionless stare. As Jean leaned over the child, she saw at once what Guylay had described. Both the child's hands from fingertips to an inch above its wrists were red, puffy, blistery masses. Clearly second-degree burns. The fact that the scalded areas ended so trimly above the wrists, like a pair of short gloves, was a clear indication that the child's hands had been forcibly immersed in scalding water long enough to create burns of such severity. No child would keep its own hands in hot water for so long.

NAI, was Dr. Scofield's immediate conclusion. *Non-Accidental Injury*. She exchanged glances with young Guylay, confirming his diagnosis, then she began her neurological examination of the tiny patient. "How old? Fourteen months? Fifteen?"

"Twenty-two," Guylay informed her.

"Twenty-two?" Jean was surprised. The child exhibited distinct lack of development for his age. She continued her examination. Her first perceptive glance detected the red scar of a healed wound almost hidden by the child's eyebrow. An incisor was missing on the same side of his mouth. His nose had evidently been smashed at one time, for it was flatter than the rest of his facial contour would indicate.

Softly, so that only Guylay could hear, Jean said, "Clear case of pugilistic puss. This child's been severely beaten. And frequently."

"Yes," Guylay agreed, self-consciously. He was black. The child and the staring mother sitting in the corner were black. Aware of Guylay's embarrassment, Jean proceeded with her examination.

Using her pocket flashlight, she intently probed the child's eyes. There were obvious signs of retinal hemorrhage, indicating the possibility of brain damage. Such findings in helpless children always outraged her.

"Did you get a history?"

"Yeah."

"What did she say?"

"The usual. She was boiling water to wash the child's feeding dish. The phone rang. She went into the other room to answer it. She heard a scream. When she came back she found the kid had plunged his hands into the hot water."

"Naturally," Jean said angrily. She had heard variations of that story too many times. "And what about his face?"

"She says he fell down the front stairs while trying to learn to walk."

"She married?"

"Yes. But her husband left her."

"You believe that?"

"No."

"Why not?" Jean asked as she used a sterile needle to test the reflexes in the child's legs and arms.

"She lives out of our district. So she's either come here to hide this from her husband or else he did it and made her bring the child here because he's afraid he'll get worse and maybe die."

"I think you're right."

"What do I do?"

"For the safety of the child keep him here. We'll find some medical reason. Do complete skeletal x-rays. I'll bet you find half a dozen healed fractures. When you do, take the case to the Child Abuse Committee."

"I'll need your corroboration."

"There's retinal damage. Neurologic deficit in the left leg. And I'll bet on x-ray you find evidence of a fine-line skull fracture. It would be criminal to turn this child back to his parents."

"What'll I tell her?" The young resident indicated the mother.

"I'll handle her," Jean said crisply. She glanced at the chart to ascertain the mother's name, then crossed to the corner of the room. "Mrs. Scott?"

The young mother looked up, staring through dazed and fearful eyes. "Yes?"

"I'm Dr. Scofield. I've just examined your son. I think his condition is serious enough for us to keep him here awhile."

"But we can't afford . . ." she started to say, then changed it suddenly, "*I* can't afford . . . hospitals so expensive like they are. . ."

"We'll take care of that. The main thing, the boy has to stay here," Jean ordered.

"How long?" the tense mother asked, her eyes flicking back and forth from Jean to the examining table where her young child whimpered in pain as Guylay applied a soothing ointment to his burned hands.

"A week. Probably longer. Depends on how his hands heal," Jean said, knowing they would keep the child longer, for his own safety.

"I don't know," the mother equivocated. "I never left him before."

"At the other hospitals?" Jean asked quickly.

The young mother realized that she had betrayed herself, but Jean's challenging look was too much for her. It would do no good to deny it. She admitted, "Yeah."

"It's my advice, and Dr. Guylay's, that this time you leave him. He'll be well looked after."

The mother hesitated, nodded, moved to the table, stared down at her son, then turned and swiftly left Emergency. Once she was gone, Jean said to Guylay, "Feed him up. He's badly undernourished. Order those x-rays. Do a complete workup. Blood, electrolytes. EEG. I'm afraid we're going to find even more than we suspect."

"Right."

"And, Preston, please don't be so self-conscious," she advised wryly.

"You know what they'll say up on the wards. Another black kid battered by another vicious black father. Or worse, by an 'uncle.' Don't whites think most black parents love their kids like other parents do?" he protested angrily.

"I said don't be self-conscious."

"My father was the gentlest, most caring man I ever knew. Never laid a hand on me in anger. But get most white people to believe that."

"Pres," Jean calmed, "let's not fight that war right now. Get this kid into a bed, put an IV on him and do those tests. I have to go down to Carey's office. Another of his 'important' meetings. Check with me when you get the results of those tests."

She had just reached the elevator on her way to Edward Carey's office when her beeper summoned her again.

While Jean Scofield was on her way to the phone, Edward Carey, Director of Administration of University Hospital, was leaning back in his chair, drumming his fingers on his costly and impressive chrome and black slate desk pad.

"Damn it, Benziger, when Dr. Scofield gets here tell her she *has* to take that appointment!"

Quietly, unemotionally, elderly Hans Benziger, Chief of the Neurology Department, stared across the desk at the Director. Benziger's aging eyes, always a bit moist and compassionate, did not reveal the amusement he was secretly enjoying. He was thinking to himself, these days hospital administrators propose, but stubborn female doctors dispose.

After his outburst, Carey softened sufficiently to ask petulantly, "Did she say anything at all to you?"

"Aside from rejecting the appointment, no."

"Didn't you try to convince her? She's strong-minded, I know, but not unreasonable. As women go, that is."

"And just how did you expect me to convince her?"

"Well, for one thing, you could have pointed out that this is a new position. The first time a woman has been offered a post of such importance in any medical department here."

"I didn't see any need to point that out," Benziger said. "After all, she knows it."

"And she still said no?" Carey asked peevishly. "Bad," he said, "very bad."

"HEW funds?" Benziger asked, still enjoying Carey's discomfort.

"They're so damned unreasonable! We're supposed to have so many women doctors in so many positions of importance. And so many minority doctors on staff. Else no Federal funding. And it doesn't matter whether they're qualified or not!"

"Well," Benziger said very deliberately, "that can't be a factor here. Dr. Scofield is extremely well qualified."

At once Carey became apologetic. "Of course. She was a student of yours. And a protege. There's no doubt about her qualifications. But these days running a hospital is like working a jigsaw puzzle designed by an insane man. You've got to fit a lot of jagged pieces into place before you can complete the picture and they just don't fit!"

Carey rose from his swivel chair and began to pace the luxurious carpet.

"I feel like a damned performing seal! It's a perpetual balancing act. Get the funding. Public and private. Keep the staff happy. Comply with all government regulations. Please the Board of Trustees. Satisfy the minorities. Worry about the personal feelings of every member of the medical staff. Some days I just say to myself, if we didn't also have to take care of the sick, I might just find time to attend to all our administrative problems.

"What if you talked to her again?" Carey asked suddenly.

"She'd say no again."

"Damn!" Carey exploded, even more furious. He resumed, this time more deviously, "Is there anyone *else* who might talk to her?"

"Yes."

"Who?"

"You," Benziger said, adding to Carey's dismay.

"I didn't mean me!" Carey said with some irritation. "I meant someone else. Someone *not* in the Neurology Department!"

"You mean you want me to talk to Dr. Braham and suggest that *he* talk to her?" Benziger asked pointedly.

"Well . . . yes. After all . . ." Carey did not complete the sentence.

"Yes. After all, Jean Scofield and Lawrence Braham are supposed to be lovers," Benziger said. "Is that it?"

"Everyone knows it," Carey defended. "They're not living together. But they might as well be! If anyone can convince her, Braham can."

"Perhaps."

"Then talk to him," Carey half ordered, half pleaded.

"Two things stand in the way," Benziger said. "First, Braham is away this week. A Pediatrics Symposium in Houston. Second, even if he were here I doubt he could convince her."

Carey shook his head, discouraged and frustrated.

"No, Edward, I think you'll have to talk to her yourself."

"I've got a call in for her now."

"Good," the elderly doctor said as he rose from his chair. For a moment he felt tempted to say something comforting to Carey, but he resisted the impulse. Since childhood he had harbored a deep resentment of authority. Partly it sprang from his early training by a father who had been a Lutheran minister in Germany during the turmoil that preceded Hitler and the more horrible times that followed. Young Hans Benziger had been taught that authority, whether it issued from governments or guns, was suspect. Man's conscience and God's word were the guides to living a decent and honorable life.

If Hans Benziger had had no strong feelings about it before, he would have after that horrible day when he had stood before an SS general and pleaded for his father's life. The gaunt minister had been discovered hiding two Jews and one Catholic in the cold, damp cellar of their modest house. The three were hauled off to a camp for their final solution. The Reverend Felix Benziger was tried, summarily convicted and sentenced to die. The only leniency extended to the Benziger family was that the life of the minister's wife was spared since their young son, Hans, was serving in the Medical Corps of the army.

Oberleutnant Doktor Hans Benziger failed to reverse the sentence meted out to his father. Lean, taciturn, defiant, Reverend Felix Benziger was shot by a firing squad in the public square as a lesson to any in their town who might consider hiding other unfortunates destined for the death camps. After that, Hans Benziger had only one ambition. To smuggle his mother and himself out of the country. With the aid of his father's fellow clergymen they were able to make it across the border into Switzerland. A refugee relief agency brought them to America. His mother died shortly after.

For the next five years, Dr. Hans Benziger, who had trained at Heidelberg and had fulfilled all the requirements which made him a full-fledged physician specializing in neurology, had had to work as an orderly and later as a lab assistant in a large hospital in Chicago until he was eligible to take his state and specialty boards and finally become once again what he had been, a physician qualified to treat patients.

The years he spent working as a male nurse and lab technician only reinforced his resentment toward bureaucracy. So whenever he could, he liked to see administrators and bureaucrats sweat a little when embroiled in their own problems.

He experienced a little such enjoyment today, when he avoided assuming Ed Carey's administrative burdens. Besides, Jean Scofield had been his most prized student and was now his most respected protege. She was not only a highly skilled, insightful neurologist, she was a woman of great inner strength. Few doctors, male or female, would have been able to go through what she had and emerge to make productive lives for themselves.

Let Carey tangle with her, Benziger thought, it will be good exercise for him.

In angry frustration, Edward Carey threw his new organization chart down on his desk. He had had it all worked out so beautifully. And, most important, to the complete satisfaction of Horace Cameron, who was not only Chairman of the Board of Trustees of the hospital but founder and president of InterElectronics, one of the leading multi-national conglomerates in the world. Which meant that Cameron had the resources to come up with those added monies that every large, modern, growing hospital needs periodically in these times of rising costs.

Carey had worked out his organization chart to meet each of Cameron's suggestions. It was a perfect plan. Every piece in place. Sunderland would become Chief of Neurology when Benziger resigned. And when the HEW enforcement inspectors asked about the progress of women at University Hospital, there would be Jean Scofield, as Associate Chief. An empty title, but good enough to satisfy HEW and clear the way to a big fat Federal grant. Now, the only crucial piece that would not fit was that woman Scofield. And Benziger, soft-spoken and professorial, had stubbornly refused to talk to her.

Before Carey dared report defeat to Cameron he would have a go at Scofield himself. There was no sense delaying. He lifted the phone.

"Martha, where is Dr. Scofield? I want her here at once!"

"Yes, sir."

Within moments Carey's phone rang.

"Dr. Scofield has an emergency at the moment. She suggests tomorrow. Or some time early next week."

"Damn it, I want this settled before the day is out! Raise her on her beeper!"

A few minutes later his intercom buzzed. "Dr. Scofield has evidently turned off her beeper," the secretary reported.

"Then have one of the floor nurses get to her."

"They have, sir."

"And?" Carey demanded.

"Well, sir, she sent back a message. Unless you're experiencing some neurological emergency, you'll have to wait."

Carey slammed down his phone and gave vent to a string of expletives in which he called Jean Scofield all the unflattering names he could level at any woman. His frustrated mind began to plot all sorts of administrative vengeance. Finally, he made his decision. If Scofield refused, there was another woman in Neurology, far less qualified, but who would be delighted to accept the appointment that Scofield had so imperiously turned down. As far as HEW was concerned, any woman in the new job would satisfy their requirements. Carey sent for the file of the other woman neurologist.

two

It was neither rudeness nor lack of concern which had caused Jean Scofield to reject Carey's summons to the impromptu meeting. It was the arrival of a new emergency case.

A young boy of five had suddenly begun to convulse. Suspecting neurological complications, the pediatrician immediately referred him to Dr. Scofield. Especially since the boy was not a regular patient of his, but one he had seen only while covering for Dr. Lawrence Braham who was away at that symposium in Houston.

As the referring pediatrician explained so glibly to Jean on the phone, "I'm sure Larry would want you to take charge of this case personally."

It was said with such studied blandness that Jean could not fail to miss the point. While she had never made any special effort to conceal her relationship with Larry Braham, she resented those who focused on it by so meticulously pretending to ignore it.

She had almost reached the ER when she heard herself being paged again. The new patient must have arrived. As Jean entered the room, the unconscious boy was being transferred from the wheeled gurney stretcher onto a treatment table. The nurse was standing by with a rubber catheter to suction any vomitus out of his throat so he would not gag. A middle-aged woman in street clothes stood by, stunned and tearful. She appeared too old to be the mother of a boy of five. Nevertheless, Jean asked, "You the mother?"

"I'm the maid. Mrs. Tatum was out when it began to happen. So I called Dr. Braham's office . . ."

"Wait outside!" Jean interrupted. As the woman hesitated, Jean turned her about firmly and ordered, "Wait outside! And try to locate his mother, if you can."

"I already have," the distraught woman called back.

Jean turned to the unconscious child. She examined his mouth. Fortunately, his teeth were not clenched.

"Rubber airway," she ordered.

Once she had slipped it between the child's teeth to make sure he had a clear air passage, she hooked up nasal oxygen. She was strapping on the blood pressure cuff to take the child's vital signs when he began to convulse again.

Assuring herself of his airway, Jean Scofield watched as the seizure proceeded. She was intent on seeing the precise manner in which it began, especially observing the child's head and eyes, which turned distinctly to the right.

It was a significant sign, indicating an irritative adversive frontal lobe seizure on the left side of his brain.

His entire body stiffened rigidly in the next, tonic phase of the seizure. Soon it was followed by the clonic phase, a rhythmic jerking of first his right hand, then his arm. Soon his entire small body was seized by it. Jean cradled the boy's head in her arms to protect him from accidentally injuring himself. She ordered the nurse to affix a light restraint to prevent his slipping off the table during the spasm's most violent phase.

Once the nurse had done that, Dr. Scofield directed her to insert a plastic intravenous catheter, making sure to enter a vein that did not cross any crease point, such as an elbow. Thus the catheter could not be broken during spasm. The nurse inserted the needle and taped the catheter to the child's lower forearm. Now, if medication proved necessary, it would be a simple, swift procedure to hook it up to the IV. The nurse again suctioned the child's airway clear.

Eventually the boy's spasmodic movement subsided. Finally, he lay quiet, unconscious. Jean Scofield relaxed her hold.

"Safety pin!"

The nurse handed her a sterilized pin. The doctor administered short, sharp stabs of the pin to the child's extremities—right arm, right leg, left arm, left leg. He responded with involuntary withdrawal movements of each limb as it was pricked. She noted that his responses were much slower and weaker on the right side than the left side. She scratched the bottom of his bare right foot. His toes turned up instead of down. Babinski's reflex, typical of a post-ictal state.

She checked his vital signs. Respiration, normal now. Blood pressure, normal. Pulse, steady. She applied her stethoscope to the boy's heart, then to his lungs. A child in seizure could inhale some of his own vomitus and contract aspiration pneumonia. His lungs sounded clear.

She placed the round metal disk of the instrument first over the right carotid artery in his neck and then over the left. There were no bruits, no gurgling sounds that would indicate a turbulent flow of blood to his brain. She examined his head carefully for signs of injury. She found none. She examined his rib cage for contusions or other evidence of trauma. None.

The boy regained consciousness. He stared at her, his pale blue eyes tearful and pathetic. Each time she touched him he became tense, drawing back from her. For the moment she dismissed it. Undoubtedly he was frightened at being alone and bewildered in this strange place, but she could not let it interfere with her examination.

She palpated his abdomen. Aside from noting that the child was rather thin, though not necessarily suffering from malnutrition, she found nothing that would help her make any determination as to cause. No rigidity. No absence of bowel sounds. She palpated the child's pelvis, squeezing gently to make sure there was no tenderness that might indicate a pelvic fracture. Most carefully she palpated his spine and neck. Lacking his history, she had to be careful not to move his head or neck precipitously until she was sure they were not traumatized, thus causing the seizures. There was no gross evidence of fracture.

That part of her examination completed, Dr. Scofield was free to proceed with the more intensive neurological phase of her search. But before she could begin, the boy's eyes and head suddenly turned to the right again. The pattern had begun to repeat. At that moment a woman's voice, high-pitched and extremely tense, was heard just outside the door of the Emergency Room.

"I have a right to see him! You can't stop me!"

The door was swung open. A young, beautiful, dark-haired woman burst into the room, demanding, "Where is my . . ." She stopped. She looked in horror at the tormented boy who was now being cradled by Dr. Scofield as he jerked from tonic rigidity into the clonic phase of the seizure that soon wracked his entire body. The young woman stared, terrified at the sight.

Two things were instantly obvious to Dr. Scofield. This was the boy's mother. And she had never witnessed him in seizure before. Unconsciously, the young mother drew back, silent, horrified and disbelieving. Then she shrieked, "Bobby!"

"Leave this room! I'll talk to you later," Dr. Scofield ordered.

The mother hesitated, then seemed relieved to turn and escape, though Jean could hear her gasping outcry before the door swung closed.

She continued to cradle the boy's head, while she ordered the nurse, "Thirty mg's phenobarb. IV. Stat!"

Instead of using the slower catheter drip, the nurse injected the medication directly into the boy's vein for the swiftest effect.

"If it recurs, give him another thirty mg's," Scofield ordered, observing the boy's seizure subside. "But be sure to watch his breathing. We don't want to throw him into respiratory arrest from overmedication."

She studied the boy, who now lay unconscious. Small for his age but handsome. His eyelids flickered while he slept. She could not forget how vacant his pale blue eyes had been during the seizure. Fortunately, when he woke he would remember none of it. Even during seizure, patients were totally unaware of what was happening.

But there was one thing of which this doctor was aware. A sudden onset of seizures could be a grim warning, a prelude to fatal disease.

As quickly as possible, she had to determine the etiology of his seizures.

There were endless causes to eliminate. Fever anywhere in his little body. Systemic infection. Central nervous system infection. Arteriovenous malformations. Congenital deformities or injuries. Trauma, especially one causing a subdural hematoma, an internal hemorrhage in the protective sac that enveloped the brain. An undiscovered subdural could cause seizures as long as a year after the initial injury. If it remained untreated it could cause paralysis, even death. Finally, in the absence of all other causes, that most dread of all possible causes, brain tumor. Benign or malignant. She hoped it was something simpler, perhaps seizures that ran in the family. Or some temporary cause, such as an overingestion of drugs. Curious children frequently climbed up onto washstands to investigate their parents' medicine cabinets, swallowing anything they found there.

Up to now, Dr. Scofield had only one clue. The boy's seizures started with rightward eye and head movement, indicating that the trouble probably originated on the opposite side of the boy's brain. Since there was such an area of specific involvement, the cause was not likely to be as generalized as a fever. More likely it was something focal, causing an irritation in one area of the left side of his brain. Possibly a mass of some kind—blood clot, abscess or tumor.

None of them welcome.

Since the maid had witnessed the first seizure, it was important to interrogate her at once. Then it would be necessary to secure a complete history. Only the mother could supply that.

As Jean came into the doorway of the waiting room both the boy's mother and the maid came toward her.

"How is he?" the mother cried out, trying to keep from weeping again.

"Resting," Jean was quick to reassure her. "Now, please sit down. I have to talk to your maid first."

"I want to see the doctor!" the mother persisted.

"I'm Doctor Scofield."

"I didn't realize . . ." the woman stammered.

Jean could not decide if the woman was reacting in surprise or disapproval. For some reason women always felt more secure in the hands of male doctors, more so even than male patients did. However women might protest it, they were the more prejudiced against their own sex.

"Now, tell me how it started," Jean asked the maid. "Did you see it begin?"

A large, middle-aged woman of Slavic extraction and not at ease with the language, the maid's lips trembled but she made no sound.

"Was he home?" Jean asked.

"Yes, he came home like every day. He goes to pre-school so he only goes half day. He comes home for lunch. I made it for him. Just like Mrs. Tatum said. Only today he didn't have no appetite."

"Today?" Jean interrupted, remembering the boy seemed thinner than he should be.

"He's not such a good eater any time," the maid admitted. "Today was worse. He just wants to go to his room and lay down."

"Does he do that often?" Jean pursued. "Ask to go to his room and rest in the middle of the day?"

"No. But today yes. I knew Mrs. Tatum would be very angry if I don't make him finish his vegetable and milk. But I let him go lie down anyway."

Dr. Scofield nodded. It was noteworthy that the child had voluntarily sought to lie down. He had undoubtedly been experiencing an aura, a premonition that the seizure was coming on.

"What happened after that?" Jean continued.

"He is so quiet I get worried. So I go up to his door. I hear this awful sound. So I go in. I find him . . . like . . . he was . . . Well, he was like you saw him. It was terrible. Terrible!"

Then she added, a bit shamefaced, as if in some way it were her fault for bringing him here in such a condition, "I guess you saw he wet himself. He don't do that. He's a very good trained boy."

"It usually happens during a seizure." Jean tried to minimize the maid's discomfort. "Don't worry about it."

But the woman continued to shake her head embarrassedly.

"You can go now. I won't need you any longer."

The maid turned to Mrs. Tatum for instructions.

The mother ignored her as she came forward. "I insist on seeing my son!" she demanded.

"You will. In a while. But first I need a complete history."

"Not until I know what's wrong with my son!" the mother persisted.

"For your son's sake, we'd better do this my way," Jean said softly but firmly.

The mother glared at the doctor, then relented.

Knowing what a shock this had been to the young mother, and expecting an emotional reaction, Jean suggested, "We can do this better in my office."

She turned to lead the way.

three

As they passed through the reception room of her suite, Jean said to her secretary, "Maggie, no phone calls for the next half hour."

She ushered Mrs. Tatum through her examining room. On one wall hung more than a dozen neatly framed diplomas and certifications of admission and qualification which Jean had amassed during her career. The other walls were devoted to glass cases, x-ray viewing boxes and bookshelves. The glass cases housed the instruments necessary to her examinations. The bookshelves bulged with thick volumes on all phases of neurology, to some of which Jean had herself contributed chapters.

Her private consultation room was large but intentionally decorated to seem intimate and relaxing. In this room no diplomas, instruments or books. On the paneled walls hung a few selected works of art which had special appeal or significance for her. The soft comfortable chairs avoided any resemblance to institutional furniture. Except for her desk and a dictating machine, it seemed in all respects like a comfortable living room. She had designed it herself, to put anxious relatives and tense patients at ease. For, in her specialty, ofttimes a patient's frame of mind was as important as his pathology. Examinations were for the examining room. This room was for the considered explanations that most neurological cases eventually required.

Jean had always felt that matters of treatment, of suggested delicate and possibly dangerous surgery, of prognosis, of affected lives, and sometimes of death, deserved proper intimate surroundings.

Her office provided this for her discussion with Mrs. Tatum.

As soon as she was seated, Marissa Tatum pulled a pack of cigarettes and an expensive gold lighter from her bag, asking, "Do you mind?"

"Not at all," Jean said, soothingly. Once the mother had lit up, Jean began the history by asking, "Your son's name?"

"Bobby. Robert Tatum, Junior."

"His age?"

"Five. Five years and three months."

"Left-handed or right-handed?"

Marissa Tatum stared back at the doctor, curious, then answered, "Right."

"Has he ever had seizures before, and if so, when did they start?"

"Seizures?" the mother repeated, frightened, though obviously unaware of the true meaning of the word.

"Seizures, Mrs. Tatum," Jean Scofield explained gently. "Convulsions. Fits, if that word is clearer."

"Convulsions? Fits? Bobby? Never!" The woman's lips quivered. Tears welled up in her eyes. But she controlled her impulse to cry.

"I know it's a great shock the first time," Jean consoled, "but after a while, when you come to know the symptoms, signs, and course of the seizures, they will be less terrifying."

"After a while?" Mrs. Tatum asked. "You mean this might happen again?"

"Until we find and remove the cause, we have to expect that they will recur," Jean said casually, aware of how traumatic such a truth could be to any mother.

Marissa Tatum stared at the doctor, suspicion and distrust evident in her eyes. "I want to see Dr. Braham!"

"Dr. Braham is out of town. And will be till late tonight," Jean informed her, without indicating how she came to know his schedule so precisely.

"Then I insist on talking to him on the phone!"

"I'm afraid that's not easy to manage. He's attending a medical symposium in Houston. But even if you did talk to him, I'm sure he'd tell you your son is in capable hands. Dr. Braham refers all his neurological cases to me."

Jean felt no need to explain their relationship to Mrs. Tatum. It had begun two years ago when Larry Braham first referred one of his young patients to Jean and was enormously impressed by her work. Subsequent referrals followed. By the sixth one, this time a young child who Jean discovered had no special need for neurological consultation, Larry had to admit, a bit sheepishly, that possibly he was more interested in the neurologist than in her medical opinion.

They began to see each other often. It was inevitable that it would develop into an affair. But Jean insisted that it in no way be permitted to affect their professional relationship. They both respected that meticulously.

Just as now it was necessary that Jean treat Mrs. Tatum as she would the mother of any patient referred to her by any other doctor.

She spoke firmly. "Mrs. Tatum, instead of waiting for Dr. Braham to return, you can do much more for your son by answering my questions as fully as you can. Is there any history of seizures in either your family or your husband's?"

"Not in mine. And I never heard Bob mention any. They're a strong, healthy family."

"Even apparently strong, healthy families can hide a history of seizures. It's important to find out and let me know."

"All right, I'll ask him."

"Has Bobby complained of headaches lately?"

"Only on mornings when he doesn't want to go to school. He finds all sorts of excuses. Sometimes it's headaches."

"Has he had nausea? Vomiting?"

"No."

"Ever complained of double vision?"

"No. Look, Doctor, what are you getting at? I have a right to know."

"Of course, and I promise as soon as I know, you'll know. But if I'm to find out, you'll have to answer all my questions," Jean urged.

Realizing the doctor was only intent on helping her son, Marissa Tatum apologized. "Of course. I'm sorry." She lit another cigarette.

"Any serious childhood illnesses?" Jean continued probing.

"Measles, that's all."

"Surgery?"

"No," the mother responded quickly, then corrected,

"He had his tonsils out, did you mean something like that?"

"Tonsillectomy," Jean noted. "At what age?"

"Three."

"Does he have trouble walking, any unsteadiness of gait?"

"No."

"Does he evidence any lack of coordination of his hands, any trouble doing simple things like buttoning his clothes?"

"No," his mother said, trying to glance across and read the doctor's notes.

"Ever complain of tingling or numbness in his fingers or anywhere?" Jean asked casually, hoping the tense mother would not suspect the import of her question.

"No."

"Difficulty swallowing or speaking?"

"No."

"Has he ever had meningitis?"

"Only measles, as I said."

"Has he run any high fevers lately?"

"No."

"Any stomach infection?"

"None."

"Has he experienced any weakness on one side of his body as compared to the other?"

"I never noticed any."

"Any trauma?" When Mrs. Tatum seemed puzzled, Jean explained, "Has he sustained any injury? Especially an injury to his head. Has he fallen off his bike? Or tripped and struck his head while running or playing? Anything like that?"

Marissa Tatum's beautifully sculptured face turned thoughtful as she tried to recollect any events in her young son's life that might be of importance to the doctor. After some moments, she shook her head.

"Was there anything special today? Anything he said to you that was different from other days?"

"No," the mother answered at once, then seemed to remember. "Yes, he did mention something early this morning about hoping his teacher wouldn't make him draw elephants again today. He wanted to draw zebras. He finds stripes more interesting."

"So there's some kind of tension at school between him and his teacher?"

"Nothing important, I can assure you. He's not a rebellious child. Quite the opposite. He's extremely easy to get along with. A perfect little gentleman. And bright. Very bright."

Suddenly Mrs. Tatum exploded with the question which was at the root of her anxiety. "This won't affect his mind, will it? He won't be like those children I see who twitch all the time and drool . . . ?"

"If he responds to treatment, I'm sure he'll be fine."

"*If* he responds . . . You mean it's possible he won't respond?"

Patiently, Jean explained, "Before we can say anything, we have to discover the etiology, the cause. Part of the process is what we're doing now. So, for the moment, please answer all my questions as fully as you can."

"I'm sorry. I'll try."

"Did anything else unusual happen today?"

"No. Nothing. He went off to school. On the bus, I assume."

"Assume?"

"I had to rush off to a meeting of the Women's Guild at Mrs. Cameron's."

Jean interrupted to ask, "Mrs. *Horace* Cameron?"

"Of course," Marissa Tatum said, pretending to be casual but quick to claim a close relationship with the wife of a man as important as the president of Inter-

Electronics. "Whenever I have to go to one of her meetings, Esther puts Bobby on the school bus. And waits for him at noontime when the bus drops him off. She gives him his lunch. Then he has an hour's rest. After that, he usually goes out to play with the other children."

"Does it happen often?"

"What?"

"That Esther puts him on the bus instead of you?" Jean asked, glancing up from her notes to study Marissa Tatum's face as she responded.

"Lately, we've been quite busy. Mrs. Cameron wants me to organize a group of women volunteers to take over certain duties here at the hospital. With rising costs, she thinks we can absorb part of the load and help keep the paid work force down."

"We could use all the help we can get," Jean agreed.

Before she could ask her next question, her phone rang.

"Excuse me." She turned to answer it. "Yes? Please tell Mr. Carey it's impossible for me to take his call now. I'll call back. He can't wait? Well, give him fifteen milligrams of Diazepan and see if it helps!" She hung up impatiently and turned back to Mrs. Tatum. "I'm sorry. This must be difficult enough for you without interruptions. Now, has Bobby had all his immunizations?" Marissa Tatum looked puzzled for a moment. "Vaccinations?" Jean explained.

"Oh. Yes, he had them all. Dr. Braham has all Bobby's previous records. You see, we've only lived here for the past two years. Bob was in the San Diego office till two years ago. That's when Mr. Cameron himself asked to have him transferred here to the office of InterElectronics."

Jean could appreciate the obvious pride the young wife took in announcing that her husband had been singled out for such a distinction by Cameron himself. Cameron's international reputation as a power in the electronics industry made such a personally selective promotion a crucial event in the career of any ambitious young executive.

Jean also realized that she was dealing with a patient in whom the Chairman of the Board of Trustees of the hospital might have a personal interest. And Cameron had a reputation for interfering in hospital affairs beyond his duties as a trustee. She would face that problem later if it should present itself. For now, the little patient's history was all that mattered.

"I'll get the records. Now, Mrs. Tatum, is Bobby allergic to anything?"

"My son is not one of those overly sensitive, allergic children," she stated with pride as well as a certain intolerance.

"Before Bobby was born," Jean began, noting that Mrs. Tatum involuntarily reacted a bit stiffly, "were you sick during the first three months of pregnancy?"

"No, I was fine."

"Did you take any medication? Sleeping pills? Tranquilizers?"

"Sometimes."

"Sometimes what?"

"Tranquilizers. Bob was away quite often. His work called for lots of travel. Still does. So when I was alone, sometimes at night it was difficult to sleep. My obstetrician prescribed a mild tranquilizer."

"Would you happen to remember which one?"

"Valium."

"How strong?"

"I don't know."

"What color were the pills?"

"White. About so small. But I didn't take them often. I never even finished the first prescription."

Jean Scofield felt relieved by that.

"During pregnancy, did you suffer any bleeding or threaten to abort?"

"No."

"Any infection of any kind?"

"None," Mrs. Tatum said, reaching into her purse for another cigarette until Jean pointed out that she already had one burning.

"Now, about Bobby's birth . . ." The look on Marissa Tatum's face changed overtly now. "There was trouble? A difficult passage through the canal? Was it overlong? Was there undue pressure on his head? Do you remember hearing your obstetrician say anything at all like that?" Jean asked, concealing her concern.

"I wouldn't know. I was under anesthetic at the time. I had a cesarean."

Jean did not respond, but noted "Difficult delivery" with no other comment save a single underlining of the word "Difficult." Then she continued, "Did they tell you if Bobby started to pink up and breathe right away? Or what his Apgars were?"

"The doctor said he came out fine. Everything normal. And there was no brain damage!" The mother was determined to make that point. Then she admitted, "Even though he was somewhat premature."

"Then he was in intensive care for the first few days?"

"For more than four weeks," Marissa Tatum corrected, "but he came out of it very well. They tested him regularly and he was fine. Fine."

"How old was he when he began to walk?"

"About a year. Thirteen months, actually. Look, he is not retarded. He is very bright!" the mother insisted fiercely.

Jean continued with her routine and pertinent questions. "And when he began to talk, how old?"

"Eleven months, almost a full year."

"How does he do in school?"

"Very well."

Jean nodded and went on to complete a review of all the boy's systems. She concluded, "That's fine. Thank you, Mrs. Tatum, you've been very helpful."

"*I* have some questions I'd like to ask," the mother said insistently.

"Of course."

"What's going to happen to Bobby now?"

"First, I think it would help you to understand what a seizure is. It is *not* all the weird things folklore says it is. It is not a curse. Nor anything mystical. It *is* a sign of some difficulty within the brain that we now have to track down. If we can. Of course, in Bobby's case he's had not one convulsion but a series of them."

"Series?" the mother asked tensely.

"He's had what we call *status epilepticus*. Which sounds worse than it really is," Jean tried to reassure her.

"You said you had to track down the cause, *if you could.* What if you *can't?*"

To avoid intensifying the distraught mother's fears, Jean Scofield ignored that question to ask, "What kind of games does Bobby's father play with him?"

"Games?" the mother asked, obviously puzzled.

"Does he lift him to his shoulders? Or toss him up in the air and pretend to let him fall, then catch him at the last moment?"

"You know how fathers are with sons. Yes, he plays games like that with him."

"Has he ever actually dropped him?" Jean asked quickly.

"Of course not! Bob would cut off his right hand before he'd let anything happen to his son!"

Jean Scofield spoke more deliberately now. "Mrs.

Tatum, of course he would never do that on purpose. I was only asking if it *might* have happened. *Accidentally.*"

"No, it never did."

"Could it have happened when you weren't there so you might never know about it?"

"It never happened! Nothing in my husband's life is more dear to him than Bobby. Because . . . well, as I told you, I had a cesarean. The doctor said I shouldn't consider having any more children. And Bob's adamant against adoption. So Bobby is all we'll ever have. Nothing must be allowed to happen to him. Nothing!"

Unable to give the mother any honest assurances and unwilling to give her false ones, Jean Scofield changed the subject. "When do you expect your husband home?"

"Friday evening. The last plane from Chicago."

"I'd like to see him as soon as possible. Saturday morning?"

"Why?" Marissa Tatum leaned forward. "Because it's so bad you don't dare tell me?"

"There's nothing to tell yet."

"Then you suspect!" Mrs. Tatum insisted. "What? I have a right to know."

"It's too early even to suspect. We need the whole picture. A complete history. All the test results. The aftereffects of his seizures. His response to the medication."

"But it could be bad," the mother ventured, desperately hoping to be contradicted.

"It could," Jean was forced to admit.

"How bad?"

Jean knew the tormented woman would be satisfied with nothing less than the complete truth, painful as that might be.

"The possibilities range all the way from seizures which can be controlled by medication and will finally disappear, to a brain tumor. Which will not disappear," Jean ended softly, trying to minimize the shock.

"Brain tumor . . ." Marissa Tatum whispered and turned away. "Oh, Bobby . . . Bobby . . . Bobby . . ."

Jean Scofield left her desk and came around to place her arm about the mother.

"Mrs. Tatum, now you know why I never like to tell the patient's mother anything before we're sure. Mothers only hear the worst prognosis. I did say your son may only be experiencing mild seizures that are completely controllable. Remember that."

The woman nodded slowly as if trying to convince herself. Suddenly she asked, "If it's a tumor, could it be malignant?"

"The odds are it isn't a tumor at all," Jean hastened to reassure her, though it was one of the possibilities. "Now I have to go back and complete my examination of your son."

"How long will he have to be here?"

"Four or five days, most likely."

"I'd like him home before Bob gets back Friday night. It will be quite a shock to find out his son is in the hospital."

"Mrs. Tatum," Jean suggested gently, "let's treat the boy, not his father. We'll send Bobby home when it's best for *him*."

"Yes, of course." The mother hesitated, then asked, "Can I see him now?"

"He's asleep."

"Just for a moment?"

"Of course. Come with me," Jean invited.

As they walked down the hall, she suggested, "Don't you think it might be advisable to call your husband and tell·him?"

"Oh, no," Marissa Tatum responded quickly. "He'd

drop everything and fly right back. And I'm afraid Mr. Cameron might not like that."

"Nevertheless, I strongly urge that you call your husband," Jean said.

Marissa Tatum approached the Emergency Room with considerable and obvious apprehension. For a moment Jean thought the mother might reconsider and not enter the room. She stared down at her sleeping son, then, taking her cue from Dr. Scofield's gesture, she slipped out of the room. Now Jean was free to proceed with her more intensive examination. She was reaching for the flashlight in her lab coat pocket when the phone light blinked. The nurse answered. It was Carey's secretary again. Dr. Scofield declined to interrupt the examination to take his call.

"Otoscope!" she requested of the nurse. She examined the boy's nose and ears for traces of blood or spinal fluid, the presence of which would indicate a recent trauma to the head. There was no evidence of either.

She used the ophthalmoscope to focus into his eyes at his optic fundi to see if she coud detect any sign of elevated brain pressure or hemorrhage. She found no such sign. The child's pupils were round as they should be, regular, equal and reacted briskly to light, directly and consensually.

Once the child became conscious she would check his eyes for accommodation.

She gently opened his eyes again, turned his head back and forth. The eyes reacted with conjugate gaze. His oculocephalic reflex was intact. She examined his neck. There was no area of focal tenderness. Once again she examined the pulses in his carotid arteries. There were no bruits, no abnormal sounds. His heart proved regular, no murmurs, no signs of enlargement. His lungs were still clear.

He still exhibited some weakness on his right side, but not so marked as before.

Her testing suggested that his cranial nerves 2 through 12 were intact. She then repeated her earlier physical and neurological examination.

Finally she wrote up her findings on the chart of *"Tatum, Junior, Robert. Patient #264 4756. Five-year-old White Male."*

At the end, she noted her clinical impression.

1. *Post-ictal secondary to 2.*
2. *Seizure disorder of unknown etiology. (a) Possible focus in left frontal lobe, i.e., presentation as adversive frontal lobe seizure with head and eyes turning toward the right and suggestion of residual right hemiparesis now rapidly clearing. (b) L/O mass lesion.*

Under *Plan,* she wrote:

1. *Admit to ICU for further care and observation.*
2. *Neurological vital signs every hour for the next 6 hours. Then every 2 hours for the next 4 hours, then every 4 hours.*
3. *If child not awake in 6 hours call me.*
4. *Clear liquids as tolerated once awake. If not, cont. IV.*
5. *Phenobarbital 30 mg intramuscularly q. 12 h.*
6. *Call me if seizures recur.*
7. *Keep IV open with 50 to 100 cc of D5 and W via micro-drips. Q. 8 h.*
8. *Dilantin 50 mg intramuscularly now, then P.O. t.i.d.*

9. *No other sedation.*

10. *Bed rest.*

11. *No bathroom privileges.*

12. *In morning ambulate with assistance of attendant.*

13. *Call if patient does not void in 8 hours.*

Diagnostic Workup:

14. *Skull x-rays, portable in a.m.*

15. *Echo-encephalogram, portable in a.m.*

16. *EEG in a.m.*

17. *Dr. Braham, pediatrician, to consult and follow case with me from pediatric standpoint.*

18. *Brain scan tomorrow afternoon.*

19. *Possible angiogram later but only if clearly indicated.*

In addition she ordered the standard lab tests. CBC. Urinalysis. Chest x-ray. Blood chemistries and screening panel.

Having noted that, she made sure the child was moved to Neurological Intensive Care. There was no more she could do before he reacted to the medication and until the results of the tests began to accumulate.

Up to the moment, "seizures of unknown origin" was the only diagnosis she could make.

She remembered that Carey was still waiting. She had meant to see him now, but reminded herself of the young child Guylay had admitted earlier. She had to stop by the wards and take another look at him. Perhaps the first of the test results were back. They might reveal something of significance.

The child was sleeping, both its hands encased in ointment-impregnated gauze. She stared down at him. The indicia of pugilistic puss were even more evident now that his face was in repose. She remembered once having had another child like that on the wards. The parents went to court to have him returned, and they won. Two months later he was dead, from an accident that she would never believe was an accident at all. *NAI.* She was determined that Guylay must not surrender this child to such a fate.

She remembered Carey again. Almost perversely, she decided to make one more stop before going to see him.

four

She stopped by ICU where Bobby Tatum now lay in a deep, peaceful sleep induced by two factors: the natural need for sleep that usually followed seizures, and the phenobarbital that she had prescribed as an anti-convulsant. She stared down at him. He was a handsome child. With his mother's black hair and some of her striking features. But there must be a good part of his father in him, too, for he was handsome in a distinctly masculine way for a boy so young.

She was reminded of another child, one who was destined never to be born, but who might well have looked like this if he had resembled his father. That belonged to another place, another life, and now was only a dull ache that she felt from time to time.

Carey's calls had been so persistent, she reminded herself, she should put him off no longer. She called his office. Though Carey was in conference, his secretary was sure he would not mind being interrupted for Dr. Scofield.

When Jean arrived, she discovered that Hans Benziger had also been invited to attend. Whenever they met for the first time on any day, Hans Benziger always greeted Jean Scofield with a warm fatherly kiss. He did so now. He spoke gently to her, the traces of his mellow German accent lending a disarming quality to his warning, "You know what he wants."

"I know," she responded, softly but with quite some steel in her voice.

"And I'm supposed to try to convince you," old Benziger said, smiling.

"Then try, Benni. Try," she said, amused.

Carey was on his feet, positively gallant in the way he greeted her. She suspected that if he hadn't considered it too flamboyant a gesture, he might have kissed her hand. Rattlesnakes rattle before striking. Carey always beamed.

"Well, my dear, you've been having a busy day. But nothing unusual about that, is there?"

Jean refused to relieve him of his anxiety by responding. She simply let the man go on.

"Now, then, what's this I hear about your refusing to accept the appointment as Associate Chief of Neurology?" He smiled indulgently, as if not taking her refusal seriously.

Jean smiled back, as pleasantly, but said. "Yes, I did refuse."

"But my dear, that position was created especially for you. Do you realize that?"

"I realize that. And more," Jean said, still smiling. "For example, the condescension in your attitude when you call me 'my dear.' I've never heard you address any male member of the medical staff in those words."

"After all, there is a difference . . ." Carey began to stammer, his face turning red.

"I'm more aware of that difference than you are!" Jean responded, abandoning her smile now. "I do not wish to be demeaned, or treated like daddy's little girl with phrases such as 'my dear.' My title, *Doctor,* will do very nicely.

"And as for jobs 'created especially for me,' don't bother. There's only one job I want. Chief of the Department of Neurology when Dr. Benziger retires."

"We've never had a woman . . . "

Jean overrode him. "That's another word I·don't want to hear. 'Never.' I don't give a damn about what's *never* happened before. I am interested in the job I am highly qualified to do. And I don't intend to be bought off with an empty title lacking the power to put into effect some of the advances we should be making around here."

Carey glanced at Hans Benziger for help. But the old doctor pretended to be staring out the window, oblivious of the distress call. Carey had to proceed on his own, as best he could.

"You understand that unless you take this new appointment we will not have fulfilled our quota of disadvantaged, under-utilized personnel. We'll be short of meeting our Federal requirements."

"And short of Federal funding."

"Exactly!" Carey continued pointedly. "After all, you should feel some gratitude toward this institution, which has done so much for you."

There was a peculiar emphasis in Carey's last phrase which made Jean Scofield wonder. Had he used it intentionally? Or was it merely a chance expression?

" 'Associate Chief of Neurology' is an empty title," Jean responded. "If you have a competent chief, you don't need an associate."

"And the matter of Federal funding?" Carey challenged.

"There's an easy way to assure yourself of that. Appoint a woman. A well-qualified woman," Jean replied, her green eyes blazing.

"Men simply do not like to work under a woman chief!" Carey declared flatly.

"There've been woman chiefs in other hospitals," Jean countered.

"Damn few!" Carey was quick to point out. "They simply don't have the qualifications. They don't publish enough research papers. Mind you," he went on, "I'm not saying I blame them. After all, medicine is not their primary interest. Most of them look forward to marriage. Some drop out of medicine completely after a while."

"As do some men!" Jean reminded sharply. "And if it's longevity you're concerned with, or continuity, let me remind you that women live longer than men and therefore have longer productive lives. So, overall, a woman doctor is likely to render *more* years of service than a man!"

"Men don't cut down their productive time with maternity leaves or to look after their children." Then, after a slight pause, Carey added, "Of course, in your case that wouldn't be a problem."

It was the second sly reference Carey had made to Jean Scofield's personal life. By now she was sure the first mention had not been entirely accidental. Even Hans Benziger, who had been enjoying the argument until now, took on a grim look.

"What does my private life have to do with this appointment?" Jean demanded.

"I was merely citing the experience other institutions have had with female doctors on staff."

"As long as we're 'citing experience,' Mr. Carey, let me cite some. No, women don't do as much scientific research as men. And it does not show up in their curricula vitae. Why? Because the committees that dole out research grants are mainly composed of men. And they do not readily give grants to women. So the fault isn't with women. Or their minds. Or their devotion. It's at the top where the money faucet is turned on or off. I was lucky. Very lucky. I had Dr. Benziger to fight for my grants. God knows how many great contributions women could have made to medicine if there had been other Benzigers sitting on other boards that control such decisions."

"Don't you see, if you take this new post, you'll have advanced the cause of women in medicine," Carey said, hoping to move her on the basis of sacrifice.

"If I take this new post I won't have accomplished one thing! Except give you an easy out, because you don't want a woman as Chief! Now, I've got to get back to Neuro ICU. There's a little boy whose condition is very puzzling and may turn out to be extremely dangerous."

Carey shook his head sadly, pretending it grieved him greatly to bring up the next subject.

"There are some important men here at the hospital who think that the pressures of being Chief might prove too much for you. Considering your past history."

Jean Scofield glared at Carey, who returned her gaze defiantly.

"Nothing about my past history bears on this appointment," she said with angry finality.

Once she had left, Hans Benziger rose from his chair.

"Edward, that was both unfair and unwarranted. That past episode has absolutely nothing to do with this appointment!"

"Still, there are men who feel that way."

"There are men who mug and rob old ladies, too. That doesn't mean you have to join them!"

Benziger strode out of the room. Outside, his own sense of guilt reproached him. From the outset, he had feared that once he proposed Jean's name as Chief of Neurology the subject of her past was bound to come up. He had assumed she was resigned to having it all aired again. Now he was not so sure. He must talk to her at once.

Since Benziger's office faced west over the city, on clear late afternoons he was blessed with an inspiring view of the sunset. If, in addition, there were a few clouds in the sky to refract the setting sun, the view became blazingly spectacular, partially blotting out the slums that had grown up around University Hospital. This was one such afternoon. Benziger opened the door of his office, stared at the bright expanse of sky, then turned to invite Jean Scofield in as he said, "That view's enough to let one forget all man-made troubles. Come, my dear, sit down." He smiled. "I trust I'm entitled to call you 'dear' without being accused of male chauvinism or whatever word the female revolution is using this month."

Benziger sat behind his desk in the high-backed chair whose rich dark brown leather provided excellent contrast for his shock of white hair. Jean sat across from him, staring at his face which reflected so many years of experience, sad and happy. It was a face any sculptor would have loved to create or recreate.

"Jean . . . Jean . . . " he began sadly, "I wonder if I've been fair to you."

"More than fair," she hastened to reassure him lovingly.

"Even urging your appointment as Chief?"

"It would have been unfair *not* to nominate me."

"I didn't mean fair in that sense."

"Oh, I see."

"It was bound to come up. We should both have expected it."

"Frankly, I thought Carey would bring up Larry," she confessed.

"Oh, he did. He suggested that I talk to Lawrence to persuade you to take that Associate Chiefship."

"We have it quite clear between us. Whatever our personal relationship, professionally we do not interfere with each other."

Benziger was always circumspect about the private lives of his staff. Yet now he presumed to ask, "Do you ever talk about marriage?"

"Larry talks about it."

"And you?"

"I . . . I *think* about it," she confessed.

"And?"

"I don't know if I can ever again marry," Jean said, turning away to stare at the last red reflections of the setting sun.

"You love him?"

"He's a good man, an honest man. I trust him. I depend on him. And yet . . . " She could not continue.

"There's something missing?" Benziger asked softly.

"He's all the things a woman searches for in a husband," she said evasively.

"But he's not Cliff."

"Or else I don't dare love with the same devotion a second time."

"Jean, my dear, we have to face it. If I leave your name in nomination, they'll bring up your past. They'll use it to attack you professionally and personally. They'll turn it into proof of your unsuitability for a taxing job. I must know if you're willing to face all that."

"Willing to face it, or *able* to face it?" she confronted Benziger.

"Have you ever detected any doubt in me?"

"No, Benni. Forgive me?" she asked softly.

"You never have to ask forgiveness from me. I simply want to know if you are willing to face the backbiting, the venomous gossip. Having the whole tragic thing come up again."

"Yes, I am!"

"I don't want your answer now, when you're in a fighting mood. Think about it."

"I won't be bought off with a phony appointment. And I won't be blackmailed!" she said determinedly.

"Think, my dear, think. There's always time to be adamant later," Benziger cautioned.

"This *is* later. The future of the Neurology Department for the next fifteen years will be determined by this appointment. I want it. Because I think I can do the best job! And I'm not fighting for women's rights. I'm alone, me, one woman, one person, who wants to take the department you built into one of the best in the country and make it even better."

Benziger couldn't argue with her on that score. If anyone could carry on his work and improve on it, Jean could. It was the personal conflict and hurt to her against which he was trying to guard. He was about to make one more effort, but the sound of the beeper in the breast pocket of Jean's lab coat summoned her to the phone.

She identified herself and listened, saying only, "Uh huh. Uh huh. Administer plasma and oxygen. And don't move her. I'll be right down."

She hung up the phone. "Another automobile emergency. Head smashed through the windshield."

"Ah, one of those," Benziger said sadly. "Go on, my dear. We'll talk more tomorrow. Meantime, tonight, think about it."

Dr. Scofield leaned over the patient, a nineteen-year-old girl, who had once been pretty but was now a mass of blood, shattered bone and pulpy tissue. Jean completed her examination swiftly.

"Arrange an emergency OR. Find Dr. Forrest and

ask him to scrub. If we want to save her from becoming a paraplegic we're going to have to go in and relieve the pressure on her spine."

Even as she said it, her cold professional mind told her that by now the pressure of the traumatized and swelling spinal cord against the bony structure of the spine had most likely done irreparable damage. Hers was a specialty which produced some tragic statistics.

Sometimes she wondered if she had chosen to stay in Neurology after Cliff's death because of the way he had died. This was one of the times when she had no time to wonder, only to devote herself to minimizing the damage to this poor, once-pretty girl, who might be lucky if she even recovered, or perhaps luckier if she didn't.

Jean had scrubbed for the operation, not to assist but to observe and verify her diagnosis. Unfortunately when Forrest went in he discovered that she was right. The damage to the spinal cord was too great to justify an optimistic prognosis. Jean was still in her OR greens when she went down to face the girl's mother and father. She was frank with them, without being unnecessarily cruel. The doctors would have to watch and see what happened to their daughter during the next few days. She warned them to expect no miracles. Neurology had not yet advanced to the stage where it could restore shattered spines.

five

She was changing from her scrub outfit back into her own clothes when she heard her beeper. She picked up the locker room phone. "Dr. Scofield."

"One moment," the operator said and connected her with the caller.

"Darling?"

It was Larry's voice. And very welcome and comforting after what she had just witnessed.

"How did your presentation go at the symposium?"

"Terrific," he said, then laughed. "I kept some of them awake for the full hour. Busy?"

"Just packing in."

"Meet me? My plane's due in at nine-fifteen."

"Okay," she promised quickly.

"You sound tired."

"Rough day. I'll tell you about it later."

"They're paging our flight. Have to go. Love you."

If she had not had so many reminders of Cliff on this hectic day, she would have responded as she usually did, "Love you, too." Instead she said only, "I know, Larry. I know." She sounded more troubled than pleased.

Lawrence Braham realized that as he hung up. She works too hard, he said to himself. She needs more of a life outside the hospital. This time, he assured himself, he would convince her.

She still had time, so she stopped off at Neurological ICU to take another look at the Tatum boy. If he were awake, she might ask him a few questions. As she walked down the deserted corridor she spied a woman seated on the bench outside ICU. The woman seemed terribly alone and forlorn, perhaps because of the lateness of the hour. As Jean drew close she recognized Marissa Tatum.

"Doctor? Has there been any change? Is Bobby worse? They won't let me wait at his bedside," she pleaded.

"My orders. You were to have a brief visit early in the evening and then let him rest through the night."

"But when he wakes he'll be frightened. He won't know how he got here or why. And I'm the only one he'll believe. The rest of you will be strangers."

Jean recalled how extremely shy and withdrawn the boy had appeared.

"Our nurses are used to dealing with children. So there's no need to worry about it. Please go home and get some rest."

"I'd rather wait."

Though she sympathized with the mother's concern, Jean felt compelled to say firmly, "I do not want the boy disturbed. You're not to go in there."

"Then I'll just wait," Marissa Tatum said, and sank back down to the bench.

Jean Scofield entered ICU, passed several cubicles and came to the one in the corner where young Bobby Tatum slept. Using her pocket flash so as not to disturb the boy, she read his chart. His vital signs were stable, pulse, blood pressure, respiration. Preliminary blood tests were back and showed no distressing departures from normal. Still no clue to the etiology of his seizures. Perhaps tomorrow's findings would reveal it. She studied the boy. All children look angelic when asleep. This boy was both angelic and quite handsome.

His mother was still waiting.

"Mrs. Tatum, it would make more sense to go home. Not only for your sake but for Bobby's. It's going to be helpful if he doesn't detect any signs of tension in you. I don't want him upset."

"I won't upset him," the young mother protested quickly.

"Children can sense the vibrations," Jean explained patiently, "especially when parents are overconcerned, overprotective. Nothing puts a child on edge more. And tension is one of the factors that can bring on seizures if a child is prone to them."

"He's not prone!" his mother interjected defensively. "This is the first time it's happened. The very first time!"

"Once a child has had a seizure we must assume he will continue to have them. We treat him on that premise. Keeping him free from stress is one of the preventives. The worried look on your face won't help."

Marissa Tatum's eyes changed suddenly from concern to anger. "Have you ever had a child?"

Impertinent and hostile though the question was, Jean's first impulse was to respond and explain. But she realized the woman was obviously too distraught to understand. So Jean said only, "No. No, I have never had a child."

"So I thought. Because it's obvious you don't know how a mother feels!" With that, she turned and started down the hall. Jean Scofield watched her go. A tall young woman, lithe, Marissa Tatum possessed the carriage of a professional model. With that finely shaped face she displayed the high degree of beauty one is used to seeing on the covers of fashion magazines. Yet, with all that, she seemed strangely insecure, Jean observed.

The airport was almost empty. A few wives waited for their husbands returning from late business trips. A young pregnant girl—probably her first child, Jean decided—was waiting too. The plane was announced and finally its landing beams appeared over the north end of the field. It made a clean sloping descent until its tires touched down with a rasping sound. The motors burst into loud reverse thrust to slow the speeding giant so the pilot could guide it off the main runway toward the terminal.

When it came to a halt it slowly disgorged its own landing steps. Most of the passengers, seasoned business travelers, came off carrying their own luggage and had no need to wait. They were claimed by wives, with whom they exchanged kisses and paired off to their respective cars. A young member of the crew claimed the pregnant girl.

Dr. Lawrence Braham came off the plane last, with Drs. Campbell and Brown, who had also attended the symposium. Since neither found his wife waiting, Larry offered them a lift, but they decided to share a cab.

As Jean was pulling her car out of the parking lot she joked, "My, how considerate."

"Who?" Larry asked, puzzled.

"Campbell and Brown. If I were your wife they'd have accepted your lift. Figuring that by now we were bored with each other and didn't particularly want to be alone. But since we're not married they think we're hotly desperate to seize every passionate moment alone, so they'd be intruding." She laughed.

"It isn't funny."

"Yes, it is," she insisted. "But I like our being treated as clandestine lovers. I'll bet every doctor's wife who's carrying on an affair must envy me. I don't have to be so secretive about it. And I can let Campbell and Brown go home feeling quite smug about how broadminded and understanding they were for having the good taste not to intrude on us."

"When you talk that way it's a sign that you're putting off the question," Larry said.

"Question?"

"I asked you to think about it again while I was away," he reminded.

"I haven't had time," she avoided.

"That particular question doesn't take time. You don't have to wait for skull x-rays to come back, or for the results of the angiogram. It's something you're aware of every waking moment. And if you aren't, there's something wrong with our relationship. Is there?"

"With me, perhaps. But not with our relationship," she admitted softly.

"Then when is it going to become something more?"

"Soon," she promised evasively.

"It's always soon. But it never gets any sooner. Why, Jeannie, why?"

Unable to respond, she stared ahead at the road, as if she needed all her concentration for driving. After a long silence, she changed the subject. "I saw a patient of yours today."

"Who?"

"Bobby Tatum."

"Bobby? With neurological difficulties?" Larry asked, startled. "What happened? An accident?"

"Convulsive seizures."

"Bobby Tatum? Convulsing suddenly? Good God!"

"On cursory examination it seems to be a left frontal lobe disturbance. Unless I can find another cause, we're going to have to go looking for the one I'd rather not find," she said. "Do you have a complete history on him?"

"I've only been treating him since they moved here two years ago. For the rest I have to rely on the records of his two previous pediatricians."

"You're his third pediatrician and he's only five years old," Jean remarked.

"They move around quite a bit. Tatum's one of the bright up-and-coming executives at InterElectronics. Cameron's been priming him for the top echelon. So he moved around from office to office. But I guess this is his last stop. The main office. Ten or fifteen years from now he'll be in contention to succeed Cameron."

"Can I see Bobby Tatum's records?" Jean asked suddenly.

"Right now?"

"Right now."

"I thought tonight you'd be a woman, not a neurologist," he reprimanded, hurt.

"I can be both," she promised. "But first, those records."

Jean Scofield examined the file of TATUM, ROBERT, JR. The prenatal history corroborated everything Marissa Tatum had told her. There were no indications of any serious illness during pregnancy that would have adversely affected the fetus. No rubella or other disease. She had been on no dangerous drugs that might imperil the health of her unborn child. There was no record of accident or physical trauma that might have affected the development of his nervous system.

The only unusual circumstance surrounding his birth was, as Marissa Tatum had reported, a premature delivery by cesarean. But, according to the notes in the file, the infant had emerged with spontaneous crying and breathing, though he required Intensive Care for several weeks.

As for the rest of his record, once released from ICU there was no indication of any difficulty that would later produce convulsive seizures.

She read through Larry's own notes on Bobby Tatum

and found little there except about periodic checkups that were favorable, plus an occasional cold and croup. One cold seemed to verge on pneumonia but was never finally diagnosed as such. For a boy of five the record was fairly uneventful.

"Well?" Larry asked.

"You were right. Nothing significant. Yet he does have those seizures. Had you ever detected any weakness on his right side before?"

"No," he admitted. "You're going to do a complete workup on him in the morning, aren't you?"

"We're doing skull x-rays, an echo-encephalogram, and an EEG first thing. Based on the results, I'll decide how much further to go."

"Keep me advised. Every step of the way."

"Of course."

"And now, what about that woman you promised me?"

Jean smiled, pulled the pins out of her hair and shook her head till her long gleaming auburn strands fell to her shoulders. He took her in his arms and kissed her. She held him tightly. It felt good to have him so close and so loving. At times she was more woman than she cared to admit, even to herself.

After a long moment of closeness, she said, "I disapprove of office love-making."

He drew back, rebuffed, until she smiled and added, "I prefer my own home and my own bed."

It was long past midnight. They had made love and it had eased her pent-up hunger as well as having drained from her all the tensions of the day. Larry was asleep. It was comforting to hear his breathing beside her. She had lived a great part of her life alone, much of it in the last dozen years. But she had never grown used to it. She needed a man. She never felt complete without one. Perhaps that was why the aftermath of Cliff's death had had such disastrous consequences.

Now she edged up in her bed, so that leaning against the headboard she could stare down at her lover sleeping beside her. Lawrence Braham was attractive by any woman's standards. His features were strong yet finely cut. His hair was curly and reminded her of Cliff. His shoulders were broad and muscular from an athletic career in college when he had had to make a choice between going on to medical school or playing professional basketball. He had opted in favor of medical school. And a good thing, Jean felt. He was an excellent pediatrician, highly regarded, and one year was voted best instructor by the students in the medical school.

He had had one marriage. Unsuccessful, because his wife refused to put up with the continuous disruption of their lives by the insistent intrusions of his little patients' parents. When she forced him to decide between his chosen practice and her and some medical specialty with more regularized hours, she was shocked that he elected to remain in Pediatrics. Secretly he was relieved that she decided to divorce him, freeing him to practice the profession he respected and loved. He realized then that his work was paramount in his life. Any wife, any woman, from now on would have to love his profession as much as he did. It was difficult enough practicing medicine conscientiously without having to defend it whenever he was home.

Love of their respective work was one of the bonds between Larry Braham and Jean Scofield. They were each understanding when the other's professional obligations disrupted their private plans. There were no recriminations, only a quiet if disappointed acceptance. Trips they had looked forward to, often were delayed or never happened. Vacations they planned together were frequently canceled. But that only made more precious the hours they did manage together.

To Jean the most lovable and loving thing about Lawrence Braham was that he respected her as a colleague in professional situations, yet was able to treat her as a woman at all other times. He was a considerate lover and a sensitive man of great passion.

In her mind there was always a kinship between Larry and Cliff. Except for some differences in their coloring and their features, they were the same: good, kind, dedicated men. Dedicated to different professions, for Cliff had entered the diplomatic service on finishing his training at Georgetown. He had devoted himself to that work with the same dedication as Larry did to medicine.

It had cost him his life. And had changed Jean's for the rest of her time.

She always thought about that more in the early hours of mornings after nights she spent with Larry. She suspected a sense of guilt, at being unfaithful to Cliff's memory. Yet she would have wanted the two to meet. They would have liked each other. Perhaps Cliff would have approved of Larry; that would have made a difference to her now. Whatever the reason, when she made love with Larry she was reminded of Cliff. The memory of him both comforted and troubled her.

six

How young and eager, how ambitious she had been about their future in the early days of her marriage to Cliff. She had come through medical school with an enviable record, had completed her internship and, as a special honor, was invited to remain and do her residency in neurology under Dr. Benziger. He had been her teacher, patron and protector all through medical school. He looked forward to her joining his department at University Hospital and moving up the academic ladder under his tutelage. A man bereft of family after his difficulties under the Nazis, Benziger had never married. He "adopted" students from time to time, training them well, then watching them depart. His "sons" and a rare "daughter" were Benziger-trained interns and residents who went on to enrich other academic institutions with the skills, knowledge, thoroughness and exacting standards they had learned under their respected professor and Chief of Neurology.

In only the most rare of instances did he try to persuade a student to remain at University Hospital. For, secretly, he was seeking among the brightest, the one who could eventually carry on when he either retired or died in service. One of the few students he had hoped to convince to remain was young Jean Scofield. She was willing and extremely flattered to be asked.

Benziger's plan and her own would have been fulfilled if Clifford Scofield, graduate of the Georgetown School of Diplomacy, young and promising assistant on the Southeast Asia desk of the State Department, hadn't been notified he was being transferred out of the country.

He had not waited till she came home to tell Jean but drove out to pick her up at the hospital. When she found him waiting in the admissions lobby she knew he had something most important on his mind. She was sure of it when he embraced her, lifted her and kissed her while waiting patients and staff stared. He wouldn't even tell her when they were in the car and on their way to the restaurant which he had selected to celebrate.

Finally, over the wine, he told her. He was being

transferred. Away from Washington, away from a desk, away from living on cabled reports and secret briefings, away from abiding by the decisions of higher-ups without ever knowing first-hand the conditions on which American foreign and military policy was being based. He was finally going out into the field. He would have contact with foreign governments and foreign peoples on a direct face-to-face basis. He was going to have responsibilities of his own. Most important, it was a signal that he had advanced far enough to be trained in the field. That was a prelude to those promotions a man needed in order to make his way upward in State.

As she listened to him, so excited by his new opportunity, she had no desire to burden him or cast shadows upon his ambitions by mentioning what they would mean to hers. She had always known that when the time came she would make whatever sacrifices she had to. She had consoled herself with the thought that there was no country that had a surfeit of trained physicians. There would always be a need for her knowledge and her science, no matter where Cliff was forced to go.

So, over dinner, she shared his enthusiasm. She welcomed the way it carried over into his love-making later that night. She had stayed awake and watched his handsome face in the dark as he slept, his black curly hair, his strong chin already showing the slight stubble which would be bristly and blue by morning. She nestled closer to him, enjoying his masculine fragrance and the warmth of him. In his sleep he slid his arm across her and gathered her to him. She would go wherever he wanted, and she would make a good life for them without any regrets. It was worth it all if only to have his arm around her this way in the middle of the night.

The next morning, first thing, she had told Benziger.

"Of course," the old man said. "I expected it all along."

He did not wish to add to her concern. He could sense how troubled she was to leave the University Hospital at a time when her own career was beginning to show such promise. Inwardly he felt the pang a father feels when his daughter tells him she is going to marry and move to some far-off place. He was losing her. Perhaps forever. Yet he knew he had no right to influence or change her decision. He must pretend that he was delighted with Cliff's promotion. He offered to write to a colleague, a man he had trained with in Heidelberg back in the oldest of old times, and who now headed up a small hospital in Saigon. Surely he would welcome Jean to his staff, or else find a place for her at some other hospital in Saigon.

"But," Jean interrupted, "Cliff won't be stationed in Saigon. He'll be out in the countryside, in the highlands, working with the peasant officials in the border areas. Some kind of unification program against the Vietcong."

"Then Werner will know what's needed out there in the line of medical help. Or else I'll contact Tom Dooley's hospital in Laos. They always need help. Out where he practices, among the peasants, a neurologist would be a godsend. And you can deliver an occasional baby, too. You haven't forgotten your obstetrics, I'm sure."

"No, no, I haven't."

"Well, then, you see, it'll be no problem at all. A small transition in your career, but an enlightening experience. There's a lot to learn in primitive areas. I've always felt that here, secluded among our tall buildings, modern laboratories and huge libraries, we tend to lose sight of the patient. Back to the basics, I say. Back to make-do medicine. It would be good for all of us."

That is what Hans Benziger said. But with each word it became more and more apparent that he was trying to keep himself and Jean from feeling too keenly the disappointment both of them shared. She let him talk on. Finally his false enthusiasm ebbed.

He said sadly, "Jean, my dear, I will be sorry to see you go. Extremely sorry. I love you as only a father could. I will miss you as the dearest of all my 'daughters' and the brightest. Write to me often?"

"Of course."

"Tell me everything. How it is going. With you and with Cliff. What you do out there. What you learn. What you need. We can send you medications, instruments, supplies. I can even arrange for you to get assistance from the hospital in Saigon. Whatever you need, let me know."

He paused, then said, "And hurry back. I will miss you."

"I'll miss you, too," Jean said.

She kissed him. It was the first time what would become their ritual had ever happened. He touched her cheek, his hand lingering there, reluctant to let her go.

In Saigon, Dr. Werner explained fully the medical situation in the countryside. There were a few peasant doctors, ill trained, undersupplied, quite primitive. The recent illness of young Dooley from cancer at a pitifully early age would leave a terrible void in Laos and Vietnam. There was much work to do. But it was hardly the place for a young female physician. She would be resented by the local doctors, out of sheer jealousy of her advanced training. She would be shunned by the natives till she proved herself. And she would be in danger always from both Vietcong guerrillas and government troops, to whom a foreign woman in such important work would be a suspect intruder.

Jean was willing to risk it. She learned sufficient native phrases to make herself understood when she gave instructions to her patients. Equipped with a small

supply of medicines and other basics, she set out in a
jeep with a guide to find one of the camps that Dooley
had earlier maintained in his time in Vietnam.

Jean's first week was spent cleaning up the place,
making it habitable again and workable. Word began to
spread. There was a new doctor, a lady doctor. She was
willing to help all comers, just as Dooley had done.
But patients were not quick to appear. She assumed it
was because she was a woman and Orientals did not
readily accept women in such exalted and mystical work
as doctoring. Yet eventually they came. She treated
their young and their old, while subjected to whispered
natives phrases which eluded her. But their amazed
stares interpreted for her. They were surprised at how
effective and able she was.

By the end of the first few months they had begun to
trust her. After a while they worshiped her. Word
spread about the lady doctor in the village near the
mouth of the river. Soon patients were being brought
down river to her from distances of many miles. It became a source of enormous satisfaction that her work
was so profoundly appreciated.

She paid a price for it, though. The times she could
get away to meet Cliff grew fewer and fewer. They had
to snatch a weekend, a day here and there, to be alone,
to rest together, to enjoy each other, to make love. His
work, his need to learn the problems and establish his
lines of communication with the local population and
their leaders meant days out in the paddies and the
villages. There was a century of distance between the
air-conditioned offices in the State Department and the
small huts in humid villages in places with strange
names like Quong Sung and My Lai.

They made the most of their rare weekends in Saigon.
They ate in excellent French restaurants, drank fine
wine, walked busy streets just beginning to abound

with American troops. They spent nights in the comfortable hotel room, making love and promising each other to spend more time together as soon as things let up. Secretly each kept from the other the fact that things were never going to let up. They lived on hope and promises. But the rarity of their hours alone made these few nights more precious. And more desperate, somehow. It was during one of those nights, when the feeling of desperation was strongest, that Jean Scofield decided it was time for her to become pregnant.

It is a strange phenomenon that in time of war the need of women to bear children increases. Whether it is a personal need or an unconscious need of the species to survive, birth rates rise at a time one would expect them to fall. Whether out of Jean's premonition of danger or out of her deep but subconscious desire to find a valid, obvious, reasonable excuse to leave her native practice in good conscience, she decided that night that she must become pregnant. She wanted it consciously, even as she desired Cliff in a passionate and sexual way. At the very height of her passion she hoped it would help to make her pregnant, though she knew scientifically that an orgasm would have no bearing on that.

She kissed Cliff good-bye in Saigon that morning, and whispered in his ear what she had been hoping.

"I seduced you," she said, laughing. "I'm going to make you the father of my child."

He laughed, lifted her off her feet, cradled her in his arms, then set her down gently on the bed. He kissed her open mouth, then whispered to her, "Just in case last night didn't take." He made love to her again. When it was over, she looked up at him, tousled his curly black hair. "What do you want? A boy or a girl? At this early stage of things we might be able to put in a request."

"Statistically," Cliff said, "there are more boy babies born in time of war than girl babies."

"But it isn't our war."

"It will be," Cliff said gravely, "it will be."

"Will it?" she asked, embracing him more tightly.

"I'm afraid so," he said, and kissed her again.

Three weeks later, she had been able to get word to Cliff. The signs were favorable. She had missed her period. By the time they met again in Saigon she was able to tell him that there was no longer any question. Cliff made her consult a gynecologist in the Saigon hospital. He also insisted she cut down on her work, that she find someone to relieve her, or perhaps replace her. She told him that it would be months before it would interfere with her work.

So he settled for making her promise that in her seventh month she would quit, come back to Saigon and spend the last two months in the city, safe, and with modern sanitary medical facilities close at hand.

He promised that he would arrange his assignment so that he was close to Saigon, if not in the city itself, when her time came.

They parted again as they had done a dozen times in the past ten months. Cliff went back out into the field. Jean returned to her primitive hospital to resume treating her native patients.

Each night when her work was done and she was finally able to retire to her own hut, she undressed and stood before the small mirror to see if she was showing. At the end of the fourth month, she was. She made a note in her diary, a record she kept to read to Cliff one day, since he could not live through the experience with her.

"Today I saw the first signs of him."

She went to sleep exhausted but happy that night.

She was in her fifth month. The native women had begun to notice and gossip about it. She understood their language better now, so she could discuss it with them, and joke, and try to explain why this was only her first child when at her age each of them had as many as five or six. Yet she was beginning to look forward to the time, not far off, when she would leave here, go back to Saigon and be with Cliff all the time, or at least more of the time than had been possible till now.

One night she fell asleep rehearsing how she would eventually tell her patients that she was leaving. It disturbed her that there had been no word about her replacement, or if indeed she would have a replacement. For she had come to love these people. The thought of leaving them totally bereft of medical attention made her feel guilty. She tried to console herself that she had at least inculcated in them good habits of health, both in pre-natal and post-natal care. She had also done some fine work in curing a number of cases of neurological disorders. Soon there would be more such cases and no one to treat them. More difficult births and no one to manage them. More infants would die in their first days who might have survived and grown to be healthy young men and women.

But there was her own son. He demanded the right to be born in safety and reared with all the advantages civilization could provide. She fell asleep with her hand resting gently on her swelling belly. She awoke, convinced that the movement of her child had wakened her.

Actually she had been disturbed by an urgent knock on the doorframe of her hut. There was silence. Then the knock came again, louder, sharper, more insistent. She was half awake when she called out in Vietnamese as she had during other nighttime emergencies, "Just a minute! The doctor is coming!"

She was drawing her light cotton robe around her when a man's voice called back, not in the excited native tongue she had grown used to, but in clear American, "Dr. Scofield?"

Startled, she went to the door, unlatched it. She peered into the darkness.

"Yes?" she asked, realizing that the man she addressed wore the dirty combat gear of a Green Beret Special Forces officer.

"Doctor, there's been a Vietcong guerrilla attack. On a local village, a province capital. They beheaded the chief. Gunned down two of his sons. . . ."

Jean interrupted, "Give me a moment to get some clothes on and put an emergency kit together. I'll go with you and see what we can do about all the wounded."

"There's only one wounded survivor," the officer said, "and he's in bad condition."

Jean pushed the door open wider to search the officer's face. "You're trying to tell me something and I don't understand."

The officer stared down at her a moment. "The attack was planned to coincide with the visit to the village chief of an American official from the State Department. A new plan to establish grass-roots contact between the people and the United . . ."

"You're saying he was there? My husband was there at the time?"

"Yes, ma'am. They fragged his hut. Two grenades. Lots of shrapnel. He sustained a bad head wound."

"Shrapnel . . . head wound . . ." All the terrible possibilities raced through her mind. "Wait, I'll go with you!"

She drew on some clothes, thinking all the while of the possible dangers presented by a head wound. She tried to reassure herself that she would help him, save him, since this was in the field of her own specialty. All during the rough and hazardous ride in the open jeep she kept rehearsing what she would look for, what tests she would make, everything that she had ever learned about the treatment of wounds and trauma to the head, the brain, the spinal column. She did that, rather than dwell on her own personal situation. This time, above all others, it was necessary to be a physician first, a woman and wife last of all.

It took almost four hours to negotiate the fifty-one miles to the village. There was still smoke rising from several of the burned-out huts. The guerrillas had devastated the homes of all those suspected of dealing with the American. As the jeep drew closer the universal wail of newly bereft widows and orphans filled the air. Jean thought, there are Americans who say that Orientals hold human life at small value. Oriental women didn't, nor Oriental children. In the family of man, grief knows no distinctions. Neither color nor culture differentiates one new widow from any other. Their outcries guided the jeep like human radar. They found one hut outside which there was no one to weep. Two Americans in combat gear with M-16's at the ready, stood guard. Jean leaped from the jeep before it drew to a halt. She raced past the guards and into the hut. On the earthen floor, in a small area cleared of debris, on a folded army blanket, lay Cliff Scofield. A medic, holding a plasma bag, stood over him, as the stuff dripped down the plastic vein into Cliff's arm. Kneeling beside him was a medical officer. He was making a desperate check of vital signs, trying to find a pulse, trying to detect respiration.

Jean rushed to Cliff, pushed the doctor aside, removed the gauze pad that covered most of Cliff's head and stared at the large gaping wound that revealed torn flesh, jagged white skullbone and grayish tissue beneath. She pulled back, stunned. She turned to the officer, who confirmed her worst fears.

"No responses. In all four limbs."

"I don't believe it," she said desperately. She proceeded to try to evoke some response. She jabbed a needle into the soles of Cliff's feet, into his thighs, into his fingers and his arms. Not the slightest response. She examined the wound again. There was still enough of the cold deliberate neurologist left in her to make her know that her skill could not save him. Yet every cell in her body was desperate to do something for him, anything, if only to keep him breathing, in the vain hope that if he remained alive perhaps something might be done back at the base hospital. Still, all the while she knew it was impossible even to attempt to move him.

Finally, all she could do was sit beside him, holding his hand, till long after the medical officer told her he was dead and they would have to take his body back to base. She was numb when she surrendered his hand. She was numb when she rode beside his body in the ambulance. She was numb when his senior State Department officer expressed the sympathy and the regret of the entire department and the Secretary of State. She was numb until, after a brief ceremony in an American military cemetery, they lowered his body into a shallow grave and fired shots over it, as if he had died in combat.

It was when they folded the flag and handed it to her that she was no longer numb but broke down in tears, and refused to be led from the graveside. She dropped to the earth and began to talk to Cliff as if he were still alive. No effort could pry her away from there. She talked in a rapid, incessant, compulsive way that led the medical officer in charge to be concerned about her condition. But she would not leave, nor would she take any sedation. Finally, he assigned a nurse to stay with her until she might finally talk herself out and be willing to depart on her own, accepting her new and sudden condition. The officer had been used to reporting deaths to wives and mothers thousands of miles from the battlefield. This was a new experience for him. He handled it as best he could.

She remained at Cliff's graveside until the rain began to fall, a monsoon-like tropical downpour. When she became aware of it, she covered his fresh grave with her body. The nurse sought to restrain her. Jean pushed her aside violently. She let the rain beat down on her, as she lay spread across the grave, his grave, her husband, her lover, the father of her unborn child.

Her pain started soon thereafter. Her delivery was premature, by some twelve to thirteen weeks. There was no chance to save the child. By that time it hardly mattered. Jean Scofield was in no condition to fully appreciate the double tragedy which had overtaken her in the course of some seventy-two hours between the time she woke, her hand on her swelling belly, and the time they took a dead child from her body.

Her father was anxious to fly over and bring her home, but the Air Force saved him that futile flight. Once she had been brought home, and he discovered her condition, he called Dr. Hans Benziger, who insisted that she be entrusted to his care. The day she was brought back to University Hospital he did a complete physical and neurological examination on her. All the examinations and lab tests proved one thing. Aside from general debilitation resulting from her refusal to take food, all her systems were unimpaired. The trouble was not in her body or her nervous system.

Benziger convened a meeting of the hospital's best men in Psychiatry. They reviewed her case and came to the conclusion that they should allow her to rest, keep her in a pressure-free environment and observe her progress. Meantime, it would be helpful if Benziger kept her on a regime of light sedation so she would get regular sleep. Perhaps they should force-feed her or else feed her intravenously so that her strength would come up to normal levels again. Many times, physical debilitation, instead of resulting from a breakdown, could cause it. They must keep her in as good condition as possible and let nature work the cure.

seven

Several weeks of sedation and feeding had produced no change. Visits from her family and friends had not brought Jean out of her deep, almost catatonic, depression. She sat in a corner and stared at the wall. She ate little, despite all their attempts to entice her and feed her. She grew thinner, her once lovely face more drawn. Her auburn hair was in distressing disarray. She presented all the classic signs of a deep, long-lasting posttraumatic depression.

The psychiatrists whom Benziger brought in on consultation offered little real aid. Cases like this might be helped by shock treatment, but it was an extreme measure rapidly falling out of favor. Some suggested narcosynthesis, chemical hypnosis, under which a patient was sometimes able to verbalize her difficulties, bring them to the surface and thus deal with them. After that, it was possible the patient might begin to recover slowly.

They all had theories, the most likely of which was that the nature of Clifford Scofield's injury was the chief source of Jean's emotional difficulty. That it was sudden and brutal surely played a part. But the most significant factor, they felt, was that his fatal injury was to the brain. Since neurology was Jean's field, they felt that her guilt at not being able to help him was thus greatly magnified. It negated her entire training, making her feel doubly guilty.

They theorized in that vein until Hans Benziger suddenly exploded. "Damn it, I don't want theories! I want a cure for that girl! And if you can't supply one, save your theories for textbooks or lectures to first-year medical students!"

They forgave his outburst. They all knew how much he loved his young protege, whom, out of his own personal need, he had emotionally adopted as the daughter he never had. But their forgiveness was of no help either. Eventually Benziger came under great pressure from the Administrator of the hospital and from the Chief of Psychiatry to consign her to a mental hospital as untreatable and to concentrate on the pressing demands of his department. He stubbornly refused.

It became a personal issue between Hans Benziger and the rest of the staff. The more pressure they exerted on him, the more stubborn he became. Behind his back they began to call him "The Prussian," and his accent didn't help. He remained unyielding. Though inwardly he did despair. He spent nights hungrily reading all the new psychiatric literature, hoping to come across a case reported by some doctor that would give him a clue as to how to breach the impenetrable wall Jean Scofield had erected in her tortured mind. He found no help in all the journals.

Yet in the back of his mind there existed a small, persistent echo of some previous bit of knowledge, of something he had heard or read in the long-ago past but could not now recapture. He tried to remember what it was, or the circumstances in which he had come across that bit of medical knowledge, but it constantly eluded him. He searched the titles in the university medical library but could find none that refreshed his memory. More weeks went by. Jean's condition did not improve. Which in itself meant she had deteriorated. The longer a depression was allowed to continue, the worse the prognosis.

One day Hans Benziger had been sitting in an inter-staff conference, half listening, half doodling on the pad before him. For a reason he could not explain, he had begun to sketch rough pyramids. These were not pyramids of a mathematical kind, but pyramids consisting of layers of stone. He dismissed the phenomenon as annoying and irrelevant, and tried to abandon it and listen to the doctor who was addressing the group on a serious problem which the Pediatrics Department was experiencing.

With the war on in Vietnam and abortion not yet legalized, the rate of illegitimate births had skyrocketed. Young girls, equally terrified of having dangerous illegal abortions and struggling to bring up fatherless infants, were having their babies under fictitious names, then abandoning them by merely slipping out of the hospital, leaving no trace of their identity. The Pediatrics Department was thus confronted by an almost insoluble problem.

There was no shortage of adoptive parents for healthy infants. But there was a frustrating legal problem. The mothers having vanished, the papers which had to be signed to make an adoption legal could not be completed without lengthy court procedures. It was during that period of time that severe damage was being inflicted on the infants. Deprived of a mother, an infant could not be embraced, kissed, or fed while held in arms. Without such close physical comfort and warmth, some infants had begun to waste. They refused to eat. They developed all the ailments one generally associated with adult emotional traumas. Skin rashes. Stomach ulcers. They failed to thrive or gain weight. In some instances, due to lack of weight gain some even sustained brain damage.

A devoted and overworked staff of pediatric nurses did what they could to fill the gap. Some stayed on hours after their tours of duty to hold the infants, to rock them in their arms, feed them their bottles. The Chief of Pediatrics had adduced statistics to prove that such infants fared better by far than the ones whom circumstance and the pressure of time had deprived of such close human contact.

The problem now, the chief was saying, seemed to be to create a program of voluntary help to replace the missing mothers. All departments of the hospital were invited to make suggestions. At this stage of the discussion Hans Benziger had abandoned his pyramids to listen intently. He understood the problem and he was sympathetic to the neurological aspects of it, since his field spanned both the physical and the psychiatric aspects of a patient's care. He was leaving the meeting when he inadvertently brushed against Dr. John Levi, Chief of Psychiatry.

The relevance of his pyramids still eluding him, Benziger asked, "John, have you ever read a paper dealing with traumatic depression that came out of Egypt?"

"The Egyptians are not very big on psychiatry. In my entire professional experience I've never seen any paper on the subject that originated there. Why do you ask?"

Rather that explain and appear foolish, Benziger did not mention his pyramids.

Quite sympathetically, Levi suggested, "In your desperation to find some therapy for your prize pupil, you seem to be going far afield. Benni, face the facts. She is, for the present and the foreseeable future, beyond our help. We'll keep her for as long as you insist. But that room could be put to better use for some other patient if we were allowed to move her to some other institution."

"No," was all Hans Benziger said. He had debated the matter too many times and too heatedly to review it now.

Benziger went from the conference room through the underground tunnels which connected the various buildings of the University Hospital till he reached the Psychiatric Building. He went up to the fifth floor where he made his twice-daily trek down the long corridor, passing wards and semi-private rooms till he came to the small private room at the end. He eased the door open softly. He peered in. He knew exactly where to look. The corner to his left.

There she was, on a stool, facing the wall. Garbed in a plain hospital gown that tied at the back, Jean Scofield sat, unaware. He looked about the room. Aside from books which he had left in the hope of enticing her to read or even gaze at the illustrations, the room held little except the bed. It was not deemed advisable to leave any instrument such as a pen or pencil which might be turned into a weapon of self-destruction. In these cases one did not take unnecessary risks.

"Jean . . ." Benziger said softly. "And how are you feeling today, my dear?"

As usual there was no answer. He moved closer to her, bent over to catch a glimpse of her face. He saw the same hollow cheeks, the same deep circles under the eyes that he saw on all other days. She flinched when he came closer to her, but she gave him no other sign of recognition. He was always disappointed, but now no longer surprised. He patted her gently on the shoulder. Perhaps he should again discuss with Levi the potentials of narcosynthesis, though Levi had never seemed too hopeful. Something, Hans Benziger kept telling himself, something had to be done. He patted her gently on the cheek, found it to be cold, terrifyingly cold. He left the room, disheartened, as he had done twice every day for many weeks.

He was walking down the hall toward the elevator when he heard himself being paged. It was a call from John Levi.

"Benni, if you once read something about Egypt and the treatment of depression it must have been papers published by British medical officers as a result of the African campaign during World War Two."

"World War Two . . ." Benziger mused. "World War Two . . ."

Now he remembered. It was during the time when he had been forced to work as an orderly and a lab assistant before he had qualified to become a doctor again. During those days he had spent much time in the hospital library, keeping up on things so as not to lose touch while working at his menial jobs. But exactly what had he read? That part still evaded him. "What about British medics and desert campaigns?"

"The war between Rommel and Alexander was so fierce and so prolonged that troops were kept in the line for periods too long and under conditions too difficult to endure. The number of battle fatigue cases mounted alarmingly. The same conditions that produced so many battle fatigue cases also prevented their proper treatment. It was impossible to bring all of them back from the battle area and give them proper rest and medical treatment."

"And so?"

"Necessity is not only the mother of invention. It sometimes leads to highly interesting medical findings as well," Levi explained. "Out of sheer inability to do otherwise, British Army physicians began to treat some battle fatigue cases right behind the lines. Twenty-four hours of sedated sleep, a good hot meal on waking, more sleep, then more good hot meals. And in forty-eight to ninety-six hours, most men were ready to go back into battle."

"Aha!" Benziger commented.

"But the really startling discovery, the one that may have been reported in the paper you vaguely recall, is this. The percentage of men returned to battle was higher when they were treated close to the line of fire than it was for those who were taken back to the hospital in Alexandria and treated under far better conditions."

"The closer to the line of fire, the better the cure rate," Benziger mused. "Can you find those papers for me, John?"

"I'm sure we have them here. I'll have the librarian hunt them up and send them to your office."

That afternoon the papers were delivered to Hans Benziger. He took them home and spent the night reading them carefully. At a little past three o'clock in the morning, he leaned back from them and stared at the most crucial sentences in all the reports.

> Since the main difference in treatment was proximity to the line of fire, it must be considered the crucial difference. Those troops who were given rest and hot food, yet could hear the sounds of combat, obviously felt a duty to their comrades to return and assist in the battle. Those men removed to hospital in Alexandria and isolated from battle felt no such obligation and, as a result, lingered far longer or became incurable fatigue cases.

Hans Benziger read those lines again and yet again. He took off the reading glasses which had worn deep grooves in the sides of his patrician nose.

So it wasn't hot food alone, it wasn't sleep alone,

though both those factors did indeed help. It was that other factor. Duty. Obligation. Whatever the word, it came to the same thing, the fact of being needed, of not being isolated from the world and from the needs of others.

He picked up a pencil and started to doodle in pyramids again.

The next morning, Dr. Hans Benziger presented himself at the office of Dr. Ernest Wilding, Chief of Pediatrics. Wilding interrupted a busy schedule to see him.

"You have some suggestion that might alleviate the problem we discussed at the conference yesterday?" Wilding asked expectantly.

"Ernest, I want you to give me the most sickly and neglected child you have in your infant ward."

"What do you propose to do?"

"You said yesterday that the problem was lack of human, personal, individual care. I shall attempt to supply that."

"How?"

"Surely you can trust me to be careful and judicious in the way I go about it."

"Hans, unofficially, and without an order of the court, I consider myself the legal guardian of all abandoned infants in my department. I would no more risk one of them than I would my own grandson. I have to know precisely what you intend to do."

Benziger hesitated, for if he revealed his plan, Wilding would likely refuse. Yet, if he didn't reveal it, Wilding would surely refuse.

"Instead of giving me the infant, let me bring the care here to your department. Do you have a small private room on the same floor as the infants' nursery?"

"Yes," Wilding said, cautiously, still unsure as to the degree of the cooperation he was willing to extend.

"Good. I will have a patient transferred here before the day is out. I want the infant placed in that room, with all the equipment to feed, bathe and change it. You may have a nurse standing by so that the infant is protected from whatever it is you fear."

Wilding stared at Benziger and hesitated.

"Please, Ernest. It is most important."

Wilding yielded, "Okay, bring your patient down from Neurological."

"Not Neurological," Benziger felt compelled to be truthful. "Psychiatric."

"Psychiatric?" Wilding protested.

"Please. For a day or two. As long as the infant is so close at hand, there's little danger."

Finally Wilding acquiesced.

Baby Smith, so designated since the mother had delivered under an assumed name, and had left without providing even a clue to a given name, was two months old. He weighed only seven pounds three ounces, after having been born full term at seven pounds fourteen ounces. He had been healthy at birth, responding to all physical and neurological tests with better than average scores. Since his birth, however, instead of a normal weight gain he actually showed a loss, exhibited a rash over most of his small, pale body and had developed difficulty keeping down any food. Though considered a prime candidate for adoption at birth, by the time some of the complicated legal work was done he had begun to evidence gross signs of neglect.

He was now in that dangerous state where he needed far more care than was available if he were even to survive. The infant's discouraging prognosis justified any risk taken to ameliorate his condition.

Baby Smith had been selected by Dr. Wilding as his patient most in need of personal care.

When the room had been prepared, Hans Benziger had Jean Scofield brought over from Psychiatric. As he escorted her down the hall, nurses who had known her in an earlier time peered out of doorways and were shocked at the sight of her. The happy, attractive, vivacious, auburn-haired young woman they had known, whose green eyes sparkled so, was now a frail, thin, hollow-eyed vestige of herself. As Hans Benziger led her down the hall toward Room 42, he moved gently with her, but not apologetically.

He brought her into the small room which held only a hospital bed, a single lounge chair and a table on which had been laid out the equipment necessary for changing and feeding an infant. In a corner of the room stood a bassinet. When Benziger had finished his inspection of the room he said, "Jean, my dear, you will be here for a while. If you want anything, tell the nurse and she will call me."

Jean Scofield did not react. It was impossible to tell if she had heard, or, having heard, if she understood. He slipped out of the room and signaled the floor nurse. She went into the nursery and came out carrying an infant surrounded by blankets. Benziger lifted the blanket and looked down at the thin, rash-red, patchy face of Baby Smith. His eyes were closed, as if shutting out a world which had been too hostile and neglectful. The look on his face was one of torment and resignation. At the age of two months he was already old, forlorn and resigned to dying.

Benziger nodded to the nurse. She went into the room, came out in a few moments, nodding to Benziger. He waited. Soon he heard the crying of the child. He listened. The crying continued. Eventually the sound of it filled the hallway, not because it was so loud but because it was so plaintive. The floor nurse came out to listen. She started for the door. Benziger intercepted her.

"Wait!"

"He needs a change or a feeding," she countered, making a move to enter.

"I said wait!"

The crying continued. The nurse made no secret of her disapproval and impatience. Benziger remained steadfast.

Inside the room, Jean Scofield sat in her chair staring at the blank white wall, unaware of the small, pathetic human being in the bassinet. She remained unaware even after the crying had begun. The crying persisted. It grew louder and more pathetic. In the only way at his command the infant was expressing his hunger, discomfort and solitude, his need for a human touch.

Later, when Jean would think back over it, ponder it, she would never be able to reconstruct the feelings and the events which followed. But finally she did become aware of the sound. It beckoned her in a strange way. It was as if in a dream, yet it had the force and effect of reality. Her son was crying. Cliff's son was crying. Their son was in need of her. She rose from her chair and turned to look about the room. For the first time she saw the table, the equipment, the bassinet, the small bundle of blanket in it.

She brushed aside the blanket and stared down at the infant, crying, squirming, its arms and legs flailing as if engaged in a battle for survival. Having cried itself almost to the point of exhaustion, it had begun to gasp. Jean Scofield stared at the infant for a long time, before she dared to reach out. She lifted it gently, as if a part of her shocked mind was reaching back into the past and guiding her. She held the pitiful little thing to her own body.

Outside the door, Hans Benziger listened gravely. The nurse was at his side, her officious look a rebuke that she did not dare to utter for fear of being accused of insubordination. Soon the crying from within the room began to subside. It grew fainter, until it finally ceased. Still, Hans Benziger did not budge except to glance at the nurse and nod. He stood there for some minutes. Then he said, "If the infant starts to cry again, call me. I'll be in my clinic."

Inside the room, Jean Scofield sat in the lounge chair holding the infant who had settled down to a slight gasping kind of breathing. Soon he ceased to gasp and fell into a light sleep. Jean looked down at him, studied his pathetic pinched little face, its color red where its skin was broken out, blue almost everywhere else. If her own son had looked like this she would have known what to do. Food, good food in regular moderate amounts. Bathe him to keep him clean. And love him to keep him happy and alive.

Had she not been so ill herself, she would have moved quickly to accomplish all that. But for now, all she could do was be aware and conscious of what was needed. The doing took more than she was able to accomplish. She held the child in her arms until, gaining solace and security from his sense of security, she herself fell into a light sleep, for the first time without the aid of sedation. She dozed only briefly, for in a while cries of hunger wakened her, startled at what she held in her arms. But after a moment of readjustment she rose, placed the infant on her bed and went to the table to prepare a bottle from the supplies in the warmer.

The demands of the task exceeded the skills she could summon. She was trying to cap the bottle with the nipple when it slipped from her hands and shattered on the floor. She broke down and began to weep. The cries of the infant grew louder. Soon the door opened and Hans Benziger entered.

"Jean!" he commanded, to quiet her crying.

She turned to him, tried to explain and apologize all at once but only broke down again, pointing to the mess on the floor.

"The child is hungry," Benziger said. "There is another bottle and more food. But no one to feed him. The nurses are all busy. The child will go hungry unless *you* feed him!"

She stared at him, hating him for the moment, but then she surrendered to his commanding look. She took a fresh bottle from the table, filled it, and this time, exercising great caution and effort, she was able to cap the bottle. She lifted the infant into her arm, pressed the nipple into his mouth. The crying became gasping, the gasping gave way to contented sucking. Soon it was the only sound in the room.

The vacant, distant look which had possessed Jean Scofield's eyes for so long began to diminish. She looked down at the infant with a sense of recognition, closeness and identity. Both of them had been sadly deprived. Both of them seemed to sense it in each other.

As the child sucked contentedly on its bottle, Hans Benziger spoke to her in a soft but pointed way, "Jean, this infant is on the borderline. If he grows worse, he will probably die. Even if he doesn't die, he might as well. Because, as he is now, a pathetic thing of rashes and other diseases, he is what is termed 'unadoptable.' That means he will, at best, live out his life in one institution after another.

"Unless we heal him. We have the knowledge but not the means. This child needs care. Much personal care. To make up for all the personal warmth and contact he has been denied. He needs a mother. To replace the one who abandoned him. Yes, Jean, abandoned. You know what that feels like. You were abandoned. Suddenly. Knowing what it is like, I want you to make up for it to this infant.

"I will know you have succeeded if this child becomes healthy enough to be adoptable. Do you understand?"

She didn't answer.

"Did you hear me, Jean?" Benziger persisted.

She nodded.

Seven weeks later Baby Smith was presented for adoption and selected by a family which lived in the suburbs. They had been checked out and approved by the hospital and the Department of Social Services. When it came time to hand Baby Smith over to his new parents, Jean Scofield asked only one thing. That she be allowed to talk to the new mother.

"He is a good baby. Not a crier. And unspoiled. But he lives on affection. It's like oxygen to him. So whatever you do for him or with him, do it with love."

"We will," the new mother promised as the infant passed from Jean's arms to her own.

"And one thing more," Jean asked, "if you haven't already decided on a name, I would appreciate it if you named him Clifford."

"Clifford, Cliff," the young woman said. "It's a nice name. I'm sure my husband will agree."

Jean watched as the young woman started down the long corridor to the front door of the hospital where her husband had pulled up in the car to wait for her.

The seven weeks had done wonders for Jean, too. Without being aware of it, in her need to tend the infant she had resumed her old habits. She had refused all sedatives, so that she could wake quickly if the infant cried during the night. She had begun to eat regularly, to keep up her own strength in order to cope with the demands of foster-motherhood. Gradually she had emerged from the depression that had gripped her ever since Cliff's death.

On the day she handed over the infant to its new parents, Jean Scofield presented herself to Hans Benziger. "I'm ready to go back to work."

Hans Benziger smiled and nodded. "I've been waiting for you," was all he said.

The entire staff was delighted at her return. She had always been respected for her ability, and loved for her kind and efficient manner. Interns and residents, sensitive about going to their seniors with problems, sought her out, knowing that she would deal with them confidentially and helpfully. The men who were her seniors liked her quiet and efficient attitude. She was trying to practice neurology, not usurp their positions.

They were as delighted with her recovery as was Benziger. Her illness became a thing of the past, forgotten, except when unusual cures were discussed.

It had not been mentioned in several years now. Until the conflict arose over who was going to succeed Hans Benziger as Chief of Neurology when he retired in six months. Then it was recalled from the past by Dr. Ralph Sunderland, an ambitious rival for the post of Chief of Neurology. He mentioned it to Edward Carey one day, citing it as proof that a woman was simply not up to the stresses involved in such a demanding job. When the pressure became too great, a woman chief would crack. In Jean's case, there was no need to add, hadn't she cracked once before and plunged into a depression for which there had seemed to be no cure?

Since Carey knew that Horace Cameron favored Sunderland's appointment, he had adopted Sunderland's argument as his own.

eight

As Jean lay awake in the middle of the night, looking down at Larry Braham's sleep-rumpled but handsome face, she wondered what it might do to them if she persisted in her ambition to become Chief. Sunderland and Carey would undoubtedly make public issue of that tragic part of her past, forcing the hospital's trustees to weigh it carefully.

Of course, Larry would defend her. But they would only impugn his motives. "She's his mistress. Why shouldn't he defend her?"

She was willing to endure her own risks and embarrassments. She did not wish to compromise or jeopardize Larry professionally. There was also another danger. If her past became an open issue, might it alter the way Larry felt about her? Loyal and loving as he was, sooner or later, out of all the slander, might some part of it worm its way into his mind, unconsciously, and corrode the love they shared now? When she contemplated that, she realized how much she loved him.

Except for the memory of Cliff, she could love Larry without any reservations.

She had put off making any definite resolves and tried to fall asleep again, when her phone rang. Larry stirred. She answered swiftly, interrupting the first ring, so he did not wake fully. She spoke in a whisper.

"Dr. Scofield."

"Doctor, this is the nurse in ICU. The Tatum boy just had another seizure."

81

"Exactly what happened?" Jean asked in a concerned whisper.

"Luckily I noticed him going from tonic to clonic, so I could insert an airway between his teeth. Then he went into a full convulsive state. It lasted almost a minute."

"Did he come out of it all right?"

"He fell asleep immediately. I just wanted to know if there's any change in orders."

"Give him his phenobarb at the regular time. I'll be in first thing in the morning."

Larry came awake at Jean's last words. "What? What happened?"

"Nothing."

"Thought I heard the phone ring," he muttered, half asleep.

"That's the penalty for having an affair with a doctor," she joked. "Now go back to sleep, darling."

He put his arm about her and drew her close. She fell asleep that way, comforted by his embrace.

They arrived at University Hospital in separate cars, and minutes apart. Shortly thereafter they met at Bobby Tatum's bedside. The youngster was awake and having breakfast. Aside from drowsiness due to medication, he seemed a healthy if unusually withdrawn five-year-old boy.

"Good morning, Bobby," Dr. Braham greeted him.

"Good morning, Dr. Larry. Why am I here?"

"You just . . . just fainted a few times. Dr. Scofield took care of you. You know her, don't you?"

"Yes, sir," Bobby said. Jean smiled at him. The boy did not smile back. "She did a lot of funny things to me."

"I may do more funny things this morning, Bobby. But none of them will hurt. So finish your breakfast."

The child pushed back his tray. By instinct or otherwise, he suspected the effort of the doctors to minimize his condition.

"I'm finished."

"Your milk, too?" Larry urged.

The boy hesitated, then finished his milk in one long gulp. But he never took his eyes off Jean, staring at her suspiciously.

"We're going to do the same tests we did yesterday, Bobby. And they won't hurt, I promise you."

He remained tense throughout the entire neurological examination yet was compliant and offered no resistance. As gently as she could, Jean repeated in every detail what she had done the evening before. The results were the same. At certain stages of the examination she invited Larry to check her findings. By the time they had finished, the portable x-ray and echo-encephalogram equipment were being wheeled into the room.

The boy lay still, rigid with fear, while the x-rays and echo were being taken.

"I want those plates stat," Jean ordered. "I'll be down to Radiology to see them as soon as I leave here."

One technician left and a second arrived with the electro-encephalogram equipment. He fixed the conductor electrodes to the boy's head and started the EEG. Both physicians watched as the pen moved jerkily across the graph paper, tracing the electrical impulses emitted by their little patient's brain. Jean saw the spiked focus which indicated the area of irritability from which the boy's seizures probably emanated. As she suspected, most likely a left frontal cerebral abnormality of some kind.

Without increasing the boy's concern, Jean directed Larry Braham's attention to the spiked reactions on the graph. Soon the EEG was finished. As the technician removed the electrodes, Jean noticed that the boy grew even more tense. Seeking to reassure him, she leaned close, reaching to pat his face. He drew back from her, his dark eyes staring at her in fear. It was an unusual reaction, even from a five-year-old in a new environment, surrounded by strangers who did unaccustomed things to him. When the technician had wiped the saline jelly from the boy's head, Jean said warmly, "Now, Bobby, we want you to rest."

"No pre-school?"

"Not today."

"Tomorrow?"

"Not tomorrow. You're going to stay with us for a few days."

The boy was thoughtful for a moment, as if debating whether to trust Jean. Finally he asked, "My mommy, will she come to see me?"

"Yes, of course."

He hesitated. "She won't like it if I'm sick."

"She'll want to help you get better," Jean reassured.

For herself, far from reassured, she was suddenly disturbed by this strange and guileless remark from a frightened five-year-old. It was not the sort of remark a neurologist would set down on a patient's chart.

But it was the sort of response an alert, observant physician would not be likely to forget soon.

Jean Scofield and Larry Braham were in the darkened Radiology room examining the skull plates of young Bobby Tatum. A radiologist stood by to interpret, his face outlined by the view box glow emitted from behind the plates.

"Look clean to me," he said. "No sign of fracture. Certainly nothing on the left side. Whatever the EEG picked up, it wasn't due to a fracture."

Back in Jean's examining room, she and Larry studied the EEG tape again. Helpful. But not helpful enough. It had located a focus of irritation but did not reveal the cause.

"Has he ever sustained an injury, a bad fall, anything that could cause internal bleeding in the brain?" Jean asked.

"Not during my time. And, from his records, not before. Of course, an x-ray isn't definitive."

"No," Jean admitted. "A fine-line fracture in a child could heal without leaving a trace." She was thoughtful for a moment. "I hate to do an angiogram on a child. It's so uncomfortable."

"And there *is* risk," Larry said, indicating he disapproved of the procedure unless it were absolutely unavoidable.

Late in the afternoon Jean stopped by to check three other patients she had on the same floor. The girl who had been in the automobile accident had died in midafternoon after a second desperate operation to relieve the pressure on her brain. Two other patients were in for diagnostic tests, one an elderly woman with a double-vision problem which might indicate suspicious pressure on the optic nerve. The other was a young man who had begun to evidence signs of Parkinsonism, rare in a man his age, but the signs were too challenging to deny.

Her last stop was at Bobby Tatum's bedside in ICU. He was drowsing, a natural state with all the medication. He became aware of her when she touched his arm and leg, lightly pinching the tendons to test for vestigial right-side post-ictal weakness. His responses were as she had expected. He opened his eyes.

"Hello, Bobby," she greeted warmly.

"Hello, Doctor." He was still tense, even under sedation. "Is Dr. Larry . . ." He seemed unable to find the next word.

"He was in to see you. You were asleep. Bobby, from now on I'm going to be your doctor, too."

The boy drew back slightly. Then, as if fearful he had offended her, he asked, "What's your name?"

"Dr. Scofield," she said. "But you can call me Dr. Jean if you like."

"Dr. Jean," he tried it out, but seemed to reject it. "Why am I here?"

It was one of the baffling but consoling aspects of seizures. The patient was unaware of them when they happened and after.

"You may be sick, and we want to find out why. But I promise we won't hurt you, Bobby."

He was not relieved. Instead he groped for a familiar small worn model car that lay at the far edge of his bed.

"I see your mommy was here."

"I was sleeping. She brought me this." He embraced his toy.

"You'll be sleeping a lot for the next few days, Bobby. But it's good for you."

"I feel all right," he protested. "I don't hurt."

"I know," Jean said. "Now, you go back to sleep till they wake you for dinner."

He finally nodded.

She studied him for a moment. Though tense, he was to all outward appearances a thin but healthy handsome boy. She did not realize she was staring until he said, "You're looking at me very funny."

She knew suddenly why she had been staring. With his black hair and blue eyes he reminded her of Cliff. She had to banish that image from her mind and concentrate on her patient. He was obviously frightened and withdrawn, suspicious of her touch, even of her attempts to befriend him. She accounted for it by the fact that she was to him a stranger and a doctor. By age five, most children had overheard enough adult conversation to know that doctors, and especially hospitals, meant serious sickness and sickness could be fatal. Five-year-olds were aware of, and some were even obsessed with, death.

Jean came out of ICU to find Marissa Tatum waiting.

"Well, Doctor?" the mother asked anxiously.

"We don't know much yet," Jean said soothingly.

"But Dr. Braham said you did all those tests."

"We haven't learned any more than we knew this morning. But we have been able to prevent any new seizures today."

"But they could come back?"

"They could," Jean admitted.

"What can we do?"

"Till we find the cause, only one thing. Medication," Jean explained.

"What if that doesn't work?" Marissa Tatum blurted out anxiously.

The woman was emotional and so suspicious that Jean decided the truth would punish her less than her own fantasies.

"We might, I say only 'might,' have to go in and do brain surgery. But that's not likely at this time."

"Brain surgery," the mother repeated, terrified.

"I said it's unlikely," Jean repeated firmly. "Chances are we can control it and he'll be fine."

"You're not to do anything to Bobby till my husband gets back!" the mother said, her voice becoming so shrill that Jean Scofield put a reassuring arm around her.

"Why don't we go to my office so we can discuss this in private?"

"I want to see Bobby!" she insisted.

"He's asleep."

"I want to see him!" she protested so loudly that visitors down the corridor turned to stare.

"All right. Go on. Have a look. I'll wait for you."

The quiet of Jean's consulting room with its soft lighting was a calming, more relaxing ambience in which to discuss the case with the nervous mother, who continued to smoke incessantly.

"Even if we never discover the cause, the usual experience is that the patient responds to medication. Then, as long as that regime continues uninterrupted, and the patient is not subjected to great stresses, he can live a normal life, have a normal marriage and most likely produce perfectly normal children."

The mother nodded continuously as she tried to absorb what Dr. Scofield was saying.

"Your job, once he gets home, will be to see that he continues to take his medication on time and in exactly the prescribed dosage. That is most important. In all other respects, he's to be treated as a normal child. Except he is to be forbidden certain activities. Swimming, climbing, bicycle riding. So if a seizure does occur he won't be thrust into sudden danger."

"What if the medication *doesn't* stop his seizures?" Marissa Tatum demanded suddenly.

It was one of those moments which doctors face too often. When a lie is professionally dishonest and eventually unwise. But the blunt truth can prove alarming to the patient or his anxious relatives. Between the two, Jean Scofield always chose the carefully stated truth. It was preferable to the possible consequences of the palliative lie.

"Intransigent seizures *can* lead to damage. Brain damage," Jean admitted.

"Intransigent . . ." Marissa Tatum evaluated the word with almost painful caution. "What Bobby had yesterday when he was brought in, one seizure after another, is that 'intransigent'?" she dared to ask.

"No, Mrs. Tatum. 'Intransigent' is when the patient continues to have seizures despite any medication we give him. Bobby responded very well to the phenobarbital."

"Then we must see that they're controlled!" Marissa Tatum declared.

"We'll do all *we* can," Jean said pointedly. "But you must never let Bobby detect how tense *you* are."

"I won't," the mother promised quickly.

"Have you called your husband yet?"

"Yes." She lowered her voice and said, "Doctor, when you explain this to my husband, please be very careful. He expects so much from Bobby, it's going to be a shock to him to find out what's happened."

"Why don't you explain it to him?"

"Bob insists on going to the source. He always does in business. He says, never deal with underlings. Go to the source. That's why he's such a successful executive."

"So I hear."

"He'll want to talk to you directly."

"And I'll be anxious to talk to him," Jean promised.

Director of Administration Edward Carey had just completed dictating into his machine when his phone rang to inform him that Dr. Lawrence Braham had arrived for their four-o'clock meeting. Since he was planning on exploiting Braham, Carey went to the door himself to make a ceremony of greeting him. Tired from a day of catching up on cases that had accumulated during his week away, Larry had little patience for ceremony. Still, knowing Carey's institutional artifices, he indulged him.

"We're in a difficult situation, Doctor. And I need your help. I needn't tell you the chairmanship of a department is the crowning achievement of every academic's career. Therefore, such rewards should go to those who have earned them. By their research, their ability to work with others, to organize themselves, and their colleagues."

Carey smiled nervously before he continued. "Unfortunately, there's hardly a man in any department who doesn't feel that he fills that bill precisely. The result? Each time we appoint a new Chief, some malcontents leave us for other institutions. It's difficult to be a colleague one day and a subordinate to the same man the next.

"You can imagine how much worse it would be if the person elevated to a chairmanship were a woman."

Thank God, he's finally come to it, Larry said to himself.

Carey continued, "Our problem is even more complicated now. The government keeps demanding that we elevate women to positions of high responsibility."

"I understand a special job has been created in Neurology to meet that demand," Larry said, impatient with Carey's circumlocution.

"And we've run into a bit of snag. As I suppose you know."

"I understand that Dr. Scofield was offered that post in place of a chiefship."

"You see how this whole thing has gotten out of focus," Carey lamented. "I made a confidential survey. Frankly, most men in Neurology do not like the idea of serving under a woman chief. It could wreck the entire department. Yet we insist on giving deserved recognition to Dr. Scofield for her excellent work. She's a most remarkable woman. But I guess I don't have to tell *you* that."

"Dr. Scofield is a most remarkable *physician!* That's the important thing, Carey!"

"Sorry. Bad choice of words. Believe me, I wouldn't hesitate for an instant to recommend her as chief to the Trustees. But my concern is the morale of the entire department. That's why I'm asking you to intercede. Explain to her, as only you can, that out of a sense of duty to this hospital, which has done so much for her, she *has* to take the new post of Associate Chief."

"I'm afraid I wouldn't have much influence with her."

Carey stared at him, then smiled. A small smile, it betrayed an aura of lewdness that was distasteful to Larry Braham.

"Carey, I'm afraid there isn't anything I can do for you. Yes, I know Dr. Scofield very well . . ."

"Shall we say 'intimately'?" Carey interrupted, now that he was sure he would receive no help from Braham.

Larry repeated with precise emphasis, "I know Dr. Scofield very well. But not so well that I could convince her to do something that she doesn't choose to do. Is that clear?"

"Yes, it's clear. Just as I hope it's clear to you that when the infighting starts, especially among the trustees, someone is bound to mention two things about Dr. Scofield. Her unfortunate depression—"

"That was years ago," Braham pointed out.

"—*and* her present relationship with you." Despite Larry's angry reaction, Carey threatened, "Someone is bound to bring it up."

"I'm sure you will," Braham shot back before he turned and walked out.

Carey leaned back in his chair, defeated for the moment, but not resigned to having lost the war. It was a war he could not afford to lose. For he had promised Horace Cameron that before the next meeting of the Board of Trustees he would resolve the matter to everyone's satisfaction. Meaning, of course, Cameron's.

A power in international business, and a self-made

success, Cameron equated all women with his own dear, long-departed mother. A good woman, religious, she had cooked, scrubbed and washed for her large family and raised sons and daughters of whom any woman could well be proud. She had worked hard and conscientiously during every day of her married life and came to her husband's bed exhausted, with no energy left to think of women's rights, needs or demands. She must have satisfied his father's demands because they had so large a family. That was as it should be. So Cameron's model for a good, proper woman was his mother.

The first time the name Jean Scofield had been mentioned as possible Chief of Neurology, Cameron responded, "Hell, Ed, are we going to have a woman chief? In our hospital? Are we?"

Carey knew those questions were a command. He received confirmation when he pointed out that the Federal government, the largest single supporter of academic hospitals, insisted on women in jobs of responsibility.

"In our business, we find ways around governments every day! Find one, Ed. Find some way around that damned woman."

Carey had thought he could. But without the help of Hans Benziger or Larry Braham that had proved futile. There must be other ways. Else Cameron might start looking for a new chief, too. A new Administrative Chief.

nine

At the first hint on the phone that his son was in the hospital, Bob Tatum insisted on flying home immediately. When Horace Cameron heard, he put his private jet at Tatum's disposal. Cameron also had his executive secretary phone Dr. Scofield to prepare her for Tatum's return. The meeting was now taking place in Jean's office with the Tatums and Larry Braham. She had finished explaining in detail all she knew about Bobby's seizures. Also, all she did not know, which, unfortunately, was still a great deal.

Tatum made no effort to conceal his shock. He looked at Marissa but was unable to say more than "God . . . poor Bobby . . . poor Bobby . . ." Then he turned to stare out the window, allowing Jean to study him closely.

He appeared to be everything Larry had described. Handsome. Tall. Broad-shouldered and obviously well-muscled. Jean especially noticed his powerful hands when he cracked his knuckles nervously. Undoubtedly those hands had helped to make him an All-American fullback with an uncanny ability to catch and hold onto swiftly thrown passes. Yet for all his physical attributes, at this crucial moment he appeared to be only another stunned, sensitive father, deeply concerned about his small, frail, sick son.

Gently, Jean prodded, "Mr. Tatum? It would help to know what you're thinking."

"Thinking?" he echoed self-consciously. "Crazy, the

things you can think of at a time like this." Then he confessed, "I was thinking, at InterElectronics we make some of the complex equipment that helped put men on the moon. Yet here we all sit helpless, defeated, when it comes to finding out what goes on in the head of just one little five-year-old boy."

Larry intervened, "Bob, Dr. Scofield didn't say we *couldn't* find out. She only said we haven't found out *yet.*"

"Well, then, *find* out! Do something! So we know how to treat this damned thing, whatever it is!"

Jean realized that Tatum's impatience was only a reflection of his fear, so she took command. "Mr. Tatum, we have to proceed cautiously. To avoid procedures that are both unnecessary *and* dangerous. The fact that we have the skill to open a child's skull and explore his brain does not mean we should rush into it."

Tatum seized on only one word. " 'Explore'? Doctor, you're hinting at some terrible possibilities."

Before his imagination could turn into panic, Jean corrected, "I haven't been 'hinting.' I've laid out the entire case. What we know. And what we don't know. Because you're wife said you're a man who likes to deal with facts. Well, now you have them. But they're not as bad as you would make them seem."

"Aren't they? You as much as said that my son's a cripple."

"I never used that word. And I won't permit you to use it about him in my presence!" Jean reprimanded sternly.

"Can't do any of the things a man looks forward to teaching his son as he grows up . . . can't go swimming . . . can't ride a bicycle . . ."

"Can't play football," Jean suggested, suspecting the real source of Tatum's disappointment. "Lots of boys become highly successful men without ever becoming All-Americans."

When Tatum glared at her, she felt she had struck precisely the right nerve. But she was taken by surprise when he responded, a bit angrily, "You, too. Nobody can forget I was All-American. But what nobody seems to remember is that I also had a three-point-seven average for four years."

When he rose to his feet, he seemed overpowering by his very presence. "Doctor, I no more got to be what I am at InterElectronics because I played football than you got to be an expert neurologist because you happen to be such an attractive woman."

He began to pace, striding with the grace of a jungle animal. "Oh, I won't deny football was the way I first came to Mr. Cameron's attention. But if I hadn't had the brain to make the most of the chance, I'd be what most other heroes become. An athletic court jester. A colorful conversation piece to have around for a while. Until another, newer, more colorful conversation piece comes along.

"Especially with Mr. Cameron, who has a very short memory for what a man did yesterday. Yes, he likes winners. But not yesterday's winners. He prides himself on picking future winners. Which is okay by me. Because that's exactly the game I'm best at. If I wasn't, I'd have gone into pro ball, made some quick money and been washed up by now. Instead of being one of only four men—yes, Doctor—one of only four men eligible to succeed to Cameron's job when he's ready to quit. By which time I intend to be one of only one man who is his logical successor.

"Football may open the doors. But only brains can *keep* them open. So if you can tell me now that my son's brain is perfect, I promise you I won't make any more demands on him than that!"

It was a declaration made in anger, but Jean was relieved to hear it nevertheless.

"Mr. Tatum, this is what I suggest. And Dr. Braham concurs. We'll keep Bobby here to see if his seizures recur. If they don't we'll let him go home on a regime of regular medication. A drug called Dilantin. When that stabilizes in his blood at the proper level, we hope he'll be seizure-free. If not, we'll have to make further tests."

"And operate?" Tatum asked quickly.

"That would be our last resort," Jean said cautiously, since she had still not been able to rule out the possibility of a brain tumor. "The main thing at home, don't make him self-conscious about what happened, or what might happen again. You mustn't make him tense."

Tatum nodded, still visibly tormented by his son's condition.

"May I see him now?"

"Of course. He's in Intensive Care."

"Intensive Care," Tatum said grimly. "That's for old men with heart attacks!"

"And young boys who need special nursing," Jean gently corrected. "You have permission to spend five minutes with him." Tatum resented the limitation. "Five minutes!" she repeated. "And don't do or say anything to disturb him."

"Go on, Bob," Larry Braham urged. "I'll join you there in a few minutes."

The Tatums started to leave but Jean Scofield called out, "Mr. Tatum?" He turned to confront her. "When Bobby was small, did you roughhouse with him? Throw him up in the air? Make believe you were going to let him fall? And then catch him at the last moment?"

"Doesn't every father do that?"

"Yes. But did you ever actually drop him?"

"No, of course not," Tatum replied resentfully.

The Tatums were gone. Jean was surprised to find how tense she had become during the interview.

"Is he always like that?" she asked Larry.

"He's always been competitive. A winner. He doesn't know how to cope with defeat."

"You call having a son like Bobby a defeat?"

"A man who has spent his whole life being best is not likely to be content with a son who is less than perfect," Larry warned. "I'd better join them."

Jean did not answer him. What she had discovered about Robert Tatum, Senior, set her off on a whole new avenue of thinking about this case.

Bob Tatum stepped cautiously into Neurological Intensive Care. He moved silently to the cubicle where his son lay dozing.

"Bobby?" Tatum whispered.

The boy opened his eyes, closed them, then opened them again to make sure. "Dad?"

"Son, I heard you weren't feeling well. So I flew right back."

"I'm okay."

"Nothing hurt?"

"No, sir."

"They treat you well here?"

"Yes, sir. I think the nurses like me."

"Why not? You're a terrific boy! You're Bobby Tatum!"

"Can I go back to school? We're going to make special Indian costumes for Thanksgiving. Is it Thanksgiving yet?"

"You'll be back in school long before Thanksgiving. And you can be an Indian. Or a Pilgrim. Or anything you want, Bobby-boy."

"Miss Halsted said Indians."

"Okay, then you'll be the best Indian of them all!"

Tatum said, taking his son's right hand. It seemed the gesture of a loving father. Actually Tatum was testing to see if he could feel the post-ictal weakness that lady doctor Scofield had mentioned. Comforted by his father's presence, Bobby closed his eyes and fell asleep.

When Tatum came out Larry greeted him, "You can see for yourself he's not in any great danger."

"As long as we don't know what causes those seizures, *I* have to consider that he *is* in danger!"

"Dr. Scofield explained that. Sometimes we never find the cause but under proper treatment it just goes away."

"What did she mean by the last thing she asked me?"

"What last thing?"

"About roughhousing with Bobby. Hell, he loves it!"

"Boys love it whenever Dad takes time to play with them," the pediatrician reassured Bob Tatum.

But as Tatum was leaving, Braham watched him thoughtfully. Tatum was a big man, unaware of his own strength. Did Jean suspect the cause of young Bobby's seizures to be a trauma to his brain, induced by over-enthusiastic horseplay with a father so physically oriented? He called Jean from the nurses' desk.

"Until I make a definite diagnosis, I suspect everything," Jean said. "I'm going to keep the boy here longer than four days."

"Tatum won't stand for it," Larry warned.

"He may not like it. But he'll stand for it," Jean said confidently.

At the end of the eighth day, Dr. Scofield studied Bobby Tatum's chart carefully, the amount of medication he had received, his vital signs, the new set of EEG's she had ordered, as well as his nuclear brain scans. There was still no clear indication of the etiology of his seizures.

One particular statistic had changed. The boy showed a noticeable weight gain since his admission. She also observed that he now seemed far less tense, was much freer and friendlier than during his first few days. Because it might prove to be significant, Jean decided not to rely solely on her own observation. She called in the nurse in charge of the floor.

"Kerner, about the Tatum boy, before we discharge him, I'd like your impressions."

Alice Kerner, a silver-haired nurse of many years of experience, said, "He shows no side effects of the medication. He's gained weight. And, of course, he's had no seizures since that one the first night he was admitted."

"What about his attitude?"

"Now that he's over his fear of being here, he's turned out to be an extremely pleasant, outgoing youngster. The floor favorite, you might say. And he likes you, Doctor. He keeps asking all the time when you're coming in."

"That's nice," Jean said, without indicating the real significance of her interest in Kerner's reactions. "He seems to have stabilized nicely. Order one more x-ray of his skull, an EEG and another scan. Then check his signs, weigh him and complete his chart. I'll have the office notify his parents."

An hour later, just before meeting Larry and the Tatums in her office, she stopped by to see Bobby herself.

"Did they tell you? You're going home this morning, Bobby."

"Yes, Dr. Jean," the small boy said. "Am I all right?"

"If you take your medicine and do what Mommy says, you'll be fine."

"I won't die?" he asked.

"Of course not," she reassured strongly, aware of the concerns of five-year-olds about death and dying.

"Can I go back to pre-school?"

"Tomorrow, if you want."

"I want to. For Thanksgiving," the boy said eagerly.

"Bobby, from now on, any time you don't feel well, or if you feel tired and want to lie down, or if you smell something funny, or hear funny noises, tell Mommy as soon as it happens. Or Esther. Or if you're in school, tell your teacher. Understand?"

The handsome dark-haired boy thought a moment, then nodded.

"We're all glad you're better, yet we're all sorry to see you go, Bobby. Did you like it here?"

"Oh, yes. After the first few days I liked it a lot. Neat," he said, remembering an expression he had heard older boys use when they were unusually enthusiastic.

"Then you can come back and visit. Every few weeks, Mommy or Dad will bring you. And you can spend a day or two here. We'll be very happy to see you." She had laid the foundation for his regular checkups, which would be essential.

During her instructions, the boy had reached out timidly toward her. Aware of it, she did not withdraw. She permitted him to run his small fingers across the soft skin of her hand. It was a silent token of affection which touched her deeply. But it was a gesture which could be revealing as well. She knew she must take a last look at his chart.

His vital statistics were all normal. The results of the neurological tests were all good. Nothing was revealed by the skull x-rays, scan or last EEG. Were it not for his seizures, now hopefully under control, he would have to be considered a perfectly healthy young child. She found the entry Kerner had made: *Weight on admission, forty-one pounds. Weight on discharge, forty-four pounds.* A significant increase in eight days for a five-year-old. It would bear watching.

She and Larry Braham were giving final instructions to the Tatums.

"He is to take his Dilantin in the prescribed doses. That means one pill by mouth three times a day. Every day. At home, traveling, in school, a sleepover at some other child's home, wherever, he must have his medication on schedule. That is not to vary for any reason," Jean stressed. "As long as the Dilantin level in his blood remains stable he shouldn't have any further seizures."

"Good!" Tatum interjected.

"I said 'shouldn't,' not 'wouldn't,' Mr. Tatum," Jean pointed out to dispel any false hopes or misunderstandings.

Tatum's smile dissolved. He nodded gravely.

"Now, his teacher, and anyone in whose charge he is placed, maid, baby sitter, grandparent, must be made aware of the possibilities. And of what to do if a seizure does occur."

She turned to the mother. "I assume you'll talk to his teacher."

Marissa Tatum nodded.

"Don't alarm her. Don't give her the impression she is dealing with a freak. Because if she's frightened, it will transmit itself to your son somehow. And eventually to his classmates. The problem of living with possible seizures is as much psychological as physical, so don't either of you give the boy any indication of your own anxieties.

"If a seizure is about to occur, it's possible Bobby may give you a signal. He may say he's tired. He may not say anything but may simply lie down on his own.

He may only experience a feeling of strangeness which he can't explain. That's the time to be alert. It's what we call an 'aura.' A prelude to a seizure.

"When that happens, you're to protect the child without inhibiting him. Hold his head to keep him from hurting himself by banging against the wall or the floor. If you can, insert a gauze-covered wooden tongue depresser between his teeth to keep him from biting his tongue. Do not insert anything metalic. That can cause broken teeth. Never insert your fingers. He can bite you severely without realizing it.

"Mainly, be sure he has an open passageway to breathe. Epileptics can choke to death on their own mucus or vomitus."

Bob Tatum stared at her hostilely.

"Yes, Mr. Tatum?"

"That word you used."

"What word?"

"Epileptic. You never before said Bobby was an epileptic. Something's changed!"

Larry interceded. "Epileptic is a general term for anyone who has seizures. It's nothing more serious than what Dr. Scofield said before."

Tatum did not argue but neither did he seem reassured or mollified.

Jean completed her instructions by saying, "And you will bring Bobby back for further testing in two weeks, when we'd like to keep him overnight."

Bob Tatum nodded stiffly. It was clear his cooperation was extended without any great enthusiasm.

That forced Jean to say, "Mr. Tatum, I think it would help if you understood the position of the neurologist. While we work with the patient's nervous system, we are also concerned with his mind, as distinguished from his brain. If from this moment on Bobby grew up physically perfect but emotionally damaged by this experience I would consider I'd failed him. I want to see a *completely* healthy boy. Not merely a boy with a healthy body.

"Just remember, he is not an invalid. Treat him like a five-year-old boy. Not a five-year-old patient. Never let him see fear in your eyes. *Or disappointment.* Either of those could stunt him for the rest of his life."

She proceeded to terminate the interview quickly.

"Miss Kerner will you give my prescription for Dilantin. And also a three-day supply to tide you over till you get your own. See you in two weeks."

"Need a lift?" Larry Braham offered, to ease the tension.

"No, thanks. Mr. Cameron sent his own limousine. But I'll call you later."

"Fine."

The Tatums were gone. The strained atmosphere Tatum had left behind made Larry apologize. "He's not a bad guy. But because he's a perfectionist he just comes on too strong sometimes."

"He's a perpetual fullback," Jean commented acidly.

To change the subject, Larry asked, "Dinner tonight?"

"I'm having the neurology residents over for a buffet. Most of them will be moving on at the end of the semester. This will be a little farewell."

"I take it I'm not invited."

"There's enough talk now, Larry. Times I think I ought to marry you just to protect your reputation," she said, laughing.

He reached out to embrace her but her phone rang. She shrugged helplessly. It was a summons to the ER. Another child with seizures had just been brought in and the admitting resident needed her help.

Before starting for the ER, she glanced at Bobby

Tatum's chart again. Putting aside any attitudes or prejudices she might have formed about Bob Tatum, there were provocative facts in the boy's record. Objective facts. He had shown a weight gain while he was in the hospital. Toward the end he had become brighter, more cheerful and more outgoing. Kerner had verified that.

Those facts, taken together, could mean little. Or they could become extremely important. She would have to wait and see. Meantime, she cautioned herself, no premature conclusions, and certainly no premature accusations. On the basis of what little she knew now, she would not even discuss it with Larry.

She started for the Emergency Room.

ten

Beatrice Fazio was no more than four, a plump child with golden curls. Her face was a bloodless white when Jean first saw her. The child was obviously terrified. The resident had done a preliminary examination, physical and neurological. He had ordered an immediate skull x-ray and an EEG. He was ready with the results when Dr. Scofield arrived. After her examination, she consulted the x-ray plates and the EEG tape. The x-ray was vague and not particularly helpful. The EEG showed an unspecified disturbance on the right side of the child's brain.

"Get some technitium into her. Let's get a scan," Jean ordered. "Then put her to bed on phenobarb."

"What's your hunch?" the resident asked.

"Let's wait for the scan. And if you're off tonight, don't forget my dinner party. Cocktails at seven," she said briskly, trying to conceal her own unhappy suspicions about this new little patient. She started to leave the ER, but turned back.

"I want an echo-encephalogram, too. Let's rule out any mid-line brain shift."

She went out to talk to the Fazios, to get a history on the child and also answer their questions as best she could.

Mrs. Fazio was short, blonded, with a round pudgy face that did not hold up well under tears. Her eyes were puffy, her hair unkempt. She was wearing a wrinkled cotton house-dress. Obviously she had rushed the child from home without waiting to change. She must have phoned her husband, who had left work to join her. He was a giant of a man, with tight curly black hair and the shoulders and arms of a physical laborer. The union button on his denim shirt identified him as a construction worker.

"How is she?" Mrs. Fazio cried out as Jean approached them. "How is my little girl?"

"Paula! Let me," her husband commanded. "All right, now, Doc. The truth. If it's serious, tell us."

"Right now you can tell me more than I can tell you. Except that her seizure is over. She's resting."

"Pain? She got pain?" the agitated father demanded.

"No pain at all."

He was greatly relieved. "She's a terrific kid. And if she got to go through some pain to get better, she can take it. But no unnecessary pain, you know what I mean, Doc?"

"I don't think she'll suffer any pain."

Fazio looked into his wife's fearful eyes. "See?"

"Mr. Fazio, do you have any other children?"

"Four. Three boys and a girl. All healthy. Healthy," he stressed.

"Has Beatrice ever had anything like this before?"

"Never sick a day in her life!" Fazio said staunchly.

His wife shook her head gingerly as if daring to disagree. "Dom . . ."

"What?" he asked, irritated.

"Mumps she had. And chicken pox."

"Mumps, chicken pox, that's nothing. The doc means real bad sickness. Don't you, Doc?"

"I mean any sickness. Has she ever had a seizure before?" When the parents both seemed puzzled, she changed her language slightly, "I mean a fit, like she had today."

"No, never!" Mrs. Fazio said.

"Has she suffered any injury, a blow on the head, a bad fall?"

"No," the father answered firmly. "That girl is handled like a doll. A little china doll. Any kid in the family lays a hand on her he knows what will happen to him."

"Children can fall accidentally while playing. They can bang their heads," Jean reminded.

"No," Fazio said, and looked to his wife for corroboration.

"No," the woman said after some thought. Then her motherly anxiety overwhelmed her. She began to weep and accuse simultaneously. "You're not telling us the truth! You think there's something wrong in her head!" She turned to her husband and cried in anguish, "Dom, oh Dom, what are we going to do?"

The big man embraced his wife protectively and looked across at Jean, his eyes apologizing for his wife's breakdown.

"Mr. Fazio, why don't you bring her into my office?"

"Thanks, Doc."

Once Jean had closed her door, Mrs. Fazio was free to weep without embarrassment. Her husband explained, "You see, Doc, we got this thing in the family. . . ."

"You mean seizures run in the family?" Jean asked, intrigued.

"No, not seizures. A curse."

"Curse?"

"Paula's mother, she ain't Catholic. She ain't even Italian. We got married, she wouldn't come to the wedding. She won't see Paula no more. She put a curse on our marriage. And on any kids we have. So Paula feels it's her fault, what happened to Beatrice."

"Mrs. Fazio, one thing I can tell you with great certainty. Your child's condition isn't due to any curse. So don't blame yourself. We'll keep your little girl here for a week or so. She'll be in no danger. And she'll be very comfortable. We'll see to that. You can come and visit her once a day."

"Me, too?" the father asked at once.

"Of course."

"Okay." He was reassured. It was obvious the child was most precious to him.

Aware that she was dealing with highly emotional parents, Jean decided it would be wise to prepare them now for some of the eventualities.

"We've done some tests but the results are not too helpful. We may have to do more tests. One of them is called an angiogram."

The Fazios glanced at each other, suspicious of the very word. Since it would be necessary to obtain their written consent, Jean explained.

"The way it works, we inject a dye into the child."

"Dye?" Dominick Fazio asked, already resistant.

"The dye spreads through the brain and gives us

much more helpful x-rays than we can get any other way."

"You mean she got to go around with dye in her brain the rest of her life?"

"Not at all," Jean reassured him. "Her body will get rid of the dye in hours. But . . ."

"But?" Fazio seized on the word, and his wife gripped his arm.

"But," Jean said with great care, "whenever we do such a procedure there is a risk."

"Like what kind of risk?"

"Danger. In rare cases, it can even result in death."

"I'm not going to let you do it!" Fazio exploded. "I'm taking my little girl home with me right now!"

"Dom . . . Dom, please."

"I don't let anybody touch her head! You hear me, Doc, nobody touches my little girl's head!"

Now Jean knew that she had been right to introduce the possibility of an angiogram early in the treatment. If the time did come when it became necessary, it would be best that the Fazios had made peace with the idea instead of having to face it fresh when the need was urgent.

"We won't do anything without your permission," she said. "And we won't do it right now in any event. But it is a possibility."

"I'll *never* let you do it!" Fazio raged.

Jean had dealt with emotional relatives often. Time was the mediating factor. She would continue to study little Beatrice Fazio, treating her with medication and doing all the non-invasive tests first. If no certain cause appeared, she would discharge her temporarily and await developments.

By the time Jean arrived at her apartment, Bessie had arranged the cold hors d'oeuvres on a tray and had the cheese puffs ready to go in the oven, just waiting to heat them so they wouldn't be done too soon and dry out. Bessie was Jean's three-times-a-week maid who could also be prevailed upon to give her one night every two weeks if she wished to entertain. Though Bessie was only two years older than Jean, she appeared and acted much older, looking after the doctor like a mother.

"I can see you're tired. It shows in your eyes. You go take a hot bath and lie down a while," Bessie dictated. She was quite domineering, particularly in matters of health and economics. Unless she did the marketing herself, she usually criticized Jean for buying too much food, and without a proper regard for price.

Jean was in her tub, luxuriating in the steamy perfumed water which would wash away both her weariness and the odor of the hospital. She often joked about it, referring to it as "washing the doctor out of me." She dried herself with a huge, thick beige towel, studying her body in the wall-sized mirror. She felt she had earned a few moments of feminine vanity. She dried her back by briskly rubbing the towel across it, then stopped to stare into the mirror and think, very good for a woman of thirty-eight. Very good for a woman of any age, she decided. It also made her quite aware of what Larry kept urging. About having a child, maybe even two, before it was too late. It was possible. Even with her heavy schedule of professional obligations. She knew it was possible when she found herself planning that she could work right up until her eighth month.

It meant she also admitted the real possibility of marrying Larry. But if it was going to mean children, she would have to decide soon. Very soon.

She was slipping into her aqua jersey hostess gown when she heard Bessie knock.

"Have they started to arrive?" Jean called out.

"No, Doctor, but I just remembered. *He* called. Before you got home. He said to call him."

Bessie always referred to Larry as "he." She had never approved of his staying over and she made no secret of it. And she would never refer to him by name unless and until they were married.

Jean decided to call back as soon as she finished brushing her hair. Then, suddenly, she put the brush down to make the call. His service answered. Dr. Braham was out on a house call but would be checking in within the hour. Any message? Just that Dr. Scofield called. Yes, of course, the service operator answered, a touch of intimacy in her voice.

There was no privacy, even from nameless, faceless telephone service operators.

She still had a few minutes to check out everything before her guests were due to arrive. In the kitchen, Bessie had laid out the hors d'oeuvre trays for her inspection. Jean couldn't resist a little rearrangement to create a more enticing and color-balanced display. She tested the tangy new pink dip Bessie had dreamed up. It was so tasty Jean could not resist dipping her finger in again and scooping up another taste.

"You hungry, I could fix you a plate before they come," Bessie practically insisted.

"It's not that I'm hungry, but it's delicious. What's in it?"

"Red caviar. Some dill. And lots and lots of sour cream."

"Sour cream?" Jean equivocated.

"Those as is on diets, you just tell them it's yogurt."

They both laughed and Jean pressed her cheek against Bessie's as she embraced her and said, "Bessie, Bessie, don't ever change."

They enjoyed these rare moments together. Bessie,

because she loved Jean and welcomed the opportunity to be easy with her. Jean, because it gave her the chance to talk about womanly things in a womanly way, as she remembered her mother doing over backyard fences in Iowa where she was born.

She checked out the living room. Large and tastefully done in gold and white with just a few touches of aqua to harmonize with her bedroom, it concealed any hint of Jean's profession. Those medical papers she brought home to study in the late hours of the night were out of sight, hidden in the antique French Provincial desk. It was a warm, comfortable, inviting room, secluded from the sounds of the city by long white and gold-threaded drapes that started at the ceiling and touched the luxurious gold and aqua Chinese rug. It was the room she had always dreamed of furnishing for Cliff when they were first married but couldn't afford it.

She was looking it over, checking the candy dishes, the nuts—salted and unsalted to suit both tastes—and, of course, the ashtrays and matches. Especially the matches, for those men who claimed to smoke pipes but really smoked matches. The doorbell rang.

The residents had begun to arrive. Between neurology and neurosurgery there were nine of them. Seven men, five white, two Africans. Two women, one white, one black. The black woman brought along her husband, a young lawyer. Two men brought their wives, one of them eight months pregnant.

Jean's earlier thoughts about Larry and marriage made her even more solicitous than usual. She saw to it that the pregnant girl had the chair that it was most easy to get into and out of.

The evening proved relaxing and delightful. The highlight was when they insisted that Jean repeat her imitation of Edward Carey. Each year one of the faculty members with a flair for entertaining was invited to be guest star at the annual Interns' Show. This year it had been Jean. She had written and performed a skit in which she imitated Edward Carey when he was being the ingratiating, conniving and obvious hospital politician. It had proved the success of the show. And it was equally successful in her living room on this night. She finished to their great laughter and applause.

By the time coffee was served there was much serious talk about the crucial decisions young doctors had to make, whether to stay in academic medicine or go into private practice.

The two African doctors wrestled with an even more difficult decision. Whether to return to their native countries or stay on and find a place in the now burgeoning black upper middle class communities in this country.

One of them, with an African name that always sounded like music to Jean, a tall, powerful man with a deep bass voice, asked, "I understand that early in your career you did some work in the back country of Vietnam?"

"Yes, yes, I did," Jean answered.

"Then tell me, is what one doctor can do in a primitive underprivileged land worth the personal sacrifice he makes? Or is it like trying to hold back a flooding river with only your bare hands?"

His bright eager eyes demanded a frank reply.

"It would be difficult for me to say," Jean admitted. "Because I can't separate two things. The practice of medicine in a primitive country. And what happened to me there."

"Yes, I heard," the black man said.

She glanced at him, trying to read in his eyes whether he knew not only of Cliff's sudden death but of her own miscarriage and breakdown. The compassion in his eyes told her he knew it all. Of course, she reminded herself, by now they must all know it all. Secretly, though not maliciously, it must be discussed by every new group of residents.

"Before my husband's death I found it exciting, most satisfying. But I think you're asking is it better to try to save a human life where the chances of saving it are greater? Or to save fewer people where the need is greater? That's a highly personal decision. I only know that when you succeed, the look in a grateful patient's eyes is the same the world over."

The black physician nodded thoughtfully. He had yet to make up his mind, but Jean had turned it in the direction of going back to Africa. When the evening was over and he stood in the doorway saying good night, he took her hand. "Dr. Scofield, wherever I go, I will remember you. Not only as a doctor, but as a woman. A very handsome woman. Sometimes I think about you and say to myself, she couldn't be so good a doctor if she wasn't so fine a woman. I could fall in love with a woman like her."

Jean felt herself blushing. He realized that, for he said softly in his deep voice, "I didn't mean to embarrass you, Doctor. It was my tribute to a fine human being."

She smiled her thanks.

They were gone. Bessie was cleaning up, putting cups, saucers and cake plates into the dishwasher, emptying ashtrays. As she worked, she muttered. She usually did when she had something on her mind.

"With all that stuff on the TV about the dangers of smoking, you'd think doctors would know better. Whew!" she exclaimed as she pulled back the drapes and threw open the windows to get rid of the oppressive odor of smoke. She resumed muttering. "That big black man. He got a lot of nerve saying some of the things he said to you."

Bessie had a most acute pair of ears, especially when it involved intimate conversations she was not supposed to hear.

"I thought he was very sweet," Jean defended him.

"You already got a man!" Bessie muttered, busying herself with her chores. "A white man, with good manners. I can tell the way he leaves things when he leaves here mornings . . ."

"Bessie!" Jean tried to interrupt.

"You don't have to go looking for no more trouble than you already got trying to make up your mind."

Before she could continue, the phone rang.

"Am I too late? Did I wake you?" Larry asked.

"No. They just left."

"Sorry I couldn't call back earlier. But I've had one emergency house call after another. It's the way anxious parents punish their pediatrician if he has the gall to leave town for a week. But all's quiet now."

"Good."

"Can I come over?"

"It's pretty late."

"I meant to stay."

"No, Larry, please, I'm tired."

"God," he laughed, "you sound like we're already married."

"It's been a rough day."

"I'd still like to come over," he urged.

"Bessie's here."

"She won't be there all night," Larry reminded her. "Darling?"

She hesitated, and while she did, Bessie called to her from the living room, "I'm all through, Doctor. I'm leaving."

"Wasn't that Bessie's voice?" he asked.

"Yes, yes it was," she admitted. Her last defense

gone, she said very softly, "All right, Larry." Then she added, "And hurry."

It was the still quiet hours of early morning. He lay close against her, his arm around her, his head pressing on her naked breast.

"What are you thinking?" he asked.

She had been thinking about the moment with her black resident and how touching it was, his words and the reverent admiring look in his eyes. But that was something private and personal, not meant to be shared.

"Thinking about us?" he asked. "Or Bobby Tatum? Or Carey?"

"Why would I spend time on Carey?"

"Because he's spending a lot of time on you."

"Is he?"

"He had me in a few days ago."

"Carey discussed it with you?"

"He thinks I have some strange power over you."

"And what did you tell him?" she asked, angry that Carey had dared to intrude on her private life.

"That the only strange power between us is the one you hold over me."

"Seriously, Larry!"

"I told him I do not interfere in your professional decisions. He started to grumble and talk about funding and the Federal government. Personally, I say it's Cameron."

"Why? Do you know him?"

"Only met him twice. At the Tatums'. Small dinner parties. Marissa's an excellent hostess."

"What kind of man *is* Cameron?"

"A decision maker. He always smokes a long graceful cigar, genuine Havana mind you, which he gets through one of InterElectronics subsidiaries in Europe. He wields it like a scepter. And he never indulges in discussions. He lets other people do that. Then he merely makes a pronouncement. It doesn't matter if the subject is international affairs, economics, politics, or running a hospital, once Cameron has spoken you can inscribe it on tablets of stone."

"That's what I like," Jean said, "a man with a nice open mind."

"I wouldn't joke about it."

"Why? Doesn't Cameron like jokes?"

"Saying no to Ed Carey is one thing. But if Carey has to go back and give that message to Cameron, that's a whole different ball game."

"Larry, my darling, tell Cameron to go fly a kite. Or use any other expression you deem apt in the circumstances. I can think of a few myself."

2

eleven

Two weeks had gone by quickly. Days always did when Jean had to race to keep up with her own admissions to the hospital and the number of patients who thronged the Neurological Clinic. There had been the usual run of cases. Patients with genuine neurological difficulties —double vision, paresis of the limbs, unremitting headaches and the like. The routine tests were carried out and the results passed on to Jean for diagnosis.

Four tumors of unknown seriousness had been discovered. Surgery would be called for. She briefed the surgeons and observed at the procedures. Three biopsies came back benign. The fourth was positive. The prognosis was poor, for the surgeon could not excise the entire mass.

She taught her classes in the medical school. She always looked forward to those. She had an excellent, eager group of students and she enjoyed teaching.

She also made her usual stops at the experimental lab where she had a dozen small monkeys in various stages of an experiment relating to the nervous system. Discoveries made in monkeys or other simians were often useful in treating humans.

This morning she arrived at her office, examined her appointment log and found that the Fazio girl and the Tatum boy were both due to return for checkups today.

She saw the Fazio child first. Both mother and father accompanied the little girl, who had been bathed and

scrubbed shiny clean. Her hair was braided into pig-
tails festooned with red ribbons. Jean wondered, are
they trying to make her appealing to the doctor and
thus earn a favorable diagnosis?

She had the child's chart before her. The indications
were not encouraging. Her skull x-ray was normal. But
the EEG showed a slowing over the right frontal temporal area, indicating her seizure focus was in that area.
The L.P. spinal tap showed an elevated protein from
80 to 150. Spinal fluid pressure was 180. There was no
blood in the fluid. No white cells. And the sugar was
normal. However, the echo-encephalogram in the file
was disturbing, though not definitive. Jean ordered it
repeated. Stat.

Little Beatrice was taken into the radiology room
where two electrodes were fastened to her head just
above and slightly ahead of her ears. Then the electronic equipment was activated. Like radar, it bounced
sound waves across the child's head to eventually reveal the position of her brain within the skull.

When the result was delivered to her, Jean studied
it while the Fazios waited anxiously. The father held
the girl between his thighs, his arms around her as if
to protect her.

The unhappy result was quite clear to Jean. The
new echo-encephalogram clearly showed that there was
a mid-line shift of the child's brain, several millimeters
to the left. Something aggressive in the right half of her
brain was pushing the left half off center. Possibly a
hemorrhage, or a mass. Jean refused to speculate on
the nature of the mass. She consoled herself that statistically in children a brain tumor more likely would
occur in another part of that complex organ. But she
could not rule out that worst of possibilities.

"Mr. Fazio, our tests reveal that there *is* something . . ."

"Not 'something,' Doctor. *What?* I got a right to know *what,*" the emotional man exploded, his huge face breaking out in a sudden sweat. He embraced his child so fiercely she had difficulty breathing until his wife cautioned, "Dom . . ." He became aware of his strangling grip on his daughter and eased his hold. "Doc?" he pleaded.

What he desperately wanted was some magic word which, unfortunately, the doctor was unable to give.

"There are signs of trouble. We're forced to make some other tests. You'll have to leave her."

"You had her here five whole days a couple of weeks ago," Fazio protested.

"And she had two more seizures after you took her home."

"That medicine! It's no good!" Fazio argued. "Don't you have some other medicine? In such a big hospital there's got to be more than one medicine for a kid like this!"

"Mr. Fazio, the medicine didn't work."

"If it was the right medicine, it would work!"

His wife pleaded, "Dom . . . Dom, listen to the doctor."

"I want to see another doctor!"

"If you'd like a man to examine her, if that would make you feel better, we can arrange it," Jean said. She had encountered that reaction many times before.

"He didn't mean that," Mrs. Fazio interceded.

"No," Fazio finally calmed, "I trust you, Doc."

"We're trying to help her, you know that, don't you?" Jean asked. The huge man nodded. It was evident he was fighting back tears. Now Jean faced the difficulty of explaining to both parents the steps she would have to take.

"First, we have to give Beatrice an injection of something we call *technitium*. It won't do her any harm.

It's a nuclear compound. When it gets inside the body it moves to the brain and settles there in areas where there might be trouble. Then we put her under a scanner . . ."

"Does it hurt?" Fazio asked at once.

"She lies on a table and the machine just passes above her. It never even touches her. But that machine tells us where there is a concentration of the technitium . . ."

"And when it does?" Mrs. Fazio asked.

"It indicates if there's something there . . . a mass or some other difficulty."

"Mass?" Fazio asked, though instinctively he knew.

"Tumor, possibly," Jean admitted.

"Cancer?"

"It might not be a tumor at all," Jean tried to reassure.

"Cancer?" Fazio pressed.

"It's too early to make a diagnosis, and too soon to rule out any possibility. If we find something on the scan, we will want to do an angiogram."

"That thing with the dye?"

"Yes. If we decide to do that, I'll want you to sign a form agreeing to the procedure," Jean said simply but firmly.

Fazio nodded, not in agreement, but indicating he grasped the gravity of the possibilities his young child faced.

"You do that scan first . . . later we see about the other thing," Fazio said.

"It may be necessary," Jean warned.

"I said we will see," Fazio answered grimly, but it was obvious he had decided against it.

"I'll have my secretary arrange to admit her to the children's ward."

"No ward!" Fazio said. "She gets her own room!"

"It's unnecessary. And very expensive," Jean cautioned.

"I don't work all my life so that when my daughter is sick she has to go into the wards!"

"You've never seen our wards. They're quite new. Only four to a room. It's not like the old days, Mr. Fazio."

"A private room!" Fazio insisted.

"She'll be very lonely."

"Private room! So we can come see her anytime!" Fazio insisted.

Jean finally acquiesced, for she observed the child had grown extremely tense in the face of her father's outburst. She buzzed for Maggie and arranged to have the child admitted and assigned a private room.

Fazio embraced his daughter. "Darling, Daddy has to go to work now. But they'll take good care of you here. The doctor will make sure. Right, Doc?"

"Yes, of course. There's nothing to worry about, Beatrice," Jean assured her.

Fazio nodded. "And Daddy will come see you every morning before he goes to work. But you will be okay. You hear? Okay! Your father promises you."

He kissed her. The child clung to him. He peered accusingly across her at Jean as if blaming the doctor for his child's condition.

She saw eight other patients after that. Aside from a man with Parkinson's, the other seven were minor neurological complaints which should respond to medication. Some further testing was indicated in two of the cases, but there were no alarming signs or symptoms.

She had just dispatched the man with Parkinson's to the Department of Neurosurgery for consultation, when Maggie announced Bobby and Mrs. Tatum. The boy entered first, gently urged forward by his mother. He was dressed in well-washed jeans and a brightly colored red and white striped T-shirt that set off his handsome face and his ringlets of black hair. Only his pale blue eyes were different, less bright, yet more active.

· "Good morning, Bobby," Jean greeted him, specifically intending to evoke a response.

"G'mornin', Do'tor," the boy managed, the last word almost indistinguishable.

She had noted previously that the boy spoke quite distinctly, more articulate than average for his age group. Without seeming to dwell on it, Jean turned to Mrs. Tatum.

"Anything unusual occur during the past two weeks?"

"No, Doctor, nothing."

"I assume there've been no seizures," Jean said.

"No."

"Any bed wetting?" Which could be a sign that Bobby had had a seizure in the middle of the night which had gone undetected.

"No."

"Good." She turned to the boy. "Come here, Bobby."

Jean watched with keen professional discernment as the boy started forward, then hesitated. He leaned back as if he would fall. His mother reached out to steady him.

"Bobby?" Jean invited again.

With some effort he moved toward her, trying to keep his balance. She held out her arms as if to embrace him but actually to catch him before he fell.

"There we are," she said reassuringly.

She stared into his pale blue eyes, which had been so clear and bright the last time she saw him. Now they jumped nervously, out of control. Nystagmus, she observed. It was adding up. Slurred speech, unsteadiness, tendency to fall backward, jumpy eyes.

"Now, Bobby, would you wait in the other room a little while?" Jean asked.

The boy hesitated, appeared rebuffed, turned to his mother. Sensing that the doctor was alarmed, Mrs. Tatum urged, "Bobby, darling, Mommy wants to talk to the doctor. Wait in there, please?"

"All right, Mommy." His words were slurred again.

Jean studied him carefully as he made his way toward the door, weaving a bit, and once more threatening to fall backward. Finally he reached the door safely.

"Mrs. Tatum, have you been giving Bobby his medication every day?"

"Of course!"

"When do you give it to him?"

"In the morning after breakfast. Noon when he comes back from school. When I'm not there, Esther gives it to him. In the evening after his dinner, before I put him to bed."

"How *much* do you give him?"

"Like you said—one pill."

"One pill . . ." Jean evaluated thoughtfully. She swung around to her phone. "Maggie, get me Dr. Forrest. If he's in surgery, get a message to him that I want to see him as soon as he's free."

As Jean hung up, Mrs. Tatum asked, "Dr. Forrest is a surgeon?"

"One of the best neurosurgeons in the city," Jean said. "Now, I have to see Bobby alone in my examining room."

Marissa Tatum rose quickly. "Doctor! What is it?"

"I don't know yet. But I want a surgeon to look at him. You wait right here!"

"Dr. Braham . . ." Mrs. Tatum started to suggest.

"Don't worry. I'll be in touch with Dr. Braham before we do anything," Jean promised.

She brought the ophthalmoscope close to the boy's right eye and stared in. She had not wanted to alarm Marissa Tatum unduly, but the boy had now begun to present a set of signs that could mean one of two things: An overdose of medication. But Mrs. Tatum had ruled that out. Or a brain tumor, a posterior fossa brain tumor involving the cerebellum. There was no apparent swelling in the optic disk of Bobby's right eye. Nor in his left.

As she completed her examination, Dr. Forrest walked in still dressed in his surgical gown. He was a tall, broad, graying man.

"Trouble, Jean?"

"Possibly." She reported the signs she had observed.

Forrest performed his own examination with the ophthalmoscope. "No papilledema. I would doubt any tumor. But with those other signs we can't be too careful. Let's get a scan."

"I've already ordered one. Two-hour delayed-view scan. I'll send him right down."

Forrest examined the boy again, asking him to walk back and forth, and interrogating him to hear the quality of his speech. Forrest glanced significantly at Jean, corroborating her fears.

"Call me as soon as you know. I can work it into my schedule first thing tomorrow morning. Just to be on the safe side, I'll reserve the OR."

Before Jean entrusted Bobby to the nurse who would take him down to the scanning room, she took a blood sample and sent it to the lab to get a serum Dilantin level. That would take twenty-four hours. The results of the scan would be more revealing and quicker.

She returned to her private office, where she found Marissa Tatum on the verge of tears.

"What is it, what did you find?"

"Nothing definitive yet," Jean said. "But we'll know in a few hours. Then we'll probably want a consultation with Dr. Braham, Dr. Forrest and your husband. Your husband's in town, isn't he?"

"Yes. But in conference all afternoon. With Mr. Cameron," she said, then demanded, "Doctor, what is it?"

"We'll have a better idea in a few hours. I'll call you as soon as we know anything."

"I want to see Bobby!" She was verging on hysteria.

"You can't see him now. He's having a brain scan. If you insist on staying, go down to the coffee shop or go for a walk for the next two hours. There's nothing else you can do."

Slowly Marissa Tatum's extreme tension began to subside. She nodded submissively and left the office.

In the dark room, Jean Scofield and surgeon Walter Forrest studied the scan for concentrations of nuclear-active technitium in the boy's brain. Forrest leaned back from the lit-up film that showed four views of Bobby's brain.

"I don't find anything. But that doesn't mean it isn't there. We may have to go in."

"No swelling in his optic disks, no increased cranial pressure and no hot spots on the scan," Jean totted up the data.

"With all the signs he exhibits, even without confirmation on examination, it could be hiding there. I've seen it before," Forrest warned. "In neurosurgery, never say never."

"Walter, would you do something for me?"

"I've always been willing to do more for you than

you've been willing to accept," he said, smiling shyly. It was an allusion to the time when he had made a gentle pass at her, which she had avoided with equal gentleness. He had apologized later. He was evidently not accustomed to having affairs with younger women. As he had said then, "I'm at the awkward age. I don't know whether to make a pass at you or adopt you." Ever since, they had been good friends and respectful colleagues.

"Walter, come back to my office and talk to the boy's mother."

"You know I'm not very diplomatic with patients' families. You want her to get all the gory details?"

"I have a hunch that, in this case, the gorier the better."

"Dr. Forrest has examined Bobby," Jean began. "I've asked him to be perfectly frank with you."

"Mrs. Terry . . ." he began.

"Tatum," Marissa corrected.

"Tatum," he repeated. "Mrs. Tatum, the signs your son exhibits are strongly indicative of a brain tumor. . . ."

She gasped. Forrest continued, "The tests don't reveal it. But the thing might be hiding there and we just can't pick it up. If his signs continue we'll have no choice but to go in and take a look."

"Go in . . . and take a look . . ." the mother repeated, breathless.

"I know how lay people feel about brain surgery. But it is a highly scientific procedure. And given half a chance we have a good record of recoveries."

"Half a chance . . ." Marissa echoed numbly.

"If there is a tumor and it's benign, we've got a good shot at getting it all out. If it's malignant—well, it depends on what we find, how much, how far it's spread, if it's encapsulated . . . a lot of things. . . . But until we turn back a flap we won't know much," he admitted.

"Turn back a flap?" Marissa Tatum mouthed the phrase.

"A flap of his skull."

She turned away. It seemed she might weep. Forrest looked to Jean Scofield. He had evidently done it again, upset some family member by his frank, straightforward approach to surgical procedures.

"There is another possibility," Jean suggested.

Marissa Tatum turned back, staring at Jean through a film of tears. "Yes?"

"Bobby does show signs that might indicate a tumor. But he fails to show others. That points to a second possibility. His eyes, his slurred speech, his unsteadiness could also mean an overdose of medication. I asked you once before, but I'm asking again. How *much* Dilantin did you give the boy?"

The mother hesitated.

"It's most important that Dr. Forrest and I know. *Now*. Before we make any further plans to do brain surgery on your son," Jean demanded pointedly. "Mrs. Tatum?"

Marissa Tatum was unable to answer.

Jean was sure now. She glanced at Forrest, then continued, "Mrs. Tatum, never try to outthink the doctor. It can be dangerous. When I prescribe 30 milligrams of Dilantin three times a day I don't mean 60 milligrams or five times a day. It's vitally important to keep the proper balance of Dilantin in his blood. Too little can bring back seizures. Too much can result in a boy who presents signs that might confuse the doctor and make her think she's dealing with a brain tumor."

Mrs. Tatum turned her gaze from Jean Scofield to stare off into space. Beneath her high cheekbones her cheeks grew more hollow, her face more tense.

"Therapy doesn't work in proportion to amount. Heat can cure. Too much heat can burn. A firm cast on a broken limb may help it to heal. Too tight a cast can bring on gangrene. The same with medication. Too much can be as harmful as not enough."

Marissa Tatum nodded vaguely.

Jean demanded, "How much *did* you give him?"

The young woman hesitated, then admitted, "Two pills."

"Two pills three times a day?"

The mother nodded. Jean glanced at Forrest, who was annoyed, yet relieved that there was no need for exploratory surgery. His look asked Jean if he could be excused. She nodded and said in a whisper, "Thanks, Walter. I had a hunch. I needed you to corroborate it."

In order not to further embarrass the unfortunate young woman, Forrest slipped out of the room quietly.

"Why?" Jean asked pointedly.

"I thought . . . what you said about the pills' preventing seizures . . . if one was good, two must be better. I didn't want that awful thing to happen again."

"Did you think *I* wanted it to happen again?"

Marissa Tatum shook her head.

"Then did you think I would underprescribe for him?"

Again, she shook her head.

"Then why?"

"I told you why," the mother insisted.

"An overdose must never occur again," Jean warned. "First, because of the effects that you've seen. And second, because we have to find the exact dose that will be best for Bobby. We can only do that if we have truthful records of how much he's getting and what effect it has. Is that understood?"

Marissa Tatum nodded. Tears did well from her black eyes. They started slowly, bringing with them streaky smudges of the mascara and eye shadow which she had so meticulously applied earlier in the day.

Jean held out a box of tissues to her.

"I . . . I didn't want Bob to see him have one of those . . . I know what it would do to him. . . ."

"Just what *would* it do to him?"

"He's a perfectionist. He has been all his life."

"Are you afraid that if he finds out his son is less than perfect he'll reject him?"

"I . . . I thought, with more medication it wouldn't happen and Bob wouldn't see it, and . . ." Her words trailed off, the thought remained unfinished but quite clear.

"I'll have to keep Bobby here five or six days. To let the effects of the Dilantin overdose wear off and to do some other tests."

"I understand," Marissa Tatum agreed.

twelve

Bobby had been settled in a bed in the Neurology ward. Dr. Scofield put in a call for Dr. Braham.

"Larry?" she greeted, crisply and professionally.

"Don't tell me," he anticipated. "When you call me 'Larry' in your proper neurologist's tone, it can mean only one thing. What about the Tatum boy?"

"When did you see him last?"

"Eight days ago. Slight cold. Fever that spiked but came down in twenty-four hours. Nothing serious. Why?"

"You wouldn't have been able to detect it eight days

ago. But he's been overmedicated. Double the pre-scribed dose."

"Marissa? Oh, no! She's not only beautiful. She's extremely bright. She wouldn't do anything so foolish."

"She wouldn't, but she did. After all, she's a mother. The brightest of them can become overemotional. Would you object if I had a talk with *Mr.* Tatum? Alone?"

"You think Bobby's prognosis is worse than origi-nally suspected?" Larry was concerned now.

"There's something in this situation that troubles me. But I can't put my finger on it."

"What do you expect to learn from Tatum? He doesn't spend nearly as much time with Bobby as Marissa does."

"Maybe that's part of the problem."

"Jeannie, don't go being a psychiatrist again," Larry warned. "Neurology is enough of a specialty."

"Freud did both."

"But he wasn't a woman."

"Lucky for you men," Jean agreed, laughing. "If he had been, he'd have been called the Mother of Psycho-analysis."

"Touché," he capitulated. "What about tonight?"

"Sorry, darling. Busy. What about Bob Tatum?"

"He doesn't appeal to me."

"I mean about my calling him?"

"No objection."

She was dictating case histories when her door opened briskly. She looked up.

"Mr. Tatum. Come in, come in."

She pushed back from her desk and turned to study him. Even at the end of a long day he appeared fresh and full of energy. When he slipped into the chair opposite her, his shoulders seemed to loom out of it like the thick branches of a huge tree.

"About Bobby," he began at once. "It's more serious than you thought. That's why you wanted to talk to me alone. Good thinking. Riss . . . Marissa can become very emotional about the boy."

Tatum was evidently a man who arrived at his own conclusions swiftly and dogmatically.

Jean would have to approach her objective in a roundabout way. She began by discussing the matter of Bobby's overmedication without making it seem quite so serious as it was. It was not her purpose to create friction or recriminations between husband and wife. Gradually, she led Tatum into describing the times he spent alone with Bobby and from that to the days of his own childhood. Eventually she had him talking about his own father.

"There was a man!" Tatum said with enormous admiration.

"You loved him very much?" Jean commented. She had expected a far different answer.

"Better than that. I *respected* him," Tatum said with sincere conviction.

"You think a father should command respect or insist on it?"

"Both!" Tatum said. "Take my father. Every break went against him. He was one hell of a halfback when he got out of high school. But just when he had four scholarships to pick from, he was drafted. World War Two. When he got out four years later it was too late for college. He was ready to get married.

"So he consoled himself with bringing up his sons to be athletes. From the time I can remember he used to say to me, 'Bobby boy, you're not going to miss like I did. You're going to be the best there is. Every college in the country is going to knock itself out to get a fullback like you.' He kept building confidence in me, in all three of us. My brother Steve, he was All-Big-Ten tackle. And Grant, he was first-string halfback at Alabama under the Bear.

"It means a lot when your dad believes in you. But it wasn't only believing. He worked with us, trained us. Made us do seven miles of roadwork every morning. He'd ride along in his truck and pace us. Every day. Rain or shine. Sun or snow. We'd run together. Steve, Grant, and me. It was a competition. I was the youngest, so in the beginning I'd have to quit and climb up into the truck alongside my dad.

"And he'd say, 'Did you mark the place, Bobby boy?', meaning where I'd dropped out. 'Well, tomorrow you're going to beat that.' And I did. It wasn't long before I was running shoulder to shoulder with Steve and Grant. When I got to high school my coach said I was the best-conditioned freshman he'd ever seen. Youngest kid on the squad and I was first string. Conditioning! How many fathers would take that much time and trouble with their sons?" Tatum asked, almost reverently.

Jean asked softly, "Did you love him?"

"Yes," Tatum replied as softly, "I loved him." He was thoughtful for a moment. "You know, I never thought of it before. But in a way my dad was the same as Mr. Cameron. With Cameron, too, training his young men is a personal thing. He doesn't leave it to others. Any more than my dad did."

"Still running behind the truck, are you?"

Tatum glanced at her resentfully.

"You think I didn't like that roadwork. Well, I did. And even if I didn't, I wanted to do it for *him*, because he wanted it for *me*. It was give and take. Father and son. That's the way it should be. When I played, I played more for him than for myself.

"And it worked. Just as he promised. It paid my way through college. Made it possible for me to meet Cameron. Gave me the opportunity that put me where I am today. I guess my old man and Cameron are the same. Cameron likes winners, too."

"What do you think your father would have done if he had had a son who wasn't capable of becoming a fullback?" Jean asked suddenly.

"Never could have happened! We were all born big-boned and strong. Like him."

"No girls in the family?"

Tatum smiled. "We had a family joke about that. Dad would never have stood for girls, so Mom just didn't have any."

"Interesting." Jean said, "That's the first time you ever mentioned your mother."

"I know," he admitted, smiling sheepishly. "Four men in the family and not another woman, she must have been lonely. Besides, she never liked football. Said she couldn't watch it, with her sons playing. For fear we'd get hurt."

Then, as if he felt sentimentality was a sign of weakness, he said, "You didn't bring me here to talk about myself."

Though that had been her real motive, Jean did not contradict him.

"About Bobby," Tatum said, very business-like again. "Brief me. All the facts. No matter how bad they are."

"We haven't made a definitive diagnosis yet. But part of that will involve giving him his medication on time and in the proper amounts."

"You have to understand Riss. She didn't do it out of any wrong motives. But she does feel guilty."

"Guilty? About what?" Jean asked with renewed interest.

"Her delivery being premature, Bobby being born

so underweight. That boy spent the first weeks of his life in a glass cage like a goldfish." Then Tatum confessed, "I was afraid he'd never make it. I never dared say so to Riss. She was blaming herself too much already."

"Why should she blame herself?"

"Too much smoking. Too much coffee. Too active. You see, I'd been transferred again. Fourth transfer in two years. And Riss, she's a fiend on decorating houses. As fussy about that as she is about the way she dresses. She just knocked herself out doing that house. That meant more cigarettes, more coffee. So when it happened the way it did, Bobby being born prematurely, she blamed herself."

"And you?"

"*I* don't blame her," Tatum said loyally.

"She didn't give you a fullback," Jean pointed out.

"That boy was just born unlucky. Too soon. Too small. Never has reached what I would call good weight."

"Yes," Jean agreed, with certain thoughts of her own about that now. "He doesn't seem the type to run behind a truck, does he?"

Tatum shook his head sadly. "I'd never ask him to."

"The things you *do* ask him to do, does he do them?"

"Absolutely. He's a terrific kid. Very obedient. No back talk."

"When he does disobey, how do you punish him?"

"I have never punished that boy," Tatum said, resentful of Jean's suggestion.

Jean nodded thoughtfully. She knew almost everything she had hoped to discover. "Fine, Mr. Tatum, and thank you for coming in."

He did not move. "Up to now I've done all the talking. Now it's your turn. I want to know about Bobby."

"There isn't anything more to know for the time being. We'll keep him here. Detoxify him. Get him back on his proper dosage. Then check up on him every few weeks."

"And I'll talk to Riss. I don't know why she'd do something like that," Tatum said gravely.

"If you'd like to see Bobby now, he may still be awake."

Jean went along with him, ostensibly to consult Bobby's chart, mainly to observe father and son together. The boy appeared happy to see his father. Tatum leaned close to him, whispered to him, little things Jean could not hear but that obviously comforted the boy. In a while he fell asleep holding his father's hand.

She returned to her office to change from her lab coat and found Benziger sitting in her chair, tilted back and reading a medical paper.

"Ah, Jean," he said, putting down the paper. "Interesting, the study on the aftereffects of cryo-surgery of the brain."

"All right, Benni," she said, suspecting he was not being as direct as usual.

Benziger smiled. "You're right. Sit down. Let's get it over with."

"Carey?"

"Carey."

"What now?"

"He still insists you accept that appointment as Associate Chief."

"I haven't changed my mind."

"I know."

"Then what do we have to talk about?"

"It seems that this afternoon you called a Mr. Tatum and had him come in for a consultation."

"He's the father of a patient. There were things I had to know."

"You're not the only one. Carey wants to know, too."

"Carey? Why?"

"Because Cameron wants to know."

"I do not discuss my patients with anyone except the immediate family. You know that, Benni."

"It seems that late this afternoon Cameron wanted to see Tatum. He discovered that he'd left the office to come here and see you. Now Cameron wants to know the boy's condition. And what he can do about it. He does not like his executives troubled by anything that takes their minds off the business of InterElectronics."

"What am *I* supposed to do, hold a TV press conference twice a day and brief the Board of Trustees on the boy's condition!" Jean said angrily. The recent practice of making public the intimate details of the illnesses of famous patients had always offended her.

Fearing she had insulted Benziger by making him seem part of the pressure, she apologized. "Sorry, Benni. I know you had to ask. Carey's entitled to that much consideration."

"That's what I'm going to welcome most when I retire. Freedom from all the hospital politics." He looked across at her. "Jean, my dear, are you sure you want to be Chief? With all the conniving, the backbiting, the power struggles that go on?"

"I'm no longer content to run behind the truck. I'm ready to come off the bench and play in the big game."

He stared at her, puzzled.

She laughed. "You would have had to be here. Okay, Carey wants to know because Cameron wants to know. How much shall we tell him?"

"Is there any reason not to tell him everything?"

"Yes," Jean said thoughtfully. "Because what we

know is quite limited. And what we *suspect* is too premature."

"And what do 'we' suspect?"

"I'd rather talk to Dr. Braham first. He's the pediatrician on the case."

Her reference to Larry by professional title did not escape either of them.

"Of course," Benziger said. "Now, about Carey?"

"Tell him the patient is under observation. No etiology has been established. When I arrive at a diagnosis, I will inform Mr. Carey." She added sarcastically, "Or, if Carey would like, I'll call Cameron directly and tell him."

Benziger laughed. "With the Board waiting for your decision, if I were you, I would avoid Mr. Cameron like the plague." He kissed her on the cheek and left.

She made her notes on Tatum. She had just jotted down, *Without saying so, patient's father, like both his own father and his boss, "likes winners." This could be significant.*

Her phone rang. An aloof, proper British secretarial voice asked, "Dr. Scofield?"

"Yes."

"One moment, please."

There was a long silence. Then another voice came on. A man's voice, by contrast soft, low and extremely confident because it never had need to be raised.

"Dr. Scofield?"

"Yes."

"Cameron speaking."

"Oh, Mr. Cameron, yes?" Jean was on guard at once.

She realized how swiftly the word had traveled. Benziger called Carey. Carey immediately reported to Cameron. Cameron was calling. All within less than fifteen minutes.

"Doctor, we've never met. But I've heard a great deal about you."

"I've heard a great deal about you, too."

There was the slightest tinge of irritation in Cameron's voice, as he continued, "I made a reasonable, well-intentioned request concerning the condition of a patient in whom I have a deep personal interest. I understand that information is not forthcoming."

"There isn't much we know. None of it definitive."

"I didn't ask for a 'definitive' diagnosis!" Cameron was openly annoyed now. "I simply want the facts. All the facts!"

"All the facts?" Jean Scofield weighed his phrase. "Are you sure?"

"Yes. I'm sure!" Cameron responded sharply.

"If you wish. 'Patient Tatum, Junior, Robert. Five-year-old white male. Clinical impression: 1. Post-ictal secondary to two. 2. Seizure disorder of unknown etiology. (a) Possible focus in left frontal lobe, i.e., presentation as adverse frontal lobe seizure with head and eyes turning toward the right . . .' "

Cameron exploded. "Damn it, Doctor! That's not what I want to know!"

Pretending to be ingenuous, Jean asked, "Would you prefer the lab reports? The results of his skull x-rays, EEG and echo-encephalogram?"

Barely controlling his fury, Cameron said, "In plain English I insist on knowing what is wrong with that boy and what I can do about it!"

"Frankly, Mr. Cameron, that's exactly what I'd like to know, too."

There was a moment of silence before Cameron hung up.

She caught Larry just as he was leaving his office. "Larry? Busy this evening?"

"Yes, but I'll break it," he offered eagerly.

Before he could assume she was availing herself of his earlier invitation, she said, "I want to discuss the Tatum case."

"Oh." His expectations had been abruptly corrected. "Of course. My office? Or dinner?"

"Dinner. But give me an hour. Something I have to do first."

"Okay. Mario's?"

"Good. In an hour."

She hesitated a moment, then dialed Radiology and spoke to the resident on duty. When she had given him specific orders, she went down to the Neurology ward where she had installed Bobby Tatum. But she discovered the boy had been transferred to a private room. On orders of Edward Carey, who no doubt was acting on orders from Chairman of Trustees Horace Cameron. She would fight that battle later. Right now, she had more urgent plans in mind.

She had an orderly roll Bobby's bed onto the elevator and up to Radiology. Within an hour she was studying the complete set of body x-rays she had ordered. Both she and the resident examined them carefully.

Suddenly he said, "You were right. There it is. Healed fine-line fracture of the fibula!"

"How long ago?"

"I'd guess about two years. Maybe three."

Jean nodded thoughtfully. She had confirmed one of her suspicions. She had needed to know that before she met Larry.

thirteen

They hadn't yet ordered dinner and were dawdling over drinks when Larry Braham realized that no subject would interest Jean except the one she had come to discuss.

"All right. About Bobby Tatum—how bad is it?"

"Have you ever gotten a call from Mr. Cameron?" she asked.

"He has no children, and consequently no grand-children. And I'm not a specialist on prostate massage." Larry laughed. "Why would Cameron call me?"

"To inquire about Bobby Tatum."

"Cameron likes to have an electronic finger on every pulse. He's a shaker and a mover. Get the job done, that's his motto. Even if you have to invent a new com-puter, change the surface of the earth, or bribe some foreign government official. It wouldn't be beyond him to put Bobby on one of his own planes and fly him anywhere in the world he thought there might be a cure. He does not accept the word 'impossible.' "

" 'With Cameron, as with God, all things are pos-sible.' " Jean paraphrased.

"How did it go? Your conversation."

"He demanded a concise report, as if he were order-ing one of his junior executives. Maybe I was a bit sharp with him," she conceded. "But even if I knew what was wrong with the boy, I have no right to tell him."

"You misunderstand him," Larry defended. "He has

142

an overpowering sense of loyalty. The men he chooses don't just work for him, he adopts them. He cares about their families, their private lives. Once when he thought Bob Tatum had been away from his wife and son too long, he put the three of them on his own jet and had them flown down to his estate in the Islands. He forced them to take a two-week vacation together."

Jean laughed. "If the government did that, the Supreme Court would call it an unwarranted interference in individual rights."

"The point is, Cameron cares about his people. He's interested in Bobby Tatum, because he's interested in his father. I think you should have considered that in talking to the old man. To say nothing . . ." Larry stopped abruptly.

"What is it that we're 'to say nothing' about?"

"Do I have to say it?"

"As Chairman of the Trustees, he's going to have a lot of influence in appointing the new Chief of Neurology."

"Cameron is never content to have 'a lot of influence.' He has *all* the influence."

Larry downed the rest of his drink, then said gravely, "It was a tactical mistake. A bad tactical mistake, Jeannie."

When he called her Jeannie, as Cliff used to do, it always touched her in a way that made her vulnerable. It weakened her resolve to discuss with him what she had intended. She wondered, could men, too, be so affected and disarmed by a single word, a single name spoken so lovingly?

She had no time to dwell on it, for Larry asked, "Now, about Bobby? Something show up on a new scan today?"

She handed him the chart of *Tatum, Junior, Robert.*

Puzzled, he stared at her. She stared back challengingly. He studied the chart in detail.

"Well?" he asked.

"You've taken care of that boy for almost two years now. Does his weight ever trouble you?"

"He tends to be underweight. But he's not suffering from malnutrition. I can assure you of that."

"In his eight days in the hospital during his first stay he gained almost four pounds."

"Why not?" Larry countered. "An active child suddenly forced to undergo bedrest, being fed three meals a day and with nurses spoiling him with milk and cookies mid-morning and mid-afternoon."

"Something else changed, too."

"What?"

"When he was admitted, he was withdrawn, placid . . ."

"Frightened," Larry interjected.

"Possibly."

"No doubt about it," Larry continued. "After a few days, when he got over his initial fear, he was bright and cheerful. He liked being there. And he liked *you*. What's wrong with that? I like you myself. I love you. Any kid would be crazy not to love you."

"He wanted to stay on," Jean said pointedly.

"He said he wanted to stay on in the hospital?" Larry asked, surprised.

"He didn't *say* it. He . . . communicated it. . . ."

"What did he do?" Larry asked sarcastically. "Send a telegram?"

"It was in his eyes. In his touch," she said softly.

"His touch?" Larry Braham repeated. Then suggested gingerly, "Jeannie, is it possible that because of her own past experience, the doctor might be reading something into the natural affection a boy would have for someone who treated him so kindly for eight days?"

"Possibly I'm vulnerable to black-haired, blue-eyed little boys. But I'm physician enough not to let my personal feelings affect my observations where a patient is concerned."

Larry reached to cover her hand with his. "Jeannie, before it's too late, let's get married. Let's have our own children. You need that. You need it very much."

"I've told you, until I can come to terms with the past, I'm not going to marry again. It wouldn't be fair. To either of us."

"You don't owe Cliff any more of your life than you've already given him."

She didn't respond. He continued, "Giving is a two-way street. For someone to give, there has to be someone to receive. Else giving is empty, futile."

"And sick?" she countered sharply.

"I didn't say that."

There was a moment of silence between them. Very few times in their intimate relationship had they ever discussed her illness, now long past.

He directed the conversation back to safer professional grounds. "You said Bobby wanted to stay on. You also made a point of his weight gain. What are you getting at?"

"You're an excellent pediatrician. You ought to know."

He glanced at her, puzzled. Then his expression changed to one of surprise and disapproval. "Good God, you can't be serious!"

"What if I am?"

"*If* I didn't know the patient. *If* I didn't know his parents. *If* I hadn't examined that boy at least once every three months for two years, then maybe, possibly, I would come to the same erroneous conclusion."

"What conclusion?" she challenged. "I want to see if you're willing to say it."

"All right. *Child abuse.* Which is the most ridiculous diagnosis I've heard in years! The Tatums are fine people. Socially and financially free of the pressures that lead to child abuse. You are simply taking a shy, sensitive boy who has a tendency to be underweight and turning it into a wild, half-baked diagnosis. Really, darling, I'm surprised at you."

Feeling he had disposed of her concern, he laughed. "If this goes on, we may have to prevent you from treating little boys." The hurt on her face made him apologize instantly, "Forgive me, Jeannie. That wasn't fair."

"I may be vulnerable to little boys, but this chart isn't. It only states facts. His weight gain is a fact."

"The boy was a preemie. Almost five weeks in ICU. He has *never* shown a normal weight gain."

"Except *once,"* Jean corrected. "With *us."*

"When you had him under sedation. In bed. And overfed!" Larry countered.

"Can you also 'explain' his change in attitude?" Jean challenged.

"What does that mean?" Larry demanded, sensitive to her reflection on his professional conclusions.

"The well-adjusted, normal child becomes depressed when confined to a hospital. Conversely, a deprived or abused child thrives in a hospital. Becomes happy and outgoing. That boy, who was shy, withdrawn and tense on admission, became happy, outgoing and warm while we had him. And don't say I'm being subjective. Just to make sure, I checked my observations with Kerner."

Larry was alarmed. "You didn't discuss this with Kerner, did you?"

"Of course not. I merely wanted her observations.

They checked with mine. That boy thrived with us. Became friendly and outgoing for a child usually docile and withdrawn."

"So, he's a docile child. Always has been. Personally, I attribute it to the trauma of his birth."

"That's a conclusion, not a fact," Jean pointed out.

"Darling," Larry said, enunciating the word with such precise care that it was obvious he was trying to contain his impatience. "You are engaging in an exercise in acrobatic diagnosis. Leaping from one questionable assumption to another to fabricate a condition that simply does not exist. I have observed that boy under all conditions, sick and well. I have never detected any evidence of abuse."

"Then maybe it's *you* who's been too close to the patient."

"Ridiculous!" he shot back.

She allowed his anger to subside for a moment before she asked, "Have you ever treated him for a fracture of the fibula?"

Larry stared at her, openly dubious.

"It's there. On his long-bone x-rays."

"When did you order a complete set of x-rays on that boy?" Larry demanded.

"This evening. After I talked with his father."

"I don't get the connection."

"He's a tough man, your Bob Tatum. Highly intelligent. But tough underneath. A winner. He was brought up that way. Without realizing it, he was one type of abused child himself. His father drove him because he liked winners. So does your Mr. Cameron."

"I have no ax to grind for Cameron!"

"I don't give a hoot about Cameron!" Jean shot back. "Until it affects one of my patients. I think it does now."

"Meaning?"

"I'm not blaming Cameron for this. But he does give us an important clue. He picked Bob Tatum for the same personality traits that make me suspect him of being a child abuser."

"Don't even think that," Larry interrupted. "It's a terribly serious and dangerous accusation to make. Especially based on incomplete and sketchy facts."

"We have two facts. A father with the earmarks of a potential abuser. And a child with enough signs to indicate he might be abused."

"A fractured fibula in a child is not that unusual. It can happen accidentally and without anyone's knowing. And it can heal without being detected or treated. There's absolutely no mention of it in his previous medical history."

"Beecher, in Radiology, thinks it could have been two or three years ago."

"Two years ago I would have known about it," Larry said. "So it must have been three years ago or more. But that doesn't prove that his previous pediatrician saw it either."

"Doesn't it?" she asked pointedly.

"What does that mean?"

"That not everything a pediatrician observes in private practice finds its way into the patient's record."

"Are you accusing *all* pediatricians?"

"No, just some of those who treat nice, upper-middle-class families which tend to abuse their children and want it kept secret," Jean said firmly.

"Are you accusing *me?*" he asked, less angry now than hurt.

"Of course not, Larry. But don't be so intolerant of my observations and conclusions."

"The Tatums are not the kind who would do anything like that," Larry defended. "They are nice, decent, intelligent people."

"If nice, decent, intelligent people could govern their emotions better than other people, there wouldn't be so many of them consulting psychiatrists! Child abuse is an emotional problem, not a cultural one."

"They're just not that kind of people," Larry insisted.

"Larry, you know that not all child abuse takes place in the slums. The statistics show up that way only because slum families don't have the intelligence or the means to hide it. They're forced to go to charity clinics, which report them. Not to private practitioners who blink at it, because they don't want to endanger and lose their 'nice, decent, intelligent' patients."

"That's a hell of an accusation to make!" Larry exploded.

Jean refused to back down. "But it *does* happen, doesn't it?"

Larry didn't answer at once. He toyed with his empty glass. "Yes. It happens. But as far as I know that's not true of the Tatums. You believe me, don't you?"

"Of course I believe *you,* Larry. But what about the pediatricians before you? How sure are we that they didn't conceal things? Like that long-bone fracture three years ago?"

"A doctor can be told a very plausible story and believe it."

"Like the reason Bobby is a failure-to-thrive child?" she asked pointedly.

"Now you *are* accusing me."

"Only of accepting a very logical deduction that could be entirely wrong. Bobby's premature birth and early history may have something to do with it. But they may *not* be the *only* reasons for his present condition."

"If I were you I'd confine myself to treating that boy for his seizures. Let me worry about the rest of him."

He seized the menu and scanned it. If he had been

hungry when he arrived, he was only angry now. Yet curious, too. Without lowering the menu he asked, "About Tatum? What *do* you think?"

She pretended to scan her menu as she answered. "He's a strong man. In personality as well as physically. No matter what he claims, he is disappointed in Bobby, who is never going to be another All-American fullback. Tatum can't accept that. His father certainly wouldn't have. So he might become impatient with the boy. Might lose his temper. Might resort to the thing that's always stood him in such good stead till now. Physical expression."

"You think he might have inflicted that fracture?"

"One possibility. The other is that he might have tried to toughen up the boy. Condition him, as he might say. By rough horseplay. The injury might have been accidental. But it's an injury that was obviously concealed nevertheless. That's almost more revealing than the injury itself."

"What do you intend to do about it?"

"Keep at it, till I discover the whole truth."

"And then?"

"If the facts justify it, I will report to the Child Abuse Committee at the hospital."

Larry Braham lowered his menu to stare across the table at her. "You can't do that."

"I have to," she countered.

"There are other ways to handle it."

"Such as concealing it? I thought you said you'd never resort to that."

"Creating a scandal won't help Bobby," he warned.

"You get Bob Tatum to accept treatment, or counseling, and I won't have to report to the Committee. Will you talk to him?"

"I'll think about it," Larry conceded.

"Do it soon, Larry. *Very* soon."

Neither of them had any appetite for dinner so Jean asked to be taken home. When he dropped her off she refused his plea to let him stay on. It was highly significant to her that he did not entreat or insist as strongly this night as he had on all others.

She was alone. Alone in a way that reminded her of all the days and nights without Cliff. There was nothing nearly so final about Larry's absence. But something had suddenly changed their relationship. Looking at it from his point of view, as she did now, she had made an accusation against his specialty. Which meant against him. Yet she hadn't intended it that way.

As a colleague, she owed him complete insight into her findings and suspicions. As a lover, she owed him the consideration she would have accorded Cliff if she had thought he was wrong. In her determination to protect Bobby Tatum she had offended and alienated Larry Braham.

She cautioned herself to be less forthright in the future. But it was her nature. Some who opposed her ambition to become Chief considered it a highly unfeminine characteristic. Meaning that such strong conduct in a man would have been perfectly acceptable, possibly even laudable.

By the time she slipped into her bed, the professional aspects of her situation had paled alongside the fact that she was alone. Alone. That small two-syllable word always frightened her.

fourteen

Dominick Fazio and his wife sat in Jean Scofield's office. The big man's face was contorted into a reflection of grim thought. He studied the consent form Jean Scofield had placed before him. She held out the pen. Fazio stared at it.

"You said she could die from this," Fazio stated, hoping to be contradicted.

Jean could not be truthful and still reassure him. "There's a very, very remote chance. But still a chance."

"I can't do it."

"Dom!" his wife reprimanded, her round puffy face about to dissolve.

He glared at her. She turned away and buried her face in her handkerchief. He put his arm about her shoulders.

"Paula, no," he pleaded. "Don't cry."

"What do you want me to do?" she asked without looking at him. "The doctor says do it and you don't want to. How can she help Beatrice if you won't help?"

"She is asking me to sign my own baby's death warrant!" he said. "You want me to do that?"

"Yes!" she said, facing him.

"I can't! Anything happens to my baby, I kill myself. I rather die than sign this!"

Jean interceded. "Mr. Fazio, if there were some way we could help your daughter by sacrificing you I would give you that choice. But there isn't. So it's foolish to

152

talk about killing yourself, or doing anything rash. Right now, the one thing we need to know only an angiogram can show us. We can't go ahead, unless you sign this consent form."

Fazio shook his head slowly but very firmly.

"Dom!" his wife cried.

He did not relent.

"Then *I'll* do it!" she said, reaching for the pen.

"No!" Fazio said. "Did you hear me? I am *ordering* you not to do it!"

Mrs. Fazio hesitated. "Dom, the doctor says it's her only chance."

"Is it?" Fazio asked. He turned to Jean Scofield. "Did you say that, Doctor?"

"I said if we did this test we might find out exactly what Beatrice is suffering from."

"And what if you find out, that's the thing I want to hear?" Fazio challenged.

"Depending on what we find, we will decide what to do," Jean said.

" 'Do' 'do' 'do'! Let me hear *cure! Cure! Cure!* That's what I want, Doctor, I want my little girl to be cured! Tell me that and I sign your form."

"We can't assure you of a cure, Mr. Fazio. You know that."

"No, but if you find something in there that can kill her, you can assure me of that, can't you?" Fazio accused fiercely.

"I can only assure you of one thing. If we *don't* do something Beatrice may die. Her best chance is to find out what we're dealing with."

She pushed the pen forward. Fazio did not take it.

"Those pills you gave her, what do they do?"

"They should control her seizures. Unless there's some underlying cause that will make them worse."

"Okay. I take that chance. We give her the medicine

and we see what happens. But I don't sign no death certificate for my daughter."

Fazio had spoken and it was obviously his last word.

"I'm sorry you feel that way, Mr. Fazio," Jean said, slipping the unsigned form back into the file of *Fazio, Beatrice.*

"Come," he said to his wife.

As they reached the door, Jean called out a warning. "Be sure to bring her back in two weeks for a checkup."

Fazio turned to glare at Jean, his face casting great doubt on that probability. Mrs. Fazio looked to Jean, pleading and apologizing at the same time. But she remained obediently silent.

Late that morning Jean Scofield was summoned to the phone by the beeper which was as much a part of her hospital uniform as her white lab coat. She was greeted not by a voice but by the sound of weeping.

"Hello! Hello! Who is this?"

There was gasping and finally a voice only sufficiently recovered from crying to be barely understood.

"Doctor? Doctor, it's me."

"Yes, Mrs. Fazio, what happened? Did Beatrice have another seizure?"

"No. But I talk to him all the way home. I beg him. He won't budge. I tell him I will go down there and sign it myself and he says, don't you dare! In the whole time we're married I never go against him. There is only one boss in this house. But now . . . now, what do I do, Doctor?"

"If she were my child, I'd sign it, Mrs. Fazio. I'd want to give her every chance."

"And if I sign, and she dies, Doctor? The rest of my life he will blame me. My children will blame me. Just tell me she won't die, Doctor. That's all I want to hear and I'll come right down and sign," the woman pleaded.

"Mrs. Fazio, angiograms can have serious side

effects. That's why it's a decision the patient's family makes, not the doctor."

There was no answer, only another burst of tears. Then the phone went dead.

Back in her office, Jean found the usual accumulation of phone messages. There was also a note Maggie had written on her calendar: "Grand Rounds, 1:30." For a moment she questioned attending. Her schedule was overcrowded. She was due in the clinic at three. There were all her own patients she had admitted to the wards and the private pavilion. It would be another long day going on into the night. But if she went without lunch she would have time to see Bobby Tatum and still attend Grand Rounds, at which some interesting cases were due to be presented.

Bobby was dozing lightly, still under the influence of over-medication.

"Bobby?"

He opened his eyes slowly. The lids fluttered, closing, then coming half open. He reached out his hand to her. She held it all the while she talked to him, to keep him awake so she could study his open eyes. They were less jumpy. He could control and focus them. If he had not been so sleepy she would have got him out of bed so he could walk for her. She wanted to see if he still had that drug-induced tendency to tilt backward and fall.

"How are you feeling, Bobby?"

"Fine."

"The nurses, are they nice to you?"

"Yes, ma'am."

"Do they give you enough to eat?"

"Yes, ma'am."

"And do you like what they give you?"

"Yes, ma'am."

The tendency to accede, to comply, to agree, to

please, to do anything but give a negative answer was typical of abused children. Even making allowances for his overdosed condition, he was too placid and submissive. No matter what Larry Braham said, Jean's instincts told her she was dealing with a child in an abnormal situation. And that unrecorded fibula fracture, now healed, and so reasonably explained away, was an undisputed fact.

She let the boy hold her hand till he slipped off to sleep again. By that time he had pressed her hand to his cheek so that extricating it was no easy matter. She did it gently, and he woke just long enough to whisper, "Doctor Jean . . ." She thought he had said it affectionately. But she realized she could have been wrong. It could have been her own need that made it sound that way.

Grand Rounds at University Hospital were conducted in impressive Cameron Hall, which had been built with a grant from the Cameron Foundation. The lavish auditorium provided a place large enough to host medical and surgical symposia of national importance and to accommodate functions such as graduations from the Medical School and the School for Nursing and the annual Intern's Show. When not used for those purposes, it was made available to each department for its Grand Rounds.

The term *Grand Rounds* had originated in Europe in the eighteen hundreds. In those days it took the form of the professor's actually making rounds of the wards, accompanied by his students. He would point out to them cases of unique importance, or baffling cases, and would, when he felt it desirable, ask his students to examine and diagnose certain of them, then agree or correct their diagnoses as part of their instruction.

These days, though the phrase and the educational purpose remained the same, Grand Rounds were held in a meeting room. Instead of the patients themselves, usually their x-rays, scans, slides and histories were presented. Cases were discussed anonymously to enlighten the staff, share information and discoveries with other physicians and surgeons, or present baffling cases to invite discussion and opinions.

The Department of Neurology held its Grand Rounds at least once every two weeks. Sometimes more often, depending on the number of unique or baffling cases which deserved attention. Today's Grand Rounds consisted of three cases. The first concerned a missed diagnosis of a lung cancer which had earlier been diagnosed as tuberculosis and came to light only after the patient began to present neurological signs. The second involved a significant change in surgical procedure in an operation on the brain. Slides were presented showing the procedure step by step. The surgeon, who had improvised the procedure when faced with an emergency during the operation, explained in detail the problem and the ingenious manner in which he had solved it.

Jean had only a limited interest in either of these cases. It was the third case that intrigued her, for she had made some observations in that area herself.

Though this was Grand Rounds for the Neurology Department, the third presentation was made by Dr. Slake, Associate Professor of Internal Medicine. His patient had first exhibited medical signs, but later the signs became neurological, which made him a subject for combined interest between the Department of Medicine and Hans Benziger's department.

A fourteen-year-old black male (no specific identification was ever given during Grand Rounds), the patient had been admitted to the wards several months ago with a fever arising from an undifferentiated cause. Treatment with antibiotics helped reduce his fever, which was kept under control for a period of five days, at which time the boy was discharged. He was readmitted four days later with a fever that spiked at 104½°. This time he responded to antibiotics but was not released until nine days had passed, fever-free. Then, just prior to his release, he ran a fever again. There had then followed a history of alternating high fevers and fever-free periods for seven weeks. There was no evidence of systemic infection. No pathology to account for a fever. Two weeks ago he had begun to present signs of a neurological nature. No diagnosis had been made by the neurologist.

Slake admitted that the Department of Internal Medicine was baffled and was inviting comment. Considerable discussion followed. Finally, Jean signified her desire to advance an opinion.

"Doctor, in which ward was this patient placed?" she asked.

Slake was obviously annoyed. The question had little relevance to his problem. He cast a glance at his assistant who had the file. The answer came back quickly: "The Seaton Pavilion."

"I expected that," Jean said.

Slake was puzzled. Jean explained:

I have been running checks of my own on Seaton. Because I noticed that we've been getting an unusual number of referrals of neurological cases from Seaton as compared with other ward buildings. Cases with hysterical symptoms. Groundless complaints of various kinds. I believe if you ask the men and women on the Psychiatric Service they will report the same phenomenon. For some reason the cure rate in Seaton is lower than it is in other wards," Jean said. "That may have some bearing on your case, Dr. Slake."

"Precisely how, may I ask?"

"I became interested in that question myself. So I decided to investigate. I discovered that cases with intransigent but undifferentiated symptoms in the Seaton Ward had certain characteristics in common. Your case seems to share them."

"Such as?"

"You said the patient is a fourteen-year-old black male. The population distribution in this city being what it is, I assume this patient comes from a slum home."

"Since he's on the wards, we can assume that," Slake conceded.

"Well, so do all the cases I've investigated. When one studies the data I've compiled, one comes to the conclusion that there's something about the Seaton Wards that leads to this condition. Since slum patients confined to older ward buildings do not reflect the same rate of recurrent symptoms and readmissions."

"What are your conclusions, Dr. Scofield?" Slake asked, intrigued now.

"First, one more fact," Jean said. "The most significant of all. Patients discharged from Seaton and readmitted to Seaton suffered recurrences. Former patients from Seaton who were readmitted to *other* ward buildings did *not* suffer recurrences. The cause is obviously in Seaton."

"But that's our newest and finest building," a voice protested from the rear of the auditorium. Jean recognized Edward Carey. He frequently made it a point to drop in on departmental Grand Rounds, hoping to pick up some morsel of medical information that might lead to a scientific paper which, when printed in a reputable medical journal, would reflect credit on University Hospital. If, in addition, it resulted in newspaper or television coverage, Carey would consider that a publicity bonanza.

"Seaton is the best and newest ward in this city!" Carey proclaimed proudly.

"That's just the point," Jean said, turning to seek out Carey.

Indignant, Carey demanded, "Dr. Scofield, do you mean to tell us that well-trained doctors, in a building with the best and latest facilities, are achieving a lower cure rate than before?"

"Well-trained doctors, with better facilities, are curing fewer patients. Yes. And patients are having longer stays in the hospital than before. Yes. But that's not what *I* say, Mr. Carey. It's what our own figures will tell you. If you take the trouble to consult them."

"You are absolutely ridiculous!" Carey said vehemently.

Hans Benziger rose slowly to say, "Mr. Carey, Grand Rounds are for the exchange of information among physicians and staff. I do not intend to have people on my service attacked by laymen who have no competence to express medical opinions."

Carey's face grew quite red with embarrassment and fury but he did not reply.

Because Benziger knew that Jean had incurred Carey's anger and would doubtless be the object of his reprisals, he had chosen to take the onus upon himself. He continued, "For myself, I am extremely interested in Dr. Scofield's theory."

Jean continued. "Mr. Carey has focused on the pivotal point. It is in the phrase he used, 'best and latest facilities.' It is my suspicion that is the precise cause of these patient recurrences. New, clean, comfortable rooms. Two or four persons to a room, not like the older wards where there are anywhere from twelve to twenty-four to a room. Bright windows. Three hot, nourishing meals a day. No rats. No roaches. None of the pressures of daily slum living. Why *shouldn't* a patient prefer that to his own home?"

No one disputed her.

"We may have made living in a hospital more attractive than living in the outside world," Jean concluded.

Slake nodded thoughtfully. "Dr. Scofield, this is extremely interesting. Would you send me a copy of your data?"

"Of course, Doctor."

Carey called from the back of the auditorium, "*I* certainly would like them!"

"Dr. Scofield?" Slake referred Carey's request.

"I would prefer to complete my observations and conclusions before making a general distribution of the data," Jean said.

"And *I* should prefer that anything which affects the administration of this hospital be kept absolutely confidential until the Board of Trustees decides what to do about it!" Carey decreed. "I dread to speculate on what the trustees will say when they hear of this!"

Having leveled that threat, Carey turned and strode out of the Cameron Auditorium.

It was late afternoon. That time when Horace Cameron turned from the demands of his multi-national empire to those activities which nourished his ego. Charitable requests, the operation of the Cameron Foundation, political contributions, support of the arts and kindred matters were reserved for the end of day. Supplicants seeking funds knew that the worst blunder was to disturb Cameron on such a matter before five. After that hour, like a medieval prince, Cameron held court for those seeking his largesse, relaxed in his huge leather chair, prepared to listen.

He was a lean man, his hands long and graceful, marked by prominent blue veins and mottled by brown patches of senile keritosis. His lips were thin and at times it was difficult to tell if he was smiling or sneering, since he wore tinted glasses which tended to obscure his eyes, giving him protection from those who would too readily read his mind. But the Horace Cameron who held court in late afternoon was a far more indulgent man than the Horace Cameron who ran a global empire.

Edward Carey knew any day when Cameron was in the city he would have no trouble seeing him if he dropped by; even unexpectedly, somewhere around six o'clock. By that hour, Cameron was usually having his eighth cigar and the first of his two rigidly rationed drinks for the day. His second drink he always had at home with his wife, before dinner.

Cameron was a man who believed in and practiced a rigid routine. On those rare occasions when his public relations counsel convinced him to grant a press interview, he always made it a point to stress discipline as his prime virtue. He had more than once been quoted as saying, "I'm not much brighter than the next man. It's just that I'm more consistent." The Justice Department had had occasion to question his "consistency" in three different antitrust actions and had discovered that he was consistent there, too, winning all three suits.

To offset his public image as a shrewd and dictatorial titan, Horace Cameron made it a studied policy to expend a great part of his wealth in cultural activities. As he was fond of saying of himself, "A man who can't give a large part of himself and his wealth to the humanities doesn't deserve the esteemed title of human being. *Making* money is no great feat. Learning how to use it for the betterment of society *is*."

He had authored a number of such self-serving homilies and repeated them so often that they had been reprinted in collections of famous quotations. He actually believed them, as well, unaware that by so doing he was filling the void in his life created by the irreversible fact that he had no natural heirs. Fully expecting to outlive his wife, since he could never consciously countenance his own mortality, Horace Cameron could look to no Camerons to succeed him.

Therefore his "future," as he chose to term it, consisted of two factors—the young men he trained to succeed him at InterElectronics and the number of cultural and charitable works which would bear his name for as long as the nation endured. Important among those works was University Hospital, many of whose buildings bore the name, acknowledging the huge contributions of the Cameron Foundation.

His wife, always unconsciously guilty at never having provided her husband with the heirs he secretly coveted, joined him in this unspoken conspiracy to make good works take the place of the children they had never had. She worked at it with the same energy her husband invested in his business empire. She had earned for herself a reputation as the originator and driving force behind many good causes which had achieved nationwide impact. In the same way as Horace adopted young executives, she commandeered and mobilized their wives, who were more than willing to serve in order to enhance their husbands' careers.

Thus both husband and wife had worked out a plan for their lives that was not only active and exciting but that subtly camouflaged the emptiness that had resulted from her inability to breed.

In his own view of himself, Horace Cameron was a fair, hard-working, just and charitable man. He ran his physical being and his private life as he ran his multi-national businesses, with unswerving discipline and resolve. He could afford every luxury the world offered. Except one. He never permitted himself to feel self-pity. The suggestion by his doctors that a man verging on seventy-one should cut down on his activities was brushed aside with a joking, "I'll outlive all you bastards! My favorite hobby is being a pall-bearer."

He could never admit, even to himself, that one of his prime interests in having University Hospital become such an advanced, well-equipped and well-staffed hospital, was the underlying fear that some day, far off perhaps, but some day, he would depend on it to save his life. For that, and other reasons that fit his style of charitable works, Cameron was always liberal with the time he granted Edward Carey.

This afternoon, once drinks had been poured, Horace Cameron loosened his tie, opened his collar and leaned back in his chair, asking pleasantly, "Well, Edward?"

Carey sighed, intending to convey the heavy weight of the burdens pressing upon him as Administrator of University Hospital. "Days like this don't happen too often, thank God."

"What now?" Cameron asked, amused, for he was accustomed to Carey's hyperboles.

"That woman again."

"Woman?" Cameron repeated casually, while he studied the smoke from his elegantly thin Havana cigar. Suddenly his eyes focused sharply as he concluded, "Scofield?"

Carey nodded.

"Scofield." Cameron disliked the very sound of it. "Did I ever tell you how rude she was to me when I called about the Tatum boy? And all I did was ask a question about a patient."

"Any other doctor would have been glad to comply," Carey volunteered.

"Women! These days, they're always pushing to

prove themselves. So concerned with their own sexist war, they don't recognize the needs and responsibilities of others," Cameron complained. "You tell me, Edward, what was wrong in my inquiring about the boy?"

Carey shook his head sadly, signifying he could not justify Dr. Scofield's insolent conduct.

"Loyalty is a two-way street," Cameron pontificated, using his cigar to emphasize his point. "If one of my young men is loyal to me, that imposes an obligation on me. His worries become my worries. Because, if they don't, after a while his worries become more important to him than InterElectronics."

He took another sip of his expensive, privately bottled Scotch. "Bob Tatum is worried about that boy. I want to do everything I can for him. But how can I, when I'm kept at arm's length by the doctor in charge of the case."

"Maybe that's the answer, Mr. Cameron."

"What?"

"We've got other excellent doctors, men, in our Neurology Department. Sunderland is the best," Carey suggested, knowing how highly Cameron regarded Sunderland.

Cameron nodded. "I will talk to Bob about that." He directed the conversation back to Carey's original complaint. "All right, now, what did she do this time?"

With the air of an innocent and aggrieved party, interested only in protecting the hospital's reputation from careless accusations by a doctor striving to make a mark for herself, Carey related the entire confrontation which took place during Grand Rounds.

Throughout, Cameron continued to sip his drink and nod grimly. When Carey was finished, Cameron declared, "Such a report could be very embarrassing. Kill it!"

"I'm afraid I don't have the power to do that," Carey said, deliberately inviting the next question.

"Who does?"

"Benziger might," Carey suggested. For future purposes it would be a good way to drive a wedge between the Chief of the Neurology Department and his obstinate protege, Scofield.

As Chief of a department, Hans Benziger had met the Chairman of the Board of Trustees on several occasions. Annually Mrs. Cameron made it a point to entertain all the Chiefs at home as an official duty.

But Benziger had never confronted Cameron face to face alone before. He was taken off guard by Cameron's detailed knowledge of the events that had taken place at Grand Rounds only a day before. He had no doubts as to Cameron's source.

Cameron squinted through his tinted lenses as he concluded, "Now, I've been told that no doctor can publish a paper without the approval of his Chief. Or *her* Chief."

Realizing that Carey had not only reported in detail, but had obviously urged a course of action as well, Benziger said, "A Chief reviews a research paper only to verify that the data and findings are accurate. And that the conclusions arrived at are reasonably in accord with the observed findings."

Impatiently, Cameron said, "Translate, Doctor! I'm a simple layman. Give it to me in words of one syllable."

"All the Chief can do is check the material. If it's correct, he gives his approval," Benziger explained.

"And if he does *not* approve?"

"That is usually the end of the matter."

"Dr. Benziger, do you remember not long ago you came to me with a request for a . . . what is that equipment?"

"CAT scanner," Benziger supplied. "A computerized scanner device that will give us the finest diagnostic equipment available."

"That's the one," Cameron seized on it quickly. "You made the request. And what did I do? Within two weeks Mrs. Cameron had eight men to dinner at the house. In that one evening I raised six hundred thousand dollars, two hundred thousand of it mine. That scanner is now on order and will be installed within the year. Well, how about a little reciprocity?"

"I don't understand," Benziger said.

"It would be embarrassing if Dr. Scofield's report were published," Cameron said.

Benziger remained silent for a moment, trying to evolve a response that would be both diplomatic and honest. Finally, he answered, his accent always a bit thicker when he was under emotional strain.

"Mr. Cameron, your comparison is not quite apt. If you were asking me to donate my time, ability, medical knowledge, which are my only possessions of value, I would be delighted to do so. Because I'm aware of the many fine things you've done, not only for my department but for the entire hospital.

"But you're asking me to depart from principle, from my ethical standards. I can't do that. I'm quite sure you wouldn't either."

Benziger thought he had put his position as inoffensively as possible.

Cameron smiled. "Doctor, in the world of business there is no principle beyond succeeding. The only point now is, for valid reasons, reasons of importance to your hospital, I think that report should be suppressed!" Cameron was no longer smiling.

"If Dr. Scofield's data prove to be correct," Benziger said simply, "I don't see how I can withhold my approval."

"Even though it makes fools of the entire medical and surgical staffs of our hospital?" Cameron demanded.

"I don't quite see how Dr. Scofield's paper would do that," Benziger demurred.

"Think of all the publicity we gave it! As the best and newest ward facility in the state. Why, the Governor was here to make the official dedication. And are you forgetting the television coverage we got?"

"I can assure you, the publicity and television coverage were not at the suggestion of the medical and surgical staffs," Benziger pointed out as delicately as he could.

"Maybe not," Cameron agreed, "but that Seaton Ward building was designed with the advice and approval of the Chiefs of every service in our hospital! Those are the wards you men wanted. And now, along comes this woman and says it's a disaster!"

"Mr. Cameron, in the first place Dr. Scofield never said it was a disaster. She did say that, for certain reasons, that new building is not accomplishing the result we had anticipated."

"You still don't understand!" Cameron exploded.

"What I do understand," Benziger said, trying to control his own temper, "is that we have a perfectly good building that with little alteration can be converted into a new semi-private pavilion. Which we desperately need. To me, that's a godsend, not a disaster."

"And what about the new wards that we also need?" Cameron demanded.

"It seems clear to me that we have to rethink our approach and make new plans for a new ward building."

"Make plans for a new ward building," Cameron mocked angrily. "As easy as that! Man, don't you realize that with increased costs a new building wouldn't cost eleven million, but twenty! And that after all that fanfare and publicity I would have to go to my money sources and say, 'Boys, I just made a little eleven-million-dollar mistake. Now we have to build another ward. So I want each of you to come up with another million or two or five!' Don't you see the impossible position that woman will put me in!"

Benziger realized it was Cameron's vanity which was at stake, even more than his concern for the hospital.

Cameron was silent only briefly before he ordered: "That report must never see the light of day!"

"I'm sorry, Mr. Cameron, I cannot compromise my ethical standards," Benziger said.

"Are you telling me that the only person who can withdraw or modify that report is Dr. Scofield?" Cameron demanded.

Much as he regretted having to place Jean in a position of increased jeopardy, Benziger had to respond, "Yes, I suppose I am saying that."

Cameron's jaw muscles were tense and rigid, until he nodded, grim and thoughtful.

fifteen

Jean Scofield had just begun to question the new patient when the blinker on her phone lit up. Since it might be an emergency and Maggie was out to lunch, Jean decided to pick up the call herself.

"Dr. Scofield?" a faintly familiar, rather imperious voice inquired.

"Yes," Jean answered cautiously, trying to recall the voice.

"This is Ms. St. John speaking." Then she added in her clipped British accent, "Mr. Cameron's executive secretary. Mr. Cameron has requested me to ask . . ."

Jean interrupted, "I'm sorry, but I'm very busy at the moment. Can you call back?"

"Oh?" Ms. St. John replied, nonplused. Evidently no one was ever too busy to talk to Horace Cameron's executive secretary, so she had no fixed response for such an unaccustomed question. Finally she settled for a curt, "Yes, of course. I shall call back."

Jean returned her complete attention to her patient, Thomas Halloran. He was thirty years old, in seeming robust health except for his right hand, which was a twisted, clenched claw. No amount of treatment had enabled him to loosen the paralysis which had afflicted him for months. His own physician had run out of modalities to suggest and had finally turned the case over to the neurologists.

Halloran had been put through every test but they found no pathological basis for his unyielding condition. Now the short, barrel-chested man sat before her, staring pathetically, caught between a powerful body that begged for hard physical labor and this twisted hand that prevented it.

"Dr. Ryan said you would help," he pleaded. But his attitude betrayed only hopelessness.

"Can you remember how it came on?" Jean began to take his history.

"Pains," Halloran said, "started with the pains."

"Did anything precede the pains? Did you hurt yourself at work? Handling some heavy piece of furniture?" she asked, for his record showed that until his affliction, he had been a warehouseman for a furniture company.

"How it began," he said, "was one morning when I

get up and I feel this pain here." He showed her the spot on his right hand. "Then it became worse and worse."

"Did it get worse in days, weeks or months?"

"Sometime between weeks and months."

"Did you do anything about it at the time?"

"No, Doctor. I thought it would be going away," he said, with a slight brogue. "I didn't want to say anything at work. Thinking they'd be sending me to the company doctor and he might say I had to lay off. We couldn't afford it. With five kids already and another on the way. So I decided to see it through. I never been sick before in my life. Never lost a day's work, except the time my middle boy was sick and I had to take him to the hospital. To me being sick was something for children and women."

His eyes flicked toward Jean's, cautiously trying to see if his inadvertent slip had antagonized her. Jean smiled to put him at ease.

He apologized in the only way he knew. "You know how it is, Doctor. A man is the strength of the family. While a woman is the soul. Leastways in Catholic families it is."

"But the pain grew worse, until you had to let someone know."

"It got so bad I couldn't hold it in no more."

"Did the paralysis start then?"

"No, it come later. I think maybe it was the doctors, you'll pardon my saying so. But the Compensation doctors, probing and all, I think they may have triggered the paralysis. Till then it was only the pain."

"And they never found any cause for it?"

"Never, as much as they told me. They have a way with them, those doctors, poking and pressing and prying and saying 'Uh huh,' but never letting the patient in on a thing. 'Specially those Compensation doctors."

Jean had studied the history his doctor had sent along, but it told her very little more. Which left her not much in the way of therapeutic elections.

She decided to delay any treatment for several days in order to make further observations.

Instead of writing out a prescription, she called the pharmacy department to send up a fairly strong tranquilizer. In that way, Thomas Halloran would have no way of knowing what he was taking, and no friendly neighborhood pharmacist could enlighten him.

She handed him the envelope, saying, "Take one of these twice a day. On retiring. On waking. There are six pills for three days. Then come back on Friday, at this same time, and let me know if you have regained any mobility at all."

"Do *you* think it can help, Doctor?" he asked fervently as he took the envelope.

"It might" was as much as Jean would say. Halloran was about to press for further assurances when her phone blinked again. "Sorry," she said, dismissing him and answering the call.

"Dr. Scofield?" It was Ms. St. John's aloof and superior voice again. "I'm afraid Mr. Cameron requires a prompt answer."

"If it's about Bobby Tatum, there's nothing more I can tell him."

"It isn't young Bobby Tatum this time. Mr. Cameron wants to know if you could hold yourself available for lunch with him this coming Friday?"

Jean was tempted to say no, merely to observe the shocked reaction of the supremely confident Ms. St. John. Instead she consulted her calendar. Friday was a day on which she taught morning classes at the medical school and her hours at the Neurology Clinic didn't begin until three o'clock. She could manage her other patients without too much juggling, so she said, "Yes, I think Friday might be possible."

As if it were necessary for Ms. St. John's sense of security that she regain the upper hand, she responded coolly, "I'm sure Mr. Cameron will be back from Iran by then. I shall be in touch."

On Friday next, Thomas Halloran sat across from Jean in her office. His entire demeanor was quite different from what it had been three days ago. His eyes seemed not so alert today. The pills had evidently done their work.

"Well, Mr. Halloran, how does it feel today? Any change?"

The man raised his paralyzed right claw. Jean reached for it. At first, he drew back. Then he surrendered it to her. She examined it, turning it over and back, pressing it, moving it at the wrist. But all that was only a diversion.

"Mr. Halloran, did you take the pills as directed?"

"Oh, yes, ma'am!" he replied staunchly.

"And nothing changed?"

"You can see for yourself, Doctor."

As casually as she could, Jean studied the patient's eyes. He seemed heavily enough sedated. She decided to venture it now.

"Mr. Halloran, have you slept well the last three evenings?"

"Like a log. My wife says it's the first good sleep I've had since the damned thing came on me."

"Right now, how do you feel?" Jean asked. "Tired? Sleepy?"

"Matter of fact, yes," the bulky man admitted.

"Good." Halloran looked at her puzzled. "Because I would like you to go to sleep now. Just relax and drift off. Sleep off the effects of those pills."

She stared into his eyes. "That's right, Mr. Halloran, go off to sleep. Don't fight it. Let go. Just drift off to sleep. Because you'll feel better afterward."

At first his eyes blinked and he fought against it. Slowly he allowed his lids to relax and close.

"Sleep will do you good. You need it. Because for months now you haven't slept well, have you? But now you can sleep. Now you want to sleep. Don't you, Mr. Halloran?"

Jean continued talking softly, soothingly. The man began to weave slightly, as if he were losing control of his body. Finally he slumped in his chair. His chin dropped to his chest. Jean sensed that he was under. To make sure, she said, "Mr. Halloran, I am going to stick you with a pin. But you will not feel it. Do you understand me?"

He made a vague nod of assent. She reached for the sterile safety pin she had prepared on her desk. She stabbed it into his healthy hand. There was no reaction. She repeated the test again. No doubt he was under. The sedative had done its work well.

"Mr. Halloran, sit up."

The man stirred, making an effort to come erect.

"Up, Mr. Halloran, up!" Jean commanded, to accustom him to responding to her orders. He pulled himself up in the chair. He leaned back, more erect than he had been in his waking state.

"Now, Mr. Halloran, I want you to extend your left arm. Extend it!"

He complied, holding it out full length.

"Now, turn it over. Palm up. Now, palm down." He obeyed her instructions. "Good. Now, Mr. Halloran, draw your left arm back and let it rest in your lap."

When he had done that, Jean felt that he was sufficiently pliable for her purpose.

"Mr. Halloran, now I want you to hold out your

right arm." For the first time he was reluctant to carry out one of her commands. "I said, *hold out your right arm.*"

Slowly, Tom Halloran raised his right arm as if it weighed more than his strong body could support. With great effort, he finally coaxed it forward, his hand still a twisted claw.

Jean was aware that the phone on her desk had begun to blink. She ignored it.

"Now, I want you to turn your hand over so that the palm is facing up." He remained motionless, as if terrified. "Did you hear me?"

He nodded his head very slightly, and only once.

"Then turn your hand over, palm up!"

At that moment Maggie was at the door, knocking.

"It'll have to wait!" Jean called out impatiently.

She turned back to the patient. "Mr. Halloran, I'm talking to you again now. Can you hear me?"

Halloran nodded.

"I want you to stretch out your right hand."

He remained motionless.

"Tom Halloran, open your hand. Finger by finger. First the thumb. Let it come away from the rest of your hand. Raise it up."

Slowly, Halloran raised his thumb from the paralyzed position it had assumed for months. It took great effort. But soon he managed to have it standing free and projecting outward.

"Now, your other fingers. One at a time. Open them. Let them stretch out. Out. Way out. One at a time."

Slowly the man began to unfold his fingers, one at a time, until all five of them were straight and his entire hand was completely open.

"Move your hand. Freely, easily, without pain. The entire hand. Open it. Close it. Open it again. Doesn't that feel good?"

He moved his hand and nodded at the same time.

"Now each finger. Move each finger, slowly. Limber them up. Let them move easily. Easily. Until you can do it without trying. Move it like in the old days. That's right. Doesn't that feel good?"

The sleeping patient nodded.

"You don't feel any pain. Do you?"

He shook his head.

She had diagnosed him correctly. A classic case of hysterical conversion. Now it was important to find the cause and eradicate it. It was not within her province to effectuate that part of the cure, but she could at least begin it.

"Now, tell me, why did you do it? Why did you find a need to punish yourself this way?"

Halloran's eyelids flickered, but his eyes remained closed. His lips moved but he did not speak.

"You hear me, don't you?"

He nodded.

"Then tell me, *why?* What made you do this to yourself?"

He began to speak, haltingly, slowly. At first he spoke in seemingly disconnected phrases.

It was many things. Five children and one more on the way. His wife wanting to make love with him but not wanting any more children. She kept urging birth control of some kind. He refused. Somehow his mother was involved. A religious woman, of the old school. She would not even go to a church where they had adopted the Mass in English. The thought of her son and his wife resorting to birth control would shock her. Torn between his wife's strong feeling and his own rigid upbringing, the conflict had evidently proved too much for him. Finding no way out, he had resorted to an unconscious, an indirect way.

"But why your right hand, Tom?"

"My hand . . . my right hand . . ." he repeated, as if probing his own mind about it. "When I reach out for her . . . at night . . . I reach with that hand." He held out his once crippled hand.

She brought him out of his hypnotic state with a suggestion that he would now be able to move his hand freely. But she knew that the cure would not prove permanent until his conflict was resolved.

When he became conscious, he stared down at his hand. He seemed afraid to try it for fear it wouldn't work.

"Go on, Tom, move it," Jean urged, smiling.

He began to move his fingers tentatively. From that he gained the courage to close and open his fist once. Then several times.

"A miracle," he said.

"A miracle is something that defies explanation. That goes counter to natural laws. This can be explained. And it is quite natural, but I'm not equipped to deal with it. I'll have to refer you to another doctor."

"But it's cured."

"We have to make sure there are no recurrences. I'll try to arrange for you to see Dr. Berkey in the Psychiatric Department."

"Psychiatric . . ." Halloran repeated, his fear of doctors who tamper with the mind quite obvious.

"It's the best thing, Mr. Halloran. Even the Church says it's perfectly acceptable. Ask your parish priest. Better still, have him call me."

Halloran was thoughtful for a moment before saying softly, "Okay, Doctor, okay."

She dialed Berkey's office.

"Dan? Jean. I've got a Mr. Halloran here, Thomas Halloran. I'd like you to see him. I've been able to treat his symptoms. An hystrical conversion expressed in a paralysis of the hand. But it's somewhat deeper. See him, won't you?"

"Of course, Jean."

She gave Halloran Berkey's office number in Psychiatric. As soon as he left, Maggie rang again.

"Doctor," Maggie said, giving a fairly good imitation of a stilted British accent, "Ms. St. John called."

"Yes, I know," Jean said, giving an even better imitation of Cameron's secretary. "My luncheon date with *Mister* Cameron." Then she added, "Maggie, do you think St. John is really her name? Or was it bestowed on her by St. Horace?"

They both laughed.

An invitation to lunch with Cameron in his private dining room at InterElectronics would normally be considered a high honor by any member of the University Hospital medical staff. However, warned by Benziger, Jean Scofield looked upon the occasion as a command performance. Still, she welcomed her first chance to see the great man up close. She had learned from experience that most fabled characters, on intimate inspection, turned out to be less imposing than their reputations.

Cameron proved a victim of the new executive health program he himself had instituted. Their lunch was as spare as if he were an athlete in training. His personal French chef had done all he could with small extra-lean filets of beef, greens, low-cholesterol cottage cheese and fruit in sugar-free syrup. Cameron ate little. Jean ate even less, waiting expectantly.

Over the caffeine-free coffee Cameron began.

"Doctor, I asked you here because I feel you're entitled to an apology."

He had intended to surprise her and he succeeded.

"I admit when it happened, I was quite upset," he

continued, "I may even have said some things that I later regretted. But you were right," Cameron granted.

"I'm sorry, I don't understand."

"That day I called, inquiring about the Tatum boy. Of course, ethically, you had no right to discuss his case with me. And you very correctly set me straight. Though I must admit I'm not used to being talked to in quite that way. Still, it was refreshing." He chuckled pleasantly. "I understand the boy is doing okay now."

"He's to be discharged soon. If he takes his medication, I trust he'll be fine," Jean said, not wishing to disclose to Cameron her private thoughts about the case.

"Good, good! Nice people, the Tatums. That young man has an unlimited future. Unlimited! And his wife— not only beautiful, but a splendid girl. Francine . . . my wife, that is . . . has just about adopted her. Makes me feel a little less sad about not having children of our own."

Jean wondered when he would come to the subject of the luncheon.

"Yours must be fascinating work, Doctor. You not only stand astride the human brain, you explore the mind as well. The soul, some people would say. Fascinating!" Cameron enthused.

He sipped his black coffee. "Equally fascinating was what I heard of your findings about our new Seaton Wards. In fact, I'm so interested that I'd like to check out your data. Is it possible for me to see them?"

"Yes," Jean found herself saying, surprised that she was so amenable when she had come here resolved to remain firm.

"Good!" Cameron said. "Then I assume you'll hold up publication until we've checked them out."

"You're assuming more than I've just agreed to," Jean corrected wryly.

"It won't take long. I've got the best brains in the country working for me. And, as for checking data, who makes better computer equipment than InterElectronics?" He laughed.

Jean cut short his laugh when she said, "I don't really need computers to corroborate what I've observed with my own eyes."

"Of course not," Cameron agreed quickly. "But your conclusions—I should think you'd want to withhold your report until they were verified by minds devoted solely to the interpretation of statistical data."

"Mr. Cameron, I think you misunderstand the scientific reason for publishing medical papers."

"Do I?" Cameron asked affably.

"The purpose of my paper, when published, will be to share information and create interest among other researchers. Inviting them either to refute my conclusion after their own research or else to suggest ways to reform the manner in which new hospital wards are built. Either way, the future of good medicine is served. That's the only reason doctors do research and publish their findings."

"I wonder, Doctor, if you realize some of the other consequences of your findings?" Cameron asked.

"I understand it might create some embarrassment for you in the raising of funds in the future."

"Unfortunately."

"I wonder, Mr. Cameron, if you have considered that this might also mean spending money more wisely and to much better effect. We might deliver better health care in the future if we learn from our mistakes now."

Cameron smiled patronizingly. "Up to now, you're the only one who keeps insisting that the Seaton Wards are a 'mistake'!"

"I don't say it. The data say it," Jean pointed out.

"Say what? That patients from the ghettoes don't wish to go back and live there once they've experienced life in a, fine, new, clean medical facility? Let's grant that for the moment, Doctor. What's your solution? To build new run-down, rat-infested hospitals?" Cameron asked, smiling.

"Of course not!" Jean protested.

"Then you leave us with only one other alternative."

"I'm afraid I don't understand."

"You're recommending we cure the poor by completely upgrading their living conditions. You're opening the door wide to more tinkering by the same social engineers who got us into the welfare mess we're in now," Cameron argued, never losing his tone of reasonableness.

"Mr. Cameron, I don't intend to make any recommendations in my paper. Merely to report my data, make observations and invite other researchers' opinions," Jean pointed out.

"That's all the Carter Administration will need," Cameron said, smiling indulgently. "I can see them now. Demanding reform while waving copies of your report in our faces. This paper of yours can not only be dangerous to our hospital, it can strike a blow at our entire social and economic system."

Cameron paused, then said, "Doctor, may I suggest that you not release that paper to any medical publication?"

"And if I do release it," Jean concluded, "there'll be no chance at all of my being considered as Chief of Neurology. Is that it?"

"Doctor, relax. I'm not in the habit of making threats. Anyone who knows me will tell you that."

Of course, Jean thought, a Cameron "suggestion" was usually enough.

Still smiling, Cameron pushed back from the table

and rose. "It's been most interesting, Doctor, most interesting."

As soon as Jean left the room, Cameron picked up the phone and dialed two digits.

"Ms. St. John, put me on my dictating machine." Once he was patched in, he began to dictate in a cold precise voice.

"I have just completed a discussion with Dr. Jean Scofield, of the Neurology Department. I find her to be quite rigid and dogmatic. She is obviously dedicated to using her medical knowledge and information to further her political and social beliefs.

"In fact, I have a suspicion that the interns' strike we faced last year might well have had her support. Though, of course, if confronted, she would deny it. It is significant, however, if I recall correctly, that she was the only faculty member invited to participate in the Interns' Show this year.

"I feel she constitutes a problem for the entire Board of Trustees to consider. Especially in light of the fact that her name has been put forth as a possible successor to Dr. Benziger when he retires. Unquote.

"Ms. St. John, see that copies are sent to all the Trustees before the next meeting."

sixteen

Once the Dilantin level in Bobby Tatum's blood had stabilized, Dr. Scofield permitted his return to school.

He attended the pre-kindergarten class at The Wilding School. It was the most expensive school in the exclusive suburb in which the Tatums lived, as did many successful executives, because the new main building of InterElectronics was situated there. Cameron had moved the offices from the inner city to escape the high taxes and other penalties of metropolitan life. Most of the students in Bobby's class were sons and daughters of other executives in Cameron's corporate complex.

Marissa Tatum had instructed Bobby's teacher, Miss Halsted, concerning the limitations which now governed her son's activity. She had also instructed Miss Halsted on the steps to take if by any chance Bobby suffered a seizure during the school day. She left with her several airways and a supply of padded tongue depressors.

Faced with this complication, which threatened the orderly manner in which she had organized her class, Miss Halsted greeted young Bobby Tatum with as much warmth as she could muster.

Once class assembled, she had them sing a welcoming song to him, as they did to all classmates who returned after an illness. They worked at finger painting during the early morning. At mid-morning, since the weather was mild, Miss Halsted led them out to the monkey bars in the schoolyard. She turned them loose to climb and play.

When Bobby moved to join them, Miss Halsted ordered, "You are not to climb, Bobby. You're to stay here with me!"

"Why, Miss Halsted? I'm all better now," the boy pleaded, for he had only recently overcome his physical shyness and begun to enjoy climbing the bars.

"Your doctor said it's best for you not to climb. You're too stay with me!"

While the other children shouted and laughed as they climbed up, down and across the iron-barred maze, Bobby and his teacher watched. At the end of twenty minutes of free play, Miss Halsted called the children in for milk and cookies. Bobby Tatum took his usual place between Allison Carr and Adam Wardell. Allison, a pretty blonde child, asked, "Bobby, you still sick?"

"I am not," he protested.

Adam intruded. "I came back after measles, I was climbing the first day. So you got to be sick."

"I am *not* sick!" he protested, tears filling his blue eyes.

"Yaah, yes, you are!" Adam insisted, in a voice loud enough to cause Miss Halsted to reprimand him. Before he was silenced, Adam called out, "Yaah, he is so sick!"

The rest of the morning passed without incident. But after class, on the way home in the Wardell station wagon, Adam said to the other children his mother was car-pooling for the week, "Bobby Tatum's sick. She wouldn't let me say it, but he's sick."

By the end of the week it was all the children talked about. Gradually they isolated Bobby. He found himself closer and closer to Miss Halsted. When the children played in the yard during their mid-morning break, he clung to her hand and stared with envious blue eyes. At night, he wept silently in his bed. He knew his father did not like any display of tears.

On the last day of Bobby's second week back at school, Marissa Tatum was late picking him up. She had spent the morning with Francine Cameron working on a Senior Citizens' project. Though Mrs. Cameron commandeered many of the wives of her husband's young executives to help in her various activities, Marissa Tatum had become her favorite. Such a beautiful woman, and so willing, Francine Cameron would remark to her husband.

On this particular day Marissa Tatum had stayed on an additional half hour to complete a list of local merchants who would be solicited for funds to refurbish the Senior Citizens' Center.

While waiting for his mother, Bobby Tatum slipped out into the schoolyard. He eyed the monkey bars from a distance. Then, knowing he was unobserved, he approached them cautiously. Rarely had he been bold enough to defy authority. Today he was tempted in order to discover just how sick he really was.

He reached out his hand to touch the iron bars. Taking one last look around, he started to climb. He reached up with his hand, seized a bar, pulled his leg up. He wrapped his arm around the bar above his head and lifted himself higher. He had finally reached the top of the ironwork skeleton. Remembering a stunt that Adam was first in the class to do, Bobby Tatum wrapped his legs over the top bar and released his hold until he hung upside down. He felt the blood rush to his head. Otherwise he felt only a surge of triumph. He had accomplished that feat for the first time. He was sorry Allison wasn't there to see him. And Adam. He'd show Adam who was sick!

At that moment Marissa Tatum pulled up in front of the building. It was school policy that no child was allowed to leave unless an authorized person was there to pick him up. Marissa blew her horn. Instead of Bobby's coming out under supervision, Miss Halsted emerged alone, surprised and puzzled. She looked about, then became frantic as she called out, "Bobby! Bobby!"

There was no sign of the boy. Marissa Tatum leaped out of her station wagon and ran up the path to the school.

"Where is he? What's happened?" she cried out.

"He was just here. Waiting for you in his classroom."

Miss Halsted started for the room, calling out, "Bobby! Bobby Tatum! If you're hiding, come out. You come right out! Your mother's here!"

They reached the classroom. It was empty.

"Bobby!" his mother cried out desperately.

It was then Miss Halsted spied him through the window. He hung head down, his legs wrapped over the top bar. Having got himself into that precarious position, he had been unable to work free. Both women raced out to the yard, Marissa Tatum calling, "Bobby! Bobby!"

Her terror transmitted itself to her young son. In his effort to free himself, he slipped and fell. His fall was impeded by the bars but he landed head down on the hard rubber mat below. Marissa raced to him, gathered him up in her arms. Terrified, he pressed against her. He heard her say over and over and over, "Don't ever do anything like that again. Do you hear me, Bobby? You're not to do anything like that ever again." She held him so close and tight he could not even nod his head to acknowledge her command.

Across her son, she shouted to Miss Halsted, "And don't you ever leave him alone again. He's a very sick child!"

She drove directly to Lawrence Braham's office. Aside from a bruise on his head and another on his arm where he had banged it against one of the bars, Bobby appeared perfectly sound. But Larry suggested Marissa consult Dr. Scofield. He called ahead to make sure Jean would be free to see them.

She checked the boy out. Beyond the two bruises, she was satisfied that he had not sustained any significant injury. However, she noticed that throughout her examination, whenever her hands were not busy, the boy held one of them as he had that night when he fell asleep pressing her hand against his face. Evidently he found some desperately needed security in the touch of her hand.

While Mrs. Tatum waited outside the examining room, Jean asked, "Bobby, didn't Mommy tell you not to climb up to high places?" The boy didn't answer. "And your teacher, she told you not to, didn't she?"

The boy remained stubbornly unresponsive, only gripped her hand more tightly. As if he feared that, since he refused to answer, she might grow angry with him and withdraw it.

"Then why did you do it, Bobby?"

The boy hesitated and then exploded suddenly. "I'm *not* sick! They said I was. But I'm *not!*"

"Is that what they said?"

The boy nodded. "I'm not sick," he kept repeating stubbornly.

Jean had witnessed such pitiful situations before. Children can be cruel and unfeeling. Little minds can inflict great hurts, not necessarily out of malice, but out of innocent ignorance. In sympathy, she tousled the boy's black hair. He looked up at her, a surge of love and warmth in his eyes. That look renewed her conviction. No matter what Larry Braham said, she felt strongly the boy was abused, by emotional neglect if not by outright physical punishment. Else why this need to seek solace from strangers? But it was still only a suspicion so far, lacking sufficient medical substantiation.

It was a sunny day. The pre-school class at Wilding was having outdoor activities. The sound of children's voices echoed across the schoolyard as they were turned loose to clamber up the monkey bars. To save Bobby the embarrassment of his restriction, Miss Halsted pretended to need his help in marking off the lanes for the potato race which she would introduce as a new activity.

She did not notice that the boy appeared a bit slower today than usual, and somewhat drowsy. Even if she had, she might not have recognized it as an aura, a forewarning.

He bent over to mark the lane as he had been instructed. Suddenly his head and eyes turned right, his small thin body became rigid. By the time Miss Halsted became aware, he was already entering the clonic phase of the seizure. His hands jerked rhythmically. His arms picked up the movement. Finally it afflicted his whole small body. Terrified, Miss Halsted raced to the classroom, found the airways and protectors, raced back to the stricken boy and tried to slip the rubber airway between his teeth and into his mouth. At the same time she called out, "Someone go to the office and get Mrs. Buttram!"

Meantime she held the boy in her arms, careful to keep his head from striking the hard earth. Eventually the spasmodic movement ceased. The boy was limp and light in her arms. From both pity and fear, she began to tremble. Mrs. Buttram, the principal, found her that way. She knelt beside the terrified young teacher and reassured her. "He's all right now. You handled it very well."

Marissa Tatum, off on an assignment for Mrs. Cameron on a project involving slum children, could not be reached. Dr. Braham's office was contacted. Larry drove out to the school to pick up the boy. An hour after his attack, Bobby was safely in a bed at University Hospital and being examined by Dr. Scofield. Larry was at her side as she tested the boy for post-ictal weakness. She could not detect any. No signs of blood or fluid in his ears or nose. She dispatched some of his blood to be tested for Dilantin level. She ran a bedside EEG and a skull x-ray.

When all the results came back negative, Larry Braham suggested, "Maybe he needs a higher dosage of Dilantin. Probably hasn't stabilized yet."

"No, I don't think that's it."

"Then what?"

"There's one significant finding this time that we haven't encountered before."

"Everything came back negative," Larry pointed out.

"*Too* negative."

"You mean no post-ictal weakness on his right side? It might have dissipated. After all, you examined him more than an hour after the seizure."

"Something else was missing, too," Jean said. "When you brought him in, he was dry. Perfectly dry. Every time Bobby's had a seizure before, he's wet himself. Except *this* time."

"Maybe it just didn't happen this time. That's possible."

"There's something else possible, too. Maybe he didn't really have a true seizure. Maybe for some reason he faked it."

"A five-year-old? I doubt it."

"Hysterical seizures are not as frequent in young children as in older patients. But there are cases reported in the literature."

"But why?" Larry asked.

"You're going to accuse me of practicing psychiatry again," Jean said. "He was in a situation fraught with great tension. That school's become a traumatic place for him since the other children began picking on him. Perhaps this was his way of escaping."

"You think he might do better in another school, where he could start out fresh?"

"I wouldn't advise changing schools just yet. If seizures are going to be part of his life, we shouldn't start him on a pattern of running away. Besides, that's only one possibility. There's another."

"What other?"

"You won't like it."

"Try me."

"Twice now we've had him here. Twice he's left here a much more open child than when he was admitted. Evidently he likes it here. Maybe unconsciously he figured that the way to get back was to have a seizure, real or faked."

Angrily Larry closed the door of her office. He spoke in a harsh whisper. "Jean, stop looking for trouble! Bob Tatum is not a child abuser. The Tatum home is not the kind where one finds child abuse!"

"It can happen in any home. Freud himself wrote, 'The unconscious wish to beat or harm children is almost universal.'"

"Freud!" Larry dismissed him. "Very few people believe in him any longer."

"Tell that to some infant who's been beaten to death by his own father!" Jean responded heatedly. Then she relented and said sadly, "Larry, oh, Larry, we're shouting at each other. Bitterly. Maybe this is what I've been afraid of all along. That we'd be better off as colleagues than as husband and wife."

"It would work," he said. "I'd make sure it would work."

He bent over to press his face against hers. "Jean?" He kissed her on the lips but she failed to respond.

"We have to come to a decision about that boy," she said thoughtfully.

Gently, cautiously, Larry said, "Darling, I don't want to upset you. But . . ."

She interrupted, "He does *not* remind me of the son I might have had!"

"I wasn't referring to that."

"What, then?"

"Your findings on the falling cure rate in the wards."

"What's that to do with this boy?" she asked.

"You're too personally involved in both problems to see it. Your findings about the new wards, that slum patients seek refuge in sickness. You're saying exactly the same thing about Bobby. That he would rather be here than in his own home."

"Yes, that *is* what I'm saying," she admitted. "But that doesn't mean I'm wrong. Material poverty isn't the only human deprivation. If someone bruised by poverty seeks refuge in a hospital, why shouldn't someone bruised by neglect or domestic friction react in the same way?"

"Domestic friction?" Larry disputed her. "If there ever was a couple that works as a team, it's Bob and Marissa Tatum. She's the perfect corporate wife. She knocks herself out to entertain, to cooperate with Francine Cameron, to do everything that helps Bob's career. There is absolutely no friction in that family. I can vouch for that!"

"Then why did Bobby have an hysterical seizure?" Jean demanded.

"We can't be sure that he did. It could simply be a seizure of unknown etiology," Larry explained, trying to sound reasonable.

"The least I can do is discuss this frankly with the Tatums."

"If you're asking my consent," he cautioned, "I don't think that would be wise."

"Larry, would it make things easier for you if I withdrew from this case?" she asked bluntly.

"Bobby trusts you. I wouldn't want to shake his confidence. Especially if he *is* having hysterical symptoms. I want you to continue on the case. But be careful. For your own sake."

"I'm going to have to face the Tatums with it," she said firmly.

seventeen

Since Bob Tatum had had to accompany Cameron to a meeting in Moscow the early part of the week, Jean's appointment with the Tatums was set for the following Thursday.

She saw them in her office in the early evening. Outside, in the corridor, the excitement and noise of the day had subsided. The hospital seemed almost empty except for the occasional whisking of a nurse's white rubber-soled shoes moving briskly down the hall. Jean was reviewing Bobby's file in preparation for the meeting when two shadows appeared in the frosted glass window that separated her private office from her examining room.

"Come in!"

Tatum allowed his wife to precede him. Jean had to admire the couple they made. He, tall, rugged, handsome, blond. She, dark, beautiful, with the grace and carriage of a model. Jean thought, she'll look striking one day when they do a series in *Vogue* or *Bazaar* on wives of well-known executives, modeling the year's latest designer fashions.

The amenities over, Tatum came directly to the point—their fears at having been summoned to the meeting.

"That last seizure means it's very serious about Bobby now, isn't it?" he began. "Well, we want the truth. Straight. Don't try to let us down easy."

Marissa reached for his hand, either to seek reassurance or to restrain him.

"It could become serious," Jean conceded. The Tatums glanced at each other, their worst fears confirmed.

"Tumor?" Marissa Tatum ventured.

"Tumors aren't the only serious things that can happen to children," Jean said.

Marissa Tatum turned to her husband. "I told you what she said about uncontrolled seizures."

"Are you telling us Bobby's had brain damage?" he asked.

"Instead of trying to guess, it would be easier if you let me discuss this my way."

"He sure doesn't act like a boy with brain damage!" was Tatum's last protest before his wife gripped his arm to silence him.

Now Jean could proceed without interruption. "For the moment forget tumors and brain damage. There's another problem. It can, in its way, be just as damaging, just as dangerous."

"And that is?" Tatum demanded.

Jean hesitated. The history of past cases had proved that abusers, like alcoholics, were quick to turn on the very persons who tried to help them. But Jean had deliberately sought this confrontation and she had to risk the consequences. She wanted to avoid only one possible result, that Bobby Tatum be removed from her care. But she had to risk that now, too.

"Your son shows a number of signs that are physical. But also a number of signs that could be psychiatric."

Tatum rebelled instinctively, but his wife's hold on his arm kept him silent.

"In situations like that, we alter our rule. We don't treat the boy. We treat the parents," Jean said.

"Situations like *what?*" Tatum demanded.

"A patient exhibits symptomatology that includes a

number of suspicious factors. Failure to thrive. Noticeable difference in weight gain between home and hospital. Noticeable difference in attitude. Namely, the patient is shy, withdrawn, totally compliant, unsmiling on admission to the hospital. Then, after a few days here, he becomes relaxed, happy, outgoing and friendly. Those factors are extremely significant."

The Tatums glanced at each other, puzzled.

"Now, this last time," Jean continued, "we admitted Bobby with all the signs of a seizure. Except one. So after my examination I drew the conclusion that he did not have a true seizure but what we call an hysterical seizure."

"That boy has never been hysterical in his life!" Tatum protested.

"I don't mean hysterical in the sense of crying or becoming uncontrollably emotional. I am using it in its medical sense. Hysteria is a term derived from the Greek, *hystéra,* for womb—since it was thought to be a condition that only afflicted females. Used in that sense, hysteria means signs and symptoms that arise in the mind, not the body. Even though they may express themselves in a physical way. I believe Bobby's last seizure was of psychological, not physical, origin. In other words, he imitated a seizure without having one. That is enormously important."

"What does it mean?" Tatum asked, now intimidated by possibilities at which he could not even guess.

"It's a matter of interpretation, of course," Jean continued. "I can only give you my own professional judgment. Dr. Braham does not agree with me. But I think that for some reason Bobby would rather be here in the hospital than anywhere else."

"He'd rather be here than with *us?*" Bob Tatum asked, making the point at which Jean chose only to hint.

"I believe so," Jean said.

Tatum leaped out of his chair. "What kind of thing is that to say?" He stood over Jean as if to intimidate her into withdrawing her accusation. "Why would any boy, with all he's got, want to be here in this hospital rather than at home?"

"That's exactly what this meeting is about." Jean looked up at him, her green eyes quite determined.

"I'm not going to take this from anyone! Certainly not from any woman doctor." He turned to his wife. "I told you I didn't like her. Especially, I didn't like her attitude about my father."

He turned on Jean. "I don't accept all this psychiatric nonsense. I don't believe that every kid goes around all his life hating his father and mother. I didn't hate my old man. And my son doesn't hate me! Because I've never given him any cause to hate me. And saying he would rather be here than at home in his own house is ridiculous! Ridiculous! Did you hear me, 'Doctor'?"

She not only heard him, she knew that everyone on the floor had probably heard him.

"Frankly, if it wasn't for the . . ." he paused to find the right words, "if it wasn't for the way Larry Braham feels about you, I'd say let's find another neurologist."

"What did you mean by 'the way Dr. Braham feels about me'?"

"If you insist."

"I insist!"

"After that meeting you and I had, I did a little investigating. It became very clear why Larry recommended you so highly."

"Whatever exists between Dr. Braham and myself, in this instance we are both concerned with only one thing. The welfare of your son. As I told you, he doesn't agree with my theory."

"And just what is your theory?" Tatum demanded.

Having already antagonized him, Jean knew her next statement could be crucial to her continuance on the case and her ability to protect Bobby Tatum.

"Mr. Tatum, your son exhibits a pattern of conduct that we generally find in cases of child abuse," she said firmly.

"I have never laid a hand on that boy! Have I?" he demanded of his wife, who had sat silent through most of the interview.

"Never," she agreed loyally.

"You show me one mark on that boy's body! One!" Tatum challenged.

Far from being intimidated, Jean said, "X-rays show a fracture of his right fibula. Now healed. But having occurred two to three years ago."

"Fracture?" Tatum disparaged at once, then recalled, "He did fall once. The day we were moving from Dayton to San Diego. The moving men were hauling the stuff down from the bedrooms. Bobby was playing on the steps. One of the men backing down with a heavy piece accidentally banged into Bobby, making him fall down the stairs. But I never knew he broke his fibula."

"Significantly, there is no record anywhere of its having been set by a doctor," Jean pointed out.

"I told you, we never even knew it was broken. It hurt him for a while, but then it went away," Tatum said. "So we never paid any more attention to it."

It was not unlike stories Jean had heard before from abusing parents. Always the child had fallen accidentally and hurt himself. Had plunged his own hand into a tub of hot water and burned himself. Or fallen off a bike and struck his head. Or fallen downstairs.

There was one factor which did give some credence to Tatum's story. He had involved others in the accident. Those moving men. If true, it defeated her theory. If untrue, he might have invented it to cover up more skillfully than most other parents who were not nearly so shrewd. Jean had to admit to herself that it was not unusual for a fracture to go undetected in a child and then heal by itself. Doctors often joked about the fact that many unset juvenile fractures healed with fewer complications than some of those that were treated.

Tatum directed her attention back to the case by asking, "Is that what you wanted to discuss with us? A leg fracture three years ago? Could that have anything to do with his seizures?"

"No," she had to admit.

"Then let's stick to that and stop looking for causes that do not exist!" Tatum warned. "If you don't know the cause, say so. But don't go inventing them to cover up your own professional ignorance!"

"Bob!" his wife reprimanded him in a low, guarded tone.

Jean had to decide whether to continue the conference or end it. Of one thing she was sure. Tatum had revealed himself to be a man of impetuous reactions. And most overbearing. Certainly the kind of father who might severely intimidate a shy young boy like Bobby Tatum.

Perhaps she was dealing with one of the more subtle forms of child abuse. Emotional and psychological abuse. Tatum could claim, and possibly with complete justification, that he had not laid a hand on the boy in anger. Yet at the same time he could have raised a son who lived terrorized all his life by this huge man who did not appreciate his own power.

It checked with her first impression, when Tatum had described his own father. A domineering man, who drove his sons in the direction he wanted them to go. Conditioned by that kind of upbringing, Bob Tatum could not be blamed for believing it was the proper way to rear a son. And a boy like Bobby, not so strong as his father, might react far differently. Whereas Tatum grew up not daring to hate his father, replacing it with an overdetermined need to claim respect for him, young Bobby might be living in that shadow area where he craved his father's affection and felt deprived of it. In which he loved his father, but feared him at the same time.

Out of such a severe conflict, a boy might well seek refuge in an hysterical seizure.

Jean debated the wisdom of discussing that with Tatum now. He was a highly intelligent man. But intelligence had never proved a bar to child abuse. Nor did it provide solutions for problems that were purely emotional. The decision to proceed was taken out of her hands when the phone blinked.

"Yes, I'm still here," she replied to the question that was asked of her by the admitting doctor in Emergency. "Oh? How bad is it? Yes, yes, I'll be right down." She turned to the Tatums. "I'm afraid I have to go. A case has just been admitted. A sixteen-year-old boy who fell off his bike and was hit by a passing car."

"Sounds bad," Tatum observed.

"It is. A head injury," Jean explained, rising to leave.

"I'm sorry," Tatum said, sincerely compassionate. The injury to the son of some unknown father seemed to have softened him.

"What makes it worse," Jean explained, "the reason he fell off his bike was that he was having a seizure. That's why we restrict their activities. We walk a fine line between restricting a patient so he can't endanger himself and giving him enough leeway so he doesn't feel like a freak."

Tatum nodded gravely.

"Now, please?" Jean invited them to leave her office.

She reached the Emergency Room. Guylay, the admitting resident, had already arranged a cardioscope to monitor the patient's heart. It showed an erratic pattern that could signify damage to the brain. She examined the unconscious boy. His skull had been fractured. More than serious, it threatened to be fatal. She ordered an operating room and called for the neurosurgical resident on duty.

She scrubbed and stood by to observe at the operation. The young surgeon worked swiftly and skillfully, racing against the erratic pattern that bounced across the screen of the oscilloscope. Suddenly the pattern leveled out with the warning tone that indicated cessation of cardiac activity. The surgeon ordered an injection of adrenaline. When the patient failed to respond, he immediately made an incision in the chest and resorted to hand pumping to restore the beat. Slowly the patient began to respond. The scope showed renewed activity. Erratic but discernible.

The surgeon completed the operation. The patient was removed to Intensive Care. While they were washing up after the operation, Jean asked, "What do you think?"

"I did all I could to relieve the pressure."

"Will he make it?"

"I wouldn't want his chances," the young surgeon said. "Why the hell do they let a kid like that ride a bike? And in traffic!"

"In some states, after a year free of seizures, they let them drive cars."

Before Jean left the hospital that evening, she stopped by at Intensive Care to have a look. The young surgeon had the same impulse. She found him at the boy's bedside. He shook his head grimly. Not a chance. As she left she passed the boy's father and mother sitting on the bench outside ICU. The mother was weeping. The father sat stunned. Soon, Jean realized, they would know the sad truth.

Times like this, Jean needed companionship. She would never grow inured to sudden death among the young. Especially to sudden preventable death. She stopped to get some dinner, ate only part of it, and hurried home to work on her paper about the Seaton Wards.

She had been at work for more than two hours, fighting sleep, and making determined promises to herself to wake early and work mornings instead of late at night. Her phone rang.

"Doctor?" a woman's voice came to her.

For a moment she was puzzled, then she recognized Marissa Tatum's voice.

"Yes? What is it, Mrs. Tatum?" Jean asked, hoping that the woman might have called with some clue that she had been reluctant to reveal in the presence of her husband. It happened that way sometimes. A patient's relative chose to speak more freely alone than in the presence of other family members.

"That boy?"

"Which boy?"

"The accident. The boy on the bike?"

"Yes."

"Is he all right?"

"He went out." Realizing medical jargon might elude Mrs. Tatum, she explained, "He died shortly after nine."

"Oh," Marissa Tatum responded. "Does it happen often? That kind of thing?"

"You mean could it happen to Bobby?"

"Yes."

"Not if we take the proper precautions. Not if we treat him and keep his seizures from recurring."

"But his *do* recur," the mother said.

"Yes," Jean agreed sadly, "they do recur."

"Doctor . . ." She hesitated.

"Yes, Mrs. Tatum?"

"One thing I want you to know. Bob was telling you the truth. He has never laid a hand on our son in anger. Never!"

"That's good to know," Jean said, though she was now more puzzled than ever.

"And . . ." The woman faltered.

"Yes, Mrs. Tatum? Anything else you wish to say?"

"Only that I feel sorry for the boy's parents. I know how they must feel. How I'd feel if anything ever happened to Bobby."

"I understand," Jean said, wondering whether any woman who had not actually suffered such a loss could know how it felt when it became a painful reality.

Though the conversation was at an end, Jean was reluctant to hang up. The call, unsolicited, must have deeper implications. The woman on the other end was troubled.

"Mrs. Tatum, *is* there something else?"

After a long silence, Marissa Tatum said softly, "That time—the overmedication . . ."

"Yes?"

"Bobby did have a seizure a few days after we brought him home."

"You never told me."

"I didn't want you to know. I didn't want Bob to know. I didn't want anyone probing into his brain. You said the medicine would help. When it didn't, I thought, the dose is wrong. I'll give him more. And then more. When he didn't have another seizure during the two weeks, I thought, it's working. I've cured him."

There was a slight gasp. And then silence.

"Mrs. Tatum?" Jean said, then waited and repeated, "Mrs. Tatum!"

"Yes, yes, I'm here."

"Are you sure that Bobby had only one seizure after you brought him home?"

There was a pause. "No, two. Both on the same day."

Jean considered that for a moment.

"Was anyone else there?"

"Just me. I did everything you said to do if he got another seizure."

"Except report to me," Jean pointed out.

"I'm sorry. I only tried to do what I thought was best for Bobby."

"What's best for Bobby is to be perfectly truthful and frank with me. Don't try to practice medicine. Is that clear?"

"Yes, Doctor." Marissa hesitated, "Did I do him any harm? Anything you can't correct?"

"Just remember, withholding the fact that you over-medicated him forced us to consider brain surgery."

"I know that now. I'm sorry. Terribly sorry."

"I understand," Jean said to comfort the distressed mother.

Jean hung up. She leaned back in her desk chair to evaluate Marissa Tatum's confession. How significant was it? In the early stages of dealing with seizure-prone children, many mothers tend to vary the doses of Dilantin, either through carelessness or through a temptation to experiment. If a child on a controlled dose goes seizure-free for a long time, one mother will grow careless and skip doses altogether. Another mother's insecurity might take over, and she might tend to overmedicate as if to ward off the devil with a modern incantation known as medication.

Marissa Tatum could be one of those. But one thing she had clarified for Jean. Bob Tatum had never physically abused his son.

The other fact had possibly greater significance. The boy had had two more seizures after he returned home. She must note it in his history.

She determined she would keep young Bobby Tatum in the hospital for a longer stay than she had originally intended.

eighteen

After a difficult afternoon Jean Scofield had returned to her office. She glanced through the messages Maggie had left on her desk. Two doctors sought her advice in consultation. An old patient called because he was suffering periodic relapses. She had expected a recurrence of his condition, which was due to a syphilitic infection undetected in his early youth. In all, it proved a routine list of messages, except for three that were bunched together. Bob Tatum had called. Larry Braham had called. Horace Cameron had called.

All of them to ask essentially the same question: What was Bobby Tatum's condition and why hadn't he yet been discharged?

Larry's interest was justified as the boy's pediatrician. Tatum's was natural, being the boy's father. Cameron's annoyed her. The meticulous but diplomatic message read, "Would Dr. Scofield consider Mr. Cameron's flying the young man to New York or Boston for another opinion? Mr. Cameron is willing to put his own jet at the doctor's disposal so she can go along." The message had obviously been dictated by Ms. St. John since it was so carefully phrased. But referring to a five-year-old boy as "the young man" sounded distinctly Cameron.

She answered only one of the three calls.

"Larry?"

"Jean?"

They were a bit distant these days, after their heated discussion of Tatum and child abuse.

"You called," she said.

"Unless you've found something, why not send Bobby home? The Tatums are becoming anxious."

"The reason I can't send him home is that I *haven't* found anything."

"What does *that* mean?"

"I want a few more days," Jean said. She had never told Larry of Marissa Tatum's confession about those two seizures at home. She considered the woman had made them in extreme confidence. There was a fine ethical line concerning the right to privacy between doctor and patient. Did it extend to keeping certain revelations from another doctor involved in the case? For the moment, Jean preferred to think that it did.

"A few more days to do what?" Larry pressed.

"Test, observe."

"You're not considering an angiogram, are you? Not without getting a signed consent."

"Of course not," Jean said emphatically.

"Then what kind of testing?"

"I want to run the entire series over again—skull x-rays, EEG's, echoes. And also another serum Dilantin level."

"That can't take days." Exasperation began to show in Larry's voice.

"I don't see that it can do any harm to keep the boy here a few more days," she said curtly.

"Oh, but it can." His answer contained a note of warning.

"How?"

"The Tatums are talking about signing Bobby out against advice."

"The Tatums? Or Cameron?"

Larry admitted, "Cameron called me personally this afternoon. He suggested taking the boy out and flying him up to Boston. 'For the best opinions,' as he put it. 'Always go with the best' is one of his mottoes."

" 'Never let a layman practice medicine' is one of mine!" Jean countered.

"He also managed to inquire about your paper on the Seaton Wards. And what you decided."

"If I can find enough time I hope to finish it this month," she responded angrily.

"His questions, not *mine,* Jeannie." Larry paused a moment. "Busy or not, you're going to have to eat dinner tonight."

"I've got some shopping to do," she evaded.

"For a new lab coat?" he asked sarcastically.

"No. Office equipment."

"Office equipment!" Larry exploded, convinced it was a ruse to avoid seeing him. "That's the job of the Procurement Department."

"Not this particular office equipment," Jean said. "Good-bye, Larry. I have to rush."

Since it was Thursday, and the downtown stores were open late, Jean Scofield could shop close to the hospital. She browsed in the toy department almost until closing time, then made three purchases. A colorful jigsaw puzzle. A story book. And a stuffed zebra. The sales girl volunteered to send them. Jean insisted on taking them along. Instead of going home, she returned to her office where she unwrapped her purchases, depositing them around the room in varying places until she was satisfied with the arrangement.

The next morning, after she had cleared her schedule of the most pressing matters, she asked that Bobby Tatum be brought in. Dressed in a hospital gown, a plain blue robe and slippers, he was delivered to Jean by a pretty young student nurse. Jean noted how the boy clung to the student's hand so that she had to extricate herself to leave.

Jean closed the door.

"Wouldn't you like to sit down, Bobby?"

The boy hesitated, then climbed into the big upholstered leather chair opposite hers. From there he could see the stuffed zebra. His delft-blue eyes widened. He was both excited and tense. His desire for the animal conflicted with his natural shyness.

"Would you like that, Bobby?"

"Yes, ma'am," he said softly but eagerly.

She handed him the zebra, realizing for the first time what had made her select it. That day of his first seizure there had been a conflict with his teacher, when he was instructed to draw elephants but preferred to draw zebras. She observed him till he was thoroughly engrossed in the toy.

"Bobby, do you like Miss Robinson?" Jean asked, referring to the pretty student nurse who had brought him.

Without taking his attention from the zebra, he said, "Yes, ma'am."

"Is she nice to you?"

"Yes, ma'am." Preoccupied, he answered her questions easily and truthfully. The toy proved a useful diversion.

Jean took the jigsaw puzzle down from the shelf. He followed her with his eyes, anxious to see, reluctant to make his curiosity obvious. Jean opened the box and turned it over so the pieces fell to her desk in disorder. She began to play with them, asking, "Are there many other people you like, Bobby?"

His attention torn now between the zebra he clutched and the colorful puzzle pieces on Jean's desk, he said only, "Uh huh."

"Who?"

"Daddy. Mommy. Esther."

"Esther?"

"Our maid," he explained, openly tempted by the puzzle on Jean's desk.

"I'm having trouble with this, Bobby. Could you help me put it together?"

Shyly the boy nodded, slipped out of his chair, still clutching the zebra. His head was just high enough to see over the desk top. Eventually he dared reach out and touch one of the pieces. Soon, he was giving the colorful pieces his complete attention. Jean leaned in close. Their heads were side by side, almost touching. His skin had the sweet smell of children. It was soft, as his silky black hair was soft.

"Has Esther ever punished you, Bobby?"

"Only sometimes," he said, almost unaware of what he was saying.

"Like what times?"

"When I come home from school and won't drink my milk."

"What does she do?" Jean asked, observing that he was a bright boy who seemed to manage the puzzle well for a child his age. But she had also gained a bit of information which led her to reconsider her own early conclusions about his father.

"She makes me drink it."

"What does she do to make you drink it?"

"She won't give me any treat."

"Is that all she does?"

The boy was too involved to answer at once.

"Bobby, is that all Esther does to you when you won't drink your milk?" Jean repeated gently.

"She makes me go up."

"Where?"

"To my room," the boy said, fitting the first two pieces together.

"Does she ever spank you?"

"No, ma'am."

"Does she ever threaten that she's going to spank you?"

The boy turned to her, his eyes reflecting puzzlement.

"Does Esther ever say, 'Bobby, if you don't drink your milk I'll whip you?' Or, 'Bobby, if you mess up your room I'll spank you?' Does she ever say anything like that?"

"No, ma'am."

The boy was trying to force an odd piece into place. Jean suggested, "Maybe that one won't fit there, Bobby. Try another one."

She let him work at the puzzle in silence for a time while she considered his answers. The thing about abused children that made it difficult for the physician was that they were extremely reluctant to admit being abused. Fear of subsequent punishment was a powerful silencer. It was difficult to determine if the boy's statements about Esther were true, or were, perversely, an indication that the maid might be the guilty person.

"Bobby, does Esther ever say to you, 'If you tell Mommy or Daddy, I'll punish you when I get you alone?' "

"Oh, no," Bobby said, in his childish way rising to Esther's defense.

"Bobby, does *anybody* ever hit you?"

"Yep."

"Who?"

"Ward."

"Who is Ward?"

"Ward," Bobby repeated, finding the right piece and fitting it into place. When he had, he turned to Jean and smiled. It was the first time she had seen him smile today. He also edged a bit closer, till he pressed against her. He seemed to want as much of her to touch him as possible, as if her body promised him warmth and security. She slipped her arm around him. He looked up at her and smiled before he turned back to work on the puzzle.

"Bobby, who's Ward?"

"Boy in my class."

"What does Ward do to you, Bobby?"

"Hits me."

"And what do you do?"

"Do?"

"Do you hit him back?"

"No, ma'am."

"Why not?"

" 'Cause he'll only hit me harder."

It was difficult to quarrel with his childish logic. But it was also significant. He was a frightened boy who did not dare to strike back at his tormentors. Typical of a child who invited abuse. Some children, especially those underweight at birth, seemed born with a predisposition to invite abuse. Others learned to be submissive from sad experience.

"Does anyone else in school ever hit you, Bobby?"

The boy thought a moment. "Cindy."

"A girl?"

"Yes, ma'am."

"Did you hit her back?"

"Yes, ma'am."

"And what did she do?"

"She just standed there," the boy said simply.

Jean turned the completed puzzle over, letting the pieces fall out. "Let's do this again, Bobby." While the boy went at the pieces more surely now, she asked, "Does anyone else ever hit you?"

"No, ma'am."

"Daddy?"

"No, ma'am."

"Mommy?"

"No, ma'am."

Denials, to be sure, but not completely unexpected if her suspicions of abuse were true.

"Did you ever fall down and hurt yourself, Bobby? I mean hurt yourself real hard?"

"No, ma'am."

"A long time ago, do you remember when you and Mommy and Daddy were moving? And the men came to take the furniture away? You were on the stairs and one of the men accidentally pushed you and you fell down the stairs? Do you remember that?"

"No, ma'am."

"Do you remember ever falling downstairs and hurting yourself, Bobby?"

"No, ma'am."

The boy appeared relaxed and at ease, clutching the stuffed zebra in one hand and working the puzzle with his other. His answers had been given free of any tension, with no apparent attempt to withhold. Yet they conflicted with what his mother and father had admitted about that long-bone fracture that showed up on his x-ray. Could he have forgotten, as he had only been two years old? Or had he deliberately blocked out the truth?

She proceeded to ask other questions which produced no pertinent or fresh information.

"Now we have to get you back to your room," she said.

"Can I stay here with you?"

"I'd like you to, Bobby. But I have other boys and girls to see, and Mommies and Daddies too. But you'll come back again and we'll play some more."

"Promise?"

"Promise."

The boy pressed his face against hers. He kissed her. Professionally, she tried to tell herself that was unfortunate. It diminished the objectivity she always strived to maintain. Personally, she was deeply touched.

She had not made the progress she hoped in their play therapy session. The boy had relaxed, engrossed enough in the toys to talk. But he had not yet reached that degree of confidence in her that enabled him to open up and talk freely and to remember. Or perhaps there was nothing of importance to remember. That was always a possibility. If her intuition were not so strong, she might have accepted the results of that one session as final. But it remained a constant, nagging point that she had to satisfy.

She was peering through the ophthalmoscope into the eye of a woman who had been referred to her by an internist. The woman suffered momentary blackouts and periods of dizziness from no apparent cause. Jean's beeper sounded. She ignored it. It continued with the insistence of an urgent call. Finally, she picked up the phone.

Larry's voice was low but agitated.

"Are you where you can talk?"

"Not too freely. Why?"

"Just got another call from Tatum. I've run out of excuses," Larry said. "How long do you intend to keep him? And why?"

"Another four or five days," she said. "Because I think he needs further observation."

"Unless you can be more specific, the Tatums won't hold off."

"I want four or five more days."

"I'll do what I can. But I'm not promising," Larry said. Then he advised gently, "Jean, darling, don't become so involved. He's their son. Not yours."

"I know, Larry. I know," she said softly, aware that she was already too deeply involved.

Less than an hour later, while Jean was dictating her preliminary findings on the woman with blackout spells, her phone rang.

"I did what I could," Larry confessed. "Either you discharge Bobby tomorrow morning or they'll sign him out against advice."

When she hung up, she sat still and pondered the choices open to her in defense of her little patient. She could, on the basis of sheer suspicion, report to the Child Abuse Committee of the hospital. But with the fragmentary facts she had at hand her suspicion might be rejected quite summarily. Intuition alone would not stand up before the Child Abuse Committee. Especially where a family like the Tatums was concerned. So if the child were indeed neglected or abused he would be returned to his parents without any chance of help. And there was that uneasy doubt, which Larry shared, that she was too involved in the case and hence too inclined to exaggerate what she found.

Perhaps what was needed was another opinion. Not, as Cameron had suggested, by flying the boy to Boston, but another opinion from doctors readily available and who would have no personal involvement with the patient. Who would, in fact, have no knowledge of the patient's identity.

She requested of Hans Benziger that she be given half an hour at Grand Rounds to present a case that was extremely baffling.

nineteen

At quarter past eight in the morning of the day of Grand Rounds, Jean arrived at her office to find her phone lighting up urgently. Mrs. Holdrith, the Social Service worker who did most of the routine work on the Child Abuse Committee, was relieved to reach Jean before she became involved in the rest of her day's schedule. They had failed to apprise her of a group consultation concerning the disposition of the Scott case.

The Scott case, Jean tried to recall. Then she remembered the little black boy, twenty-two months old, brought in with evidence of gross abuse, glove burn and pugilistic puss. She had examined him again several weeks ago to determine if he had suffered any permanent neurological deficits.

The committee wanted her opinion on the future course of action to take on the boy. Could she see and examine him once more, then attend the conference?

She saw him in one of the examining rooms in the clinic. The first thing she noticed was that he had grown appreciably since she had seen him last. He looked more nearly normal in size for his age. While his features presented vestiges of the punishment he had absorbed in his brief lifetime, his hands had cleared, leaving only slight scars and traces of what had been serious burns.

When first brought into the room he clung devotedly to the nurse who accompanied him. While Jean conducted her neurological testing he felt secure only while holding the nurse's hand. During the weeks in the hospital he had obviously formed a strong attachment to her.

"Really a nice kid," the nurse remarked. "Very loving. Needs people."

"Needs parents," Jean observed as she examined the child's eyes, ears, reflexes.

"I hope nothing more happens to him," the young nurse said. "Next time . . ." She did not complete her dire prediction.

"They told me his parents are coming along. Cooperating."

"God, I hope so," the nurse said fervently. "He won't let go of my hand now, but do you know how long it took for him to let me touch him in the beginning?"

Jean had completed her examination. From all that she could determine, there were no residual neurological deficits as a result of the punishment the child had suffered. The x-rays had proved what she had originally suspected on her first examination, including a previous fine-line fracture. But, fortunately, there had been no internal bleeding to create a subdural hematoma. Neurologically, at least, the little patient had a chance at a normal development. She would not hazard a guess as to the psychological prognosis.

She attended the consultation. In her opinon, if not subjected to further abuse, the child should do well. It would be better to have him returned to his family if it was safe now, rather than consign him to charitable or welfare institutions for the rest of his childhood. Depending on the progress his parents had made toward rehabilitation, she would recommend discharging the boy.

On the way back to her office, her concern made her stop by the Pediatric wards where the Scott boy was being kept during his stay. She stood in the doorway glancing down the long room to where he played with two other children. He seemed happy and alert, far from the dazed, burned, tormented child he had been that first day of his admission.

Within the next few months they would discover if their judgment had been correct. Maybe they would never hear of him again. Or he might become one of those stomach-wrenching items in the morning paper, an infant killed by his own mother or father.

It was no small responsibility. Jean tried to be free of it by reminding herself she was a neurologist, not a social worker, a psychiatrist, or an officer of the court. But the obligation weighed heavily on her and she hoped she had been right.

Dr. Ralph Sunderland, along with Jean one of the leading contenders to succeed Hans Benziger to the post of Chief, presided over Grand Rounds on this afternoon. His duties were formal and limited to introducing the cases which would be discussed. He presented the first physician and the subject of his case, then took a seat in the front row so that he could view all the slides, x-rays and angiograms which were part of the presentation. While the first case was being presented other neurologists and neurosurgeons slipped into darkened Cameron Hall, most carrying sandwiches and coffee in plastic cups in place of the lunch they had to forgo to sit in on the meeting. Physicians with busy schedules were constantly juggling their time in a desperate effort to keep abreast of the ever-changing specialties they practiced.

Midway through the first presentation, Hans Benziger entered the auditorium. Just before Jean began her presentation of the case of an unnamed five-year-old boy with seizures, Larry Braham, in white lab coat, carefully nursing a cup of hot coffee, entered and took a seat in the last row.

Jean launched into her presentation, describing in detail the signs and symptoms the patient had presented on admission to the hospital. She presented his echoencephalograms, EEG's, and the observations of herself and Kerner, the floor nurse, as to his progress. She also noted his overdose of Dilantin, the later occurence of what she diagnosed to be an hysterical seizure, and the seizure-free period during his hospital stay, as well as several confirmed seizures since his return home. She also mentioned the finding of an old long-bone fracture.

Without expressing her own suspicions, she threw the case open for questioning and suggestions.

One of the older men, an attending neurologist with a large private practice and hence sensitive to the high cost of malpractice insurance, was first to respond.

"By no means would I insist on an angiogram under those conditions. Though the odds of morbidity or mortality are small, one unexpected reaction in the patient can be enough to drag you into court for two years and God knows how much expense in increased insurance after that. I would definitely advise against an angiogram unless his condition grows worse. And then I would make it very clear what the risks are."

He had completely missed the point of Jean's presentation, but she did not take time to correct him. One of the other men spoke up.

"I disagree. I think it's the neurologist's duty to insist on angio. There's enough here to create a suspicion of a condition which, the longer it exists, the more likely it is to become a source of permanent damage."

"And what condition would you expect to find on an angio?"

"Why, a subdural hematoma," the doctor responded.

Another doctor argued, "I wouldn't be quite so quick or so dogmatic. I say it's jumping to conclusions to suspect a subdural, especially with no history at all of trauma to the head."

The discussion had tended away from the question of child abuse and onto the relative merits of doing an angiogram, until Hans Benziger spoke out from the rear row.

"If I may . . ." He eased his way into the discussion. "Could I have a brief review of the case under discussion?"

Jean recited the pertinent facts. As she did, the rear door of Cameron Hall opened. Edward Carey was showing a Federal inspector around the hospital. The woman represented the Health, Education and Welfare Department. It was her job to monitor compliance with regulations that involved the employment and up-grading of minorities and women in jobs of responsibility.

Carey had deliberately chosen to drop in on Grand Rounds for he was aware that Dr. Scofield was scheduled to present a case. That was bound to make a good impression on the inspector, thus helping him gloss over those areas in which the hospital's compliance was considerably less than satisfactory.

Once Jean had completed her brief review, Benziger said, "Aside from the question of an angiogram, there are several other interesting aspects to this case. For example, that hysterical seizure. Unique. In my experience I have encountered very few hysterical seizures in young children.

"And to me the unique is always medically significant. Taken together with another interesting fact, a pattern begins to emerge. As I understand it, once the child is admitted to the hospital after his first seizures he never again suffers a seizure while he is *in* the hospital. But he's had seizures once in school and twice at home. Evidently the pressures of his home life seem to be a factor conducive to seizures.

"I assume this is one of the cases in the clinic?" Benziger asked.

"This is a private patient referred by a pediatrician attached to the hospital," Jean explained.

"Strange," Benziger remarked, nonplused. "It has all the earmarks of a case of child abuse, coming from a lower class home in which parental tension in the household might bring on seizures. These days, with high unemployment and other economic difficulties, abuse of children is becoming epidemic. But I see I was wrong. And yet . . ." he said, reluctant to abandon his conclusion.

Suddenly he asked, "Is there any evidence at all of physical abuse?"

"That long-bone fracture, which the parents explained."

"Parents always have an 'explanation' for such 'accidents.' If we *are* confronted with a subdural here, it would have had to be from an injury in the past six months. A year at the most. Is there anything suspicious during that period?"

"Nothing I could uncover," Jean said.

"Yet it is possible. And, of course, the parents would deny it. Still, that doesn't absolve the doctor from pursuing the issue. My approach would be, an angiogram is indicated. But, in the meantime, as long as the issue is unresolved, safeguard the child. Keep him in hospital, under any pretext."

"That's the reason for presenting this case. Is there

sufficient evidence on which to make such a report to the Child Abuse Committee?"

Aware that Carey was now in the auditorium, Sunderland joined the discussion.

"If I may be permitted a personal aside. It seems to me that Dr. Scofield is exhibiting what is, for her, a remarkable degree of reticence in this matter. I've seen her act far more quickly and decisively in other cases where she suspected abuse. Her caution in this case may be another of those 'unique' aspects to which Dr. Benziger referred."

Benziger responded angrily, "Grand Rounds is not a place to air personal differences or to campaign for promotions."

"Where a doctor's personal interests impinge on her professional judgment, I believe it is justified," Sunderland shot back, hoping that Carey had grasped his meaning.

"Dr. Sunderland . . ." Benziger tried to interrupt.

"If the truth be told, I think Dr. Scofield is using us. And I for one resent it."

"What do you mean, 'using'?" Jean demanded furiously.

"It is quite transparent who your patient is. That's why you're reluctant to take sole responsibility. You want us to make the decision for you. Then if there's any flak, you can say that we all shared in the opinion!"

"That's not true!" Jean responded.

"It should be quite obvious to anyone in the Neurology Department that the patient is young Bobby Tatum," Sunderland said. "And the parents you're accusing are the Tatums."

Edward Carey, embarrassed that this outbreak of personal antagonism was taking place in the presence of the Federal inspector, was shocked by Sunderland's charge. He was even more disturbed when Jean replied.

"The identity of the patient has no medical significance. I regret you felt compelled to mention it," thereby confirming Sunderland's identification.

Carey nudged his companion. They both slipped out of the hall.

"Extremely regrettable," Carey said. "That woman is so emotional. Possibly too emotional for a key job."

Thus he laid the foundation for overcoming any possible legal complications that might arise when Jean Scofield was passed over for Sunderland, who was Cameron's selection for Chief.

As soon as he could gracefully disengage himself from the Federal inspector, Carey placed a call to Horace Cameron, seeking a meeting for this afternoon so he could report.

But Cameron was in Japan, visiting one of his plants there, and was not expected to return for several days.

twenty

Jean Scofield was striding swiftly toward her office, having just completed a session with her students. She had discussed a case in which the patient, a woman in her forties, had presented double vision. After intensive testing it was discovered that she had a malignant tumor pressing on her optic nerve. A biopsy revealed it was a secondary mass which had metastasized from the primary in her breast which had gone undetected in her routine physicals. Many times neurologists had to deal with the unhappy consequences of other physicians' errors. Such cases always infuriated her.

Suddenly from behind her there was a loud, desperate outcry, "Doctor!"

Jean turned to stare down the long corridor. A man raced toward her, carrying a young child in his arms. As he drew closer she recognized Dominick Fazio.

"Doctor, Doctor!" he called as he approached. Behind him his plump wife raced to keep up.

He reached Jean and held out little Beatrice to her. "Please, Doctor? Please!"

"Bring her into my examining room."

Fazio followed, pursued by his wife. He placed the child on the examining table.

"Now leave me alone with her." Fazio did not move. "Please, Mr. Fazio, leave us!"

Before he left the room the distraught father kissed the little girl on the head. Jean commenced a routine neurological examination, testing for weakness on both sides, examining her eyes, nose, ears. There were no gross signs. Once she questioned the child, she was sure there was no pain. She had time now to talk, to discover the reason for Fazio's panic.

"Now, Mr. Fazio, tell me what happened?"

The man attempted to talk but couldn't, giving way to tears. His stout little wife spoke for him. "He saw it. He finally saw it for himself."

"What?"

"He was home today when she had a fit. So he saw it for the first time."

"It's terrible!" Fazio cried. "My little girl shaking and twisting, her eyes rolling up. Terrible! Terrible! And I couldn't do nothing for her. Nothing. I can't let it happen again. Not to my baby. Whatever you say to do, Doc, I do. Whatever you want me to sign, I sign. Anything. Only help her. Keep it from happening anymore. Save her!"

"Mr. Fazio, remember what we were talking about the last time. . . ."

He interrupted her. "I'm sorry, Doc, I didn't mean to be so rough the last time. But when you said I had to sign something and my little girl could die, I couldn't. I couldn't. But now, anything . . . anything."

"Mr. Fazio," Jean began again, "what we want to do now is only a test, not a treatment. It won't prevent Beatrice from having seizures. But we hope it will tell us why she's having them. Then we may be able to prevent them in the future. So I want to be quite clear about it. Just by signing this paper you're not going to cure her."

"Even if it's only the first step, do it. Do it now! Today!" the frantic father insisted.

"I have to arrange for it. We'll probably do it early tomorrow. Meantime, let me admit her and do some other testing overnight."

"All right, Doctor, all right," Fazio said, agreeing to anything to wipe that terrifying picture from his mind.

He signed the consent form, kissed his daughter and started down the corridor, weeping again. His stout little wife walked alongside trying to comfort him. "Dom, Dom, please . . . people are watching."

"Let them watch! Who cares? Beatrice . . . we got to save Beatrice."

Fortunately Beatrice Fazio withstood the angiogram procedure well. Of the many complications that might ensue—cardiac arrest, arterial spasm, anaphylactic reactions to the dye—she suffered none.

Within an hour after it was completed, Jean and the neuroradiologist stood before the view box in his office examining the plates produced by the two cameras in the bi-level x-ray. A suspicious shadow of considerable size was evident.

"We better have a surgeon look at these," Jean said. "I'll get Forrest at once."

Forrest studied the films for some minutes. "We have to go in. Right away. I don't like the location of that thing."

"Malignant?"

"Won't know till I get there. But eventually pressure alone will kill that child if we don't do something."

Jean Scofield now had the task of informing Mr. and Mrs. Fazio. When they entered her office she could read in their eyes that they anticipated the gravity of what she was about to tell them.

As gently as she could, she explained that they had found incontrovertible evidence of a mass. Whether it was benign or malignant they did not know.

"In either case," Jean said, "it's necessary to go in and remove as much of it as we can."

"As much as you can?" Fazio asked.

"It depends on the exact location. How enmeshed it is in her brain tissue."

"Brain. . . . He's going to cut out part of her brain?" Fazio was alarmed.

"He's going to remove as much of the tumor as he can without doing damage to her brain."

He shook his head. His wife read it as a sign of resistance.

"Dom, we got to. The doctor says it's the only way."

He closed his eyes, shook his head and murmured, "Why? Such a nice sweet little girl. Why, Doctor?"

"Doctors don't know why," Jean said gently. "All we know is what we find, and what we have to do."

"And if you do?" Fazio asked, eyes still closed, as if to blot out the ugly truth.

"Mr. Fazio, in this kind of surgery, we do not make any promises. We'll know soon enough."

Tears escaped from between his clenched eyelids and

traced down his cheeks. "All right, all right, all right," he whispered.

"It'll be necessary to sign another consent."

He said softly to his wife, "Paula, you do it. I can't."

The pudgy little woman took the pen, hesitated for an instant, then scratched her signature on the bottom of the document.

"When?" Fazio asked.

"Tomorrow morning."

Fazio nodded, opened his eyes. Wearily, he lifted his great bulk out of the chair and turned to leave. When his wife did not follow, he called back to her, "Paula?"

"Yes, Dom." But she didn't move.

"Come. We got to go to church," he said as he left the room.

Mrs. Fazio lingered to apologize for her husband. "He's not a weak man. He's very strong. Only when it comes to Beatrice. She's his whole life. He loves his boys. But she's his whole life."

"I understand," Jean said. Mrs. Fazio was gone. Jean dialed Forrest's office to say she had obtained consent. The surgery on the Fazio girl could now be scheduled.

Before they left the hospital, the Fazios stopped off to see Beatrice, to prepare her for what was to come.

"And the nice lady doctor is going to take you to another doctor. And he is going to make you all well," her mother said.

"But it won't hurt, darling," her father was quick to reassure her. "They put you to sleep. You never even know. And when you wake up you're all better! Like magic. Just like you see on the TV." He managed a big encouraging smile. "Just like on the TV," he repeated, because he could find no other words to reassure her.

The girl smiled and twisted one of her golden curls.

It made her father feel better, much better. He leaned his stubbly face against her cheek and kissed her. She rubbed her hand over his cheek. "It scratches," she said. But it was not a rebuke, just a game they had played many times under far happier circumstances. It only served to twist his nervous stomach into a knot of spasmodic pain. His wife could read the signs. "Dom, the doctor said not to stay too long."

He nodded, kissed his daughter once more and lingered a bit longer before he could break away. He waved to her from the door. She smiled and waved back.

"There's nothing to worry about, sweetheart," he called to her. "Nothing! The operation will make you as good as new. So don't be afraid."

Her parents were gone. The girl was alone, for the moment feeling reassured, and thinking how nice it would be to be home again with all her toys, instead of the single favorite Raggedy Ann they had let her bring with her. She was also frightened, for she had heard the word *operation* spoken by adults before. Always in a way that indicated pain, danger and even death. She grasped her doll more tightly and lay staring up at the white ceiling, alone and frightened.

In a while there was the scuffling sound of slippers on the highly polished floor. She rolled onto her side to look toward the door. A five-year-old boy in a navy-colored robe and slippers to match was staring at her. He was black-haired and blue-eyed. He was shy, but loneliness had endowed him with the courage to go seeking another child's company and comfort.

"Hi," he said. The little blonde girl smiled at him. "My name is Bobby. What's yours?"

"Beatrice."

"That's a funny name," he said, for he had never before met anyone with that name.

"It is *not* funny." Then she asked, "Are you sick?"

"Uh huh," he admitted.

"Me too," she said. "But I'm going to get all better. My daddy said the doctor is going to opa . . . opa . . ." She could not remember the complete word.

"Operation?"

"Operation," she recalled now. "Then I'll be all better. And I can go home."

The boy drew closer to her bed. "You go to school?"

"Next year. Mommy says next year I'm going. When I'm all better. Kindergarten. She told me all about the games and everything."

"Pre-school," the boy said proudly, "I go to pre-school."

"You too small to go to school."

"I am not!" he said staunchly.

"Yes, you are."

"I am not! When my Mom comes she'll tell you. I go to pre-school."

"You don't go now."

"When I get better I'll go back."

"You going to get a operation too?"

"I don't know," he admitted.

"Then how you going to get better?"

"I'm just going to get better," the boy said. "My Mom said so. And Dr. Jean said so."

"I like her."

"Me too," the boy said. "She said I'm going to get all better."

"Me too. After I have my opa . . ." Again she struggled with the word.

"Operation."

"Operation," she managed.

They were quiet for a moment, until the boy asked, "What's a operation?"

"I don't know," she admitted. "Something the doc-

tor does. And my papa said it don't hurt. You don't
even know it. And you get all better."

"That your favorest doll?"

"Yeah."

"Can I see it?" he asked.

After a moment's consideration she relinquished her
tight grasp and held it out. He took it and rubbed
his fingers over the cloth face. He twisted the yellow
rope hair. He held it close to himself.

"I don't have a doll," he said wistfully.

"I have a lot of dolls," she informed him proudly.

He embraced it, until she reached out. Reluctantly,
he gave it back.

"Can you get out and play?" he asked.

"The nurse won't let me."

"Not even a little bit?"

"No," the girl said sadly.

The little boy turned and started for the door. She
called out, "Can't we play if I stay in bed?"

"It could be an airplane and I'm the pilot."

"Okay," she said.

"You ever been in an airplane?"

"No. You?"

"Yep," he said. "When we moved from San Diego."

"San Diego? What's that?"

"A place," he said.

"What kind of place?"

"Just a place," he explained.

"Can we go there?"

"Sure."

He stood at the foot of the bed facing away from her
pretending he was the pilot. He made noises that
sounded to him like the jet plane on which he had
flown from San Diego. While he was playing the nurse
came into the room to say it was time for milk and
cookies. Though Bobby pleaded to remain and have

his refreshment in the girl's room, the nurse took him by the hand. As he left the room, he called back. "I'll come see you again."

The little girl lay clutching her Raggedy Ann and thinking how nice it would be once she had her operation and was all better and could play with the boy again. She began to look forward to that mysterious thing called an operation.

At seven o'clock in the morning Beatrice Fazio, wrapped in a blanket, a tiny passenger on a mobile operating table, was wheeled into Operating Room D. Her head was no longer crowned by the soft golden curls she had loved to twist. It was now shaved clean and encased in a white hospital towel.

Dr. Forrest and his team were waiting. The anesthetist put the child under. When the sensors had been attached so they could monitor her condition throughout the procedure, Forrest, guided by x-rays and scans, selected the place for his incision. After turning back the scalp, he proceeded to work carefully and with great precision with the high-powered surgical saw to remove a flap of her skull.

By the time Jean Scofield entered the observers' gallery, Forrest was already into the child's brain. Behind his face mask, with his magnifying spectacles on, Forrest seemed like a pair of huge eyes. Impassive, cold, scrutinizing eyes. He leaned over the field of the operation, issuing curt instructions to the nurse, accepting instruments, using them, discarding them. When his concentration caused a tension knot in his shoulder, he straightened up momentarily, drew his shoulders back and rotated his head to fight off the pain. In so doing, glancing over his glasses, he spied Jean. But his eyes revealed little for his thick glasses obscured them from that distance. He resumed his work.

He had removed a small bit of the tumor tissue and

placed it in a steel basin. An assisting nurse raced out to obtain a frozen section for a swift, if not entirely conclusive, diagnosis. While they waited, Forrest leaned back from the table, exhaled wearily and turned to look up at Jean. He shook his head in warning. He would not make a definitive judgment on his own, but he had his suspicions.

Minutes later, the phone rang. A nurse answered it. Forrest approached the phone. She held it for him so he could listen without touching it.

"Well?" he asked.

"Positive."

"Primary?"

"Primary," the pathologist confirmed.

Forrest nodded. He turned back to the table. He went to work again to remove what he could of the deadly invader.

An hour later, he was free to discuss the findings with Jean Scofield.

"Did you get it all?"

"Couldn't. Not encapsulated, and deeply embedded."

"What do you think?"

"We've reduced the mass. You might consider chemotherapy."

"Is it worth putting a child that age through chemotherapy?" Jean asked.

"In my opinion, no," Forrest said simply. "She hasn't got a chance. One month, maybe two, and that's it. Why torture her?"

Jean nodded. It was a decision she would have to make in consultation with the chemotherapist. But no matter the therapy or lack of it, she would have to tell the Fazios what Forrest had found.

The Fazios listened numbly. This time no tears. They held hands, stared vaguely as Dr. Scofield told them simply but truthfully what the surgery had revealed, how little it had been able to accomplish.

"I knew it," Fazio said. "All along, I knew it."

He moved from his chair, embraced his wife who pressed her face against his huge chest. "Dom . . . Dom . . ." she kept saying softly, bereft of words and empty of tears by now. They stood embraced for a time.

"Can we see her?" he asked.

"Yes. But only for a few minutes. She's in Intensive Care."

"Okay. Only for a few minutes," Fazio agreed.

Awed by the battery of electronic equipment that monitored all the patients, the Fazios tiptoed into ICU, trying not to stare at the other patients. Neither of them spoke, but both harbored the same thought: So much equipment and still they couldn't do anything for our little girl.

They stood by her bed, staring down at her. Her head was turbaned in white bandages. Her eyes were closed. A wire led from the sensor on her arm to the oscilloscope just behind her bed. A green light moved across it, tracing the pattern of her heart beats.

Fazio stared at his wife; she stared back. Should they make their presence known or was the child sleeping? Fazio reached out gently to touch his daughter's cheek. She opened her eyes. He smiled down at her. She tried to smile back but was too weak. Fazio took her hand in his and patted it gently till he felt that she had gone back to sleep. Mrs. Fazio leaned over the bed and kissed her child on the cheek.

Outside ICU, he said softly, "I'm glad she went to sleep again."

"Yes," his wife agreed. "If she asked any questions, what would we tell her?"

"We would lie," Fazio said.

They started down the corridor.

3

twenty-one

"Benziger was the first doctor to mention child abuse?" Horace Cameron asked grimly of Edward Carey, as they nursed their late-afternoon drinks in the old man's office.

"I think they had it arranged that way," Carey said. "It's so obvious. She presents the case, but Benziger makes the scandalous diagnosis. That way he takes the onus off her and upon himself."

"Of course," Cameron agreed. "After all, at his age and with his standing, what does he have to risk?"

"So they must have agreed between them. I think that's why Sunderland felt compelled to expose the whole thing."

Cameron nodded, then said suddenly, "Thank you, Edward," bringing the distasteful meeting to an end.

Once alone, Cameron sat back in his capacious leather chair behind the desk from which he commanded his empire. He took one last sip of his drink before he gave vent to his feelings.

"Damned woman!" he muttered finally. She would not accept the post created for her. She was determined to have that Chiefship or destroy anyone who stood in her path. She had the audacity to persist in writing that paper about the low cure rate in the new Seaton Wards. Obviously, after he had exerted the least bit of subtle pressure on her, she had sought some means of vengeance. Evidently, she thought she had found it. She was determined to slander the name of InterElectronics by attributing the most distasteful of crimes to one of his most promising young executives. This was the kind of scandal that could attract important news coverage.

Horace Cameron paid an excellent public relations firm more than half a million dollars a year to accomplish two things. Keep the names Cameron and InterElectronics before the public in a favorable light. Or, when not favorable, keep the names Cameron and InterElectronics hidden from public view. They succeeded extremely well in an era when other large corporations were being pilloried in the press. But this sort of personal scandal was really not in their line. Some nosy hostile local newspaperman, looking to make a name for himself, might pick up a hint of this story and run with it. There had been at least a dozen physicians in Grand Rounds. The seal of confidentiality did not strictly apply to them. By now the story that woman had planted about the Tatums must be a juicy bit of vitriolic gossip making the rounds of the hospital. That very evening doctors must have been telling it to their wives and guests over the dinner table. Soon it would be all over the city.

He reached for his phone. "Get me Tatum!"

Within minutes, Bob Tatum, who was en route back to the city in one of InterElectronics' jets, was on the radiophone.

"Yes, sir?"

"When can you be here?"

"Pilot says our ETA is seven-o-nine."

"I want you in my library at home no later than seven-thirty!" Cameron said and cut off any response.

The library of the Cameron home was a room of such dimensions that only a ceiling two stories high could give it graceful proportion. From floor to ceiling it was lined with books. A walkway ran around the room halfway up the walls to give easy access to the volumes on the upper level. The room was kept at precisely the correct degree of temperature and humidity year round, to protect Cameron's collection of rare books and manuscripts.

The floor was covered with costly Oriental rugs except where polished hand-pegged oak floors showed through. There were two huge fireplaces, one at either end of the room, each high enough for a tall man to stand in without stooping.

Set against one carved oak-paneled wall, with a wealth of luxurious antique leather bindings as a rich and colorful background, was the huge desk of Horace Cameron. He was seated there in an original Chippendale chair when Bob Tatum entered. Tatum made the long walk across the huge Persian rugs before he reached the desk.

"Good evening, sir."

"Tatum . . ." Cameron began.

Accustomed to being addressed more warmly, Bob Tatum knew that he was suddenly confronted by a crisis of consequence to his career.

"Tatum," Cameron resumed, "I like to think that I've always been fair with you."

"Yes, sir, more than fair."

"And Francine has always been generous with your wife."

"They get along very well. Marissa worships her. She considers her the perfect woman."

Cameron let that bit of flattery pass without comment. "Then I think I deserve a reasonable degree of honesty from you now."

"I've always been honest with you, sir," Bob Tatum said, suspecting that in his absence some corporate infighting had taken place in which he had been made the victim. "Anyone who says I've lied to you, is lying himself."

Ignoring Tatum's protestations for the moment, Cameron turned to the shelf behind him and drew down a volume.

"Tatum, a shocking accusation has been made against you. I hope it isn't true. I devoutly hope so."

"What is it, sir?"

"No charge has been formally made. But the suspicion is strong that your son has been the victim of abuse. By you."

"That's a lie!" Tatum exploded in a far greater show of emotion than he had ever before permitted himself in Cameron's presence. "She tried to get me to admit that once before. I told her it was a lie!"

"She?" Cameron asked quickly, anxious to validate his suspicion.

"Scofield. She put me through a long examination about my family. As if she were trying to build a case against me. She even hinted that I might have hurt the boy while playing with him, roughhousing with him. Never happened! And I told her so."

"Am I to understand you deny ever whipping that boy hard enough to injure him?" Cameron asked pointedly.

"I have never whipped that boy at all!" Tatum said flatly. "He's a fragile boy, has been since he was born. What kind of monster do you think I am?"

Cameron stared at Tatum for a moment before he raised the book. "I want you to put your hand on this Bible and swear that you have never abused that boy."

Without hesitation Tatum placed his left hand on the Bible which Cameron held. "I swear, sir, I have never laid a hand on that boy to punish him."

"Thank you, Bob."

Tatum was free to leave. Once the door closed, Cameron lifted his phone and ordered the InterElectronics operator to reach Dr. Braham, no matter where he was. In a few minutes his phone rang.

"Doctor?"

"Yes."

"Doctor, do you make house calls?"

Knowing Cameron had no grandchildren, Larry was puzzled for a moment. "Yes, Mr. Cameron, but there's no one at your house who'd have need of my specialty."

"*I* need you. It is urgent I speak with you. At once!"

"Mr. Cameron, with all due respect, these days pediatricians are busy enough with their patients . . ."

Cameron interrupted. "This affects one of your patients. I deem it mandatory as well as urgent that you meet me here."

"As soon as I've covered my other calls."

"Shall we say nine-thirty?" Cameron asked. He was most punctual and penurious with his own time.

Promptly at nine-thirty Dr. Lawrence Braham arrived at the Cameron mansion. He was shown to the library, where Cameron was studying reports from his own private intelligence sources as to conditions—financial, industrial and political—in all countries where InterElectronics maintained plants or offices.

"I don't blame you for looking so puzzled, Braham. But it's essential that I receive first-hand corroboration about a matter in which I'm vitally interested."

"If I can help . . . and if it's something I'm free to discuss."

"There are no ethical restrictions in this instance. The Tatum family will give you permission to speak quite freely. You've examined the boy?"

"Of course, many times."

"Tell me, Doctor, during the course of your examinations have you ever found on him any mark, bruise or sign that he had been beaten beyond what one would consider normal discipline for a child his age?"

That one question suddenly put the interview into focus for Larry Braham. He knew why he was here, and what must have preceded Cameron's call. He was also aware of the effect on Jean of his truthful answer. Still, he had to reply frankly.

"I've never detected any signs of abuse on the boy."

"Thank you!" Cameron said briskly, as if that closed the interview.

"However," Larry persisted, "the fact that I haven't found any signs of abuse does not invalidate Dr. Scofield's conclusions. She is a neurologist and a physician of enormous skill, instinct and intuition. And her dedication is beyond question."

Cameron smiled knowingly. "I'm quite aware of your relationship with Dr. Scofield."

"My professional opinion of her work has nothing to do with the way I feel about her personally!" Larry answered angrily.

"Dr. Braham, I know how great a conflict my question has imposed on you. There's no need to explain or to defend her. In your place, I'd do the same."

Cameron smiled in his superior way. "Braham, would you like the advice of an older, more experienced man? Instead of spending so much effort defending her, consider this. Could there be any connection between her unusual reaction to this little boy and her refusal to marry you? I'd think about that, if I were you."

Resenting his intrusion into their private relationship, Larry said, "If you have no further questions, I'd like to go."

Braham left. Cameron lifted the phone and put through a call to the Tatum house.

"Bob!" he ordered, "I want you to remove that boy

from Dr. Scofield's care. I would suggest that you turn him over to Sunderland. An excellant man. And the next Chief of the department."

He hung up. He reached for his dictating machine, which fed a line directly to his office where one of his private secretaries would type up his messages in the morning.

"Note," he began. "A letter must be circulated to all members of the Board of Trustees of the hospital. At our very next meeting we are to act swiftly to demand and secure the resignation from staff of Dr. Jean Scofield."

He felt quite satisfied now. By overreaching herself the woman had presented him with the opportunity to solve two vexing problems. She had removed herself from any consideration as Chief of Neurology. She had also destroyed the effect of her projected paper on the failure of the new Seaton Wards. He would make it sound logical that once terminated from the hospital staff, she had reacted like a disgruntled ex-employee by writing a baseless and spurious paper criticizing the new wards.

Now he had a perfectly logical case to present to the Board.

The next morning when Dr. Scofield arrived at her office she found a visitor waiting. Before Jean could even close the door, Marissa Tatum demanded fiercely, "What do you have against us?"

Without giving her a chance to answer, the beautiful young woman, obviously under enormous tension from a sleepless night, accused, "Since the first time you had any contact with Bobby, you've had this antagonism. Mainly, against me. The first day, when I tried to be with my son in the Emergency Room, you shut me out. You were angry then. You made no secret of it. Well, I don't intend to let you destroy my family or my husband's career. We've worked too long and sacrificed too much for the opportunity he has now. I refuse to have it jeopardized by anyone, least of all *you!*"

Completely taken aback by the ferocity of the attack, Jean said, "Mrs. Tatum, I've no wish to jeopordize your husband's career."

"Then why did you spread those vicious rumors about him?"

"Please understand, I spread no rumors. I named no names," Jean explained as gently as she could, hoping to pacify the obviously distraught woman.

"You didn't have to!" Marissa continued to accuse. "You only had to do what you did. And you did it, damn you, you did it!"

The wild look in the woman's eyes made Jean realize she was on the verge of an anxiety panic. Jean had dealt with too many patients and their relatives in that condition to attempt to argue or even to defend herself. Instead, she said, "If I've done anything to harm you or your husband, I'm terribly sorry. And if there's anything I can do to make amends, just calm down and tell me and I'll do whatever you ask."

Her apology accomplished its purpose. The anger in Marissa's eyes slowly seemed to drain away. Her lips began to quiver as a prelude to tears. Before she could start to weep, Jean resumed, coaxing gently.

"Tell me about it, please?"

Marissa Tatum did not respond at once.

"Would you care for a cigarette?" Jean suggested.

Marissa nodded, opened her purse, dug about frantically and finally came up with her pack. When she could not find her lighter, Jean supplied a match from her desk drawer. She could see that Marissa's hands were trembling, so she struck the match for her. As the woman leaned close to take the light, Jean had a chance to study her eyes more closely. There was no doubt, the seeds

of panic were there. Short of forced sedation, there was
only one way to abort it. Get her to talk, freely, until
it was all drained out of her. Once Marissa had taken
several long deep draws on her cigarette, Jean commenced to accomplish that.

"Tell me. Everything. I want to know. It's important
—for Bobby's sake, and for yours.

Now, when she resumed talking, Marissa Tatum was
less bitter and accusatory, but seemed to be seeking understanding.

"Do you know what Mr. Cameron made Bob do?
Made him take on oath on a Bible that he didn't abuse
Bobby. Do you realize what that meant?"

Before Jean could answer, Marissa continued, "Give
Cameron reason to trust you, he'll trust you all the way.
But give him the slightest reason to doubt you, and he'll
never really trust you again. He does not promote or
advance men he doesn't trust."

The young woman turned away from Jean and began
to talk in a voice strange and a bit distant as well. Jean
sensed she was reaching to another time, to another life.

"It isn't only Bob's career, Bob's life. It's mine, too.
I've sacrificed and fought right along with him for us to
get to where we are. I don't intend to give all that up
now."

She took a deep drag on her cigarette and continued.
"Because it hasn't been easy. Don't let surface impressions mislead you. I know what you see now. A young,
very well groomed woman. Because I am. I know it.
Part of it I was born with. The rest is what I made of
myself. How can a girl will herself to be beautiful? If
you have to, you just do. And I had to. Had to," she
repeated in a strange mixture of determination and long-
ing that made Jean sympathize with her and seek to
understand her better.

"I had this example before me. Of what can happen to

a woman. My mother was once just as beautiful as I, even more. I have pictures of her.

"And I have pictures of her later. After." Marissa Tatum's voice changed as she recalled the change in her mother's life.

"After she had become pregnant. For some reason my father couldn't face that. So the week I was born, he left. Disappeared. I wondered all my life, did he see me and was he disappointed? Is that what made him desert us? Or did he want a son so much that he could never love a daughter? Or didn't he want a child at all? One day you're sure it's one thing, another day you're sure it's another. In the end you're sure of nothing except the facts of what happened. I was born. He deserted us. The connection is clear.

"The connection isn't the only thing that becomes clear. From my earliest days I remember my mother's working in her little store all day and living in the back at night. She'd been left penniless. No one to fall back on. Of course, she could have become a secretary again. But who'd take care of me? An uncle who was fond of her lent her enough money to open a small dress shop in the neighborhood. I remember her being busy in front in the store all day. At night she would talk me to sleep while she did alterations. There wasn't enough business then to justify her hiring an alteration lady.

"So she did it all. Sold the dresses. Raised the hems. Let out the seams. I would lie there and wonder, when is she going to put aside that damned dress and hug me, kiss me? There was never enough time, never enough."

Marissa Tatum turned to face Jean Scofield. Jean could see the panic had dissipated, replaced by a plea for understanding.

"I was very young, but I wasn't blind to what was happening to her. I would look at her wedding photos. Then I'd steal looks at her. You could see how the beauty had drained out of her. Her face, so much like mine, the high cheekbones, the slightly hollowed cheeks, the nose, all those features gradually grew sharper, more exaggerated, until she became a tense, ugly caricature of herself. Bitter, old before her time. She became a shrewd businesswoman. And a very determined mother. Bent on making sure her daughter wouldn't repeat her mistakes."

Jean detected almost the same kind of pride in her mother that Bob Tatum felt for his father.

"From the beginning she trained me. She taught me how to dress, how to walk, how to carry myself. By the time I was fourteen I was modeling clothes in her shop. When I was fifteen she changed my name from Mary to Marissa. It sounded more exotic. She had special photographs made of me and took them downtown to the big department store, Kirkenthal's. She got me a part-time job as a model in the expensive dress department. Then they began to use me in ads. In time I became a model who appeared in some of the best national magazines. You may have seen me."

Jean nodded, to keep her talking freely.

"But Mother kept impressing on me that that was no end in itself. It was only a beginning. The thing for me to do was find a man, a man who had ambition. But, above all, a sense of responsibility. A man with a future. She used to say, 'It's as easy to fall in love with a good man as a bad one. Don't waste yourself, Marissa,' she'd say. 'Don't waste yourself.' I remember her eyes, so fixed and determined. What had happened to her was never going to happen to her little girl.

"She'd gone through her whole life feeling that the one man she loved never did love her. But it was me he never loved. When I was born he couldn't share her with me. Well, I determined that it was never going to happen to me.

"When I married Bob, I deliberately decided that his life would become my life. His career would become my career. So that when we had children he'd have no reason to be jealous of them.

"In those days I used to think it would be children. A boy, then a girl, then possibly another boy." She smiled faintly, self-conscious about her own youthful naiveté. "An ideal magazine-type family. Besides, Bob wanted sons. At least more than one," she admitted regretfully.

"What did he say when he discovered there wouldn't be 'sons'?" Jean asked, curious as well as sympathetic.

"He's more sensitive than you'd think for a man so physical. He'd never say anything to hurt me. But I could feel it. He was enormously disappointed when the doctor told him."

"Disappointed enough so that he might run off and leave you?" Jean suggested as gently as she could.

Marissa didn't answer. She turned away from Jean. All the doctor could see was her lovely profile, which was now very determined, her head uptilted and proud.

"Bob would never leave me," she said with great conviction. Jean believed her until she added, "Never!" which was overdetermined and evidence of her fear.

"Has he ever said anything because you haven't given him another fullback?"

"No, Marissa Tatum said. "And he does love Bobby. No matter what you may think."

"I've never said he doesn't love the boy." Jean tried to reassure her.

"You said Bob abused him."

"I presented an anonymous case and asked for the opinions of my colleagues. I made no accusations."

"Unfortunately, Mr. Cameron thinks you did!" With the mention of that name, the hostility returned to her voice. She rose to stare at Jean in angry determination.

Jean was now less concerned with her anger than with the opportunity she presented. She was intent on pursuing it.

"Mrs. Tatum, once you decided, but before you actually became pregnant, did it ever worry you that Bob might react to a child in the same way as your father?"

"Never! We talked it over. We both wanted it. We did it quite deliberately."

"And you never once entertained the fear that he might leave you?" Jean persisted.

"He loves me," the young woman said proudly. "I've made sure of that."

"Just how does a woman make 'sure' of something like that?"

"I told you. I've made his life my life."

"When you went into labor prematurely, and had reason to fear it might go wrong, that you might not give Bob the son he wanted, did you have any doubts then?"

"Doubts? About Bob? No!"

"You were raised to be a very determined young woman. You set high goals. You make demands on yourself. Stringent demands. I wonder what happens when you fail?" Jean asked, studying the young woman's face intently.

"But I haven't failed. Bob and I have come far. Together. Very far. And we're going all the way. All the way. That's what I came here to tell you, Doctor. Don't do anything to hurt Bob's career. Or I'll see that you pay for it."

Rather than becoming intimidated, Jean asked, "What if it were Bobby who 'interfered'? If Bobby hurt his father's career?"

"How could a little boy interfere with his father's career?" Marissa scoffed.

"Be born before he was expected. Be a source of worry. Have to spend weeks in an incubator. Be a disappointment to his father. Infants can prove a very serious disruption in the lives and careers of parents."

"Let me put your mind at ease about *that,* Doctor," Marissa Tatum reponded sharply. "And also about the other thought that is obviously lurking behind your insinuations."

"Lurking?" Jean asked, curious to see if Marissa had made the same significant connection.

"Mr. Cameron was extremely solicitous. He paid all the expenses for Bobby's being in Pediatric Intensive Care. Which you know can be an exorbitant amount. He also made sure that Bob was home every weekend. To be with me, so I wouldn't become depressed or morose. If anything, that experience brought us closer to the Camerons. So Bobby was no 'distraction,' I can assure you."

Marissa Tatum's eyes became fiercely protective as she concluded, "Our relationship with the Camerons has been excellent. Until *you* decided to destroy it. With your vicious rumors. I warn you, don't try it again!"

With that, she turned and strode out. Despite the animus the woman displayed, Jean Scofield felt compelled to admire the way she carried herself, proud and erect, the perfect carriage for a beautiful woman who still retained all her youthful glamour.

The slam of the door put an end to those thoughts. Dr. Scofield had more urgent business. Whatever Marissa Tatum had come here to say, she had revealed infinitely more than she had intended. Jean Scofield began to dictate every detail she remembered from the informative interview.

twenty-two

A copy of Horace Cameron's confidential memorandum to the Board concerning the dismissal of Dr. Jean Scofield had reached Amos Farr, a trustee as well as counsel to University Hospital. He phoned the chairman immediately.

"Horace, you have to withdraw that memo! Recall every copy!"

"Give me one good reason!" Cameron shot back irately, a man who never liked to be told what to do, even by experienced attorneys.

"Tenure!" Farr said, as if one word covered the entire situation.

"What about tenure?"

"Dr. Scofield has tenure. She can't be fired peremptorily. We'd have to prove some act of outrageous conduct on her part."

"I understand she's sleeping with that doctor, Braham."

"Horace, if you fired every doctor who's sleeping with another doctor or a nurse, we wouldn't have any staff at all. That is not the kind of conduct that justifies removing a tenured professor."

"Then what is?" Cameron demanded. "Name it. I've got lots of grounds."

"Such as?"

"There's a paper she's writing about our Seaton Wards. Claims we have a worse cure rate in our new wards than in the old ones. Isn't that ridiculous?"

247

"Only if she hasn't got proof," Farr cautioned, for he could tell that Cameron, usually a cold, unemotional man, had become personally involved in the matter and was likely to make a serious mistake as a result. "Anything else?"

Cameron would have preferred to avoid the subject, but it was his trump card. "She's made an outrageous accusation against one of my young men. She accuses him of child abuse. Can you imagine that? Why, she can be sued for that, can't she? Damn it, maybe that's the way to get rid of her."

"I wouldn't advise it. That could create more scandal than it would resolve. Besides, there's the law."

"What law?"

"In this state, and in many others, a doctor can't be sued for reporting anyone for child abuse, provided the report is made in good faith."

"Good faith, eh?" Cameron considered. "How the hell do you determine something like that?"

"Do other doctors agree with her?"

"No," Cameron said, "not even the one she's sleeping with."

"That's a point. Messy. But a point," Farr considered.

Then Cameron recalled, "Of course, Benziger did agree with her in Grand Rounds."

"Benziger?" Farr reacted at once. "It would be tough to prove lack of good faith if a doctor of Benziger's standing agreed with her."

"Damn it, Amos! I don't want a long legal lecture. I just want that woman out of my hospital."

There was a brief and noteworthy silence during which Farr restrained himself from reminding Cameron that it was not his personal hospital, though he acted that way most times. Cameron realized it, too, for he continued in a tone somewhat chastened and much milder. "Amos, how do you suggest we go about this?"

"We can't simply remove her. None of the accusations you made would be good enough grounds. Besides, she might refuse to leave."

"Knowing her, I'm sure she'd refuse. For a woman who looks so soft and feminine, she's tough as nails."

"That could leave us with a lawsuit as our only hope of forcing her to leave," Farr advised. "Or worse."

"Worse?" Cameron asked.

"If we terminated her, *she* could sue *us*," Farr explained. "And stand a damned good chance of collecting. No, this has to be done very, very carefully."

"Okay. How?"

"Let me think about it. Meantime, retrieve those memos. Every copy!"

Having recovered from the immediate effects of surgery, Beatrice Fazio was removed from Intensive Care and returned to her room in Neurological. Her head was turbaned in bandages and would remain that way for some days. Though Bobby Tatum had inquired about her often, he was told that he would not be allowed to go into her room and play just yet. Always he was put off with promises that soon it would be all right.

Today it was finally all right. When the moment came to enter her room, he turned reluctant suddenly, frightened at having to face anyone who had had that mysterious thing called an operation. He stood in the doorway a long time, staring at her head, wrapped in white bandages. She was unaware of him until he finally came to the foot of her bed and asked, "Does it hurt?"

"No way," she said, as she had heard her older brothers say.

"It didn't hurt, never?" he asked, to make absolutely sure.

"Uh uh," she reiterated weakly.

Encouraged, he moved closer to her side. He stared at the Raggedy Ann in her arms.

"Where did you go?" he asked.

"I didn't go nowhere."

"Couple of days you were gone."

"Oh," she remembered now. "I was in Tensive Care."

"Tensive Care?" Bobby asked. "What's it like?"

"You sleep mostly. There's lots of nurses. And they have all kinds of funny TV."

"TV?" His eyes brightened. "My Mom and Dad don't let me watch TV too much. But Esther does. She's always saying, 'Go watch TV.' Cartoons. You like cartoons?"

"Uh huh."

"Me too," he agreed. "They have good cartoons in Tensive Care?"

"No," she said sadly. "Just little balls bouncing up and down and across."

"That's all?"

"Uh huh," she said, drifting off to sleep under the effects of the regular sedation which she had been given to keep her quiet during the early stages of her recovery.

"You all better now?" he asked. She didn't answer. So he asked again, "You all better?"

She lay still, eyes closed. He drew closer, his eyes just level with the height of her bed. He stared at the white bandages that completely enshrouded her head. It was not only strange but a bit terrifying. It was necessary for him to know positively.

"You all better?" he asked, in an even louder voice.

She stirred, came awake and made a sound which was a drowsy question.

"You all better?" he asked precisely because he needed a precise answer.

"Uh huh," she said.

"You going home soon?"

"Uh huh," she said, still drowsy and ready to drift off.

"When?"

"I don't know."

"Didn't your Mom tell you when?"

"Soon."

"When is soon?"

"I don't know."

"My Dad always tells me how many days. Like when he's going away and coming back, he tells me how many days so I can count them on my fingers. Like this time, he's coming back on the thumb. Doesn't your Dad tell you that?" Bobby asked.

"Only soon," the girl said, drifting off again. This time he could not wake her. After a while he gently freed the doll from her grasp, embraced it and took it with him to his own room.

When his mother came to visit and discovered the doll, she made him return it. They went to Beatrice's room together. Mrs. Fazio was there. Marissa Tatum could tell from her first sight of the anguished mother's eyes how grave the situation was. They exchanged introductions and tried to talk pleasantly. But though their children got on well together, the two women could find little to say to each other.

The children played airplane and pilot again, Bobby making all the required noises. When Marissa Tatum saw how difficult it was for Mrs. Fazio, she reminded Bobby that it was time to go back to his own room and that he could come play with Beatrice again tomorrow.

Mrs. Fazio was visibly relieved to see them depart. She turned her forced smile on Beatrice and encouraged her to go to sleep again, reassuring her in gentle whispers that she would be well again. When the child was asleep, Mrs. Fazio permitted herself the luxury of weeping freely.

By the time her husband arrived for his end-of-day visit, she had recovered sufficiently so that with the aid of some powder and a touch of rouge, she seemed presentable. Though she could not disguise the redness of her eyes, Fazio pretended not to notice. He stood at his daughter's bedside, waiting for her to wake so he could tell her more comforting lies.

In a whisper, he said to his wife, "We got to bring the boys soon."

She did not respond.

"They got to see her. At least once," Fazio said. Now that he had adjusted to the inevitability of things he had become the stronger of the two.

Mrs. Fazio finally nodded.

"And we got to ask."

"What?"

"About a priest."

"No!" she protested instinctively, for it was the final acceptance of what she could not accept.

"Paula, we must!"

She acquiesced with a series of tiny nods, turned away to hide her face in her handkerchief.

"Paula, no matter what, I don't blame you. All the papers, it's the same as if I signed them myself. I don't blame you."

He moved to his wife and placed his huge hands on her fleshy shoulders to reassure her. She leaned against him, needing his closeness.

After considerable thought on the matter of Dr. Jean Scofield, Amos Farr called back.

"Horace, I think I have it."

"Shoot!"

"We do not remove Dr. Scofield. Or even attempt to remove her. We don't go into the matter of child abuse or anything that can create legal repercussions for the hospital. We can, and we do, deprive her of the right to admit patients to the hospital. That will just about kill off her practice and force her to quit."

"Good!" Cameron agreed.

"It might also raise enough questions about her professional fitness to make her want to quietly slip away and seek a position in some other city."

"Exellent!" Cameron exulted. "How do I go about it?"

"Canvass several of the trustees individually. By phone. I don't want any written evidence floating around. Explain that the situation is quite delicate and get their private agreement. But don't make it an official Board matter."

"Why not?"

"An official action always opens the way for legal appeals and reviews. Do it my way," Farr advised.

By the end of the day Cameron had recaptured every copy of his memo and had spoken to more than half the trustees. With their approval, he ordered Edward Carey to carry out the plan in the manner and at the time Cameron had ordained. Carey was most eager to cooperate.

Dr. Jean Scofield was making her usual morning rounds between early classes at the Medical School. She came down the corridor of the Neurological wing, stopping briefly at each room where she had a patient. She had found nothing unexpected. The man slated for neurosurgery this afternoon seemed a bit apprehensive and it was reflected in his elevated pulse rate. She reassured him and went on to the private room three doors down where Bobby Tatum had been installed at Horace Cameron's insistence.

Cameron's imperious attitude always reminded Jean of the hospital anecdote about the rich mother who, on hearing that her son had been given artificial respiration, indignantly demanded, "Artificial respiration? Give him the real thing! We can afford it!"

It would have been much better for the Tatum boy to be in a room with other children. He was a youngster who cried out for company, for warmth, especially for children who, themselves ill, might have compassion instead of scorn for his condition.

Pretending to appear more cheerful than she felt after having been up half the night working on her paper about the Seaton Wards, Jean opened the door, smiling and calling out, "Good morning, Bobby!" But she discovered Marissa Tatum standing protectively at the foot of Bobby's bed. Bending over the boy was Dr. Ralph Sunderland.

Sunderland appeared self-conscious at being discovered examining the boy without first having checked with the original doctor on the case. Marissa Tatum was more aggressive.

"Dr. Scofield, I have to inform you that you've been replaced on this case."

"Replaced? Who made that decision?"

"My husband and I. And for obvious reasons. So there's really nothing further for you to do here."

Even Sunderland was embarrassed at the rude manner in which Mrs. Tatum handled the moment. He turned to Jean. "The family thought another opinion . . . a different approach to the case . . ."

"The *family* thought . . ." Jean echoed, making no secret of her suspicion that Cameron was the prime mover in the affair, Sunderland being his candidate for Chief. Then, "Of course," she agreed, so as not to alarm Bobby, who was already tense and beckoning to her through his frightened blue eyes. "I'm sure it will all be for the best."

"I'm sure it will," Marissa Tatum said with precise finality.

Jean withdrew, closing the door softly. She finished her rounds, went directly to her office intending to call Larry Braham. But she found him waiting. He could read her face at once.

"I guess you know," he said.

"I shouldn't have had to find out that way."

"It was done over my objection," Larry tried to explain. "But they insisted."

"*They* insisted?"

Larry shrugged; her suspicions were his suspicions too. "Nothing was said, but Bob and Riss were both so agitated that I'm sure it was Cameron's idea."

"Did they remove you from the case, too?"

"Not yet. But it wouldn't surprise me. Not after that meeting I had with Cameron."

"Do whatever you can to stay on. I don't want Bobby totally in the control of doctors who are more bent on pleasing Cameron than saving the boy."

"Sunderland is a good neurologist."

"Sunderland is also a very ambitious neurologist," Jean countered. "Ambition has a way of warping a doctor's judgment."

"He wouldn't deliberately do anything to harm a patient."

"How do you know, or how does even Sunderland know, when his judgment is being influenced by what Cameron wants to hear?" Jean demanded. "Larry, I'm extremely worried about that boy!"

"We all are."

"No one else wants to admit the serious possibilities,"

Jean explained. "I was about to demand the right to do an angiogram."

"The Tatums would have refused."

"That wouldn't have relieved me of the obligation of demanding it," Jean said angrily. Then she accepted the inevitability of the situation. "Keep me advised of how Bobby progresses?"

"Of course."

"Drop in and see him. Often. He seems so alone."

Because he knew how much her own loneliness afflicted her at times, he moved to take her in his arms, but they were interrupted. Old Benziger opened the door, a single sheet of paper in his hand, on his face a grim look that made him seem even older than his years.

"Oh," he made a single syllable apology for having intruded on the two of them.

"Come in," Jean invited, wondering what tragedy had afflicted the old man that he seemed so grieved. "Benni?"

He handed her the paper. She glanced at it, then passed it on to Larry. He took one look, then, outraged, demanded, "Take away her admitting privileges? But why?"

The distressed old man dropped into a chair before he explained, "Grand Rounds. The Tatum boy. Cameron considers that an act of revenge. Because he opposed Jean as Chief, she tried to even the score by slandering one of his proteges. His mind works that way, so he thinks everyone's does."

"I presented the case to invite other opinions," Jean defended.

"It was an unfortunate mistake, my dear," Benziger said. "But this . . . this . . ." he said, referring to the letter. "I never expected it would go this far."

Suddenly the old man said, "And I hear Sunderland is on the case now."

"Yes, yes he is," Jean said, taking the letter to study it carefully.

. . . for numerous reasons—including personality difficulties which have caused her to attempt to damage innocent persons and thus place this hospital in legal and financial jeopardy, it is our considered opinion that Dr. Scofield should be deprived of any future admitting privileges at this hospital.

"The old bastard's got you boxed in," Larry said.

"There *is* one choice," Jean said thoughtfully.

"What, my dear?" Benziger asked.

"Demand what they've refused to give me."

"Which is?"

"A hearing before the Board. Let them decide in full session, officially, that my professional conduct justifies this!"

"Don't do anything impulsive," Larry warned. "If you exercised the same care about your own life that you do when a patient is involved . . ." Larry didn't complete the thought. It would only divert them from this crucial professional emergency to their own personal relationship.

Benziger covered the awkward moment by pointing out, "My dear, if you ask for a hearing there will be much gossip, and eventually much publicity. It can only make your situation more widely known and your motives more open to question."

"I am going to insist on a full hearing before the entire Board of Trustees," she persisted.

"Larry . . ." Benziger pleaded for him to intervene.

"When she speaks in that tone of voice, it's futile, Benni. No one can talk her out of it."

"I wish someone could," the old man said regretfully. Then he became more practical. "We shall have to organize some sort of defense."

"Defense?" Jean challenged. "I intend to attack!"

"My dear, when you ask for such a hearing, first the other side will have to present its reasons. Then you will have to defend against them. Believe me, we should organize a defense for you. And find someone to present your case to the Board."

"I suppose I wouldn't be the best choice, would I?" Larry asked.

Jean smiled wryly. "You might be considered just a little prejudiced."

"We'll find someone . . . someone . . ." Benziger said. "It's not out of the question to be represented by counsel in such a matter. After all, your professional reputation is at stake. Yes, perhaps an attorney would be the wisest choice."

"If I have to be defended, I'll do it myself," Jean said firmly.

"I forbid it!" Larry exploded. "You know what attorneys always say, 'A lawyer who defends himself has a fool for a client.' How much worse it would be for you, as emotional as you are about this case."

Jean turned on him. "Just how emotional *am* I? Yes, I lost a child. Does that mean that I'm to be barred forever from having sound medical opinions about other children? Why not bar me from having opinions about all male patients because I lost a husband as well? No, I refuse to have my conclusions challenged on the ground that I'm too 'involved' or too 'emotional.' Maybe my observations and conclusions are sounder *because* I'm involved!"

There was a moment of painful silence. Jean was

sorry she had exploded at Larry. Benziger was embarrassed and pained by the fact that hospital politics were not only menacing his protege's professional life, but her private life as well. He terminated the meeting by saying, "You will be receiving your own copy of this notice soon enough. I'd like to keep this one."

He folded the paper and stuffed it into the pocket of his lab coat as if it were an unwelcome pathology report which spelled the doom of one of his friends.

"Don't do anything rash, my dear. And consider what I said about being represented by counsel," he urged.

For the past two days, Bobby Tatum had not been allowed to enter Beatrice Fazio's room. Though he asked many times, he was put off by the nurses and by his mother with many excuses, none of which he quite accepted. He was permitted to take walks down the hall, alone or accompanied by his mother. And he could see that Beatrice Fazio's door was closed all the time. Those who went into the room and came out did so in utmost quiet, not letting the door slip closed but holding it till it did. One time he saw two boys, older than himself, go into the room. Their faces were very grave and they were frightened, so frightened that he sensed they really did not want to go in at all.

Once he saw a man dressed in black and not wearing any tie around his white collar. He carried a long purple cloth and a small black book. Bobby stopped to stare. His mother urged him along, saying, "Come, darling, let's go out to the solarium. It's nice and sunny."

He went, but not without looking back at the closed door.

The next morning when his mother came to visit and take him to the solarium, he started out. But in the doorway he stopped.

"Bobby?" his mother asked, puzzled.

She glanced into the corridor. The door of the Fazio girl's room was open and a stretcher was being wheeled out. On it, completely covered in a white sheet, was an object the size of a small girl. Bobby stared as the orderly wheeled the stretcher down the hall toward the elevators. He reached for his mother's hand and clutched it.

"Mommy, why is she all covered up?"

"She . . . she's going away."

"Away? Why? Is she all better now?"

Marissa Tatum hesitated, wondering if a lie were permissible in such circumstances. But remembering what she had read in the child-rearing books, she decided to deal with it as best she could.

"She died, Bobby."

"Like Grandma Tatum?"

"Yes, Bobby, like Grandma Tatum."

"You said only old people die."

"Sometimes . . . not often . . . little children die. But only sometimes."

"Will I die too?"

"Oh, no!" she said quickly.

He remained thoughtful for a time, then he asked, "Did she take her Raggedy Ann with her?"

"I think so, Bobby."

"Oh," he said, disappointed, since he would have liked to have her doll.

They went out to the solarium but he showed no interest in playing games or watching the television set which droned on endlessly. He wanted to go back to his room. When they passed the Fazio room the door was open. He dared to look in. A nurse was stripping the bed. He reached for his mother's hand and led her back to his room. He made her sit in the armchair. He crawled up and lay in her lap. His arm around her, he pressed his head against her breast.

In a while he asked, "Where's Dr. Jean?"

"You have a different doctor now, Bobby. Dr. Sunderland. Dr. Ralph."

"I like Dr. Jean," he said, but didn't pursue it any further, as if afraid to pursue a subject his mother found disagreeable.

twenty-three

Larry called in late afternoon. "I have to see you. Now!" he insisted.

"I'm busy."

"Then dinner."

"I'm working on my paper tonight. I've got to get it finished. I've already submitted an outline to several journals."

"That's part of what I want to see you about. I've been thinking about it since Benni showed us that letter. You've got to drop writing that paper."

"I won't drop it!"

"Then postpone it."

"Larry!" The single word expressed not only her anger at his intrusion into her professional life, but her disappointment at his desire to have her bow to the pressures being exerted on her.

"Sorry, darling," he said, "but I'm thinking of *us*. If that hearing goes against you, and Cameron has his way, you'll leave here."

"I'd have no choice."

"I don't mean just the hospital, I mean this city. Who knows where your next offer would come from? New York. La Jolla. Houston. I can't let you go. I won't!"

"Larry . . ." she tried to interrupt.

"I will not let you go!"

"I know how you feel. And how I feel. But I won't submit to professional blackmail. They can remove that boy from my care. That doesn't free me from caring. And the same goes for my paper. It's something I have to do!"

It was past two o'clock in the morning. Despite her most determined resolutions, she had had dinner with Larry. When he had insisted on taking her home, she had relented. When he had held her in his arms and made love to her, she had known it was what she had wanted all during the long and difficult day.

Once he drifted off to sleep, as she watched his handsome face in repose, she became aware, painfully aware, of what he had been urging earlier. If she lost her hearing, she *would* have to leave. She would have to accept another offer that might take Larry out of her life. And for her there would never be another man. Other men might be willing and anxious for her. But she couldn't open her emotions and her life to another man, couldn't love as she had loved before and then lose once more. She would forgo all love rather than risk losing one more time. Nor could she ask Larry to jeopardize his career for hers.

She kissed him tenderly on the cheek before she slipped out of bed and went into the living room to resume working on her paper. She was determined to finish it before she became embroiled in the bitter and emotionally consuming confrontation of that Trustees' hearing. Cameron would probably prevail. He always did. But she was determined not to make it easy for him.

She wrote and rewrote for almost three hours. The light was just seeping in under the living room draperies when she fell asleep, while curled up on the couch rereading the draft of her paper.

Larry found her that way. He lifted her tenderly and carried her back to bed. He covered her well and went out to the kitchen to fix the coffee. While he was waiting for it to perk, he picked up her draft. "Social Conditions and Cure Rates."

Curious, he intended only to glance through it. After the first page he went back, started from the top and read with great care. By the time he was half through he became aware of the aroma of coffee perking. He took the script into the kitchen and finished it over several cups of coffee.

He leaned back from the table and let the realization settle in on him. No matter what he had said before, he knew he had no right to dissuade her from publishing this paper. It was a solid piece of work. The facts were here. Her conclusions were sound. Detractors might accuse her of politicizing medicine, but they could not disagree with her observations. No doubt it would enrage Cameron. But the only relationship between Cameron's reaction and this paper was that the enormity of his rage might be the best proof of the validity of Jean's conclusions.

What depressed him, of course, was the realization that with this paper went any chance that she might be allowed to stay on. This morning when he arrived at his office he might well begin making discreet inquiries. Perhaps there was an opening for an excellent academic neurologist in a good university hospital somewhere close, at least closer than Houston or the West Coast.

Jean Scofield carried out her duties of the day with an unaccustomed grimness that made the other doctors and nurses remark on it behind her back. By late morning everyone learned why she was so unsmiling and determined. Gossip about an impending hearing had made its insidious way around the floor.

She was in her office, dictating her orders and observations on the ward cases she had seen earlier. Her door was gently eased open. Without looking up from her file, she interrupted dictating only long enough to say, "Five minutes, Maggie, till I'm finished with this case."

Instead of the usual and efficient, "Yes, Doctor," Jean heard no voice, no sound. She put aside the file and her hand microphone and turned to the open door. Instead of the secretary she expected to find, there stood a small five-year-old boy, dressed in his navy blue robe, the sash so unevenly tied that she knew he had done it by himself.

"Bobby?"

"Dr. Jean . . . " the boy said. "Can I . . . can I come in?"

"Bobby, Dr. Sunderland is your doctor now. You know that, don't you?"

"Yes, ma'am."

"Are you sure you want to come in?"

"Yes, ma'am," the boy said, still not daring to move toward her.

Jean hesitated, then acceded. "All right, Bobby."

Timidly he started toward her, shuffling in his slippers. At her desk he stood silent for a moment. Cautiously, he reached for her hand and placed it against his cheek. She had to resist embracing him. The source of her need was obvious. The source of his troubled her.

"Do you have any toys?" he asked, hoping she would bring out those that had intrigued him so in their play session.

It would do no good to encourage him. He would have to accept the fact that she was no longer his doctor.

"No, Bobby, no more toys," Jean said gently. "Does anyone know you're here? Did you get permission to leave your room?" The boy did not answer at once. "Did you?" she persisted.

"You won't send me back?" the boy pleaded.

"I won't send you back Bobby. I'll take you back." She reached for his hand to lead him out of the room.

"The zebra . . . can't I even have my zebra?" ..

There was no harm in giving him the cherished little animal. She reached into the lower desk drawer where she had stored the toys, thinking to use them again with some other child in another play session. She brought out zebra, puzzle and story book. She pushed the animal forward so that he could reach it. He held it off to admire it, then hugged it close to his chest in a tight, affectionate embrace.

"Now, Bobby," she said, holding out her hand so she could take him back to his room. She was determined to be firm about it. But the look in his eyes made her reconsider. Instead of taking his hand, she went to the door and closed it. She half turned away, then turned back and locked the door securely and returned to her desk.

"Bobby, wouldn't you like to sit down?"

Delighted, the boy snuggled his way into the armchair, still clutching his precious toy.

"Would you like to play a new game today, Bobby? A wonderful new game?" Jean began. "Instead of putting pieces together in a puzzle, we're going to make believe."

"I make believe. Me and Esther, we do sometimes.'

"Good," Jean encouraged. "We're going to make believe you're home. In your own bed. And I'm reading you to sleep."

"But it isn't dark."

"We can make it dark," Jean said, rising to draw the draperies. "Better?"

"Uh huh," the boy said, eager for the new game.

"Now close your eyes. Make believe it's night and I'm reading you to sleep."

With her pocket flashlight focused on the first page Jean began to read from the story book she had bought. He was obviously familiar with it, for she could see him smile as he kept his eyes tightly clenched to play along with her. Eventually she departed from the text and began inserting language of her own.

"It's night time, Bobby. Time for you to go to sleep. The better you play the game, the more asleep you are. Play that you're going into a deep sleep. Let's see if you can fall asleep faster than I can. You should be asleep now, Bobby. Deep asleep. With your eyes closed tight. Very tight."

She stared across at the boy, trying to determine if his breathing rhythm had changed. In the darkened room he was a mere shadow. Only the little striped animal stood out in contrast to his navy blue robe. He seemed perfectly still until his tiny hand relaxed its grip on the toy. He might be under. To make sure she turned the small flashlight on his face. His eyes were closed, but no longer clenched. It was a good sign.

She spoke more softly now, still urging sleep. Meantime, she reached across, lifted his free hand. It was limp and unresisting. Carefully she removed the little zebra from his grasp. He surrendered it without resistance. She knew he was under.

She began by asking simple questions about his days in school, his days at home, his friends in the neighborhood. It was a necessary prelude to her eventual purpose. When she had accustomed him to that, she suggested, "Now, Bobby, we are going to play birthdays."

"Birthdays?" the sleeping boy asked vaguely.

"Do you have a birthday when you are five?"

"Uh huh," the boy replied.

"Do you have a party? A big party?"

"Uh huh."

"Who's there at your party, Bobby? Who's there right now?"

The boy's face lit up as he said, "Gwen. And Tony. Angela. Judy."

"Is that all, Bobby?"

"Granma Pearson."

"Is she Mommy's Mommy?"

"Uh huh," the sleeping boy responded.

"No grandpas?" Jean asked.

"I got no granpas."

"Is it a nice party, Bobby?"

"Cake. Big chocolate cake. With white writing on it. 'Happy Birthday, Bobby.' Good cake. Lots of icing." The boy smiled, his eyes remained closed.

"Now, Bobby, it's your four-year-old birthday party. Isn't that a nice party?"

"Uh huh," he agreed, the evidence of his enjoyment on his small smiling face.

"And who's there, Bobby?"

"Mommy. Daddy. Tony. Angela. Judy."

"Not Gwen?"

"She's sick in bed."

"And Grandma Pearson?"

"No . . ." the boy said, seeming a bit dubious.

"And is it a nice party?"

"Uh huh. White cake, with chocolate writing on. And ice cream. Twice," he said reliving the enjoyment of that indulgence.

"And now you're three, Bobby. And do you have a birthday party when you're three?" When he hesitated, she urged, "You remember that you're three, don't you, Bobby?"

"Uh, huh," the boy agreed. "Three years old." His speech began to take on the characteristics it had possessed at that age.

"It's your three-year-old birthday party, Bobby. Who's there?"

"Mommy. And Daddy."

"Grandma Pearson?"

"No."

"And your friends?"

"Don't have no friends."

"No friends at all, Bobby?"

"No . . ."

"Why?"

"We move to San . . . San Diego." As a three-year-old he had had trouble with the name.

But he had mentioned San Diego, one of the critical openings Jean was searching for.

"Bobby, it's just before you move to San Diego. You remember, Bobby. You live in a place called Dayton. Dayton. Remember?"

"Yes, ma'am."

"You are almost three years old, Bobby. It's the day you and Mommy and Daddy are all getting ready to move to San Diego. What happens, Bobby? Who comes to the house? What do they do?"

"Men come. Mommy wakes me up early." His voice and diction were now that of a younger child.

"What does Mommy say when she wakes you up?"

" 'Time to get up, darling. Men coming to take your bed. And your toys. And your play table. We're moving to San Diego today.' "

"And now the moving men are coming, Bobby. What are they doing?"

"Taking down. Everything down. Boxes. Big boxes."

"And what are you doing, Bobby?"

"Playing."

"Where?"

"On the floor."

"In your room?"

"The big room. Downstairs."

"What room, Bobby? What does Mommy call that room?"

"Living room."

"Are you playing there all the time the men are taking everything down?" Jean asked, curiously awaiting the boy's reply.

"No . . ."

"What do you do, Bobby?"

"Go up the stairs."

"And what happens?"

Suddenly he called, in imitation of his mother's angry voice and tone, " 'Bobby, you stay away from those stairs! How many times do I have to tell you? Do you hear me? Go back into the living room and play. Stay out of the way. Unless you want to be punished.' "

"Do you go back?"

"Yes, ma'am." Then the boy confessed, "Till . . ."

"Till what, Bobby?"

"I want my teddy bear."

"Now what do you do, Bobby?"

"I . . . " The boy paused, for now he was feeling the same guilt he had felt then. "I . . . I go back."

"Back up the stairs?"

"Yes."

"And?" The boy did not respond. "What happens, Bobby?"

"I go up . . . one at a time . . . " He held out his hand as if grasping the stair rail. "One . . . two . . . three . . . four . . . " he counted up to nine and then stopped.

"What happens at step nine, Bobby?"

"The man . . . "

"Man?"

"Mover man."

"What does the mover man do?"

"Carrying this big thing down."

"And then, Bobby?" Jean asked, reconciled to hearing the same explanation the Tatums had given her.

But the boy let out a scream, just as he had when he had hurtled down those stairs. He began to cry, the same crying that must have occurred on that day of the accident. Jean was not diverted.

"Why are you crying, Bobby?"

"Hurts."

"What hurts?"

"Foot," he said, but he pointed to the outside of his leg. The fibula of his right leg, where his healed fracture had shown up on x-ray.

"And Mommy?"

"She takes me in her arms and says," again he imitated her, " 'I'm sorry, darling. Mommy is very, very sorry. She didn't mean to do it.' "

Jean edged a bit closer to the boy. "Does she say what she didn't mean to do, Bobby?"

"No."

"Bobby, the man on the stairs, does he bang into you?"

"No."

"Or touch you in any way?"

"No."

"But still you fall down the stairs. Why, Bobby? Why?"

"Mommy is very angry."

"Why?"

"She catches me on the stairs and told me not to."

"Now what does Mommy do?"

"She . . . " The boy could not articulate it but swung out just as his furious mother must have struck out at him that day. "And I . . . I . . . " He screamed and seemed to fall backward. Then he reached out to touch the place on his leg where the pain had been so intense moments before. He touched it and began to weep again.

"Why are you crying, Bobby?"

"Hurts. Hurts."

It was interesting to Jean, how the events of that day had been altered just enough to conceal what had actually happened. True, they had been moving. There had been moving men. And the boy had been caught on the stairs. But, unlike what Bob Tatum had reported, no moving man had even touched the boy. Only his mother had. And from the boy's painful recall, she had struck him in a fury.

"Bobby, is Daddy there when it happens?"

"No, ma'am."

So Bob Tatum's knowledge of the episode was based entirely on what Marissa had told him, Jean realized. It only served to urge her on. The leg fracture was long ago healed and no longer harmful. But there might be other injuries which, if more recent, could have aftereffects that might still prove extremely dangerous.

"Bobby, are there other times when Mommy gets angry with you?"

"Uh huh . . ." he admitted softly.

"Times since you moved here, since you've lived in your new house?"

"Uh huh . . . "

"When Mommy gets angry, what does she do? Bobby?" Jean pressed, since he seemed reluctant to talk about it. "Bobby, tell me, what does Mommy do?"

"Hits me."

"Does it hurt?"

"Yes, ma'am."

"Bobby, can you remember what she says and does?"

"After?"

"Yes, Bobby, it's after, and Mommy has just hit you hard. What does she say?"

"She . . . she cries . . . "

"Cries?" Jean asked.

"Yes, ma'am."

"Does she say anything?"

"Yes, ma'am. She cries and says she's sorry. . . ." He began to imitate his mother, " 'It'll never happen again, Bobby, never. So don't tell anyone. Don't ever tell anyone. Especially Daddy. Promise, Bobby, promise.' " Then he assumed his own voice again as he pleaded with his mother, "I promise, Mommy. Only don't cry, don't cry. I love you, so don't cry . . ."

Jean was tempted to take the pathetic little boy into her arms and comfort him. But there was more she had to know.

"Bobby, we're going to remember another time. It's now. You're living in your new house. A time when you hurt your head. Do you remember that time?" Jean speculated, hoping to stimulate a memory.

The boy responded negatively.

"No bumps on your head. No hurt anywhere on your head?"

He shook his head, but continued to sob.

"Do you ever get a big bump on your head? Can you remember that? Try, Bobby, try."

The boy's weeping subsided and finally ceased.

"Bobby?"

He reached up and cautiously touched the left side of his head, reacting in great pain.

"Does that hurt, Bobby?"

"Yes."

"Very much?"

"A lot."

"Is there a bump there?"

"Yes."

She leaned across to touch his head. Naturally, she felt no bump, but the boy drew back in great pain.

"When do you get that bump, Bobby?" she asked; it was important to establish the time since it might be a vital clue to his present seizures.

"Christmas."

"On Christmas day?"

"Before."

"How long before, Bobby?"

" 'Fore Daddy comes home."

"Daddy is coming home for Christmas?"

"Yes."

"What happens?" She waited, then had to urge, "Bobby?"

"Mommy going out."

"Is that all, Bobby?"

The boy hesitated.

"Bobby, is that all?"

"Mommy and me, we trim the tree. Big shiny ormanents," he mispronounced.

"And then?"

His voice became apologetic as he confessed, "I break one of the ormanents. Big shiny red one."

Jean leaned closer to him. "And what does Mommy do? Does she punish you again, Bobby?"

"No," the boy said simply, frustrating Jean's expectations.

"And then, Bobby? After you break the 'ormanent'?"

"Mommy is going out. All dressed up," the boy relived.

"Do you know where Mommy is going?"

"Mommy is going out," was all the boy could supply. Until he added again, "All dressed up."

"And what do you do, Bobby?"

"Ask her not to go."

"And what does she say?"

"She has to go. Esther will put me to bed. Then Mommy kisses me."

"And then, Bobby?"

A look of bitter distaste came over his tormented face. "I . . . "

"You what, Bobby?"

"I . . . I get sick," he said. As he relived the moment, his lips reacted to the bitter taste of it.

"And what does Mommy do?"

"Hits me."

"For getting sick?"

"Yes."

It was difficult for Jean to accept. She tried again. "Is that why she hits you, Bobby? Because you get sick?"

"Yes."

"How does she hit you?"

The boy swung out fiercely in imitation of an action he now remembered very well.

"And then what happens, Bobby?"

The boy did not answer.

"Bobby?"

Still the boy remained silent, as if that were the end of the episode.

"Do you remember what happens after that, Bobby?"

The boy did not answer but began to tremble. He continued to tremble until Jean took him in her arms and held him close. "There's nothing to be afraid of now. Can you remember what happens after Mommy hits you?"

The boy buried his face in Jean's soft warm shoulder.

"Can you remember, Bobby?"

Pressed close against her, he managed nevertheless to shake his head.

"And is that how you get the bump on your head?"

Without relinquishing his desperate embrace, the boy nodded. She recalled now the boy's saying to her once, "Mommy won't like it if I'm sick."

She brought him out of his hypnotic state, then said, "Come, Bobby, I'll take you back to your room." She had to free herself from his embrace. Awake, he stared longingly at the toy zebra. "You may have it, Bobby. It's yours to keep."

Eagerly he swooped up the animal, holding it close to his chest. Jean took his hand and led him out to the corridor. Halfway down toward the boy's room, Jean heard the voice of an angry woman behind them.

"There he is! She took him!"

It was Marissa Tatum, fiercely accusatory. "Bobby! Let go of that woman's hand! You come right here to your mother!"

The boy looked up at Jean, tears forming in his eyes.

"Does that mean I have to give this back?" he asked simply.

"No, Bobby, keep it. It's yours. Now, go to your mother."

He went to her. Marissa dropped to one knee to embrace her son. Looking over his shoulder at Jean, she accused, "Doctor, I think your conduct is very unprofessional. Absolutely outrageous. And I will report it at once!"

twenty-four

"Good God, Jeannie, you didn't bring that boy into your office? After being removed from the case? No wonder Marissa was furious."

Instead of responding directly to Larry's agitation, Jean said, "Since I'm no longer on the case, it's up to *you*."

"What?"

"Demand an immediate angio on that boy!"

"Why the sudden need for an angio?"

"I may have discovered the etiology of his seizures."

"You know the cause?"

"I only said *may* have discovered," she corrected.

"What did you discover? How?"

She told him about her findings on hypnosis.

"You hypnotized that boy without parental consent?" was Larry's immediate and irate reaction.

"As far as I know, there's nothing legal or medical that requires informed consent for hypnosis."

"Yes, I know but   . ." Larry left his objection hanging.

"But what?" she demanded. "The Tatums' feelings will be hurt? Well, they're not my patients."

"Neither is Bobby," Larry reminded.

"He was," she insisted. "And in some ways he still is."

"Jean . . ." he warned, without reminding her of his feeling that she was too personally involved already.

"Larry," she countered, "insist on an angio. Because, aside from a computerized CAT scan, which we don't have yet, it's the only test that will give us a definitive diagnosis. And if it turns out to be a subdural hematoma, he'll need surgery. Without delay!"

"At most, even if you were able to prove it, the boy only said he was hit by his mother. It won't be the first time a four-year-old has been punished by his mother."

"For getting sick?" Jean asked.

"I don't accept that part of it. There must have been more," Larry insisted.

"A patient does not usually lie under hypnosis."

"It doesn't make sense. That Marissa would punish him for getting sick."

"It does if you read up on the literature about NAI. Bobby's case is typical."

"Of what?"

"Normally, when a child is ill, parents tend to be overly kind and loving. But an abusing parent tends to be frustrated and angered by a child's sickness."

"So you've switched from accusing Bob to accusing Marissa? All because of one incident related by a little boy saying that his mother once punished him. Really, Jean." He was trying to control his exasperation.

"And what about *his* version of that long-bone fracture?" Jean challenged.

"The way it happened, it *could* have been the moving man. All I know, at the time you say he received a head trauma, *I* was his pediatrician. *I* never saw any sign of it. Never heard anything about it. As far as I'm concerned, it never happened."

"Larry, a boy doesn't get a painful bump on his head by being punished. Unless he's been hit hard enough to fall and strike his head."

"Did he say that? Even under hypnosis?"

"No."

"Then you're jumping to conclusions again."

"If we had an angio we wouldn't have to jump to conclusions," she reminded.

"On the basis of what we know, I can't justify the risk."

"I can," she insisted. "Go way back to the earliest literature on NAI. In 1946 Caffey reported on the relationship between long-bone fractures and subdural hematomas. In cases of child abuse, where you found one you generally found the other."

Already sensitive over having missed a significant fact about one of his patients, Larry answered in controlled fury, "Don't tell a pediatrician about Caffey's work on child abuse! In the cases he reported on, the children were unwanted, clearly unwanted. And there were other factors that are not presented here."

"There's one factor here that I can't brush aside. Under hypnosis, the boy couldn't remember anything that happened after his mother struck him."

"Meaning what?"

"He blacked out. Was unconscious. He can't remember. A blow like that *could* cause a subdural. Larry, insist on an angio!" she said intensely.

"I want to talk to Bobby first."

"He's your patient, not mine. You don't need my permission."

The conversation ended on that note. Crisp, professional, impersonal. She regretted it, but felt more strongly than ever that she must keep the two parts of her life separate.

If, finally, this case meant losing Larry, she would have to face that. Perhaps, without being aware of it, she had passed that point in her life when she was part physician, part woman. Maybe she was purely the physician now. She would have accepted that more readily if she had not felt a strong need for him now, though he had left her office moments ago and in great anger.

Larry Braham tried to make his visit to the boy's room seem like the usual drop-in.

"Hi, Bobby!"

"Hi, Dr. Larry." The boy was delighted to see him, though he resumed smoothing the coat of the little zebra.

"How do you feel?"

"Fine," he reported, with no particular emphasis.

"Do you like it here, Bobby?"

"Yes, fine."

"Wouldn't you rather be home and with your friends?"

"I have a friend here."

Thinking he referred to the unfortunate little Fazio girl, Larry said, "But she's not here anymore."

"Yes, she is."

"Who?"

"Dr. Jean. She's not my doctor anymore, so she must be my friend."

"Oh, I see. Well, the main thing now is we're going to see that you get home for Thanksgiving."

"Don't they have Thanksgiving here?" the boy asked naively.

"Yes. But it's better to have Thanksgiving at home." He directed the conversation toward the point he wished to make, "Just like Christmas. You like Christmas at home, don't you?"

"Yep," he said.

"The presents. And trimming the tree. You always help Mommy trim the tree, don't you?"

"Uh huh," the boy said, but his concentration was on smoothing the coat of his cherished toy.

"Bobby . . . do you like trimming the tree?"

"Yep."

"Even when you break one of the 'ormanents'?" Larry asked, using the precise mispronounced word Jean had reported to him.

The boy smiled. "You said that wrong. It's not 'ormanent.' 'Ornament.' "

"Oh." Larry pretended to accept his correction. "Well, did you ever break an ornament?"

"No."

"Not ever?"

"Not ever."

Surprised by such a complete and spontaneous contradiction, Larry felt obliged to come directly to the point. "Bobby, did anyone punish you last Christmas?"

"No . . ."

"Didn't Mommy punish you for getting sick?"

"Uh uh," the boy denied, more deeply involved in his toy now.

"Did you ever get a bump on your head? A bump that hurt a lot? Try to remember, Bobby."

The boy gave every overt evidence of thinking hard. "I never got no bump on my head."

Larry Braham studied the boy's face. There was no hint that he was dissembling or speaking anything but the truth. He patted the boy on the cheek, then pressed

his thin bicep in a gesture of affection. Larry Braham
was now a very troubled physician.

"Jeannie, don't you see how impossible your situation will be if you pursue this? Even the boy you're
concerned about will dispute you," Larry warned.

"What the boy recalled under hypnosis is the truth.
In his conscious state he's inhibited. Afraid to remember. Fear of more abuse can do that to a child."

"If you go before the Child Abuse Committee, or
have to defend yourself at the Trustee's hearing, which
you insisted on, what are you going to tell them? That
you put the boy under hypnosis without permission?"

"After all, I didn't expose him to any side effects,"
she defended.

"What if the Trustees insist on questioning the boy?
And he tells them the same thing he told me. He never
got sick. His mother never punished him. What then?"

She could not answer.

"Jeannie, just six months ago there was an article in
the *Pediatric Journal* about a judge who refused to
let a five-year-old testify in court. Even though she
presented gross physical evidence of abuse. He ruled
that a child of five couldn't be relied upon to tell the
same story the same way twice in a courtroom. And
you can't even prove physical abuse."

"I might, if you'd have them do an angio on that
boy."

He lost patience with her. "Jean! Forget it's me.
Pretend you're talking to another pediatrician. A
stranger. You're treating his patient, a five-year-old
who has not had a seizure for days. Who gives every
evidence of being stabilized on Dilantin. Would you
ask him to get consent to do an angio?

"Besides," he added discouragingly, "if I ask the
Tatums, I'm going to have to tell them why."

"Tell them!" she shot back.

"Now? Before your hearing? And give Cameron one more charge to make against you?"

She realized the import of his last question.

"In fact," Larry continued, "if it's not too late, call off that hearing."

"That would be a virtual admission of Cameron's charges."

"Yes," he admitted grimly. "Yes, it would."

Larry had left. Discouraged, but determined, Jean sat down at her typewriter and wrote a number of brief letters. Since the subject matter was highly confidential, she did not wish to entrust them to Maggie. She addressed each letter to the Record Department of each of the other hospitals in the city, twenty-nine in all.

Her request was simple and based on professional courtesy. She would appreciate any information in their files concerning the emergency admission to the hospital of a boy named Robert Tatum, Junior, during the previous December, most likely between the eighteenth and the twenty-third of the month.

If there was substance to the boy's recall under hypnosis, as she was sure there was, then he must have blacked out on being struck. His mother would have been desperate. She had only one of two choices. To call her own pediatrician, Larry Braham, which would have meant having to explain. Or rush the boy to the Emergency Room of a hospital. University Hospital was the last place she was likely to choose, because of Larry's affiliation, and even more because of Cameron's. Obviously, she must have chosen another hospital. Jean was determined to discover which hospital and to get the record of that emergency admission.

She addressed, stamped and mailed the envelopes herself.

It used to take weeks before such letters would bring a response. These days, with hospital records computerized—ironically, with InterElectronics equipment —she should get the information very soon.

Hopefully, before the day of her hearing.

Within the week she received replies from all twenty-nine hospitals. None of them showed any admission of a patient named Robert Tatum, Junior during the month of December last. There were two admissions of persons named Tatum. One a man in his sixties. One a woman of twenty-four, the victim of a mugging who required emergency treatment and was released.

There was no admission of a Robert Tatum of any age recorded anywhere in the city.

The results unsettled her. It left her with the unhappy suspicion that Marissa Tatum might have taken the boy to another private pediatrician, a stranger. If that had happened, it would be impossible to trace.

Jean would have to face the Trustees without any confirmation of her findings. Worse, when challenged, she would have to withdraw her suspicions of Bob Tatum in view of what she had discovered during her hypnosis of his son. Larry's earlier advice seemed not only reasonable but imperative. She could not face the Trustees and make new charges, which, though they might be true, she could not substantiate.

Knowing what such an action would inevitably mean, Jean had no choice but to write the Trustees withdrawing her request for the hearing.

On receiving word, Horace Cameron convened the Board of Trustees nevertheless. He wanted his victory to carry official sanction.

twenty-five

Two days later when Dr. Scofield returned to her office from her duties at the clinic she found on her desk a sealed inter-office envelope.

She sensed what it was even before she opened it. Formal notification from Edward Carey. The Board of Trustees had voted officially to deprive her of admitting privileges to the hospital. The letter said nothing about continuing to teach in the Medical School or about tenure. But those mattered little if she could not continue to practice as well.

Her first reaction was to fight. Now that there was official action by the Trustees, she could appeal the matter to the courts. But after her initial surge of fury wore off, and despite the fact that she had expected the action, the finality of it shook her so severely that she closed her door, sat down at her desk and began to weep.

Her phone rang. She recovered sufficiently to answer, "Dr. Scofield."

"Jeannie?" It was Larry. "You been crying?"

"No," she protested vainly.

"You got the word."

"Yes." Her voice was muffled.

"You shouldn't be alone now. I'm coming to take you home. Wait there for me."

"All right, I'll wait." She was relieved to agree. She needed him more now than ever. It had been years since she had felt so defeated and insecure. Before she hung up, she asked, "Larry? Please, do something for me."

"Anything!"

"Bring Bobby Tatum's file with you."

"Why?"

"Just bring it."

"Jeannie, darling, don't tear yourself apart over this case. It's cost you too much already. Put it out of your mind!" he advised heatedly.

"Larry! Please?"

"Okay," he reluctantly agreed.

Before Larry arrived Hans Benziger came in. He took one look at her eyes.

"You received official word," he concluded. "So did I." He embraced her tenderly and kissed her on the cheek. "I wish there were something I could do. Something," he said hopelessly.

To ease the old man's anguish, she assured, "There'll be other appointments, other hospitals."

"But it will never be the same," Benziger said. She could not disagree.

She examined Bobby's file while Larry mixed them drinks. She would not touch hers until she had searched every entry, every lab report. Eventually she closed the file and shook her head.

"Here," Larry handed her a drink. As she sipped it, he studied her diagnostically until she caught him when she glanced over the rim of her frosty glass.

"What are you thinking?" she demanded.

"Nothing."

"The way you were staring at me it was more than nothing."

"I think you ought to get away for a while, rest up a bit. I know. We should go on a trip. Get away from this place and this case."

"Is that all? Just 'get away'?" she asked pointedly.

"What does that mean?" he countered, though he knew what she meant.

"The way you were studying me. You're afraid I'll have another breakdown. Aren't you?" She demanded a frank answer, no evasions.

"The Trustees' action is no minor defeat. It could mean losing the most important thing in your life since Cliff. I've never deluded myself into believing I'm as important to you as your career. I've accepted you on your terms. But when I see you looking tired and despairing, when I read in your eyes how tormented you are, yes, I ask myself, could it happen all over again? And I have a right to ask. Being in love with you gives me that right. Even Benni . . ." He had not meant to reveal that.

"You discussed this with Benni?"

"*He* discussed it with me."

"Is it that obvious?"

Larry did not answer except to take her in his arms. After a comforting moment there, she spoke in a small voice like a little girl.

"Today I cried. The first time in a long time," she admitted.

"You can cry now, if you want to. I'll understand."

"Just hold me." And he did. In a while she said, "So Benni is worried too?"

"Yes."

"He shouldn't be. Psychiatrists will tell you that the people who recover from breakdowns usually come out of it stronger than they were before."

"'Usually' is not enough, when you're worried about the woman you love. And we love you, Benni and I, each in his own way."

"I know, I know." She sounded sad as she said it.

He took her to bed. She went willingly. But in the

middle of the night she slipped out and went back to the living room. She spent almost an hour studying Bobby Tatum's file. It offered her no corroboration.

She was not only frustrated but depressed. Larry's concern had made her realize something for the first time. It was not only loyalty to Cliff that stood in the way of her remarrying. It was a false island of protection she had created for herself. As long as she was not married, she had told herself, she could never again suffer the same shattering loss. Now, unmarried, she knew she had lost again. And it hurt, deeply. Because this time it was of her own doing.

She, not Larry, had precipitated the events that would cause the two of them to be split apart. Unless she were willing to compromise her career. She could remain in the city and go into private practice. There was no dishonor in that. But neither would there be the satisfaction she derived from her teaching and her research. She had contributions yet to make in both areas. She was determined to make them. Despite the price in pain and loneliness that she would have to start paying again.

In the morning, before he left, Larry made her promise that she would ease up. She was to teach her classes at the medical school, do her scheduled hours at the clinic, then take some time off and, especially, get away from the hospital.

"And do what?"

"Whatever women do when they have time to themselves," he said. "What do they do?"

"Go shopping," she said, smiling. "Or else go to lunch. Women are great on going to lunch."

"That's the way I like to see you. Smiling."

He kissed her, then he left for his office. Poor Larry, she thought, still trying to pretend that it's going to work out. It's like children playing house. And it was her fault. She had made him a partner in the security game she had been playing all along. Now she felt not only lonely but guilty as well.

There were four police prowl cars pulled up in the driveway of University Hospital, their red and white warning lights rotating in the misty night. Several officers waited outside the entrance, talking among themselves. Visitors passing into and out of the huge complex stopped to stare with concern at the need for such a concentration of police presence.

Inside the hospital, in Edward Carey's commodious office, Horace Cameron was in command. He had appropriated Carey's desk, using both phones to make and receive calls.

Marissa Tatum sat off in a corner, her eyes dry but red from too many tears. She had twisted her damp handkerchief until it was only a tiny ball of soggy linen. She seemed alone and terribly in need of comforting.

Cameron did his best to reassure her. "Bob's on his way. Another two hours and he should be here." She nodded, but it was difficult to know if she really comprehended, for she seemed remote and cut off from everyone. Her lips trembled and she kept mouthing a single word over and over. "Bobby . . . Bobby . . . Bobby . . ."

Suddenly she started up from her chair and cried out, "They have to find him! They have to!"

Cameron had never been able to cope with emotional women, even his own wife. "Damn it, Carey, do something! Get a doctor to give her a shot."

At that moment Larry Braham entered.

"Well?" Cameron demanded.

"No one saw the boy. Not when he left his room. Not when he left the hospital."

"We don't know if he left the hospital," Carey interrupted, seeking to protect his institution from the accusation that a five-year-old boy could slip out without being detected. "We're doing a search of every floor, every room, every utility closet right this minute!"

Marissa Tatum suddenly cried out, "Search the elevator shafts! He likes to play with elevator buttons. He may have opened the doors somehow!"

Larry Braham embraced her to calm her. "Riss, it won't help to get hysterical. If he did touch an elevator button, the doors wouldn't open till the car was there. So he couldn't have fallen."

"These things happen. You read about them all the time," she protested.

Larry stared past her at Cameron, inquiringly.

"Bob's on his way back. He was running an engineering and sales convention in San Francisco. The company jet will be here in a few hours at most."

Cameron turned to plainclothes Detective Inspector Greer. "Ever had one like this before?"

"One like what?" the tall, lean inspector asked.

"A child kidnaped right out of a hospital?"

"Mr. Cameron, we don't know if he *was* kidnaped. Personally, I doubt it."

"It could happen," Cameron insisted.

"If some psycho nurse or nurse's aide took him, you don't have to worry. We always find them. And that type takes good care of the kid. That's why they snatch them in the first place. To have something to take care of. A doll might do almost as well."

"That's not the kind of kidnaping I meant."

"You mean ransom?" the inspector asked. "I doubt it."

"Why not?" Cameron asked. "I'd be a logical target for something like that."

"He's not your child," the inspector reminded.

"If there was a ransom demand, where do you think the money would come from? Anyone who knows me knows that."

"Maybe," the inspector agreed, realizing now how personally Cameron was taking the unfortunate matter.

Ralph Sunderland arrived, quite tired and hopeless. "Can't understand. Someone must have seen him. Between his afternoon milk and cookies and the time the student nurse came to bring his dinner someone should have seen him. But nobody did. Nobody."

"Kids!" the inspector said. "They like to play games. They hide to scare adults. Did he ever play games like that?" He had directed this last at Marissa.

"Sometimes. When he was younger," the frantic mother said.

"He wouldn't be hiding all this time," Larry Braham said.

"Then *you* think he *was* kidnaped," Cameron said, seeking support for his own theory.

"Look, Mr. Cameron," Greer intervened because he feared the emotional consequences to Marissa Tatum, "if this was a kidnaping and several hours had gone by we'd have had some word from the kidnaper. They work fast. Do the job, get the money, and blow, that's their MO. They know the longer the involvement the greater the risk. But there's been no hint of ransom." He turned to Marissa. "Call home. Maybe he's shown up there. Better still, what's the number?"

There was little possibility the boy was there, but Greer knew if a ransom call did come it would most likely be made to the Tatum home. Esther answered. No, Bobby was not there. He was in the hospital as far as she knew. Why, was there something wrong?"

Greer didn't respond. He only asked, "Have there been any calls? From strangers? Anything unusual?"

"No calls at all, except one. A call from a doctor."

"Oh? Who?"

"Dr. Scofield."

"What did he say?"

"She," the maid corrected.

"All right, she! What did *she* say?" Greer asked impatiently.

"Just she wanted to talk to Mrs. Tatum."

"That's all?"

"That's all. Why?"

"Thanks. Thanks a lot," the inspector said. He hung up. "Who is Dr. Scofield?"

"Why?" Larry demanded at once.

"Only one call at the Tatum house this afternoon. From a woman who said she was Dr. Scofield," the inspector replied, quite suspicious now.

"Of course!" Cameron seized on it. "That explains it!"

"What?" Greer asked, eager now that he had his first lead to the boy's disappearance. "Was she going to operate on him or something?"

"No," Cameron said. "What you said about a nurse or nurse's aide needing a child to mother."

"Yeah, what about it?"

"Those cases always involve women, don't they?"

"I never worked on one that didn't," Greer agreed.

"What if it was a *doctor* who had that kind of need?"

"I suppose that could happen."

"There you have it!" Cameron concluded. "She's exactly the kind of woman who would do that."

"That's an outrageous accusation!" Larry Braham exploded.

"It's the only logical explanation we've had so far.

I'll bet right now you can't find her. Not in her office. Not in her home. She's off somewhere with that boy, hiding him, having him all to herself. Which is what she always aimed to do!"

To prove Cameron wrong, Larry picked up the phone and dialed Jean's private number at her office, a phone only she would answer. There was no response. He hesitated a moment, then reluctantly he dialed her apartment. She did not answer, but her service did. By this time Cameron, Sunderland and Greer were staring at him. He made one more call.

"Benni? Larry Braham. Have you seen or talked to Jean in the last few hours? I see. I see. Left right after her clinic hours. Thanks, Benni. Wrong? The Tatum boy is missing. Then you know. Still no sign. None."

He turned to face the three men who glared at him, accusing, as he tried to explain, "I told her to take the afternoon off and go somewhere by herself. She was very upset," he addressed Cameron, "about having her admitting privileges canceled. It's tantamount to being fired, kicked out. She's taking it very hard. I wanted her to get away from the oppressive atmosphere here."

The more Larry Braham tried to explain, the more he gave credence to Cameron's accusation. By making his calls in an effort to absolve her, Larry had only incriminated her.

"Inspector, shouldn't we put out an alarm for that woman?"

"If this ever gets into the paper or on TV it could do enormous damage to Dr. Scofield's career," Larry interjected. "She could sue all of you."

"Let her," Cameron replied defiantly, "if she wants to risk a suit like that with her past record." He turned to Greer. "Inspector!"

Greer dialed a code number, "Klein? Oh, Hruska. Hruska, put out an APB on a doctor, female, Caucasian." He turned to Larry. "Full name?"

When Larry hesitated, Cameron supplied, "Jean. Jean Scofield."

"Description?"

"Woman. Medium height. About thirty-five, thirty-six," Cameron said.

"Thirty-eight," Larry corrected, then realized he would have to complete the description. "Five-five. Auburn hair, green eyes. Very attractive."

The inspector relayed the information. "She will most likely be seen in the company of a small boy, about five years old, dark hair, blue eyes. The boy's name is Robert Tatum, Junior. No, they're not related. Yeah, it's one of those."

The chief of Hospital Security arrived to report, "We've made a complete search of this building. And of every building our tunnels connect with. No sign."

Exasperated, Greer exploded. "Let's go back over this whole damn thing. You're sure the kid wasn't due to have something done to him? Some operation or examination that might scare him? Kids, if they're scared, can do the weirdest things."

"Inspector, we've already told you, he wasn't due for anything but to be discharged," Cameron said. "Dr. Sunderland had approved his release from the hospital because there were no further procedures planned for him."

"A kid who's due to go home doesn't disappear," Greer insisted doggedly. "Is it possible he was afraid you weren't telling him the truth?"

"But we *were* telling him the truth!" Sunderland persisted. "I'd given the orders. When his Dilantin level came back from the lab, if it was within the proper limits, tomorrow his mother was free to take him home." Turning to Marissa he asked, "Didn't I say that to him in your presence only this morning?"

"Yes."

Cameron intruded himself into the discussion. "I think it was that woman who filled his little head with fears."

"That's not true!" Larry defended.

"Then why are she and the boy both missing? Tell me that!" Cameron demanded.

Marissa Tatum, still involved with the last question Greer had asked her, suddenly said, "That stretcher. That could have done it."

They all turned to her.

"What stretcher?" Larry asked. "Riss?"

"A week ago. I thought he'd like to go for a walk down to the solarium. Maybe even stop in one or two of the rooms where there are children. He misses other children," she said as discreetly as she could. For it had been Cameron's decision that the boy be confined to a private room. "I put his robe on him and we started out. When he reached the door, he stopped suddenly. I looked out. An orderly was wheeling a stretcher down the hall. There was a small body on it, completely covered. He held tight to my hand and looked up at me and asked why it was covered so, head and all.

"I tried to explain so as not to frighten him. I thought I had succeeded. But after that he didn't want to stay out very long. He just wanted to go back to his room and sit in my lap. From time to time he would ask questions about dying. And where people went after they died. Finally, after he had been quiet a long time, he asked what would happen to him if he died. Of course I said he wouldn't die. But he was quiet and very troubled the rest of the day."

"Could it have scared him enough to make him run away?" the inspector asked.

"I don't know. But does it matter why? Just find him. Find him!"

Before she could break down, Larry Braham gripped her arms. "Riss, please. They'll find him. He can't have gone far." But it was empty assurance, not based on anything but hope.

"What if he has a seizure, and there's no one to help him? He could die, he could choke to death. . . ."

"He probably won't have a seizure," Larry said. Actually that had been the fear uppermost in his mind from the moment he heard Bobby was missing. Alone, if the boy had a seizure, he might well suffer severe injury or even death from the fall, or suffocation from inhaling his own vomitus. And if the seizure were prolonged enough, there could be damage to his brain. While Larry did his best to reassure Marissa, who was now verging on panic, he and Sunderland exchanged glances which expressed their professional fears.

Suddenly Marissa said, "Tension! She warned me once that tension could bring it on. If he's alone and frightened that could bring it on. Couldn't it?"

"Riss, you're not helping with these unreasonable fears," Larry warned, though her fears were well founded. If the boy were deprived of his Dilantin long enough it could open the door to all the dread possibilities that tormented his mother.

In his frustration, Larry went to the phone and dialed Jean's office number again. There was still no answer. He tried her home. This time Bessie answered. But she knew nothing of the doctor's whereabouts. Larry found himself considering the possibility he had so vehemently denied earlier. The boy was missing. So, evidently, was Jean. It could be merely an unfortunate coincidence. But it could be more than that.

In his own fashion Larry tried to analyze her state of mind. This hospital had been the place and the means of her own recovery. It was essential to her security, both professional and emotional. Being deprived of it, suddenly and without justification, perhaps could have caused her to react in an unpredictable fashion.

He made one more phone call, to Jean's answering service. Finally, he had some word. Yes, Dr. Scofield had called. She had picked up his messages. At least she knew that he was trying to reach her. As he hung up one phone, the second phone rang. It was Carey's secretary to announce that Dr. Scofield was on her way in.

Marissa Tatum rose to confront her, crying out as the door opened, "What have you done with him?"

"I haven't seen him," Jean said. "But I know we have to find him. At once!"

"Jean?" Larry demanded an explanation.

"Never mind why, for the moment. Just find him!" she insisted.

"Damn it, woman," Cameron interceded, "what do you think we've been trying to do? We were sure he was with you."

"I wish he were," Jean retorted.

The inspector intervened, "Doctor, do you have any idea where he might have gone? The boy is very attached to you, I understand."

"If he left his room he might have come seeking me. I had some toys he liked to play with. Did you search my office?"

"He wasn't there."

"In that case, I wouldn't know," Jean said, gravely concerned.

The inspector lifted the phone and dialed. "Hruska, kill the APB on that doctor. Just concentrate on the boy."

Jean looked to Larry, whose eyes admitted the kind of speculation that had been rife in the room until she appeared. She turned and left. Inspector Greer called after her, "Keep in touch. Any ideas you have, let me know. We're going to need all the help we can get to find that boy."

"We're going to need more help than that when we *do* find him!" Jean responded, and she was gone.

Cameron looked to Larry Braham. "What did she mean by that?"

"I don't know." He started after her.

Jean went directly to her own floor. She stopped at the floor nurses' desk to make inquiries. She found she was only asking the same questions that had been asked before. No one—nurse, orderly, nurse's aide or porter—had seen the boy or given him directions to Jean's office. Of course there had been a change of shift since the boy was discovered missing. They had tried to reach all personnel who had been on duty at the time it might have happened. Those they had succeeded in contacting had no information about the boy.

Jean reached her office harboring a fear that far exceeded those the others had. Whatever their concerns, and they were well founded, her own new knowledge magnified her fears greatly. Larry found her at her desk, in deep, concerned thought.

"Jeannie?"

"They've got to find him!"

"They will," he reassured her, with no real conviction.

"It's urgent."

"Why more urgent now than it was before?"

"Because I found it."

"Found what?"

"I'm sure now, even without an angiogram. I'm sure he's suffering from a subdural hematoma due to trauma to the head."

"You didn't receive any confirmation from any hospital. You admitted that."

"That was day before yesterday," Jean said. "That's why I wanted another look at your file on Bobby."

"Nothing in there would substantiate the presence of a subdural."

"No," she agreed, "but it did provide a place to start."

"What place?"

"Pearson" was all Jean said.

"Pearson?" Larry asked, completely puzzled.

"Marissa Tatum's maiden name."

"Yes," he remembered vaguely. "What about it?"

"I've been doing lots of reading in the pediatric literature on child abuse. There's a prevalent pattern that emerges. Middle and upper class abusing mothers, when confronted with an emergency, as a rule, do not go to their own pediatricians. They seek out a hospital or a doctor to whom their identity is not known. They do not pay the fee or the hospital bill by check or medical insurance. They pay cash, to avoid any chance of identification. *And* they almost always use another name."

"What does Marissa's maiden name have to do with it?"

"Somehow, by some psychological quirk, such mothers very often use their maiden names instead of a completely fictitious one."

Larry conjectured, "Maybe they're trying to cover

up, while at the same time hoping to be caught and stopped from repeating the experience."

"Some psychiatrists say that."

"Now what about the name 'Pearson'?"

"That's where I've been all afternoon. I went back to each hospital who wrote that they had no record of admitting a Robert Tatum, Junior."

"And?"

"Back in December of last year, a four-year-old boy named *Charles Pearson* was brought to Emergency Admitting at West Side Memorial. He had suffered a trauma to the head, resulting in a marked swelling. He was kept overnight, observed, found to have no other signs of damage. The next day his mother took him home. She paid the bill in cash. One hundred sixty-seven dollars."

"Back in December," Larry considered.

"Three days before Christmas," Jean said. "According to the record, the mother's story was that she and the boy were trimming the tree. While she had gone to answer the phone, the boy climbed the ladder and fell off, striking his head on the floor. The admitting doctor evidently believed her story because he entered no other comments on the chart."

"That's almost ten months before he had his first seizure," Larry commented significantly.

"Well within the time span when a subdural could begin evidencing itself in seizures," Jean agreed. "If it *is* a subdural and it's beginning to act up now, it could have disastrous consequences if we don't take steps at once. If *you* don't take steps," she corrected, realizing she was no longer on the case.

"I should have acted on your hunch and insisted on permission to do that angio."

"Let's hope it isn't too late. They've got to find him, before it is."

twenty-six

It was long past ten o'clock that night when Personnel finally heard from the last nurse's aide who had been on duty during the hours when Bobby Tatum disappeared. She had seen the boy in the corridor. He asked for Dr. Scofield's office. She directed him down the hall, asking if he could count off eight doors. He said he could. She admired him as he trudged down the hall in his robe and slippers, counting off the doors. She saw him disappear into the right office. She continued about her duties, assuming the boy was expected and that Dr. Scofield was there to receive him. She saw no further sign of him and went off duty at four o'clock as scheduled. She knew nothing more till she turned on her radio later that night and heard about the missing boy. She had called the hospital at once.

Her information was interesting but not helpful. It only supplied a possible motive for the boy's leaving his room. Where he might have gone after failing to find Dr. Scofield was still unknown.

Bob Tatum had returned from San Francisco and was insisting on all sorts of police measures, most of which had already been tried and failed. He took to searching the hospital neighborhood in the prowl car Inspector Greer put at his disposal. Occasionally, if he saw some suspicious shadow, he would order the driver to stop. A number of times he bolted from the car even before it came to a halt and raced to the spot

where he thought he had seen some object that might
be the figure of a small boy. His sightings turned out
to be illusions caused by the confluence of street
lights and shadows.

During their patrol they passed other prowl cars
on the same mission. The police radio in the car maintained a steady reportage of distress calls, crimes and
emergencies along with the discouraging news that the
Tatum boy was still missing. No sign of him had been
reported. This, despite the public appeal made on
television news shows which gave a special police
number for anyone to call who had seen a boy resem-
bling Bobby Tatum at any time since late afternoon.

Horace Cameron had left the hospital after giving
instructions that he was to be wakened no matter the
hour of night as soon as there was some definite word
about the boy. Francine Cameron arrived and insisted
on remaining to comfort Marissa Tatum. However,
the presence of the older woman did little to help.
The distressed mother had become so tense that she
verged on hysteria. It was deemed advisable to inject
her with strong sedation and put her to bed.

In the small all-night staff cafeteria, Jean Scofield
and Larry Braham were having what seemed like their
hundredth cup of coffee. They had said all that they
could say, and had repeated most of it. Silence was
their only refuge now.

Their coffee had grown cold. It had stood un-
touched so long that it had formed permanent rings
around their cups.

Larry said suddenly, "You mustn't be too harsh
with her. Believe me, she tries to be a good wife and
mother. No one tries harder."

"I hope they find him soon. For her sake as much

as his. If she has to live with the possible results of
Bobby's disappearance she'll never make it."

"They'll find him . . . they'll find him," Larry kept
saying. He knew those were words of desperation.
"Are you going to confront her with what you discovered?"

"She doesn't need any more punishment than she's
already giving herself."

Seeking to divert Larry from staring at her, Jean
stirred her cold coffee as she confessed, "Even if a
woman's done nothing wrong, she always blames herself
for any tragedy that befalls her man or her child. During
those days after Cliff, I kept reliving the million little
things that I might have done that would have prevented his death. If I had loved him more and never
let him go. If I hadn't gone back to my little hospital.
If I had insisted we go back to the States as soon as
I found I was pregnant. I created endless computa-
tions of the possibilities that could have kept him
alive.

"I did nothing wrong. Everyone knew that. *Except
me.* Imagine how Marissa must feel now. How much
worse it is for her."

"She doesn't know that what she did ten months
ago could be what's threatening her son now," Larry
said.

"She knows," Jean disputed sadly. Intuition. Guilt.
Her unconscious mind. Whatever you call it, inside
her there is something that knows. That's why I don't
want to add to her guilt now."

At that moment a young black orderly appeared
in the cafeteria doorway, scanned the room, then approached them swiftly.

"Doctor," he addressed Larry, "they want you in
Emergency Admitting."

"They found him?"

"There's a report of a boy being found. Some man taking his dog out for his late night run found a boy lying in his driveway. A police car is bringing him in now."

"Did they say anything about his condition?" Jean asked.

"That's all we know."

"How can they be so vague?" Larry asked, irritated. " 'A boy being found.' Bobby can surely identify himself. You'd think that would be the first thing they'd ask him."

"Maybe they did," Jean said thoughtfully.

"And he wouldn't answer?"

"Maybe he couldn't answer," Jean said.

Bob Tatum, Ralph Sunderland, Larry Braham and Jean Scofield waited in Emergency Admitting. The prowl car pulled up at the dock, its siren muted because of the late hour, but its lights ablaze and rotating. The car door burst open. A uniformed policeman emerged carrying in his arms a small boy, black-haired, dressed in a wrinkled dirty blue robe, one slipper missing from his bare foot. He handed the boy over to his father. Bob Tatum rushed his young son into Emergency where three doctors waited to assess his condition.

Tatum laid his son on the examining table gently. For a single awkward moment both Jean and Ralph Sunderland moved to examine him. She drew back, realizing she was no longer the doctor on the case. Bob Tatum leaned close to his son and murmured into his ear, "Bobby! Bobby boy, you're safe now. You're all right. You're going to be fine. Bobby, do you hear me? Daddy is talking to you, son. Do you hear me, Bobby?"

It was obvious the boy did not hear. But he was not asleep. He was unconscious.

"Undoubtedly had another seizure," Sunderland concluded as he took over from the father.

Jean Scofield focused not on the boy's eyes or his face but on his right hand, which had assumed an unusual position. Meanwhile, Sunderland proceeded with the routine. He tested for the boy's vital signs. Blood pressure slightly on the low side. Pulse elevated. Respiratory pattern normal. All seemed to confirm his original diagnosis: the boy had had another seizure.

He fixed the boy's head in a position facing upward and gently forced his eyes open to test his oculo-cephalic reflexes. He turned his head to one side, then the other. "Doll's eye reflex," Sunderland announced, meaning that the boy's eyes did not turn on movement but stared straight up. Confirmation of unconsciousness.

Sunderland now noticed the condition on which Jean had been concentrating. The boy's left arm and leg moved in subtle spontaneous reactions. But his right arm and leg did not. Sunderland ran his fingernails lightly across the plantar surface of the boy's left foot. The big toe went down, his other toes curled in. He turned his attention to the boy's right foot. That large toe turned up, the others fanned out.

"Positive plantar response," he observed unhappily. He turned to the emergency nurse in charge. "Kit!"

She handed him a sterile kit. He drew some blood. He sealed the test tube and ordered, "Electrolytes! Stat!" The nurse dispatched an orderly to the lab with the blood sample.

Sunderland turned back to his little unconscious patient, thought for a moment, then ordered,

"Twenty-five percent glucose. Push IV. After so long, he could be hypoglycemic."

The nurse prepared the glucose and began to administer it. Sunderland picked up the phone and called Radiology. At this late hour only a resident was there. Sunderland glanced at Jean, exchanging with her their mutual regret that a more experienced man was not on duty. But with time important, he ordered the procedure nevertheless.

"I want a bedside echo. Stat. In Emergency. And also bedside skull and cervical spine x-rays."

Sunderland's attitude, his crisp orders for the various tests, the concern he evidenced all had a mounting effect on Bob Tatum. When Sunderland repeated his examination on the soles of Bobby's feet, and shook his head with great concern, Tatum could no longer restrain himself.

"Damn it, Doctor, what is it?"

"Nothing to be alarmed about," Sunderland tried to reassure him.

"Then why are *you* so alarmed?" Tatum demanded.

"Please, Mr. Tatum! Obviously the boy had another seizure just before he was found. He's unconscious. But he'll come out of it. This time, however . . ." Sunderland turned to Jean. "Has he ever presented Todd's before?"

Before Jean could answer, Tatum demanded fiercely, "What the hell is Todd's?" He turned to Jean. "I never heard you say that."

"He's never presented it before," Jean admitted.

"He's getting worse! Someone better bring him out of it," Tatum demanded, so agitated it seemed he might become violent.

Larry Braham stepped in to take over, meanwhile beckoning to Cameron who had just returned. The older man reached out to calm Bob Tatum with a firm hand on his shoulder.

Sunderland explained. "Todd's Phenomenon sounds more imposing than it is. In the post-ictal state the patient will generally have a weakness on one side, the side opposite the place of brain involvement."

"But this is more than weakness!" Tatum argued.

"That's what I'm trying to explain. Todd's Phenomenon is a temporary paralysis that can set in after a seizure. Just as the weakness can."

"How long does it last?" the suspicious father asked.

"A day. A few days at most."

"Then he'll be all right again?" Tatum demanded skeptically. "His leg and his arm, he'll be able to move them? Normally?"

"Absolutely!"

Relieved, Bob Tatum sank down to a white metal stool and breathed deeply and swiftly, as if he had just run forty yards with a football under his arm against tough opposition. Jean watched unobtrusively, thinking, whatever his shortcomings as a father, whatever his demanding nature had inflicted on the boy, Bob Tatum loved his son and would have sacrificed himself for him.

But she also wondered how much more in the way of love, kindness and indulgence this father was capable of. For she was not so sanguine as Dr. Sunderland. Todd's Phenomenon was the readiest and most comforting diagnosis to make.

There were others. Far less reassuring.

The boy's lids flickered and opened. His blue eyes were dull as if waking from a long sleep. He stared up at the faces that hovered over him. Dr. Larry. Dr. Jean. Dr. Sunderland. Mr. Cameron. He made an effort to reach out to Jean, who was at his right side. He was puzzled, then terrified as he discovered his arm did not respond. His lips moved. But he could not formulate any words. He finally reached across to her with his left hand. There was an obvious look of disapproval on Cameron's face, but he said nothing.

"Bobby?" his father intervened. "Bobby, can you hear me? This is Dad. Bobby?"

The boy turned to his father. Bob Tatum leaned close, pressed his face against the boy's soft cheek. At that moment a technician arrived with the equipment to make the tests that Sunderland had ordered. They all gave way while the x-rays were made of his head and his spine. The resident arrived to perform the echo-encephalogram, to see if there had been any shift of the boy's brain in his skull.

As the equipment was being cleared from the Emergency Room the lab reports came back on the boy's electrolytes. Sunderland glanced at them. As a matter of courtesy he passed them to Jean.

"Sodium—136. Potassium—3.8. Blood, Urea, Nitrogen—6. Glucose—68."

His glucose and the B.U.N. were lower than normal, but only slightly so. Sodium and potassium were both within the range of normal. There was nothing definitive in the entire report.

"Todd's," Sunderland reiterated. "We'll put the boy to bed, resume his Dilantin and observe him for the next forty-eight hours. By then I'm sure the paralysis will clear up. Meantime, we should have the x-rays and the echo in another half hour. Right now, I think what he needs is medication, rest and freedom from tension."

The boy was placed on a gurney and wheeled back to his room. Marissa Tatum had been wakened. In her drowsy sedated state she received the news. She insisted on sitting at Bobby's bedside the rest of the night. No one, not even her husband, could convince her to leave. She kept repeating, "When he wakes up, first thing he'll want to see is me."

Larry offered to drive Jean home, but she decided to wait until the results of the tests could be examined. Within the hour they were delivered. Sunderland placed the x-rays in the view box. They examined them together. The plates revealed nothing abnormal in the skull or the cervical spine. It was temporarily comforting but by no means definitive.

The echo, which would have been more indicative, was not at all satisfactory. The resident admitted that he could not get a good mid-line trace. There was no way of telling whether the boy's brain had been forced off center. A new echo by a more experienced doctor would have to determine that. But that must wait till morning.

It was past three when Larry drove Jean home. They were both exhausted from the night of uncertainty and tension. The personal conflicts that surrounded the case had added to the unhappy experience.

"I could see Cameron resenting every moment that Bobby held your hand," Larry said.

"I'm sure he thinks I cast some spell over the boy," Jean tried to joke. But after a long and harrowing night, her words sounded flat, not funny.

"You don't agree with Sunderland's diagnosis, do you? You don't think it's Todd's?"

"Remember, I know something Sunderland doesn't. That emergency admission of ten months ago."

"Then you should have told him."

"In front of the Tatums? In front of Cameron? It could destroy their marriage. And their family. Unless it's handled very carefully. Then, of course, there are the damned ethics of our profession. Sunderland is on the case. I'm not."

Jean was silent for a moment before admitting, "Of course, there's always the remote possibility that the name Pearson is a coincidence. I have to be very sure before I say anything. But when it clearly affects Bobby's prognosis, then to hell with professional etiquette and the effect on the lives of adults. I am going to speak up. My obligation is to him. After all, he was my patient."

The next morning Bobby Tatum woke early. He found his mother at his bedside smiling down at him. He tried to smile back. Hoping there had been some change in his condition overnight, she held out her hand, coaxing him to reach his right hand to her.

"Try, Bobby. Try, darling," she urged, still smiling though becoming desperately tense and adding to his fears.

The harder he tried, the less able he was to accomplish it. Tears welled up in his soft blue eyes and ran down the sides of his cheeks, wetting his pillow. Marissa Tatum left the room and stood outside his door, pressed against the wall, frightened and weeping now herself. The floor nurse passing by took her to the empty visitors' room, where she could give vent to her emotions with more privacy. The nurse returned to Bobby's room. She smiled at the tormented little patient, trying to reassure him. His lips moved, but made no sound. She urged him on. "Try, Bobby. Just try, my dear. I think you can."

The boy stared up, seemed to mobilize all his effort and finally brought forth a sound. Heartened, he tried again, and was barely able to enunciate, "Dr. Jean . . ." The nurse patted him and nodded. She went directly to the floor phone and paged Dr. Braham to report his patient's request. Braham called Bob Tatum and urged restoring Jean to the case.

"I think she was responsible for his disappearance!" Tatum accused.

"We know that isn't true."

"He left his room to go looking for her. She's got my son under a spell of some kind!"

Larry was struck by the irony of Tatum's words. What Jean had said the night before as an impossible sardonic joke was being seriously accepted now by the irate father.

One other thought also registered sharply on Larry Braham. He chose not to discuss it. Only last evening, while the boy was missing, someone said he had no reason to be missing. Everything about his condition was so favorable. Dr. Sunderland said that he was ready to be released from the hospital. For the first time something became startlingly clear to Larry Braham. The mention of being sent home could have been the precipitating factor in Bobby's disappearance. Deprived of Jean once she was removed from the case, fearing that he would never see her again if he were sent home, he might well have gone seeking her. Then through some unexplained accident he found himself out on the street and lost, a wanderer, until he collapsed in a seizure in the driveway of the home where he was found.

Larry recalled reading in the pediatric literature that a doctor in New York, who specialized in child abuse cases, said physical abuse was not the sole or even the most destructive kind. Prolonged parental deprivation could have serious and lifelong emotional effects. Nor did it matter if the neglect was that of a drug-addicted parent or of an ambitious and successful professional parent who did not have time to lavish love on an infant or a child.

For the first time Larry Braham was convinced of Jean Scofield's diagnosis. All the qualities of the good executive wife that he had found so admirable in Marissa Tatum were suddenly revealed to him as possible destructive factors in her shy young son's condition. He knew now that it was more than desirable to have Jean restored to the case. It was vital.

Because it would mean so much to the boy, and because merely dropping by to visit could not be construed as a breach of professional ethics, Larry was able to prevail upon Jean to see Bobby.

She had intended to visit him only briefly, on her way to her class. But the boy held her hand tightly and pressed it against his cheek desperately.

The door opened. Sunderland was staring at Jean, anger plain on his face. Jean rose to greet him.

"Good morning, Doctor."

"Good morning, Doctor," he answered coolly, his attitude demanding an explanation.

"Purely social visit," Jean said. "The patient asked to see me."

"If you'll excuse us, Doctor, I'd like to examine my patient."

Jean had no choice but to free her hand from Bobby's grasp and leave. She had to avoid his pleading blue eyes.

Sunderland repeated his neurological examination. He thought he detected a bit more mobility in the right leg, though the arm was no better than it had been the night before. He was satisfied with the progress and with his diagnosis. Once out in the corridor, he said to Larry Braham, "Of course, we'll run the echo and the EEG as a matter of routine. I'll call you later, once I see the results."

"Do you think it might be advisable to do an angio?" Larry suggested, hoping he could implement

Jean's recommendation without provoking a professional crisis.

"Last resort," Sunderland said dogmatically. "The risks are too great. And the indications are not persuasive enough."

"Then you're still sure it's Todd's?"

"More certain now than I was last night. It's clearing up, isn't it?" Sunderland demanded, annoyed that a mere pediatrician would question his expert judgment.

Still hoping to influence Sunderland, Larry made a point Jean had made just before she drifted off to sleep in the early hours of the morning. "We still can't prove the boy actually had a seizure last night."

"The odds are very strong that he did," Sunderland said, openly irritated now. "He had post-ictal unconsciousness, didn't he?"

"On the off chance that he didn't, how would you explain Todd's Phenomenon in the absence of a seizure?"

"Braham, this may be the first case of this kind you've had. But I've had dozens. So let me do this my way. We'll run the test and by this evening we'll see."

"What if it can't wait till then?" Larry asked pointedly.

"Oh, I see!" Sunderland said, smiling. "You've discussed all this with Dr. Scofield. That must have made for an interesting night!"

Larry Braham reached out to seize Sunderland by the lapels of his white lab coat. "We're not discussing my private life! Only my patient. Let's keep it that way!"

Sunderland blanched. Gradually Larry released his hold.

"What if it can't wait?" Larry reiterated.

"You may be quite sure that if I see any need to resort to an angiogram or any other invasive procedure, I will do so. When *I* think the time is right," Sunderland said coolly as he straightened his coat. With that he started down the corridor.

Larry reported his conversation to Jean, omitting Sunderland's personal remarks, and his own physical reaction.

"I'm going to insist on an angiogram at once!"

"How?" Larry asked, bringing her face to face with the realities.

"There's only one way."

"What way?"

"The only way left," Jean said thoughtfully.

twenty-seven

Marissa Tatum was still at her son's bedside when the nurse came in to hand her a message. It instructed her to call a certain extension within the hospital. She felt it might be unwise to make such a call in Bobby's hearing. Perhaps it was Sunderland and the word was not favorable. She used the phone at the floor desk.

"This is Mrs. Tatum. Someone at this extension asked me to call."

"I did," Jean Scofield said.

"You! What do you want now?"

"If you love your son, if you're concerned about his health, maybe even his life, come and see me. *At once!*"

"His case is in Dr. Sunderland's hands now," the tense young mother answered brusquely.

"I'll wait in my office for fifteen minutes. *Be here!*" Jean said firmly, then hung up.

When fifteen minutes had gone by with no sign of Marissa Tatum, Jean realized that she had failed. She might as well do her rounds of the last patients she had admitted to the hospital before her privileges were canceled. She had just started away from her office door when she heard a voice call out, "Doctor!"

Jean turned to face Marissa Tatum. The women stared at each other for a moment. Jean opened the door to her private office, allowed Marissa to enter. She locked the door from the inside, to avoid being interrupted during what could be a crucial session for the little patient and a painful one for both mother and doctor.

"You may smoke if you wish," Jean began.

"Thank you," Marissa said archly, resenting any show of courtesy or warmth from this doctor she had come to resent. But she did avail herself of the comfort of a cigarette. Jean had to admire the graceful way Marissa handled a habit that was essentially ungraceful. She would always be the correct model, no matter what she did. It was a part she played extremely well.

"Mrs. Tatum, you must believe that I have only one interest. Bobby. His health. And his future. I talk to you now only because I think he's in great danger."

"Dr. Sunderland doesn't think so!"

"I do. And I feel it's my duty to tell someone."

The mother made a pretense of listening, but her hostile attitude reflected her rigid state of mind.

"I do not agree with Dr. Sunderland's diagnosis," Jean said flatly. "I don't think Bobby is presenting

Todd's Phenomenon. Even if his paralysis were to clear up in a day or two, I don't think that's what it is."

"You think it's something more dangerous."

"I do," Jean said. "And I want you to remember what I say. Or if you wish I'll write it down for you. But I think your son is suffering from a *subdural hematoma. . . .*"

"Subdural hematoma," Marissa Tatum repeated. The strange words had no meaning for her.

"Tell Sunderland that he should not discount a subdural hematoma in his diagnosis. It's important. *Now.* I think what's going on in your son's brain at this moment can spell life or death."

The tense young mother grew pale and breathless. Her lips quivered as the smoke trailed aimlessly from her finely shaped nostrils.

"You're trying to frighten me. So we'll put you back on the case."

"I'm not trying to frighten you. But it's something to be frightened about," Jean said, making no effort to minimize the urgency she felt.

"If it's that dangerous, why doesn't Sunderland know about it?" Marissa Tatum demanded. "He's a good man. One of the best. Mr. Cameron says he's going to be the next Chief of the Department."

Jean had to make her decision now. She did.

"Mrs. Tatum, I think I know certain facts about this case that Dr. Sunderland doesn't."

"Wasn't it your professional duty to tell him everything you knew when you turned the case over to him?" the angry mother demanded. "I think I should report this to the proper authorities."

"When I turned the case over I didn't know what I know now," Jean said, with a pointed significance that forced Marissa to stare at her and listen.

"Mrs. Tatum, does the name 'Pearson' mean anything to you?"

"It was my maiden name."

"Have you ever used it since you've been married?"

"For a short time. I continued to model during the early months of our marriage. Once Bob was selected for Cameron's training squad I gave up my work and never used that name again."

"Never?"

"Never," Marissa Tatum repeated, believing absolutely that she was telling the truth.

"The name 'Charles Pearson,' does that mean anything?" Jean asked, hoping to refresh her memory.

"That was my father's name."

"Mrs. Tatum, did *you* ever have occasion to use the name Charles Pearson?"

"Only on employment applications," she said bitterly. "I had to put something down where it asked 'Father's name.' "

"I mean recently. Within the last year," Jean said pointedly.

"The last year? Of course not," Marissa Tatum started to deny. She stopped, her face in a fixed and tense pose, as if her features had suddenly lost all mobility.

Gently as she could, Jean asked, "For Bobby's sake I must know. I give you my word I won't tell anyone else without your permission. Did you sign him into West Side Memorial one night late last December with a head injury? It's vital."

Marissa Tatum did not respond.

"And was he held overnight and released to you the next morning, this four-year-old 'Charles Pearson'? And did you pay his bill in cash?"

Marissa Tatum answered in a breathless whisper, "It can't mean anything. I asked a number of times and the doctor there kept saying, 'He's all right. Far as we can tell, he's fine.' So what difference can that make now?"

"An enormous difference. It completely changes the diagnosis and treatment of Bobby's case. Especially now, when I don't think we have any time to lose."

"You're threatening me again."

"Yes, I am threatening you," Jean admitted. "Unless your son has an immediate angiogram I am very fearful about his future."

"What . . . what do you want me to do? What do you want me to say?"

"You don't have to tell anyone what happened. Not even me. But you must go to Sunderland and insist he do an angiogram on Bobby!"

Alarmed, as Jean had meant her to be, Marissa Tatum called her husband at once. Within twenty minutes, Bob and Marissa Tatum, accompanied by a concerned and agitated Horace Cameron, confronted Ralph Sunderland in his office at the hospital. If Cameron had not been present, Sunderland would have been openly irritated and nasty. Due to the presence of the Chairman of the Board of Trustees, he treated Marissa's concern indulgently and lightly.

"The trouble with parents," Sunderland said, smiling at Cameron but obviously referring to Marissa Tatum, "they read an article in some magazine or see something on television or hear some gossip from some other woman whose child has had a totally dissimilar ailment and they become hysterical."

He turned to Marissa. "Mrs. Tatum, exactly what do you know about angiograms and why are you insisting on one now?"

Unable to speak freely, she said, "Well, as I understand it, this Todd's thing . . ."

"Todd's Phenomenon," Sunderland supplied condescendingly.

"This Todd's Phenomenon can be mistaken for something else. And one can't always be sure."

"Of course, one can't always be sure, my dear. That's why we make a tentative diagnosis and watch the patient's progress carefully. We'll get our complete reports on those tests I ordered this morning, then we'll know even more. But the one thing we don't do is go rushing into an angiogram. I can imagine who suggested it. Dr. Braham? Right?"

Because it was easier to lie about it than admit the truth, she said, "Yes, yes, he did."

"Damn it, I told him not to meddle!" Sunderland expressed his dismay with a look toward Cameron who seemed to understand. Then, with an intolerant smile, Sunderland said, "You don't learn all about neurology by osmosis." He left no uncertainty in Cameron's mind that he was referring to the relationship between Larry Braham and Jean Scofield.

Sunderland turned back to Marissa. "My dear girl, do you have any idea what side effects an angiogram can produce?"

"No," she admitted unsurely. "Is it dangerous?"

"Dangerous? Let me give you a small idea." Sunderland proceeded to expostulate to Tatum and Cameron. "The doctor can do everything right and still an angiogram can produce bizarre and unpredictable results. Some are minor. Such as an irregular heartbeat. But there can also be total cardiac arrest.

"Since it involves passing a plastic catheter into one of the arteries, it can also result in a spasm of the artery, cutting off the supply of blood to a leg or an arm, resulting in an amputation. It can create an embolism by causing a bit of matter to flake off an artery wall. When that reaches the heart, that's it! Instantaneously. Why do you think we insist on a signed consent? So you see, we do not do angiograms whenever the whim seizes someone."

He took Marissa Tatum's hand and patted it comfortingly. "Mother, let's not get hysterical. Your son is reacting well. His Todd's is clearing up."

Torn between her fears and her need for secrecy, her loyalty to her son forced her to interrupt Sunderland. "What if he had some injury to his head? Would that change your opinion?"

"There's no record of such an injury in his file," Sunderland said. He returned to Tatum. *"Did* the boy suffer a head injury any time in the last year or so?"

"No," Tatum said firmly.

His wife did not have the courage to contradict him. But she did manage to say, "I suggest that we bring Dr. Scofield back on the case."

"Marissa!" her husband exploded. "You disapproved of her as much as I did. Now you want her back? Why?"

Unable to articulate her real reason, she said, "Because she knows Bobby better. And he likes her. I think he needs all the confidence and security we can give him now."

Tatum looked to Cameron, who openly disapproved.

"Marissa . . ." Bob Tatum began to remonstrate. But she interrupted.

"Bob! Please? This one time, do it? For me? Because *I* want it?" she pleaded.

Bob Tatum shrugged.

"Bob, I want her to take care of my son!" Marissa Tatum said firmly, but her eyes glistened with tears.

In all previous disagreements between them, he had always prevailed. His judgments and his opinions were virtually supreme. Now, whether it was her tears waiting to be shed or his belief that this was vitally important to her, Bob Tatum decided he had to risk Cameron's disapproval for the first time. "If Marissa feels so strongly about it, I want to call Dr. Scofield back on the case."

"It would be impossible for us to work together," Sunderland threatened. "I hope you realize that."

"I would still like her back on the case."

"Well!" Sunderland said, dismayed and embarrassed. "I no longer assume any responsibility for the patient." With a look to Cameron, as if asking his permission, Sunderland strode out of the room.

"I wouldn't have done that, Bob," Cameron said.

"Marissa doesn't insist often. When she does I have to respect that. Sorry, Mr. Cameron."

"It's quite all right, I understand," Cameron replied, making it clear his sensitivities had been grossly offended. He started out.

"Mr. Cameron!" Cameron turned, fixed his gaze on Bob Tatum, staring at him through his tinted lenses. "May I come see you at the office when I'm finished here?"

"My door is always open to you," Cameron said coolly.

Bob Tatum turned to his wife.

"Thanks, darling." She began to cry.

He embraced her. "I'd better call Dr. Scofield."

Even before she examined the boy, Dr. Scofield sent for the EEG and the echo-encephalogram results. Together with Larry Braham she studied them.

The EEG showed no great changes. There was now a trace of voltage depression which could substantiate her suspicion of a subdural hematoma, though it did not rule out other and even more serious possibilities.

The new echo-encephalogram left no doubt about the seriousness of the boy's condition. The fresh plate clearly showed that the pressure on the left side of his brain had caused it to shift from mid-line by four to five millimeters. She was positive now they were not dealing with Todd's Phenomenon. A subdural or a brain tumor could cause such a mid-line shift.

"We must do an angio," she said to Larry. "And we have no time to lose."

"Sunderland's scared the hell out of the Tatums about an angio."

"It's still a lesser risk than surgery. If it will make them feel any more secure I'll do it myself. Do you want to get their consent or should I?"

"We can both do it, if you'd rather."

"I'd rather."

When she had compared for the Tatums the possible risks of doing an angiogram against the far greater risks of not doing one, Tatum agreed to sign, asking only, "Don't hurt him. He's a sensitive, fragile boy."

"We won't hurt him," Jean promised. "And maybe this is the first step toward making him less sensitive and less fragile."

Tatum's reaction called for an explanation, which Jean avoided. For that was a vital matter that could not be subsidiary to any other. It would have to be handled with utmost tact if lives were not to be disrupted or even destroyed.

Jean Scofield and the assisting neuroradiologist scrubbed in the Radiology Department since the procedure would demand certain equipment that could only be found there. When she had slipped into her sterile gown and moved into the small operating room, she found that Bobby Tatum had already been wheeled in on a stretcher. The paralysis limited movement on his right side but the rest of his body seemed unduly active, reflecting his apprehension about this strange room and its equipment.

The little Fazio girl's sad ending had left its mark. Jean knew that she would have to sedate him strongly. An active, overtense child could create unwelcome developments during the course of a procedure that presented sufficient hazards to make it treacherous.

She herself injected the hypo of Seconal and Thorazine since she knew he would accept it from her without question. Once the sedative began to take effect, she was ready to commence the procedure, which involved inserting a needle and a thin rubber catheter into the boy's femoral artery and gently directing it from his groin up the artery into the aortic arch. Then, carefully, it must be eased into his left carotid artery. A thin wire encased in the catheter enabled the doctor to guide it on the desired course. With an adult the procedure would have been briefer; since the insertion of the catheter could be made directly into the carotid. But a child's carotid was too narrow for a direct approach.

It was a delicate, dangerous procedure. But Jean would be able to follow the instrument's course on the image intensifier, a screen that looked not much different from a conventional television screen. It revealed the patient's entire arterial system so the doctor could monitor the course of the intruding catheter continuously from the moment it was inserted. To allow the doctor to watch it best, the room was kept in dim light.

However, no image intensifier could predict when an artery was about to go into spasm. No image intensifier could detect when some bit of tissue or some embolism attached to an artery wall would be dislodged, break loose and race to the heart with fatal results. Nor could the image intensifier predict if and when a patient's heart would go into bizarre rhythm with unforseeable and sometimes irreversible results.

Sure that the boy had been sufficiently pacified by the sedation, Jean reached for the needle to which the thin catheter was attached. She gently inserted it into his femoral artery. She worked slowly, glancing at the image intensifier opposite her. The needle and the catheter showed up clearly as they passed through the artery slowly, like a benign worm making its way.

Periodically she stopped to monitor the pulse in his legs, then in his arms. A falling pulse rate could be the signal for the most dangerous of complications. If he lost pulse completely in a leg or an arm it would mean a spasm of the artery in that limb and could lead to consequences as disastrous as an amputation. The image intensifier continued to reveal the course of the needle and catheter. The boy's pulse rate revealed his ability to endure the procedure.

Carefully monitoring its progress on the screen, Jean continued the insertion. It seemed to proceed without complications. She stopped again to check the boy's pulse. It had grown a bit weaker. Hastily she checked the pulse in both his legs. She could find it, feel it, measure its rate. Slower than it was, but not yet within danger range. She had to consider stopping or even withdrawing the catheter. There were patients who for this reason or others could never be angioed. Perhaps Bobby would prove to be one of those.

When his pulse rate did not fall any lower, she decided to continue. The screen revealed that the catheter had finally reached his aortic arch. Now it would take careful maneuvering to move it in the direction of the left carotid artery where it would be in position to accomplish its ultimate purpose—to carry to his brain the dye which would allow the bi-plane cameras to photograph his brain simultaneously, one from the side and one from above his head, and thus hopefully reveal the root of his seizures, and his paralysis.

Her eyes fixed on the screen, her hands obeying her impulses, she finally maneuvered the catheter to the point where it reached the carotid artery on the left side of the boy's neck. She had arrived at another highly critical moment in the procedure. The injection of reno-graphin, the dye which would serve as a contrast and allow the cameras to carry out their function.

Not all patients could tolerate the dye. There were cases in which a strong allergic reaction set in. In some it had proved fatal. Jean acted cautiously and injected only half a cc of renographin. Now she watched not the screen but her little patient. If he commenced to gasp or exhibit any difficulty in breathing, or if his little body broke out in hives, it would indicate that he could not accept the dye without severe adverse, possibly fatal, consequences and the entire procedure would have to be aborted. A small dose would also warn her if the needle had by chance lodged in the wall of the artery, making passage of the dye into the brain arteries impossible.

She allowed the small dose of dye to settle. She observed the boy, who was dozing under the effects of the hypo she had given him. His breathing continued shallow and regular. He evidenced no hives, blotches or other allergic reactions. The dye did not accumulate in the artery walls. She nodded to the neuro-radiologist. They would inject the entire dosage.

The radiologist set both cameras in operation. They did their work swiftly. There was nothing for Jean to do but watch over her patient. No results could be detected yet. That would have to wait until the plates were developed. The films were removed and sent to the lab.

Slowly Jean reversed the procedure until the catheter and needle had been withdrawn. She could relax a bit now, for the procedure had been carried out without dangerous reactions. The boy was in light sleep, unaware of the bit of skillful medical magic by which one could read the inside of the human brain without opening the skull. Jean checked his pulse again. Regular, slow, only a bit weaker than usual. He had weathered the procedure fairly well.

The question now was what steps would be dictated by those films.

Fifteen minutes later Jean Scofield, the neuroradiologist, and Larry Braham stood before the view box and stared at the plates which revealed the inside of Bobby Tatum's skull. The arteries were sharply traced on the x-ray films. The middle cerebral artery stood out clearly. Even the mid-line shift of the brain was discernible. But in the left side of the boy's brain, which appeared on the right as the doctors studied it, there was a cloudy gray mass.

"Middle cerebral artery depressed two or three centimeters," the radiologist observed.

"Arteries on the left side very depressed," Jean said. "No question it's a subdural hematoma."

"And an ugly one," the radiologist agreed. "Certainly could cause his paralysis."

"Surprising that a subdural like that didn't cause any . . . " Jean started to observe. Then she stopped.

"Jean?" Larry prodded.

"Now that I think of it, the first time I interviewed Marissa Tatum she said he *did* have morning headaches. She attributed them to his not wanting to go to school. I shouldn't have missed that. That subdural's got to be removed before it kills. I'll check Forrest's schedule. This should be done today, if possible. Tomorrow at the latest."

4

twenty-eight

The Tatums were waiting at Bobby's bedside. The boy had overcome the effects of the sedation and was playing with a small sponge-rubber football his father had brought him. He almost managed to get his left hand around one end of it and needed his right hand for added holding power. But try as he did to please his father, the boy could not raise his right hand. It lay inert and useless.

"It's all right, Bobby boy," his father tried to encourage him. He realized, as did Jean and Larry, that the boy was more anguished at disappointing him than at his own paralysis. "The doctors are going to make it all right, Bobby. Aren't you?" He looked beseechingly across the boy at Jean Scofield and Larry Braham.

Larry indicated they wanted to speak to him urgently but privately.

Tatum glanced up sharply. The assurance he had tried so hard to instill in his son now deserted him. He no longer wore the encouraging smile. Yet he tried not to alarm the boy.

"Sure," he said. "Riss, you wait here."

Jean interposed firmly, "No, I think she should come, too."

Marissa hesitated, glanced at Jean Scofield, whose eyes tried to assure the tormented woman that there would be no disclosure of any secrets. Marissa kissed

329

her son. "We'll be back in a little while, darling. You play with the football Daddy brought you."

But the grimness of the moment was not lost on the boy. He stared at them as they filed out of the room. He hugged the ball his father had brought him but his little body began to tremble in fright.

Jean conducted the consultation in her office, where a view box was available. Tatum, a man who prided himself on always demanding facts, would only be convinced by seeing for himself. In the darkened room Jean traced the affected area of Bobby's brain. She pointed out how the pressure on the left side of his brain was causing the paralysis on his right. If allowed to continue it must enlarge, and most likely become fatal.

"But his speech . . . " Tatum argued. "He recovered his ability to speak."

"Temporarily, Bob," Larry said. "These things do not cure themselves. Not at this stage. They only become worse."

Strong an image as he liked to project, Tatum had to take his wife's icy cold hand before he could ask, "What do we have to do?"

"Operate," Larry said. "Right away."

"I checked with Walter Forrest," Jean added. "Fortunately he can fit it into his schedule first thing in the morning."

"Fit it into his schedule . . . " Bob Tatum repeated bitterly. "God, you doctors are so casual! It's like getting your car serviced! You call the station. And if the service manager is a nice guy and likes you, he says, 'You're in luck, Mr. Tatum, I can fit you in first thing in the morning.' This is my son you're talking about! And some surgeon is going to dig into his brain, and all you can say is, he can fit him in in the morning."

"Bob, please!" His wife tried to stop him.

"No, damn it! He ought to take more time. He ought to study the case. He ought to know what he's doing!" Tatum exploded.

"Forrest does know what he's doing," Larry tried to explain. "He's one of the best neurosurgeons in this part of the country."

Bob Tatum turned away, disconsolate, angry, but most of all afraid. Afraid for his son. And doubly so because he himself felt helpless—neither money, nor position, nor corporate clout could help him now.

Jean explained, "Mr. Tatum, all a good surgeon like Dr. Forrest needs to know is on these plates. They show clearly where the trouble is. And what he has to do about it."

Without turning back to face them, Bob Tatum asked the question that had been gnawing at him from the outset. "Is there a chance . . . I mean, is it possible in these cases that they find something they didn't expect?"

"Like a tumor?" Jean completed the thought Tatum was too afraid to express.

"Yes, like a tumor?"

"That would be unlikely," she tried to reassure him.

"I don't want 'unlikely.' I don't want percentages. I want an answer. A straight, simple answer. Is it possible?"

"Mr. Tatum, we have a rule. In neurosurgery, never say never. In any surgical procedure there can be complications. Factors unknown to the doctors at the outset. I won't try to minimize the dangers. I can only tell you your son will be in capable hands."

"Will he be cured?"

Jean recalled Dominick Fazio's words. Lowly laborer or highly intelligent successful executive, fathers were fathers.

"That will depend on what Forrest finds when he gets in there."

" 'Gets in there'!" Tatum exploded. "Damn it, you people have a funny language for something as terrible as this."

Turning more severe, Jean said, "Mr. Tatum! We have no time for emotionalism! We need your consent. We need it now, if Forrest is to proceed!"

Tatum nodded slowly, not agreeing, but giving the matter his most sober consideration. "I . . . I have to talk to Mr. Cameron first."

"Bobby is your son," Jean said pointedly.

"I know," the big, strong man said, a bit helplessly, "but I have to talk to Mr. Cameron."

"Then do it quickly!" She could not help saying to herself, he still needs a father, still needs a truck to run behind. For all his strength, intelligence and seeming confidence, Bob Tatum had never outgrown that need. Maybe he never would. What would happen, she wondered, when he had to face the other problem, concerning his wife's part in all this. There were three lives at stake here, not one. And the one whom everyone assumed to be strongest might turn out to be weakest of all. She could sympathize with Marissa and the pressures with which she had to live.

Bob Tatum turned and walked out of the office. Jean signaled Larry to go after him and urge him to come to a decision swiftly. Only the two women were left in the dark, shadowed room. As Jean reached to raise the window blind, Marissa Tatum interrupted, "Please don't!"

Marissa moved to the view box where the plate of her son's brain was so clearly displayed. Her finger traced the entire brain, the middle artery, and finally came to rest on the gray area which was the seat of his sickness.

"Did *I* do this?"

"Right now what matters is getting rid of it."

"Did I?"

"You can answer that better than I," Jean said. "But I would advise you not to try it now. You've enough to worry you without that."

"But he'll know . . . "

"Your husband?"

"Dr. Forrest. Isn't he the same one you called in before? When I gave Bobby that overdose?"

"Yes."

"When he finds this, he'll know."

"Know what?"

"That it was me," the woman said in a whisper that was both breathy and pained.

"How would he know that?" Jean asked.

"He'll know why I gave Bobby the overdose and if he knows that he'll know everything. Everything."

Jean realized it was her guilt talking. Marissa was indicting and convicting herself and attributing it to Forrest.

"He'll never guess. And I won't tell him," Jean tried to reassure. "A surgeon doesn't have to know *why* or *how*. Only *what*, and what he can do about it."

But it was less than Marissa Tatum needed. She could no longer contain her torment. Her beautiful face began to disintegrate in a flood of mascara-streaked tears. Jean pushed a box of tissues toward the distressed woman.

Marissa Tatum had been quiet but tearful for a time. Twice, Jean's phone blinked persistently. She refused to answer it. For she suspected that just as tomorrow morning Dr. Forrest would try to remove the results of the wound that afflicted Bobby Tatum's brain, now his mother was steeling herself to finally probe the secret wound from which her son's affliction had originated.

She began suddenly, in a spurt of words that reflected her inner torment. "You'll despise me! You'll think I'm not fit to be a mother, not fit to belong to the human race!"

Jean made no attempt to console her. It was necessary for Marissa to condemn and punish herself before she could go on.

"I never meant to do it. It just . . . just happened. No, it didn't just 'happen.' I must stop using that word. I've been telling myself for the last ten months that it just 'happened.' It didn't. *I did it.* I have to face that. *I did it!*"

Jean considered offering her a tranquilizer, but it would be better in the end if the woman reexperienced the full horror of it. To confront one's self with enormous guilt was basically a solitary process. One might need a sounding board, but always the process involved recognition of one's own actions, crimes and guilts. To speak the words aloud, for the first time, was like opening an abscess in the brain and allowing the infection within to pour out and thus relieve the pressure. As in all surgery of the brain or of the mind, the healing part could only take place later and at a much slower pace.

Without expressing any judgment, Jean asked softly, "Exactly *what* did you do?"

"Christmas," Marissa began strangely, "I have always had this terrible feeling about Christmas."

"Holiday depressions are a common phenomenon. We always see more cases in Neurology around Christmas time. And in Psychiatric it's even more marked."

"Yes, but in my case . . . " As most troubled people do, Marissa felt her guilts and torments were unique and unlike those of the rest of humanity. But Jean did not interrupt to point that out.

"In my case it was different. It's always been different. I can remember the first time, in kindergarten, when the teacher said, 'Let's all tell about our Christmas.' Every child in the class had to get up and tell what Santa Claus brought them. What Mommy cooked. And what Daddy did. How he played with their toys, or fixed them after they were broken. How Daddy took them out on Christmas day, to play with their new sleds. How Daddy took them for hot chocolate or brought them in from the cold and Mommy made them hot cocoa. Every child except one talked about Daddy. That one was me.

"When my turn came, I said . . . I said my Daddy had to work Christmas day so he wasn't home. The teacher must have suspected, because she looked at me questioningly. But she didn't say anything.

"It was like that every Christmas. After a while I would tell myself that one day my father would come back. He never did, of course. Charles Pearson went off and deserted his only child. All he left her was his name, Pearson."

She wiped back the tears from her eyes with her fingers and tried to smile at the irony. "In the end it was *his* name that trapped me. Isn't that funny?"

"You have to stop thinking of yourself as being trapped," Jean said. "This could be the beginning of becoming free."

The woman shook her head, denying the possibility. "When you hear what I have to tell you, you'll take my baby away from me."

"Nobody wants to do that."

"You will, you will. Because I . . . " She faltered and could not continue.

"If you say it just once, it might not be so bad. We tend to be our own worst judges."

"I had always promised myself, long before I was married, long before I ever had a child, that when I did I would make Christmas the most wonderful day of her life. My child, my daughter, I always thought it would be a girl, my daughter would be able to stand up in school and boast of her mother and father and how they made the best Christmas in the world for her. I owed it to that little girl who had to lie in kindergarten.

"You see, all my life I've been playing parts. The little girl with the father who didn't exist. The model in the fine clothes. The beautiful woman. Which I really am not. I can show you a dozen flaws in my face. But I do so much with what I have that everyone thinks me beautiful. Just as I'm not Mary but Marissa. It's a part I play so well. I have to. Otherwise I would have to face the fact that Bob could go off and leave me, as my father deserted my mother."

She was silent after that confession. Until Jean prodded her gently, "Did you feel that way before Bobby was born?"

Marissa nodded. "I was into my second month before I told him. Then I had to steel myself to say it. I had to make up a way, like they do in films, to be cute and coy about it. I couldn't come right out and say, with great excitement, 'Bob, we're going to have a baby.' Even then, though I pretended to be happy, because I knew how much he wanted a son, I was afraid to tell him. Behind my smile, my eyes were studying his face, to see the reaction there. Always that fear. He would run off and leave me.

"As the time drew near and I became big and ungainly and my face changed shape, I kept saying to myself, he can't love me now. I'm ugly. Ugly!"

"Did you notice any change in him?"

"Yes."

Jean was surprised but refrained from reacting.

"He became more tender, more loving. But I only suspected him more. He must be covering up, I said to myself. Yes, he is big and strong. But times he can be so considerate, gentle, kind. And he was. All during my pregnancy. Only I couldn't accept it. Those times when he went on business trips I would check on him."

She admitted, "I would make up pretexts and reasons to call him when he was away. Until it became a company joke."

She smiled wanly. "Once, Mr. Cameron said to me, 'Little lady,' he talks like that, 'little lady, you must be the most loving and devoted wife in the world.' He never guessed I was the most frightened and insecure wife in the world. Every time Bob went on a trip while I was pregnant, I had this fear that he would never come back. Until, I think . . . "

She was forced to gather all her resources before she was able to say, "Until, after a while, I think, I came to hate that baby even before it was born."

She waited, expecting recrimination from Jean. "Doesn't that shock you?"

"After what you'd been through, no."

"I mean, *you* . . ."

"What about *me?*" Jean asked.

"From what I heard, you so much wanted to have your baby and never did. I can imagine how you must despise me after what I just admitted."

The young woman was still begging for judgment and condemnation. Jean did not feel it wise to give her that release.

"I sometimes think that in some way, I'm not sure how, I had Bobby prematurely because I just wanted to get him out of me. Is it possible that a woman can *will* herself to have her baby prematurely? Is it?" she demanded.

"We really have no answer to that."

"I always blamed it on the moving. Bob was being transferred from one InterElectronics office to another To him it was exciting. He was doing what he had always wanted to do and succeeding at it. When Cameron picked him for his own personal training squad, he knew he was on his way. To me that meant another move, another job of setting up a home. And I was getting bigger, more ugly every day. I kept thinking, the further Bob goes, the faster he goes, the more the chance that he'll leave me. And all the while I was drudging away, trying to make a home for us. I no sooner made one than it was time to move again.

"That's when it happened. Just as we were moving for the third time in four years, I had Bobby. Seven and a half months. Just on the borderline. Small and so frail. I was allowed to see him twice during all those days he was in his Isolette in Intensive Care. Small, scrawny, shriveled, like a little old man. With black and blue splotches on his body, especially around his umbilical cord. I said to myself, my God, that isn't a baby at all. It's not the kind you see in the baby food ads. I thought, he won't survive. Nothing that small and pathetic can survive. I see now that was more my hope than my fear," she admitted.

"Did they let you hold him?"

She shook her head. "Even if they had, I wouldn't have been able to. I wouldn't have known what to do with it. That's the way I thought of it, not 'my baby' but 'it.' "

"How long before you were able to hold him?"

"Weeks."

"How many?"

"About five. He was very sick. For a long time they didn't think he'd make it."

She seemed to recall now. "The first time I held him was the day we came to bring him home from the hospital. He was still scrawny. We had to keep him on a special weight-gaining diet for months. But he never did seem to catch up."

Jean recalled how well the boy had fared during his recent hospital stays.

"He never will catch up," Marissa Tatum said. "We're resigned to that, Bob and I. He doesn't say much about it anymore. But I disappointed him. He wanted sons. Strong sons. I gave him one son. And you can see he's not what his father dreamed of."

"He loves the boy. And the boy loves him. I saw it yesterday."

"Still, there's the disappointment," Marissa Tatum said pathetically. "I can see it. Times his old coach asks him to scout some promising young high school player. Bob goes to see him play and then visits with the boy. When he comes home and tells me about him, what great potential he has, I can read the disappointment in him about his own son."

"Is it his disappointment or yours?" Jean asked pointedly.

Marissa Tatum considered it for a moment. "Does it matter? I feel it. That's bad enough."

"There is a difference between feeling something that exists, and something that doesn't."

"How would you know? Your husband loved you till the day he died. You never had reason to doubt him. So you don't know. Even Larry . . . " Marissa Tatum blurted out, then became silent, regretting that she had brought his name into the discussion.

"What about Dr. Braham?"

"I know how he feels about you."

"He's discussed me with you?" Jean asked, surprised.

"He didn't have to. When a man feels that way about a woman, you can read it in the way he looks when he mentions her. That Christmas . . . that awful Christmas when it happened to Bobby . . . I invited Larry to come to our party. The Camerons would be there. So I invited a small group of friends we thought would make a good impression on them. That was always important, to make a good impression on the Camerons. It was the first time they would be coming to our new house. Bob wanted everything to be perfect. Every detail. Including the hand-picked guest list. I invited Larry. He said that he could come, if he could bring someone. I asked who, Bob being so particular about the guest list. Larry described you. He never said what your relationship was. But the way he talked about you, I knew how much he loved you. And I was jealous."

She stared at Jean and repeated, "Yes. Jealous. God, I said to myself, if only some man loved me that much. Two men have loved you like that, so you can't know the way I feel." Suddenly she said, "Marry him. Before it's too late." She shook her head and apologized, "I shouldn't have said that."

Ignoring the statement, Jean realized the poor woman was using every pretext she could to avoid talking about it. It was time she was made to face it. "That Christmas, Mrs. Tatum, was that the one that followed Bobby's admission to West Side Memorial for one night?"

Marissa nodded.

"You will have to tell someone sometime," Jean insisted.

By habit, Marissa's hand went to her purse, found a cigarette and her elegant gold lighter. She had to smoke the cigarette halfway down before she could talk again.

"Mrs. Cameron . . . " she began. "You have to understand how important she is. It's well known at InterElectronics, if she takes a fancy to a man's wife, his career suddenly blossoms. The best thing that can happen is for her to take charge of your life. Well, I can please people when I make up my mind to. God knows, I've had lots of practice. Pleasing is my profession, in a way.

"So she took to me at once. Bob was delighted. I felt, at last I'm doing something that helps him. I can be of use to him. He might even need me. So I gave myself to all her charitable activities. Completely.

"I know what you're thinking. Bobby. Yes, he did suffer because of it. He was neglected. But I kept saying to myself, in the long run he'll benefit from it. It will insure Bob's future. And Bobby's. Even now, some of Bob's stock options are in Bobby's name. And for a Christmas present last year Mr. Cameron gave Bobby a hundred shares of InterElectronic stock."

"What about Mrs. Cameron?" Jean brought her back to the one night she was avoiding.

"Christmas . . . "

"Yes, Christmas. . . . "

"Two nights before . . . it was mad. I had my own party to prepare for. And Mrs. Cameron had her reception for the Foundling Home. One of her most cherished activities. Especially in these times. When white babies are scarce and fought for by adoptive parents, black and mixed babies are shunned and keep piling up in the Foundling Home. She gives this big party for the babies, the sponsors and the trustees. There are gifts for the children, and clowns, ice cream and cake, a big tree. Then after the children are put to bed, Mrs. Cameron makes her appeal for funds. Her entire budget for the year is raised that night."

"What about *you?*" Jean insisted.

"I . . . I was one of the young wives she chose to assist her. We act as hostesses to greet her guests. Then we help with the pledge cards. It's an honor for her to ask. She only chooses four wives each year. Naturally I agreed. But there were the preparations for my party. Bob was away, not due back till the afternoon of Christmas Eve. It was hectic. Terribly hectic. I was trying to get dressed. Bobby was crying. Even though he likes Esther, he didn't want to be left alone again."

"Again?"

"I told you it had been a hectic time. I was out quite a lot, doing my own shopping and helping Mrs. Cameron on a dozen of her committees. I guess I'd been out almost every afternoon and evening for quite a spell. You have to understand!"

"I'm trying to understand," Jean said sympathetically. "It was a difficult time. Hectic. Bobby didn't make it any easier, wanting a share of your time, wanting you to stay home."

"I explained it to him a hundred times," Marissa justified herself.

"Some things one can never explain to the satisfaction of a child. You know that better than anyone."

"Yes," Marissa dropped her voice as she admitted it, "but not that night. I was so determined to make good for Bob that I became cross with Bobby. Impatient. I shouted at him. Sent him to his room. I finished dressing. In a new dress that I had bought especially for Mrs. Cameron's party. Bob had said, 'Spend anything you like. Only, make a good impression! It's important!'

"So I bought a Halston original. Five hundred

seventy-five dollars. Bob didn't mind. He called it 'an investment.'

"I was all dressed and ready to leave. I could hear Bobby in his room, still sobbing. I went in to kiss him good night, to tell him I'd be home as soon as I could. And to be a good boy and go to sleep. But he kept crying. Then, when I bent over to kiss him, he . . . " She stopped suddenly.

"He what?"

"Whether it was nerves, or something he ate, or just sheer spite, he threw up. All over my new dress," Marissa Tatum said, then added strangely, "He destroyed everything . . . everything. . . . "

"Everything you'd worked so hard and patiently to achieve."

Marissa Tatum nodded. "The dress. Mrs. Cameron. Bob's career. My marriage. When Bob found out what happened, he would never forgive me. Never. Everything that we had planned and sacrificed for . . . everything . . . gone in one single moment. It was as if Bobby had done it deliberately."

"Of course, he didn't do it deliberately."

"At that moment I couldn't think anything else," Marissa Tatum admitted softly. "So I . . . without thinking . . . without wanting to . . . without . . ." Finally she was able to admit, "I lashed out at him. With all my fury, I hit him. So hard that he crashed against the wall alongside his bed. Then he was suddenly still. Very still."

"Unconscious?" Jean asked.

"For a moment I was sure I had killed him." Marissa repeated the words in a whisper as though she could not now believe what she had done, "Killed him.

"I was terrified! I didn't know what to do. My first thought was, call Larry! But I couldn't. Not without telling him how it had happened. I wanted to call Bob. Till I realized he was the one person I could never tell.

"But I had to get help for my son. Without letting anyone know what I'd done. So I got into fresh clothes. I took Bobby in my arms, put him in the car and then it dawned on me. How could I get help without anyone knowing? That's when I decided on West Side Memorial. The hospital farthest from our part of town. No one would know me there. And I wouldn't use the name Tatum.

"On the way I kept thinking of names. The name Charles Pearson kept coming up. Yes, I decided, the sonofabitch, it would serve him right to have his name used that way. It was the only thing he'd ever done for me. Given me a name to use at a terrible time like that.

"Bobby was still unconscious. The doctor examined him and brought him around. He gave him tests that showed that he wasn't suffering from a skull fracture. He said to leave him overnight. That he seemed okay, but they wanted to make sure. I finally agreed. And I gave them the information they wanted. Name. Charles Pearson. Address. I made up a fictitious address. And I made up a lie about his falling off the ladder while trying to trim the Christmas tree.

"Then I was suddenly standing outside this unfamiliar hospital. Alone. No husband. No son. Just alone. It was the worst moment of my life. Worse even than being a child and having to lie about Christmas."

"What about Mrs. Cameron?"

"I called. I said Bobby was ill and I couldn't leave him."

"And what did she say?"

"That was the strangest part of all. She was just as sweet and concerned as she could be. She said, 'Of course, my dear, I understand. Your first obligation is to your son. We'll do it again next year. And give him a kiss good night for me."

"It was all so simple and easy for her. After I hung up I started to cry. I cried for hours. Why couldn't life be that simple for me? Why did I have to go on racing forever against all sorts of hazards and dangers? As if life was one long obstacle course that I would never finish."

"The next day, Mrs. Tatum?"

"I went back. The doctor said Bobby was fine. No sign of any damage. I paid the bill. In cash. And took Bobby home. He never said a word to anyone. Never told Bob. Never mentioned the entire experience. So no one ever knew. No one ever had need to know."

"I asked you about any head traumas when he was first brought here," Jean reminded.

"I said to myself, there couldn't be any connection. The other doctor said he was fine. It was so many months ago. Why bring it up now?"

"These things sometimes take long to develop. And when they do . . . "

"They lead to brain surgery?"

"I'm afraid they do."

"He mustn't know," Marissa protested suddenly. "Bob must never know. He'll hate me! He'll leave me!" She regained control and said sadly, "Strange, the thing I feared so, that having a child would cause him to leave me. That didn't. But it's what I did that will. I fulfilled my own worst fears."

"We all have a way of doing that, I'm afraid," Jean said. "Still, I think he has to know."

"You can't tell him!" Marissa protested. "You're a doctor. You must respect my confidence!"

"I didn't say that I would tell him," Jean reminded her. "I only said he should know."

"You mean that I . . . " Marissa could not face having to make such an admission to her husband. She sat numb and silent, then shook her head, slowly, persistently. "They'll take my baby away from me. They'll take him away. I can't tell anyone. I can't."

"Mrs. Tatum, it would have been far better if you'd told someone long ago. Subdurals don't remain static. They tend to enlarge. The longer they endure the greater the chance that the effects will become permanent." It was a harsh truth, and would add to the poor mother's guilt. But she had best know it. "If you don't tell someone, I'll have to."

"But professional confidentiality . . . "

" . . . obtains in all cases except child abuse. Under the law it's my duty to report it. That's why *you* have to do it. Think about telling your husband. You have till tomorrow."

"Tomorrow?"

"In the morning. Dr. Forrest. The surgery."

"Yes. The surgery. He'll come through it all right? He won't have those terrible seizures anymore, will he?" She begged for reassurance.

"We won't know anything until we see how his brain reacts to the surgery" was all that Jean could honestly say.

"His seizures, his paralysis, he could have that for the rest of his life?"

"The problem now is to remove the immediate danger. The kind of pressure that can cause seizures and paralysis can also kill, unless it's relieved."

"And I did it. I did it," the distraught woman kept repeating.

She had come this far, but it was necessary to uncover the whole truth, so Jean asked, "Mrs. Tatum, that time on the stairs, Bobby's leg fracture, was it really the moving man's fault, as your husband said?"

The woman shook her head, "Bob was only telling you what I told him."

"Have there been other times? Times that left no permanent results?" There was no answer. Jean persisted, "Have there?"

Marissa nodded.

"Many times?"

"Other times" was all the mother would admit. Then she sought Jean's understanding, "You have to know the feeling. What makes you do it. You tear yourself to bits trying to please everyone. Trying to have everyone love you. And then suddenly, there are moments when it's too much. Too much for you to cope with. And you take out all your fears and frustrations on the one person who really does love you. Your own child.

"That's the worst of it. Not just losing control. Not crying afterward. Not even their crying. It's the look. The look in their eyes that pleads, Mommy, why did you do that? I love you. Why did you do that to me? Why?

"You can't explain. You can never explain. Not to your child. Not to anyone. But suddenly you're seeing yourself as a child. You see all your fears, all your sadness in your own child's eyes. And you hate yourself. You promise never to do it again. But you do ... you do ... you do. ... " her voice trailed off sadly.

She was silent for a moment, until she said, "They'll send me to prison. They should."

Jean placed a hand on Marissa's arm. "We don't try to send parents to prison. We try to save families, Mrs. Tatum. Remember that."

twenty-nine

At six o'clock the next morning, Dr. Jean Scofield appeared at University Hospital. It was two hours earlier than her usual time, but today she had to scrub to attend brain surgery on Bobby Tatum. Aware of the boy's fear of operations, Jean planned on seeing him before going up to the Operating Room.

At six o'clock, the hospital barber was just beginning to cut away Bobby's shiny black hair. The boy appeared forlorn and frightened, as he watched handfuls of his hair fall to the sheet that was tucked around him. With no mirror to look into, his curiosity got the better of him. His sound left hand ventured up to touch his shorn scalp until the barber warned, "Uh uh! I run a pretty sharp scissors. You don't want to get cut, do you?"

The timid boy quickly withdrew his hand and watched his hair come cascading down. When the barber was finished cutting, Bobby reached up and felt the bristly remains of what had been his silky black hair. At that moment Jean Scofield opened the door.

"Good morning, Bobby."

"Morning, Dr. Jean. Look what they did to me," he said apologetically.

"It'll grow back, Bobby. A few weeks and it'll be the same as it was."

With little concept of time, the thought of weeks seemed eternity to the boy.

The barber said, "All right, sonny. Now we're going

to give you a shave. Bet you never had a shave before. But you've watched Daddy. Well, this is the same only we'll be shaving your head. So don't reach up no more."

The barber shook up a can of lather, applied it to the boy's scalp and began the slow and careful process of shaving the boy's head until it was completely devoid of hair. The boy held still, stiffly so, as if afraid to breathe. When he spoke, it seemed he was rationing his breath so he would not create any unnecessary movement. He stared at Jean.

"Feels cold."

"That's because your hair is gone, Bobby."

"Am I naked on top? Real naked? Can I see?"

"Do you really want to?" she asked.

The boy hesitated, then said, "No." He was silent for a moment. "This a real operation this time?" he asked carefully.

"It's not like the one yesterday, Bobby. But you don't have to be afraid. I'll be there. Dr. Larry will be there. We'll all be there making sure that you're safe."

"That little girl . . . "

"Yes?"

"I remember . . . "

"What, Bobby?"

"I 'member her name now. *Beetrice.* I never before knew a girl named Beetrice. I know Amy. And Sally. And Linda," he named the girls in his class.

"It's really a nice name, Bobby," Jean said, enunciating it slowly and giving value to all the letters, "Be-a-trice."

The boy repeated, "Be-a-trice." The sound pleased him. While he smiled, he reached out his left hand to Jean, but very cautiously, lest he move and incur the barber's disapproval. She held his hand until the barber said, "Okay. Finished. Beautiful job!" and he laughed. "You going to be okay, sonny."

They were alone. The boy. And his doctor. He still clutched her hand. She could feel how cold and damp he was.

"Not all kids die?" he asked. "I mean, old people die. But not kids? Do they?"

"Every day in this hospital, and all hospitals, little boys and girls have operations and get well and don't die," Jean comforted.

He tried to accept the doctor's assurance, but his blue eyes betrayed him. Jean could not resist. She took him in her arms and held him tight. He pressed against her breast, his tiny shaven head making him seem more a pathetic waif than usual.

"You're going to be fine, Bobby, fine! You'll be able to use your right hand again. And your leg. You'll be able to walk and run again," she promised.

"Will I be able to climb on the jungle gym in pre-school?"

"Of course!"

He brightened, then remembered. "I won't be going to pre-school next year. I'll be in kindergarten. That's what Mommy says."

"Well, then, you'll be able to climb on the jungle bars in kindergarten."

That delighted him. She could look down and see the smile on his face as he pressed against her. He would have been content to remain in her arms and close to her, but there was a sound at the door. An orderly and a nurse arrived with a gurney to take the boy up to the OR.

The nurse realized she had intruded on a most intimate moment. She joked to hide it, "Which one is the patient here?"

"I am," the boy spoke up quickly. "This is Dr. Jean. She's my doctor," the boy said proudly.

"And a very good doctor, too," the nurse answered. "Now, young man, we have to go for a ride."

"I know," he said, growing tense again. He looked up at Jean as if she could give him a dispensation at the last moment.

"Yes, Bobby, you have to go for a ride. And I have to go up and scrub. Then I'll be able to be with you all through the operation. Even when you're asleep and won't know it, I'll be there. Right next to you. And so will Dr. Larry. Watching over you every minute."

Jean looked to the nurse, giving her a signal to perform her duty quickly. The young nurse reached out and gathered the boy in her arms. "Up we go!" She deposited him on the stretcher. The orderly folded the waiting blanket over his body. The stretcher was half-way out the door when they heard a cry.

"Bobby! Darling!" Marissa Tatum cried out from a considerable distance down the hall. She raced toward the stretcher. She embraced the boy, half lifting him out of the protecting blanket. The nurse tried to intervene, protesting, "Please, he's due up in the OR."

The frantic woman would not release the boy. Jean intervened and gently freed him from his mother's embrace. Whatever had been done to calm his fears, Marissa's frenetic conduct had undone. He started to cry.

"Take him up," Jean said curtly.

Doctor and mother watched the stretcher disappear into the elevator. Marissa Tatum kept saying, "I'm sorry . . . sorry . . . I couldn't help it. . . ."

It was obvious the poor woman had not slept at all. Premonitions of disaster plus guilt have a terrifying synergistic effect.

"I have to go up and scrub. I promised Bobby."

"He'll be all right, won't he?" the woman begged.

"He's in most capable hands. We just have to wait and see."

Marissa Tatum nodded numbly.

"Why don't you go back home? I'll call you," Jean suggested. "It'll take several hours."

"I'll wait."

"Then go down to the cafeteria and get some breakfast."

"I'll wait," the mother said, "in his room."

"You can't do any good up here. Please?" Jean urged for the woman's sake.

"I'll wait," Marissa insisted grimly.

As she turned to go, the elevator door opened. Bob Tatum emerged hurriedly. He raced down the corridor with the air of a man seeking someone. When he saw the two women he called out, "Marissa!" He approached them, embraced his wife at once and held her tight. "You scared the hell out of me. You didn't sleep all night. When I woke this morning you were gone. I didn't know what to think. I raced over hoping you were here. But I wasn't sure. I wasn't sure."

He glanced across his wife at Jean Scofield, his eyes transmitting the fact that he was greatly concerned over Marissa's condition. Jean tried to detect some indication of whether Marissa had told her husband of their conversation of yesterday. She had to conclude that she had not.

"I have to go scrub," Jean excused herself.

Marissa Tatum turned and went into Bobby's room. Bob followed Jean Scofield, overtaking her at the elevator.

"Doctor!"

"Yes?"

"The truth," Tatum demanded quietly.

"We've been telling you the truth all along," Jean said.

"I'm sorry," he said. "But it isn't just my son's life that's involved. If anything happens to him, it'll destroy her. You're really treating two patients. And I don't want to lose either one of them. I love them both. Both."

Jean was sure now that Marissa Tatum had not told her husband. She would go on tormenting herself. But Tatum's diagnosis of the situation was correct. Marissa was beginning to exhibit signs of a total nervous collapse. If anything untoward took place in that operating room, it would surely catapult her over the edge.

"Mr. Tatum, go back and take care of your wife. She needs all the love and understanding you can give her now. We'll take care of Bobby."

"But if anything happens . . . "

"We'll do our best."

"I had a coach who used to say, 'When a man claims he did his best, he's only apologizing for failure.' "

"This isn't a football game, Mr. Tatum. We *will* do our best. The odds should be in Bobby's favor. I can't say any more than that."

Tatum nodded, accepting the cold fact. "I hope you won't hold it against me. Sunderland and replacing you."

"My personal feelings will have no effect on the outcome of the surgery."

"Mr. Cameron said if the boy comes through all right, he might be willing to change his mind about you."

"Trying to buy a good result, is he? I'm going up there to scrub, and observe. And to hope for the best. Like you and Mrs. Tatum."

The elevator door opened and she stepped in.

Poor little kid, Bob Tatum said to himself, five years old and in such trouble. Up there all alone without me, without his mother. All those doctors. All that staff. All that equipment. And one poor little kid, paralyzed and with something terribly wrong in his brain.

The injustice of it plagued him.

When he opened the door of Bobby's room he was greeted by a cloud of cigarette smoke. He went to the window and shoved it as high as he could with such force that the panes shook.

"Marissa! Darling! You can't go on smoking this way!" he exploded. He took the cigarette from her hand and snuffed out the burning end with his fingers. "I know, I know," he apologized, "I shouldn't keep after you about it. But it's for your own good. You've got to be strong now. For Bobby's sake. And for my sake, too. If anything happens to him, we're going to need each other. More than ever. In fact, I was thinking last night . . . if the worst happens . . . "

"Bob, no!"

"If the worst happens," he persisted, "I would change my mind."

"About what?" she asked, suddenly gripped by new fears.

"Adoption. Before, when we talked about it, I was always against it. I wanted my own sons, or no sons. Well, that's selfish. You need a child. Maybe a couple of children. It was wrong of me to deprive you."

She did not dare to answer, automatically reaching for her purse and another cigarette.

"No more, please, Riss?"

"Okay, no more." She had to turn away, unable to face him.

"I've been thinking of something else too. I didn't do much more sleeping last night than you did. That's how I know you were awake all night. It was past four this morning before I finally drifted off. What I was thinking mostly was . . . about Bobby. It could be my fault."

"Your fault?" she asked.

"Things I haven't told you. Maybe I should have."

"What things?"

"Family things."

"Like what?"

"You know how we always liked to kid about Mom and her four men. How she didn't have a daughter because Dad wouldn't approve. That isn't exactly true."

"What do you mean?"

"There *was* a girl . . . a daughter. Between Brad and me, my mother was pregnant again. She delivered prematurely."

"What happened to the baby?"

"For days they didn't know. Then she died. The doctor said it was the best thing that could have happened."

"What's that to do with Bobby?"

"I suspect we may have some genetic weakness in the family. Maybe I should have been completely open and honest about it and we should have adopted a baby right from the start."

"Is that what kept you awake all night?"

"It wasn't fair. I never had a right to put you through all this. Will you ever forgive me?"

She shook her head, not in disapproval, but sadly. He rose to embrace her.

"Will you?" he repeated.

"What?"

"Forgive me?"

"Yes," she said strangely. "Yes, I'll forgive you." She began to cry.

"I'm sorry . . . sorry," he said.

"Don't, Bob. Don't say any more," she pleaded,

fearful that his honesty would force her into a confession of her own, far more pertinent and devastating.

Outside Operating Room C of the Neurological Section of University Hospital, Walter Forrest, Jean Scofield and Lawrence Braham had just finished scrubbing. They were being assisted into their sterile gowns. Forrest, a bulky man, who had the frame of the oarsman he had been in college, plus the weight he had added since, was silent as he usually was before surgery. He was a man whose craft lay within his nimble hands and his astute mind. He was known for his blunt opinions and his delicate surgery. Those patients to whom he had had to give bad news considered him a hard, unfeeling man. Those whom he had worked on and brought back from the edge of death considered him God. This morning he seemed unusually silent and grim. It was the early hour, Jean thought. Though she had assisted Forrest on other early morning operations and even some late night emergencies, when he had been more talkative.

She remembered that with the Fazio girl he had been just as grim and silent. She attributed that to the fact that Forrest had had a grandchild who needed brain surgery and whom he had entrusted to a colleague he considered a most able surgeon. The boy had shot an embolism on the table and died immediately. All the surgical skill in the world could not have prevented it. It was one of those accidents that made all good physicians wary of any invasive procedure. Since that time, Walter Forrest approached surgery on children with extreme caution and uneasy foreboding.

The only thing he said to Jean and Larry was in the nature of an afterthought.

"I conferred with Killinin last night. He's using

nitrous oxide by endotrachial tube, Demerol by injection."

They entered the operating room. The staff was ready, nurses and aides, all under the strict command of Alice Drews, chief operating room nurse. She was known to other nurses as Mrs. Simon Legree and to all surgeons as the most dependable OR nurse in the hospital. Her sharp gray eyes stared over her mask at Dr. Forrest when he entered the room. She nodded to him. He nodded in return. She gave an order and two nurses went to the opposite door and swung it open. An orderly in OR greens wheeled in the mobile operating table on which a tiny figure lay inert and asleep. The anesthetic had already begun its work.

Killinin, the anesthetist, hooked up his sensors to the boy's body so he could monitor his vital signs on the oscilloscope. Drews, meantime, draped the boy's bald head in towels and sheets and fixed it in permanent position on foam rubber blocks. She affixed a sterile band across his forehead to keep his head completely immobile. The strong white light shone down on the pale shaved scalp of young Robert Tatum, Junior.

Forrest stared through his glasses at the angiograms mounted on the wall view box. He had studied them the night before. He knew exactly where the source of the boy's paralysis was located. But before making any entry into the boy's head he studied them again. He was a meticulous man. He trusted little to memory. So he stared at the angio plates as if for the first time.

Jean was at his side. She could not tell whether he was talking to her or himself as he muttered, "Depression posterior temporal region. Subdural under parietal convexity." He approached his subject, reached out his hand. Drews handed him a long-pronged shiny steel forceps with a wad of cotton which she had dipped into the brown betadine solution. Forrest swabbed the solution over the boy's scalp. He had made his battlefield antiseptically safe. He discarded the swab and held out his hand again. Drews did not need instructions. She had assisted Forrest on most of his operations and knew each instrument and the order of its use during any given neurosurgical procedure. She handed him a felt-tipped pen that had been gas-sterilized. He made two small, precise crosses on the left side of his little patient's skull.

Now he took the scalpel which Drews held out. He leaned over Bobby Tatum and made his first incision at the point of the lowest cross. A small but precise incision down to the bone. One and one quarter inches long. Blood spurted from between the two edges of the flesh-colored wound, as if from between two small lips. He used another instrument to scrape the periosteum. Then he said, "Retract," to Jean.

Drews handed her the sterile steel retractor. Jean spread skin and periosteum apart, revealing a white patch of bone one inch long, one inch wide—Bobby Tatum's skull. Drews now passed him a compact, shiny, sterilized electric drill. The sound of the drill as it made impact with the boy's skull was shrill and not much different from a workman's drill cutting into some inanimate piece of lumber or metal. Carefully, Forrest drilled through the white bone of the boy's skull, making a hole one half inch in diameter. He was finally looking at the dura, the membrane that encased and protected the boy's brain. A normal dura should be whitish in color. But in the presence of an active subdural hematoma, the dura could be as blue as human veins. Bobby Tatum's dura was exceedingly blue.

The surgeon reached out his hand, palm up. Drews slapped a scalpel into it. Very carefully Forrest made a small incision into the dura, making sure not to cut into the subdural membrane where the trouble lay. He motioned to Drews to bring a light into position so he could stare down into the hole at the subdural membrane. He found a thick, well-organized outer subdural membrane which confirmed Jean's earlier suspicions.

"You were right. This thing's been here eight or nine months at least. Well, here goes."

With the bright light still trained on the spot, Forrest made an incision in the outer subdural tissue. It evoked a sudden gush of thick fluid that looked not like blood at all. It was a mixture of dark brown and yellow that neurosurgeons term "machinery-oil-colored material." With the spurt of material came small clots of dried blood, the residuals of the internal bleeding the boy had experienced that night when his head struck the wall. After the first gush and subsequent flow of discolored liquid, eventually came the bright red of pure, clean arterial blood. Sponging it away from time to time, Forrest let it drain. Then he ordered, "Cottonoid." Drews was ready with a tampon of surgical cotton. Forrest placed it in the opening to slow down the draining process, for he had more work to do.

He turned his attention to a second cross he had marked on the area farther back on the boy's scalp. He repeated the same steps. Incision into the scalp. Scrape periosteum. Retract. Drill small hole with the high-speed drill. Cut through the dura. Down to the subdura. Then open the subdural membrane. Again, his incision provoked a gush of "machinery oil." He permitted the incision to disgorge itself of the brownish yellow mix, spotted with small clots of dried blood. Once more that was followed by bright red blood. He let both holes drain, intervening occasionally with suction to drain away the material as it oozed through the cottonoids.

"Irrigation," he announced to Nurse Drews.

She was ready with a syringe full of a cleansing solution of physiosol. He placed the tip of the syringe in the upper hole in the boy's skull and carefully injected the fluid so that it drained out of the lower hole, carrying with it more clots of dried blood. He repeated the process a number of times, injecting the solution into the top hole in the boy's skull, watching it drain out of the bottom hole, until he had washed the entire damaging blood clot out of the boy's brain.

But all this was only preparation. The crucial moment in the entire procedure came now. Once the solution began to emerge clean, no longer carrying any discolored clots, Forrest glanced over his mask at Jean and Larry, who were across the table from him. From this moment on, there was little Forrest or anyone could do to help the boy. The question now was how much of a brain depression there had been and how his brain would react to the relief Forrest had provided by his surgical intervention.

Once the hematoma had been removed, the boy's brain could react in one of three ways. It could rush immediately to fill the area which had just been evacuated. It could be extremely slow to do so. Or it might do so at a moderate rate. The boy's future rested on the reaction of his own brain, with which no one could assist him.

Forrest motioned to Drews to focus the light over the holes in the boy's skull. Forrest, Jean and Larry leaned in to watch.

If Bobby's brain rushed to fill the empty area it would be a sign that there was additional pressure within, which could mean as yet undiscovered dangers. If the brain reacted too slowly it meant that the depression of the last months had done permanent damage. Only if the brain came back slowly and gently to fill the cavity and resume its normal position, shape and size would the boy have a chance at complete recovery.

Three pairs of eyes watched hopefully but with professional dispassion.

Now, freed of the intruding force of the hematoma, the brain began to expand again. It did so at a rate that fortunately did not create the suspicion of further pressure from within. However, it seemed sluggish at first, and led to the suspicion that the damage had been more permanent than they hoped. Then they began to see it assume a somewhat quicker rate of expansion. Finally it appeared to resume its normal place within the boy's skull.

Jean glanced across at Forrest. Her own observations might have been buoyed by her emotions. She wanted his cold appraisal. Forrest nodded. "Good! Damn good!"

Forrest had now to make a decision whether to close up the wound completely or insert a drain to draw off any further flow of material. He decided on a drain. He placed a small rubber catheter in the back hole in the boy's skull. Then he made a small stab wound in the scalp to let the catheter slip through and drain. After that, the procedure virtually complete, Forrest proceeded to close up both the scalp wounds. There was no need to fill in the burr holes in the skull. The boy's body, young and still growing, would eventually do that.

Once he had finished, Forrest leaned back from the table. "I'll leave the drain in place for about twenty-four hours. Then I'll come by and remove it. Meantime, let it drain into a closed bottle which should be fixed below the level of the boy's head."

Forrest started out of the surgery, then stopped and turned back. "Let me know if you detect any change in his paralysis."

"Of course," Jean said, greatly relieved that the procedure was over and the boy had come through. Once

Forrest's assistant had completed bandaging the boy's head, two nurses and an orderly lifted the sleeping boy from the operating table onto a gurney and he was wheeled out.

thirty

Patient Tatum, Junior, Robert was moved down to Neurological Intensive Care and placed in a small, isolated, glass-enclosed room from which he could be closely observed by the nursing staff. Sensors were attached to his body so that his vital signs were continually reported to the monitoring station. He slept, unaware of the care and the intricate procedures being employed on his behalf.

At the same time, Jean Scofield and Larry Braham, still in surgical greens, had come down to find Bob and Marissa Tatum.

The distraught mother was beyond tears by now. Though relieved that his wife had stopped crying, Bob Tatum was alarmed by the fact that she sat in the large leather chair and stared, eyes hollow and fixed.

He welcomed the slight whisper of the door as it opened. Any sound, almost any word, would be welcome now. When he saw Jean's smiling face he had to turn away to hide his own tears of relief.

"It went fine," Jean said. "Just fine."

Bob Tatum nodded, still hiding his face in his handkerchief. Marissa Tatum stared, as if she had not heard the news. Jean lifted her face so they could look at one another.

"I said he's fine!"

She could see the fear in Marissa Tatum's eyes. Surgery was only the beginning of the curative process. The more difficult and dangerous part for Marissa Tatum would come now.

"His paralysis? Will that be okay now?" Bob Tatum asked.

"We can't tell until he wakes," Larry explained. "Even then it might take several days before we can be sure."

"And those . . . those seizures," Tatum dared to ask.

"We hope they'll be gone. But no one can say," Jean answered truthfully.

"When can we see him?"

"He's in ICU. But still under. If you just want to look I think it would be all right."

"I want to see him. Now." He turned to his wife. "Riss?" She did not respond at once. "Darling? They said we can see him."

He held out his hand to her. As they passed Jean, Marissa's eyes begged, help me, don't make me tell him, Jean remained impassive.

The nurse in charge of ICU reported that Bobby was responding well. They looked into the glass-enclosed room before entering, for a nurse was adjusting the bottle into which the drainage from his brain emptied. She became aware of them, nodded, inviting them in.

Silently they slipped into the room to stare down at the small sleeping patient. His head swathed in a surgical turban of white bandages, he looked smaller and more fragile than usual. But his handsome features were more prominent.

As if aware of their presence, his eyelids twitched, then flickered. Eventually they parted to reveal his eyes, delft blue, now vague and uncertain. They fixed briefly as he recognized his father and mother, then closed again. Tatum looked to Jean Scofield for reassurance.

"It's just the anesthetic."

Tatum leaned close to his son. "Bobby . . . we're here . . . Mom and Dad. The doctors all say you're going to be fine. Good as new."

The boy did not respond.

"Is there anything we can bring you, Bobby boy? Some of your toys from home?"

The boy murmured so softly he was inaudible. His mother summoned up the courage to move close, leaning over him. "Bobby . . . Bobby . . . "

The boy opened his eyes again, stared up at her. She reached for his right hand, clasped it, hoping to evoke some reaction. But his hand and arm were as limp as they had been before the surgery. She looked to Jean Scofield. Jean was unable to give her any promises. Marissa turned away from her son's bed. Bob leaned over to pat the boy on the cheek. He put his arm around his wife and led her from the room.

Once outside ICU, Marissa said, "You said the surgery would cure it."

"We said it *should,* not would," Jean said. "Besides, it's too early to tell."

"But you said the results could be immediate."

"He's still under the influence of the anesthetic. That alone would inhibit any movement," Jean explained. "It could take hours. Maybe even a few days before we know for sure."

"Are there cases where it doesn't work?"

"It's possible."

"Then it won't happen," Marissa said stolidly. "Not in a few days. Not ever."

"Riss! No!" Her husband said in a low hoarse voice. "We've got to hold on, believe. Cameron said if it didn't work here, he'd send Bobby to the best doctors in Boston, in New York. This isn't the end!"

"But it is." Her eyes seemed to stare beyond his,

beyond Jean who was trying to establish contact with her. "Punishment. This is my punishment." She slumped against him. He embraced her gently. He looked across her at Jean, who gave no hint of what Marissa Tatum's trouble might be. It was obvious to her that Bob Tatum had never seen his wife in this state before. She had always been the willing, dependable, adaptable wife, up to every challenge, able to face any difficulty, a woman to rely on, a woman who always understood, who never complained. The perfect wife for a man with consuming ambition. The perfect protege for Mrs. Horace Cameron. The perfect model of the corporate wife by the severe standards laid down by Horace Cameron.

"Doctor, can't you give her something?" Bob pleaded.

"Medication might help. Temporarily. But it will take more than than," Jean said.

"Whatever it takes," Tatum insisted.

"Whatever it takes?" Jean challenged, doubting his ability to face the truth.

"When it comes to my wife and my son, whatever it takes, whatever it costs. If I can't afford it now, Cameron will make sure I get it."

"Cameron is the one person who can't help in this situation."

"What do you mean?" When Jean didn't answer, he stared down at his wife. "Marissa?"

She pressed her head against his chest, rolling it back and forth with unreasoning persistence.

"Give me fifteen minutes with her," Jean said.

Bewildered by the bizarre, unprecedented conduct of his wife, Bob Tatum reluctantly released her. Jean led her down the corridor toward her office.

"Mrs. Tatum, you can't avoid this any longer. And even if you could, I can't."

"He'll hate me," she pleaded.

"Then I'll have to tell him. Or Dr. Braham will."

"I'll tell him," she finally agreed. "But I have to face him alone."

Jean found Tatum at Bobby's bedside. The boy was asleep and perspiring lightly. Tatum leaned over the boy, gently wiping the perspiration away from his pale cheeks with a gauze pad. When he saw Jean he came out of the glass-enclosed cubicle.

"Is she all right now?"

"She's in my office. She wants to talk to you. But before you go in there, I want your word that you'll see me before you do or say anything to anyone else."

"Why?"

"I want your word! It's important. To you, to your wife, and most especially to your son!"

"All right."

He started down the corridor. Jean watched until he had disappeared into her office. She went back into the tiny room where her patient lay, head swathed in bandages, an oscilloscope just behind his bed, tracing his heartbeat. She stood over the boy, watching his right arm to see if she could detect any change. Though she knew it was probably too soon, she couldn't avoid staring and hoping. Perhaps in his sleep he would make some involuntary movement that would indicate improvement. There was none.

thirty-one

In Dr. Jean Scofield's office, Marissa Tatum held the flame of her gold lighter to her cigarette with an air of such determination that Bob knew she was under severe tension. Misreading the cause of her anxiety, he reassured, "He's going to be fine. Dr. Scofield thinks his paralysis will clear up."

"Does she?" Marissa evaded. There was no way for her to begin.

"Well, she seemed very hopeful," Bob admitted more truthfully. Seeking something affirmative with which to reassure her, he added, "At least there was no tumor. Kids, you know, can get brain tumors. I asked the doctor in charge of our company medical plan. Yes, kids, little kids, can get cancer of the brain. So we're damn lucky. He's going to be okay. You can stop worrying. And please, darling, please stop smoking! I mean, this would be a good time to make a commitment. Bobby's going to be okay, you give up smoking as a kind of thanksgiving," he urged hopefully.

She knew she had to come to it now or he would discover her secret in other ways.

"Bob . . ." Then she faltered.

Sensing that she needed him, he took her in his arms. She shook her head, forbiddingly.

"Riss?"

"Don't come near me. Don't touch me. Don't . . . don't do anything, but promise one thing."

"Anything."

"No, not *any*thing. One thing," Marissa insisted firmly.

"Okay, whatever . . ."

"No, Bob, not whatever. But *one* thing."

"What?"

"No matter what I tell you, I want you not to say a word. Until you've heard it all and had a chance to think about it."

"Okay!" he gave his assurance glibly.

Too glibly to put her fears at rest. She felt an overpowering compulsion to brush by him and run from the room. Remembering she had at least one source of help in Jean Scofield, she determined to face it now.

"Bobby . . . his condition . . . his attacks . . . fits . . . whatever they call them."

"Seizures."

"Seizures," she repeated. "They didn't just come on. They weren't something he inherited from your side of the family or mine."

"I know," he said, relieved. "Dr. Scofield explained the very first time. Sometimes they never discover what they come from. Well, in Bobby's case, we're lucky. They found out and they removed the cause."

"Not the real cause," his wife tried to explain.

"Of course, darling. That's why they operated. And they removed it."

"Bob! Please! Just be silent and listen!" Marissa interrupted, on the verge of hysteria. She regained control of herself. "The cause, the thing that made the operation necessary, was *me*," she finally confessed.

"Hell, angel, we've been through that a million times! It wasn't your fault you gave birth prematurely. Or that you had Bobby by cesarean. I know one of your doctors said something about women who smoke having smaller babies or having a tendency to premature deliveries. But that's only a statistic. We deal in statistics all the time at InterElectronics, so we know better than anyone that statistics do not apply to individual cases. *Nobody* knows why you delivered early. No one. I asked a dozen doctors. Not one of them could be sure. So stop blaming yourself," he said resolutely. Then he added a softer note of caution, "You know what almost happened the last time."

Whenever he spoke of "the last time," it meant that time when Bobby was days old, then weeks old and still a tiny, scrawny thing in Pediatric ICU, attached to life by wires and oxygen tubes. She had blamed herself then to the point where the doctor warned Bob that unless she came out of it, she could sink into a post-partum depression of such severity that there might be no returning.

"I'm not talking about 'the last time.' I'm talking about *now*. About what's been happening to Bobby these last weeks. What was in his brain that caused it. Mainly about how it got there."

"How *what* got there?"

"You promised you wouldn't say anything until I was done and you had a chance to think it over."

"Okay, okay."

She paused, then said slowly, "It was something *I* did."

"You?" he asked, disbelieving. "What?"

"I . . . I didn't mean to do it. But that night was too much . . . too much. . . ."

"What was too much? What happened?" he demanded, reaching out to take her by the arms so forcefully that his strong fingers were inflicting great pain. But she was thankful for even this small measure of punishment.

"I hit him," she admitted simply.

"Hit him?" Bob asked, puzzled. "Is that all? Hell,

kids get hit all the time. And most times have it coming. Times, I feel that way," he confessed. "Yes, times
I get so frustrated with him I'd like to beat him myself.
And I would, if I thought he was strong enough to
take it. I've often wanted to hit him."

"But not . . . not the way I hit him that time," she
said, pressing her head against his chest so she would
not have to see his eyes when she said it. "I hit him
so hard that he . . . he crashed against the wall."

"Against the wall?"

"His head . . . his head smashed against the wall.
I'll never forget the sound. Then he lay there, so still.
I . . . I thought he was dead. . . ."

"Riss?" he demanded, trying to hold her off and
look into her eyes. But she clung to him so desperately he could not move her.

"You said you would listen . . . you promised,"
she pleaded.

"All right, all right, I'll listen." By now his angry
intolerance was quite evident. "But tell me. *Everything!*"

"Yes . . . everything."

She told him of that fateful evening, beginning with
the stresses and strains of trying to please Mrs. Cameron. Up to the final furtive details of picking up
"Charles Pearson" at the hospital the next morning
and paying the hospital bill in cash to wipe out any
trace of Bobby's identity. Assured by the doctor at
West Side Memorial that Bobby was fine, she felt
that the episode was over for all time. Submissive,
frightened child that he was, he had faithfully abided
by her instructions never to say anything about it to
anyone.

"There," she said, in a painful whisper, "now you
know *everything.*"

She paused, breathless, still clinging to him, awaiting his judgment.

He did not respond at once. Then, with firm, strong, vindictive hands he removed her arms from around him. He grasped her hands in a punishing grip as he held her off and stared into her eyes.

"You're not a mother, you're a monster! How could you do that to my son?"

His voice was now so loud and accusatory it drowned out her pleas and cries to be heard. "You said you would listen, would try to understand."

"Understand? How can any man understand something like that? You could have killed him! You were only a step away from being a murderer. A murderer of your own son! Christ, animals do that! Not human beings!"

She made no further effort to defend herself or mitigate her crime. She broke down and wept, slipping into a chair. He stood over her, straining to keep from inflicting violent physical retribution on her. She would have welcomed that. Slowly the avenging anger of punishment superseded the anger of judgment.

"You know what this means, don't you?" he asked coldly.

She nodded. But it was not enough for him. He had to say it, and to hear himself saying it.

"You are never going to see that boy again!"

"Bob . . ."

"You know me. Once I come to a decision, that's it! You are never going to see him again. Or me either. And if you fight the divorce, I'll tell the whole world what you really are!"

"Bob, no! Please, please, I beg you . . . Don't!"

He slammed the door with such force the sound echoed down the corridor. People turned to stare.

Jean Scofield was in Neurological ICU watching the

oscilloscope monitor Bobby Tatum's vital signs. They were stable, and that was hopeful. The boy had wakened and smiled at her before giving way again to the effects of the anesthetic. He had made no move, voluntary or otherwise, to indicate that his paralysis had abated. The sound of that door slam alerted Jean. She had a foreboding suspicion of what it meant. She emerged from ICU to see the tall, robust figure of Bob Tatum striding down the corridor alone, on his way to the elevators. She raced down the hall to her office.

She could hear the pathetic sound of distraught Marissa Tatum. Past the first full flush of crying, she was whimpering like a small child, perhaps the small child who in her early years wept secretly, wondering what was wrong with her that her father had deserted her. Jean's first and most terrifying reaction was that the breakdown which had seemed incipient in Marissa Tatum had, under the blows of the last few weeks, finally occurred. She reached out to the unfortunate young woman to comfort her. Marissa Tatum drew back, staring at her venomously.

"Tell him, you said. He has to know. Now I have no husband, and no son."

"It was only a momentary reaction. He'll think it over. He'll understand."

"You don't know him. Once he makes up his mind . . ." She didn't have to complete the thought.

The defeated young woman, no longer beautiful, controlled and regal in her bearing, turned and slowly walked to the door.

"Did you explain . . . about Mrs. Cameron . . . about how important that evening was for his career?"

"My husband is the wrong man to 'explain' to. He was brought up that way. His father used to tell him, 'Bob, the perfect play doesn't need any explanations.' To him everything that happens between people is like a football play. If it works, no explanations are necessary. If it doesn't, no explanations will suffice."

A thin, bitter smile crossed her tear-stained face. "The first time we made love. Before we were married. It was wonderful. For both of us. In the after-talk I remember his saying, 'It worked. It's going to be great between us, because it worked.' To him sex was like football. I had been in the game. I had proved myself. I had made the team. His team. In bed. So it was okay for us to be married. Well, I'm no longer on the team. I fumbled on a crucial play. There is no place for losers in his scheme of things."

For the next few hours Jean Scofield was immersed in her duties in the clinic. She had examined twenty-eight patients, made nineteen diagnoses, referred a number of patients to Neurosurgery for further study, and discovered four cases of suspicious origin which she suspected were psychiatric, not neurological, in origin. It had been a routine afternoon in the Neurological Clinic.

The only event that brightened her day was a call from the *Journal of Clinical Medicine*. The editorial staff had reviewed her paper on the patient return rate in the Seaton Wards. It had been passed by three editors and accepted, with the usual suggested revisions, of course.

She realized this offered her a last chance to withdraw it without creating any professional gossip. She could refuse to make any revisions. That would be the end of it. Then she could quietly put it away and deny credence to the lie Carey and Cameron must be spreading throughout the medical community, that her article was an act of revenge.

Normally, she knew she would have responded defiantly and resolved, damn it, let them publish! That she did not brought her face to face with the fact that nothing she had experienced since early morning in this crowded, eventful day had made any deep personal impression on her. In mind and spirit she was still with Marissa Tatum, who in one short day had lost both her husband and her son.

There was an affinity between them now. Jean, too, had suffered such a double loss long ago. What had happened to her thereafter would undoubtedly happen now to a much more insecure Marissa Tatum. Or worse. She had no dear and devoted Hans Benziger to care for her. No one to depend on. She had made her whole life Bob Tatum's life. Without him, she was cut loose, she had no one. She was the deserted, insecure little girl again.

Jean felt a strong sense of responsibility. On her advice, Marissa had told her husband. Her bitter accusation before she left the office had much truth in it. "Tell him, you said. He has to know."

Jean had uncovered the secret, had used it to force permission to do the angiogram. It had saved Bobby's life, but destroyed his family. Jean's first thought was to call Larry and have him intercede with Bob Tatum. That would mean asking Larry to undo what she had done. Hardly fair. Hardly professional, either.

Instead, she dialed Bob Tatum's office.

"Mr. Tatum!" she demanded.

"I'm sorry, he's not in his office at the moment."

"Then get him!"

"I can't do that. He's in a meeting with Mr. Cameron."

"Then switch me to Mr. Cameron's office."

"Oh, I couldn't interrupt them," Tatum's secretary said, aghast at the thought that anyone would make such a request. In the midst of the secretary's explanation about the sanctity of Mr. Cameron's office, Jean hung up.

She paused thoughtfully for a few seconds, then dialed the private number that Cameron's secretary, Ms. St. John, had once left for her. An efficient-sounding voice answered the phone crisply, "Mr. Cameron's office."

"I wish to talk to Mr. Tatum."

"I'm afraid that's impossible. He's in with Mr. Cameron."

"Then I'll talk with Mr. Cameron."

"We never interrupt Mr. Cameron when he's in conference," the secretary informed regally.

"You will interrupt him now. You will tell him Dr. Scofield is calling. That it is urgent that I talk to Mr. Tatum at once!"

Quite aware that both Cameron and Tatum had been greatly distressed by the boy's surgery early in the day, the secretary said, "Well, that's different. One moment, Doctor."

When the voice of Horace Cameron came on the phone, Jean could picture him brandishing his cigar and peering through his tinted lenses with laser-like penetration.

"Doctor?" Cameron asked. "What's the word about the young man? Bob tells me he wasn't quite awake so you didn't know about his paralysis. How is he now?"

"The boy's condition is the same. Stable and hopeful. But that is not what I want to discuss with Mr. Tatum. Put him on, please!" she commanded.

"There's nothing you have to say that you can't say to me."

"I'm afraid there is!" Jean said. "I insist on speaking to him."

After a moment of resentful hesitation, Cameron turned the phone over to Bob Tatum.

"Yes?" Tatum demanded brusquely, all his anger still in his voice.

"Mr. Tatum, it is vital that I talk to you at once. In private."

"About what?"

"I think you know."

"I refuse to discuss that with anyone."

"Even with Mr. Cameron?" Jean challenged. "Or have you told him already?"

Tatum's silence was answer enough.

"In that case, I insist on talking to both of you," Jean said.

"That's impossible."

"Mr. Tatum, your wife's life is at stake here. Unless we help her. The first step is your understanding. If it's necessary to convince Mr. Cameron to get that, I will convince him. Put him back on the phone!"

She heard a click and then silence. Her impulse now was to call Larry. Perhaps a man would carry more weight in a situation like this. She sat drumming her fingers on the desk top, then came to a decision. She took off her white lab coat, grabbed her own coat from the rack. She stopped at Maggie's desk only long enough to say, "I will be out for the rest of the afternoon. I can't be reached. I'm on an emergency."

thirty-two

When Jean presented herself at Horace Cameron's office twenty minutes later, his receptionist was not only surprised, she was protectively hostile. No one dared come to this office without an appointment. She was finally persuaded to call Cameron's officious executive secretary, Ms. St. John. Tall, thin, efficient, she wore severe black-framed spectacles and looked like she had long ago forgotten how to smile.

In her clipped British manner, she explained that Mr. Cameron's day was booked. Completely booked. As it was, he was running late, more than an hour behind his rigorous schedule. It would be impossible to see him today. Or tomorrow, it turned out, once she consulted the black leather-bound appointment book she carried. Perhaps if the doctor wrote or phoned a time could be set, say, next week. No, on second thought, next week Mr. Cameron was due to make a trip to London. But the week after. Better still, next month seemed more feasible.

"What I have to say won't keep till next month, next week. Or even tomorrow. I insist on seeing him now. While Mr. Tatum is still in his office."

That Jean knew who Cameron's visitor was changed Ms. St. John's attitude markedly.

"One moment," she said. She disappeared into her office. She returned to say, "Mr. Cameron will see you. But briefly. He's under great pressure of time."

"So am I," Jean said, brushing by the woman.

Horace Cameron was behind his desk, assuming the severe but elegant posture of a reigning monarch. At his side stood Bob Tatum, obviously hostile and defiant. Jean knew it would not be easy to do what she had to. But the memory of her last view of Marissa Tatum gave her the determination.

"Doctor . . ." Cameron opened the meeting. It was a challenge, not an invitation.

"I assume Mr. Tatum has told you everything his wife told him." Cameron did not deny it. "This is nasty business. Shocking business. Certainly not the kind of thing that *nice, refined, upper class people* like us are used to discussing."

Her irony did not escape Cameron. His face was beginning to develop a noticeable flush of anger.

"We assume that the upper strata cease to be vulnerable to emotional weaknesses once they attain a certain economic or social level. That assumption is wrong. Certainly as it relates to the care of children, it is wrong. I have seen poor and oppressed people who love their children in ways you wouldn't even appreciate. I have also seen rich and intelligent parents inflict the cruelest and most destructive deprivations on their overindulged children.

"The abuse of a child is a personal matter. Not a class matter. It is, Mr. Tatum, a *family* matter. Not an *individual* matter."

Both Tatum and Cameron reacted to this as to an accusation. Jean intended it to be.

"Yes, Mr. Tatum, we rarely find only one abusing parent. There is always connivance, open or implied, on the part of the other parent. So before you judge your wife, a little self-examination is in order."

"If you came here to defend Marissa by accusing me, it won't work!" Tatum shot back.

"I'm not here to defend or accuse. Only to get you to take a good look at yourself. And at what you've done to the two people in this world who I'm sure you think you love the most."

"That's all past. After today, there is only one way."

"And that way?" Jean demanded.

"She is no longer fit to take care of my son. Or to be my wife. Both things will be arranged legally. If she fights me, I'll have this whole thing brought out in court! She wouldn't dare."

Cameron nodded sharply. It was clear he and Bob Tatum had decided on this course of action. They had decided to fire Marissa Tatum as they would an unworthy employee. And do it in such a way as to prevent any hint of scandal from besmirching the name InterElectronics. If need be, blackmail the victim into silence, as Marissa Tatum would now be blackmailed.

"Gentlemen, you're not taking into account *my* position in this case. Or Dr. Braham's."

"What has Braham to do with this?" Cameron demanded, taking over.

"He and I are both bound by law to do something about this."

"What do you mean 'bound by law'?" For the first time Cameron betrayed a hint of insecurity.

"A doctor who discovers clinical evidence of child abuse is obligated to report it. But these matters can be handled confidentially. Because the intent of the law is not to disgrace the parents, but to protect the child. So you make the choice. If *you* are going to victimize this woman, *I* will make the matter public. But if you want to help her, both Dr. Braham and I will do everything we can to see that she gets help."

Tatum turned to Cameron, seeking his advice. The old man stared straight ahead, ignoring both Tatum and Jean Scofield. Image, he was thinking. How would such a public scandal affect the image of Inter-Electronics? Nasty, distasteful business, child abuse. Shocking. If it became public he would undoubtedly have to get rid of Bob Tatum. Tatum had become an asset, well trained, one of the young men who was ambitious enough, demanding enough of himself and others to take up the reins of InterElectronics one day, or at least of one of its major subsidiaries. Men with his intelligence and dedicated drive were hard to come by. Even if, as a last resort, Cameron rid himself of Tatum, it would still not ensure that the scandal could be avoided. Scofield was blackmailing him as he had intended to blackmail Marissa Tatum. Damn this woman, he had resented her from the first time he ever heard of her.

She had defied him on the position of Associate Chief. She had defied him on the matter of the Seaton Wards. What irked him even more, he had secretly secured a copy of her data and turned it over to his own statisticians, only to have them confirm her conclusions. He had never let Carey know that. Or Benziger. But, according to his own experts, the damned woman was right. But the thing that irritated Cameron most, she was tough. As tough as any man he had ever dealt with. Necessity forced him to affect the appearance of reasonableness.

"Bob, I think we should listen to what the doctor has to say."

Surprised at first, Bob Tatum acceded to his boss. He slipped into a chair but sat forward, tensely ready to combat her every step of the way.

Jean began, "In medicine we have a shorthand of our own. NAI. Non-Accidental Injury. Child abuse. It doesn't only mean striking a child in such a way as to injure him. It can also mean the *failure* to do something. Depriving a child. Both forms of abuse can be equally destructive.

"Your wife is a victim, Mr. Tatum. She was deprived. Severely deprived during her entire childhood. Of a father who couldn't face responsibility and deserted her mother after she gave birth."

"Yes, I know," Tatum replied, but with no great tolerance. "Times that's all she talked about. Finding him. Making him face up to it. After all these years."

"She must have talked about him almost as much as *you* talk about *your* father," Jean said, pointedly and purposefully.

"There was one hell of a difference between my father and hers! My dad devoted himself to us. He trained us, brought us up to be what we are."

"So you could run behind the truck forever. Only this time it's Mr. Cameron's truck!" Jean pointed out.

Cameron's face grew more flushed. Jean was not deterred.

"I'm sure your father thought he was doing the right thing. But the price, Mr. Tatum. The price of that ambition is where it crosses the line from constructive ambition to abuse.

"I said that NAI is a family matter. Somehow, for reasons we don't yet understand, individuals who have been abused in childhood have a way of finding each other. They marry. And when they have children, those children tend to be abused. There is a quiet, insidious acquiescence, an unconscious conspiracy between the parents. Somehow they feed on one another. Provoke one another. Drive one another.

"You did that to your wife," Jean accused.

"No man has worked harder to give his wife everything she could want!" Tatum defended. "Security. A good home. Position in life."

"And made her run behind the truck at the same

time," Jean pointed out. "Economic pressure doesn't only exist in the slums."

"I never asked *anything* of her."

"You didn't have to. She asked *everything* of herself. Don't you see, Mr. Tatum, that poor girl was hanging on to your marriage, to your life style, your career, hanging on by her fingernails in a desperate effort to keep the one thing she had never had before. A family. A complete family. Mother, father and child. That wasn't so much to ask, was it?"

"But she had it!" Tatum protested.

"Did she? What security was there in picking up stakes and moving every time you received a promotion? For a girl whose life was a search for roots, it was a rootless existence. And those endless days and nights alone when you were traveling on business. Each time you left there was always the fear, would you come back?"

"I always did."

"That wasn't the only pressure on her. She had *all* the cards stacked against her. Premature deliveries lead to isolation in Intensive Care. In Bobby's case for weeks. Well, mother love isn't born fully developed with the infant as it emerges. It comes with physical closeness. With caring for her child. Fondling it. Feeding it. For some reason, mothers deprived of that closeness tend to become abusers. As do women who have difficult deliveries. Why? Maybe because during the delivery the mother feels the child is endangering her own life. In your wife's case, fear of losing you complicated her difficult delivery even more. The pressures were too many and too great. And under enough pressure almost any mother can abuse her child.

"There is something you intolerant men never remember. The mother is with her child almost all the time. She is constantly subject to the frustrations, the day-to-day challenges and pressures. Fathers are not. I wonder, Mr. Tatum, how you would have coped if you had had to do more than render all your fatherly duties in that one hour before the boy was sent off to bed?"

Somber and thoughtful, Bob Tatum turned away from Jean. For the first time he began to understand the forces at work in the mind of the tormented woman whom he had loved, the mother of his son who now lay half asleep and paralyzed in Neurological Intensive Care.

Jean Scofield turned to Horace Cameron, whose very posture betrayed his severe judgmental attitude, now directed toward Bob Tatum.

"You played a part in it too, Mr. Cameron," she accused.

Cameron bristled but did not dignify her accusation with a reply. He was not used to being rebuked, not by employees, associates, politicians, statesmen, or even heads of state. Certainly not by a woman. He had once walked out on a meeting with the Prime Minister of India when she made unkind references to his country and his business practices.

"Your price is too high, Mr. Cameron," Jean said. "The loyalty you demand exceeds the rewards you have to offer. Not that Marissa Tatum wasn't willing to pay the price. She would do anything for her husband and her marriage. But there was also the need to please your wife to further Bob's career.

"What precipitated this tragedy had to do with you, and Mrs. Cameron. Bobby needed his mother that night. Just as those orphans your wife is concerned about need their Christmas party. How do children express their needs? By asking. By crying. By pretending to be sick. At any other time Marissa Tatum would have done what any other mother would do. She would have cleaned up her little boy and dressed him in fresh pajamas, comforted him and read him to sleep. And that would have been the end of it.

"But that night it wasn't just mother and child. It was mother, husband, career, Cameron, Mrs. Cameron, and only then, finally, child. It was the honor, plus the obligation, to have been chosen by Mrs. Cameron to assist her. It was all the plans and expectations. All the attention and care focused on that new dress to make just the right impression on Mrs. Cameron. When that dress was ruined, it seemed to her that her marriage was ruined. She had missed a fateful rung on the corporate ladder. She stood in danger of losing, of being deserted again.

"Each of us has limits. I discovered that I had mine. Maybe that's why I'm here now. I don't judge Marissa Tatum. She'll judge herself. Which is worse. She needs help. She needs it now."

She turned to Bob Tatum. "Most of all she needs you. *And* her son. She will never make it alone."

"What she did to Bobby . . ." Tatum protested.

"Was not much worse than what *you* did to him," Jean reminded. "It's one thing for a father to *try* to be kind and loving. It's another thing to actually *be* kind and loving. He is never going to be a fullback, Mr. Tatum. But he is a bright, intelligent, sensitive human being of unlimited potential. If you can truly love that, you'll have yourself quite a son. Believe me."

"His right arm and leg . . ." Tatum sought reassurance.

"You have to love that boy whatever way he is. If you can't, *you've* failed, not *he*. God knows, he loves you despite your disappointment in him. He never stops trying to please you. Give him a chance. Give her a chance, too," Jean urged.

"Do you know where she is now?"

"At the hospital. She won't leave till she knows the boy is all right. After that, I don't know."

"I'll find her," Tatum promised. He looked at Cameron for permission to be excused.

"Just go!" Jean exploded. "You don't need permission. You don't need anything but to know your wife and your son need you!"

Tatum started for the door. Cameron edged forward in his chair in a reflex action as if to issue some minute order to demonstrate his continued dominance. Then he eased back slowly.

"If you report this, there's bound to be a scandal," Cameron began. "Surely there must be some diplomatic way to handle it."

"Mr. Cameron, I assure you it will be handled with complete confidentiality. Not out of concern for your corporate image, but because I have no desire to punish Marissa Tatum. But I will report it."

"The Chiefship of the Neurology Department is still open," Cameron reminded.

"I will still report it. And I might as well tell you that my paper on the Seaton Wards has been accepted by the *Journal of Clinical Medicine*."

Cameron exploded. "Damn it, what is it about you?"

"About *me?*"

"Any man would realize the advantages he could derive from being reasonable in a situation like this. That's why I like to deal with men. They're practical. They're realists. Women . . ." He dismissed them without another word.

"*Any* man?"

"*Most* men."

"Most men?" Jean persisted.

"Well, many men," Cameron conceded gruffly.

"Don't you really mean the kind of men you select?"

Cameron did not answer. Eventually he conceded, "Sunderland would have known how to handle this. No fuss. No scandal."

He took off his tinted glasses and rubbed his eyes. Without those forbidding lenses his eyes were revealed as a tired brown. The wrinkles around them showed his age quite clearly. He was silent for a moment before he admitted grudgingly, "But then Sunderland completely missed the diagnosis on the Tatum boy, didn't he?"

"It happens. To all of us. It's no disgrace," Jean explained.

"All I know, the Scofield diagnosis was right."

"Yes. I know. You like winners," Jean said wryly, not accepting his judgment as praise.

Cameron smiled, then confessed, "Despite you, I managed to get a copy of your data on the Seaton Wards."

"Of course."

"How did you know?" Cameron asked, surprised.

"I didn't," Jean said, herself smiling now. "I just assumed you would. You had to prove me wrong. After all, who defies Horace Cameron and gets away with it?"

Cameron's tired face relaxed in a smile. "I'm glad I don't have to deal with you every day." Then he admitted, "My man agrees with your conclusions. The Seaton Wards do present us with a new problem."

"What are you going to do about it?"

"I already have a staff at the Cameron Foundation working on the problem. I didn't want to tell you or Benziger. Vanity, I suppose."

It was the most profuse apology Horace Cameron had made to anyone in many, many years.

The sharp trader in him could not surrender without one last try. "Look, if I broke my rule, if I myself nominated you for Chief, would you . . ." He stopped, shook his head. "No," he concluded, "you wouldn't agree not to report the Tatum matter if I made you Chief, would you?"

"No, I would not."

thirty-three

Horace Cameron did not receive his next visitor at once. He sat back in his huge chair, very thoughtful. The lights on his battery of phones continued to flash. He ignored them, even the red one that signified problems of great urgency, which could only be resolved by his personal decision.

When he did lift a phone, it was the private wire to Ms. St. John. He instructed her to reach Dr. Hans Benziger at once, no matter where he was.

His secretary located Dr. Benziger examining a patient who had been referred to him because several neurologists on staff had disagreed on the diagnosis. Benziger waved aside his secretary, though she appeared most insistent when she announced that an important call was waiting. Benziger completed his examination and called back some ten minutes later.

"Benziger?"

"Cameron?"

"Yes!"

"What can I do for you?" Benziger asked.

"Two things. I don't want to ask Dr. Scofield, but

I do want a report on the Tatum boy. On whether his paralysis is clearing."

"I'm not the doctor on the case," Benziger reminded him.

"Please, Benziger! Don't make me humiliate myself to that woman. I'm anxious about the boy. I'd like to know. But I don't want to ask her."

"If the Tatums give their permission, I'm sure she'd be willing to keep you advised of the boy's condition."

"It isn't that," Cameron confessed. "But if I ask her and she does tell me, she's going to be sure that's why I've changed my mind. And that the Chiefship is a bribe."

"Do I understand you correctly?" Benziger asked.

"I'm going to put that damn woman's name before the Board myself!" Cameron blurted out. "Much as I hate to admit it, she's a winner. And you know how I feel about winners."

Benziger smiled and suggested gently, "Mr. Cameron, I wouldn't let her know that was your reason. I don't think she's as devoted to winners as you are."

"I found that out."

"People and their weaknesses are more in her line," Benziger said. "It's what makes her such an excellent doctor."

"Find out, please? About the boy?"

"Of course."

"Thanks, thanks very much." Just before Cameron hung up he asked, "As Chief, she's not going to be a continuous pain in the butt to the trustees, is she?"

"She will be," Benziger said. "That's why she's going to make such a good head of the Department."

Jean Scofield, in white lab coat, strode down the corridor of the Neurological pavilion on her way to

ICU. She was about to enter that wing when she changed her mind and headed for the visitors' lounge.

In the far corner sat Marissa Tatum, her husband at her side. She was turned away from him. He spoke in a voice so low neither Jean nor anyone else could overhear. But it was obvious he was seeking to convince her. It was also obvious he was not succeeding. When he caught sight of Jean in the doorway he left his wife's side.

In a discouraged whisper he said, "I can't reach her. No matter what I promise, she won't listen. Am I too late?"

"Does she say anything at all?"

"Just 'Bobby . . . Bobby . . . Bobby.' "

Jean glanced up at the clock on the lounge wall. It was seven hours since the boy had come out of surgery. The anesthetic should have worn off. If he were going to recover the use of his right arm and leg, some signs should become apparent soon. The question in Jean's mind was what dangerous effect there would be on Marissa Tatum if her son did not evidence signs of recovery. It could be the final shattering blow.

Forrest's surgery had been faultless. But there were always factors which could prevent a complete recovery. Jean had to take a calculated risk. She approached Marissa Tatum, put her arm around her. The distraught woman recoiled. She still harbored the delusion that but for Jean she would have been able to conceal her secret forever.

"We have to go see Bobby."

Brushing aside Jean's help, Marissa rose and started for the door. She raced past her husband's outstretched arms. She had to face this truth by herself. She made her way to ICU and passed the small glass-enclosed cubicles to enter the one closest to the window.

Bob Tatum followed her until Jean beckoned to him not to enter the room. They could see all they had to through the glass wall.

The boy lay still, his oscilloscope reporting that his vital signs were stable. His eyes were closed. Finally he sensed a presence in the room. He opened his eyes, saw his mother and smiled. Marissa Tatum reached for his left and nearest hand. She pressed it to her lips and kissed it. Though the boy did not sense the reason for her impulse, her closeness and her devotion made him reach out with his right hand to stroke her cheek.

As he had said to her so many times in the past, "You're the prettiest one, Mommy. The prettiest one."

She began to weep, not at his words, but at the touch of his right hand, which now moved with no remembrance of ever having lost its ability.

Jean said to Bob Tatum, "It's okay to go in now."

"Then what happens?"

"We find the right kind of help. I think she'll be fine. Fine," Jean assured him.

She returned to her office to find three messages there. One from Dr. Benziger, which underscored the word *urgent*. One from Larry Braham. One from Emergency Admitting. An eighteen-month-old child had been brought in with a fracture of the skull. The mother's story was suspicious. But at the moment the cause was not as important as the therapy. It was urgent that Jean consult with the admitting resident. She ignored the other messages and rushed down to Emergency.

She had just completed her examination of the newly admitted victim when Larry Braham found her. Before she would speak to him she completed her consultation with the resident, advised immediate surgery and demanded a complete history from the mother. She would see that this child remained in the hospital long after it recovered from the skull fracture.

Now, finally she had time for Larry. A situation he was never happy with, but to which he was resigned.

"Don't you ever return calls, Dr. Scofield?" he asked.

"There was an emergency."

"There'll always be an emergency," Larry conceded. "You never called Benni back either."

"I told you . . ."

Larry interrupted. "Yes, *I* know. There was an emergency. But what *you* don't know, Cameron is proposing to put your name before the Board of Trustees as the new Chief of Neurology."

"What does he want in exchange?"

"Not a thing, from what Benni told me."

"Cameron?" Jean asked, openly dubious.

"Benni warned me not to tell you his reason. But I will. Cameron thinks you're a winner." Larry laughed. "You'll accept anyhow, won't you?"

"That depends," Jean said thoughtfully.

"Depends?" he asked, puzzled.

"On how you feel about winners."

Larry Braham's look changed from puzzled to deeply disappointed. "Are you saying if you take the Chiefship that's the end of any possibility of marriage?"

"It'll mean more work. Even less time together," she pointed out.

"I realize that."

"It won't be fair. And I've been too unfair to you as it is," she said.

"Have I ever accused you of being unfair?"

"No," she conceded.

"Then?" he demanded.

She hesitated before she admitted, "I've always compared you to Cliff."

"And I've always known that."

"I kept trying to discover what special quality Cliff had that I couldn't find in you."

"I wanted to know the same thing. I even asked Benni," Larry confessed. She reacted in obvious surprise. "Yes," he admitted, then continued, "He said Cliff was an unusual man, a very terrific guy. Well, there's nothing I can do about that, Jeannie. I'm what I am. But evidently I'm just not up to Cliff."

"Don't ever say that!" she protested quickly. "Because these past days I discovered the only difference between Cliff and you. I had lost him so I wanted him back. Desperately. When I faced losing you, I realized I felt the same way. I wanted you back. I wanted . . ."

She stopped, then confided softly, "I want your arm around me at night. Every night. A man might not understand that. But it's the only way I can say it. So, darling, if you're not averse to marrying a woman chief . . ."

"I wouldn't marry any other kind," Larry said, smiling again. *"When?"*

"Just as soon as I let Cameron know that I accept his offer. If he accepts my terms."

"You are going to lay down terms to Horace Cameron?" Larry asked.

"Damn right. I want it very clear. He runs Inter-Electronics. I run the Neurology Service!"